"GABRIELLE!"

If she heard him, she gave no sign, and continued to shove her way forward, her linen nightgown catching on branch after branch.

Bryce reached her in seconds. "Gabrielle." He seized her arm, but she yanked it free, her slender body trembling with cold, shaking with sobs.

"No!" she gasped, shaking her head wildly from side to side "Mama . . . Papa . . . No!" Her words were garbled, but chillingly recognizable.

"Gaby." He caught her by the waist, dragging her against him.

She was clutching an object to her chest. The glistening alabaster color, the size, the shape—Bryce knew immediately it was her music box.

"Mama . . ." she whispered brokenly.

Gazing into her face, the vacant look in her eyes, Bryce realized with a sickening sensation that she was asleep.

UNFORGETTABLE ROMANCE . . .
UNBEATABLE SUSPENSE
PRAISE FOR *LEGACY OF THE DIAMOND*

"Andrea Kane is brilliant! An unforgettable story that will have you waiting on line for the second book in this series. . . . A classic has been born."

—*Rendezvous*

"A sparkling gem of Regency romantic suspense. The lead characters are charming, the action is nonstop, and the intrigue so plentiful it would satisfy any adventure fan. Andrea Kane raises the mark of quality for both the Regency and romantic suspense genres with her latest novel."

—Harriet Klausner, *Painted Rock*

"Andrea Kane starts her Black Diamond series with a bang! It has everything: action, adventure, sensuality, and the gripping style of storytelling that has become her trademark."

—*Affaire de Coeur*

"Once again Andrea Kane dazzles readers with a riveting tale of historical romantic suspense. . . . A deliciously romantic tale. . . . A must-read for fans of the Gothics."

—*Romantic Times*

"Breathtaking! Andrea Kane keeps me turning the pages, and loving every word."

—Lana Mills, Something Novel

"The tale is well-plotted, keeping readers properly in the dark to its end. *Legacy of the Diamond* promises to keep readers engrossed and eager to while away the time it takes to reach the last satisfying page."

—Camilla Coleman, *Gothic Journal*

Books by Andrea Kane

My Heart's Desire
Dream Castle
Masque of Betrayal
Echoes in the Mist
Samantha
The Last Duke
Emerald Garden
Wishes in the Wind
Legacy of the Diamond
The Black Diamond
The Music Box
"Yuletide Treasure"—Gift of Love Anthology

Published by POCKET BOOKS

ANDREA KANE

THE MUSIC BOX

POCKET BOOKS

New York London Toronto Sydney Tokyo Singapore

NOTE TO THE READER

This is an advance uncorrected proof for recipient's use; material and/or information contained herein is not in final form and should not be relied upon without the publisher's prior authorization. If any material from this book is to be quoted in a review, the quotation should be checked against the printed book.

An *Original* Publication of POCKET BOOKS

POCKET BOOKS, a division of Simon & Schuster Inc.
1230 Avenue of the Americas, New York, NY 10020

ISBN: 0-671-53484-X

Pocket Books Advance Reader copy printing October 1997

POCKET and colophon are registered trademarks of
Simon & Schuster Inc.

Printed in the U.S.A.

To each of us who has ever felt like a misfit—
find your heart and you'll find your home.

THE
MUSIC BOX

Prologue

Hertfordshire, England
May 1862

VIOLENT COUGHING TORE AT HER LUNGS, JARRED HER awake.

She sat up, rubbing her fist across her face as she tried to clear the cobwebs from her head, the burning mist from her eyes.

Where was she?

Not in her room. Not safe. Not tucked in her bed as she'd been when she last recalled.

The robins. The nest.

The shed.

She remembered now.

A bright glow slashed the room, along with a fierce surge of heat. She scrambled to her knees, her pupils wide, dilating with bewilderment.

Sunlight? It couldn't be. 'Twas night. An unusually cold night. That was why she'd sought shelter. She'd been shivering when she slipped into the shed and snuggled into the pile of old blankets. Yet now she was unbearably hot, her hair plastered to the nape of her neck, her nightgown clinging to her skin like a soggy piece of candy. Why?

The glow intensified, a wall of flames leaping at her like a predatory tiger.

Fire.

The shed was on fire.

Whimpering with fear, she cowered in the corner, pressing a blanket to her cheek for comfort. Her harsh rasps mingled with the flames' ominous crackling, the sound a terrifying contrast to the lilting melody that had lulled her to sleep.

The music box. Her stomach tightened with dread. *Where's the music box?*

Frantically she groped on the floor. There, she thought, snatching it up with trembling fingers. Just as she'd left it, only silent now, having performed its customary miracle earlier that night. The silvery tones had danced through the treetops, soothing the newborn robins, then accompanying her into the shed, nestling beside her, and serenading her to sleep.

Only to awaken to a nightmare.

As she stared across the flame-lit room, the full horror of the situation struck home. Even her music box could not protect her from this. If she stayed here, she'd die.

She didn't want to die.

"Mama," she whispered instinctively, only to realize how foolish she was being. How could she pray for her mama to save her when neither of her parents had any idea where she was?

No, 'twas up to her to save herself.

Small chin set, she struggled to her feet, clutching the music box and casting the blanket to the floor. Her eyes stung with tears, but she dashed them away, knowing she had but a brief time before the fire took over, robbing her of any chance for escape. She had to act now.

She made her way across the shed, bumping into one storage crate after another, wincing at the resulting pain but refusing to allow herself to cry out. To do that would mean to stop holding her breath. And that would mean inhaling the smoke that clamored at her nose and lungs.

Stubbornly she kept her lips pressed tightly together, biting back the silent sobs that shook her.

After ten steps that felt more like a hundred, she reached the door.

The handle was scalding hot, burning her fingers so badly she yanked them away. She tried again, but it was no use. She couldn't withstand the pain long enough to open the door.

Her lungs were bursting. She had to get out.

Her gaze fell on the sleeve of her nightgown, and an image sprang to mind of her mama using kitchen cloths as aids to remove hot pie pans from the oven. Perhaps her nightgown could serve that same purpose.

Determinedly she yanked down her nightgown sleeve until it covered her entire hand. That done, she grasped the door handle, feeling the heat radiate through the fine linen as she gave the handle a frantic twist. At the same time she flung her slight frame against the wooden door with every ounce of strength she possessed.

The door swung open, releasing her from her fiery prison.

Cold night air slapped her face, laced with the scent of musk and burning timber, and she stumbled outside, gasping in one grateful breath after another. Unsteadily she made her way across the grass, one slippered foot at a time, until her strength gave out, her knees tumbling her to the ground—and to safety.

Still clutching the music box, she managed to turn her head, shaking her wild tangle of hair from her face so she could see the full impact of the blaze from which she'd just escaped.

Flames were everywhere. They seemed to gobble up the entire row of structures that led from the shed to the outdoor staff's servants' quarters.

The servants' quarters . . .

God, no!

"Mama!" White fear descended like a monstrous dragon from a fairy tale. She battled her way to her feet, tripping over the hem of her nightgown and falling to the ground. Shoving herself upright, she abandoned the music box, cupping her hands to her mouth and calling, "Papa!" Dizziness swam through her head, but she ignored it, taking three tentative steps toward the wall of smoke and flame.

She never reached it.

"Mama . . ." She began to weave, her movements dragging strangely, everything unraveling in a series of slow, eerie motions. Abruptly her legs refused to obey the commands of her smoke-veiled mind, and then the grass was rushing up toward her at an alarming rate. She called for her parents again, but her voice sounded funny, and it seemed to come from somewhere far away. "Mama . . . Papa . . ." This time what emerged was a croak.

Her eyes slid shut, unconsciousness stifling her pleas and her resistance, wild flames completing their deadly mission as she slumped just beyond their portals.

One by one the buildings were swallowed up by the raging inferno.

Spared from its hideous destruction, she lay insensate, the music box resting in the grass behind her.

Secure and unscathed it lay, its mother-of-pearl uncharred, its gilt trim untainted.

Its melody utterly silent.

Chapter 1

April 1875

WHY IN GOD'S NAME HAD SHE REQUESTED THIS MEETING?

For the hundredth time, Bryce Lyndley asked himself that question, pondering the motive behind what was about to occur even as he steered his phaeton through the iron gates of Lady Nevon's elegant country estate. Tension knotted inside him, having escalated with each passing segment of his twenty-five-mile journey from London to Hertford.

He had yet to find an answer that suited him.

Damn. This chapter of his life had been closed decades ago, and he had no intention of allowing it to be reopened—especially not by the death of the very scoundrel who'd authored its pages.

Still, it *was* Lady Nevon who'd sent for him, Bryce reminded himself. And, even though his sole contact with her all these years had been through letters, the idea of refusing her fervent summons was unthinkable. He owed her a huge debt of gratitude—one that no number of visits could repay.

No number of visits? he thought wryly. In truth, this was the first time she'd ever requested his presence at her home. Until now she hadn't dared see him, much less invite him to Nevon Manor.

Oh, he knew precisely why. He knew, he understood, and he accepted.

He was also aware that, as of a week ago, the reason prompting her restraint was gone, having died along with the man who'd created it—the very man who'd been the insurmountable obstacle thwarting Lady Nevon's wishes, barring Bryce from his past.

Fine. So now Lady Nevon could send for him.

The question remained: why would she want to?

She, better than anyone, knew the past could not be undone. Like the cruelty and lies that defined it, the past and all its ills had long since been cast in stone. An eternity had elapsed, lives had been formed, and nothing and no one could alter those hard realities.

So what had prompted her to request this meeting? And why had her tone sounded so urgent?

"My brother is dead," her note had read. "Come to Nevon Manor at once. I've asked nothing of you in the past. Please don't refuse me now."

Bryce's jaw worked as he contemplated the information conveyed by her words. The fact that the Duke of Whitshire was dead meant as little to him as the blood they'd shared. The latter was no more than a cruel accident of fate, the former the inevitable culmination of life. After all, every man, saint and sinner alike, had to die. Even a soul as black as Whitshire's would therefore be reclaimed—doubtless to be sent straight to hell.

Abruptly Bryce's legal mind inserted itself, posing a new possibility. Death necessitated the disbursement of an estate, an intricate procedure, given the late duke's renowned wealth and assets. And while Whitshire had doubtless bequeathed his title and estate to his heir apparent—in this case, his legitimate son, Thane—that said nothing of any further provisos his will might have contained. Had that son of a bitch specified something to adversely affect Lady Nevon?

Was that the reason behind her unexpected summons? Did she require Bryce's help?

Doubtful. From all reports, Hermione Nevon's relationship with her brother had been a smooth one . . . so long as she complied with his wishes. Which, presumably, she did—with the exception of one pivotal undiscovered deception. Further, if there was anything amiss in Whitshire's will, Bryce would be the last person Lady Nevon would contact to dispute it, given his lack of objectivity.

Unless it was Bryce she meant to protect.

That prospect struck like a blow. Was it possible that, through his death, the duke had found a way to inflict some new plague on Bryce's life, one Lady Nevon intended to warn him of?

Impossible. Whitshire had believed Bryce dead. Lady Nevon herself had seen to that more than thirty years ago, convincing her brother that the bane of his existence had been cast into the streets, where he'd starved and perished.

Which eliminated Whitshire's will as a possible cause for today's summons.

Leaving the same nagging questions in its wake.

Easing his horses round the drive, Bryce abandoned his speculations. The manor loomed just ahead. Whatever Lady Nevon wanted, he'd learn about it soon enough. And whatever her request was, he'd find a way to oblige her—without dredging up the ugliness of the past.

He'd hardly made his decision when a small white streak shot across the drive, directly into the path of Bryce's oncoming phaeton. The streak—which revealed itself to be a swift but thoroughly terrified rabbit—froze for a moment, staring fearfully about before completing its mad dash to the opposite side of the drive, where it disappeared into the woods.

Bryce's horses went wild.

Whinnying their distress, they came to a screeching halt, rearing up and tossing their heads in protest.

"Easy!" Bryce commanded, tightening his grip on the reins and fighting to bring the horses under control as the carriage pulled precariously to the left.

After a brief struggle, the skittish mounts complied, and the carriage eased to a stop, teetering at the very edge of the drive. "Damn," Bryce muttered. Peering to his right, he scanned the woods, the fluttering leaves on the trees the only sign that they'd been recently disturbed.

"Sir! Pardon me—sir!"

Bryce's head snapped about at the approaching sound of the feminine voice breathlessly accosting him from the same direction as had the white streak. "Yes?" He blinked as a delicate young woman sprinted toward the carriage, a cascade of chestnut hair billowing out around her smudged, fine-boned face, her eyes—a brilliant cornflower blue—filled with worry.

"Did you see a white rabbit go by?" she panted, looking furtively about.

Despite the lingering effects of the past moments' tension, Bryce felt his lips twitch.

"Pardon me," the girl repeated, gazing at Bryce as if trying to assess his ability to hear. "Did you see a white rabbit go by? I spied him heading in this direction. I only pray your vehicle didn't strike him." With that, she forced herself to peer into the drive, her shoulders sagging with relief when she saw it was devoid of an injured animal. "Thank goodness. Still, I'm sure the commotion startled him. Lord knows where he went. I must find him before he gets hurt. He's too inquisitive for his own good. Oh, why did I doze off? I know Crumpet delights in racing off the first chance he gets. Are you sure you didn't see him—a rather bewildered-looking white rabbit who rushes about as if he's in a frightful hurry?"

That did it.

Bryce's shoulders began shaking with laughter. "I'm not certain," he managed. "Was this rabbit wearing a waistcoat? Contemplating a pocket watch, perhaps?"

At first the young woman's brows drew together, distress precluding comprehension. Then realization struck and her eyes began to twinkle. "No. Actually, he was quite bare."

"Ah. In that case, I can put your fears to rest. The scamp who, mere seconds ago, tore across the drive, terrorizing my horses and nearly catapulting my carriage from the road, was definitely white and assuredly bare. My guess is he's the rabbit you're searching for. If so, he's quite intact." Bryce pointed. "He darted into those woods, right beyond that elm." Another grin. "Will you be going in after him?"

One dimple appeared in each smudged cheek. "I think not. As long as he's in the woods, he's safe. So I'll let him have his fun. He'll be scolded later."

"With a scolding to look forward to, I doubt he'll return."

"Oh, he'll return—when the desire to eat overcomes the fear of reprimand." The girl tucked a strand of hair behind her ear. *"Or* when he consults his fictitious pocket watch and learns that it's mealtime," she added, laughter lacing her tone. Tilting back her head, she regarded Bryce with undisguised interest. "You must be Bryce Lyndley. Aunt Hermione's been expecting you."

Aunt Hermione? Now, that was an unknown scrap of information.

"Indeed I am," he said aloud. "I'm also at an obvious disadvantage. You know my name, but I haven't a clue as to yours. Unless, of course, it's Alice."

She flashed him another smile. "No. It's Gaby— Gaby Denning. Nevon Manor is my home." She backed away as she spoke. "Let's avoid making this an official introduction. Aunt Hermione would be most upset if she were to learn I'd met you when I was in such a disheveled state. She's very proud of you, you know. You *and* your accomplishments. She wants all of us to look and act our best when we're introduced to you. So I'd best hurry inside and make myself presentable. I'll see you . . . meet you"—she corrected herself—"shortly."

With that she darted toward the manor.

Bryce stared after her, amused by the encounter, intrigued by what he'd learned.

So Lady Nevon had a niece. Odd, he'd never known of her existence until now. Then again, he hadn't exactly been apprised of family matters. Evidently that was about to change, if all Lady Nevon's niece had just said was true. If what she'd blurted out was any indication of what lay ahead, he was about to meet an unknown number of people, all of whom had been advised to make a favorable impression on him.

Why?

There was only one way to find out.

Taking up the reins, Bryce urged the horses toward the manor.

"Good day, Mr. Lyndley. Lady Nevon is expecting you." A tall, stately butler opened the door, giving Bryce a lightning-quick head-to-toe perusal that, had Bryce been a tad less observant, would have escaped him. "Welcome to Nevon Manor," he continued with a practiced bow. Straightening, he held his chin high, his dark hair and pencil-thin mustache impeccably groomed, just barely tinged with gray. "My name is Chaunce. Anything you require, please let me know and I'll see that you get it."

"Thank you, Chaunce," Bryce responded, intrigued once again by the enthusiasm of his welcome, though still baffled by its cause. From the corner of his eye he spied a line of footmen, all darting about in a sudden flurry of motion, some carrying trays, others polishing the wood, all of them casting curious glances in his direction. Dryly, he wondered if they intended to line up and throw rose petals at his feet as he strolled the halls. "I truly require nothing, other than knowing where Lady Nevon is, that is."

"She's in the library, sir. I'll take you there myself, then see to your refreshment." The butler cleared his throat purposefully. "Correct me if I'm wrong, sir. As I understand it, you prefer coffee to tea. You take it black, no cream or sugar. As for what accompanies it, you fancy cinnamon cakes—with raspberry jelly, of course—rather than scones." A pause. "Any errors, sir?"

"Not a one." Bryce inclined his head, a fascinated gleam lighting his eyes. "Tell me, is there anything about me you don't know, Chaunce?"

"I try to be thorough, sir. Lady Nevon prefers it that way. Now, if you'll follow me." The butler gestured grandly, then turned and, hands clasped behind his back, headed down the polished hallway.

Bryce followed, feeling suddenly and uncustomarily off-balance. It took a great deal to unnerve him, which was why he was so bloody good at his profession. Yet now, preparing to face the woman who'd spared his life and ensured his future, he felt oddly uneasy, plagued by an awareness that old demons were on the verge of being confronted.

First a bantering session with a girl straight from the pages of a novel, now this.

For a man who was ruled by fact, rooted in thought rather than emotion, this day was turning out to be most unsettling.

"Yes?" a delicate voice responded to Chaunce's knock.

"Forgive me, madam," the butler began, opening the library door a crack, "but Mr. Lyndley is here."

"Thank God," Bryce heard her murmur to herself. Then: "Please, Chaunce, show him in."

Chaunce threw the door wide and gestured for Bryce to enter.

Slowly Bryce complied, wondering if the memory he'd carried with him all these years—of a tiny lady with aristocratic features and a knot of upswept honey blond hair—would match the woman he was about to see for the first time in twenty-three years.

"Bryce." The elderly matron who approached him, hands outstretched, was a replica of his memory, save the color of her hair—now snow white—and the previously absent lines of age set into her cheeks and brow. "Oh, Bryce." Tears shone in her pale blue eyes as she drank him in feature by feature, nodding her approval and clasping his hands in hers. "You look wonderful. Tall. Handsome. Even I couldn't anticipate . . ." She broke off. "Forgive me."

"It's good to see you too, my lady," Bryce returned, his voice raw as childhood memories slammed from past to present at a breakneck pace. "You're looking well—precisely as I remembered you, in fact." He kissed her hand.

"Hardly. But bless you for saying that." Her lips curved, and she released his hands with great reluctance. "Please, sit. Chaunce will fetch our refreshment. Then we'll talk."

Nodding, Bryce waited for her to be seated, then lowered himself into a library chair. "I came as soon as I got your message."

"Yes. I hoped you would." She fell silent as Chaunce reentered and placed a tray on the side table.

"Shall I pour, my lady?" the butler inquired.

"No, thank you, Chaunce. I'll pour."

"Very good. Will there be anything else?"

"Not at this time. I'll summon you shortly."

"Of course, my lady." Chaunce bowed. "Enjoy your visit."

Lady Nevon waited until the door had closed behind him. Then she turned her attention back to Bryce. "I have so very much to say to you. I always have, though I never could. But now, with Richard dead . . ."

"Please accept my sympathy on your loss."

Her brows rose. "Why would you offer something you can't possibly feel?"

"I beg to differ with you. I do indeed feel sympathy. Granted, it's for you, not the duke. But my personal opinion of him detracts nothing from the fact that he was your brother. The sympathy I'm offering is therefore quite genuine, I assure you."

A small smile curved Lady Nevon's lips. "You haven't changed, Bryce. You're still as straightforward and honest as ever. *And* as skilled at driving home your point. 'Tis no wonder no other barrister in England can compare with you. I thank you for your kind wishes. As for my feelings, they're mixed. You, better than anyone, know how very different my brother and I were. I loved him—but I very seldom liked him. To be frank, a part of me feels naught but relief at his death." She inclined her head. "Do I sound like a monster?"

"No, Lady Nevon. You sound human."

In reply, she took up the coffeepot, poured two steaming cups. "Lady Nevon. How very formal. Tell me, Bryce, after all these years, do you think you might call me Hermione?"

"If it would please you."

"It would." She handed him a cup, along with the tray of cinnamon cakes. "I trust these are still your favorites?"

"They are."

"Excellent. My cook has made dozens. Please help yourself."

Bryce placed two cakes on his plate, lounging back in a posture that was deceptively casual. "Forgive me, my lady, but am I the fly and you the spider?"

Lady Nevon's lips paused at the rim of her cup. "What on earth do you mean?"

"Only that you and your staff seem to be making the most extraordinary effort to please me. Am I being led to slaughter?"

A breath of laughter greeted his assessment. "No, Bryce. I assure you, you're quite safe." Her laughter faded, replaced by a sad, wistful look. " 'Tis only that I thought this day might never come, that I might never open my home to you as I have my heart. If I've gone too far . . . caused you any discomfort . . ."

"Of course not." Bryce felt a stab of remorse—and more than a twinge of guilt. "I apologize. My comment was rude and ungrateful." He pursed his lips, staring into his coffee. "To be frank, I'm not certain how to act. I owe you my childhood, my schooling, my career—my very life. But your message made me distinctly uneasy."

"My message, or me?"

"That depends upon your reason for sending it."

"I thought as much." Hermione emitted a long, resigned sigh. "You're furious with me." Setting down her saucer, she added, "I don't blame you. I've neglected you all these years, left you virtually alone since the Lyndleys died. My only excuse is that I'm weak. I feared for your life—and my own. I hadn't the strength to combat Richard's reaction had he guessed what I'd done, what I continued to do. So I kept my distance, to protect you—and myself. I'm a coward, Bryce. And because of it, you've had to grow up with only my letters for family. Can you ever forgive me?"

Bryce shoved his plate aside, amazed and appalled by such unwarranted self-censure. "Forgive you—for what? Sparing me the horrors of being cast into the streets to die like an animal? Secreting me in a place where Whitshire couldn't find me? Giving me two fine parents, a life, and a future?"

"Perhaps merely for having so heartless a man for a sibling," she replied quietly.

"Lineage is an accident of fate. I, better than anyone, know that—from firsthand experience. Let's compare my *blood* ties with my actual ones. Whitshire, the man who sired me, not only refused to acknowledge me but did all he could to guarantee my demise—and all so he could be spared the embarrassment of a bastard son. And my mother? She was either too weak, too frightened, or too selfish to keep me. She abandoned me on your doorstep and rushed back to the stage and her flourishing career. So much for bonds of the flesh. Now let's discuss true bonds. The Lyndleys raised me. They were fine, decent people who taught me right from wrong, conveyed to me—by example as well as by word—the importance of hard work, gave me a sense of belonging. *They* were my actual parents, Hermione—in every way that matters. They still would be, had that wave of influenza not killed them when I was ten."

"A tragedy I should have relayed to you, along with the rest of the disconcerting truth, in person, not by way of some cold, passionless letter."

"Your letter was neither cold nor passionless." Bryce visualized the bewildered ten-year-old boy who'd pored over an explanation that had forever altered his life. "It was filled with pain and sorrow—and a fervent wish that things could have been different."

"Do you have any idea how badly I wanted to come to you? To ride to Eton and sit beside you as I explained the details of your parentage, answered whatever questions I could? To assure you, time and again, that you were precisely the same extraordinary young man you'd always been—that nothing and no one could change that fact?"

Hermione pressed her trembling palms together. "But I didn't dare. Richard's connections extended to every prestigious member of Eton's admissions committee. There was but one man, Edward Strong, I trusted, and that was because he'd been a longstanding friend of my late husband, John. Edward was the person through whom I made all my anonymous payments for your schooling. As for the others—if any of them had seen me, there's not a doubt Richard would have heard about it. My brother was far from stupid. He'd have questioned me, delved until he discovered the truth. I couldn't risk it. I also wanted you to have more than my word on your true lineage. I wanted you to have written confirmation, should a situation ever arise in which verifying your true identity would prove necessary or useful. So, along with my letter, I had my messenger deliver all the papers your mother provided me when she abandoned you on my doorstep. I sent all those documents off to you—and then I waited, half praying you'd contact me, knowing full well you wouldn't."

"You implored me not to," Bryce reminded her, his tone more strained than he intended. "You wrote that we could have no contact other than through your letters. You said you feared for my life if Whitshire were to learn the truth."

"I most certainly did." Hermione paused. "And if I hadn't? Would you have contacted me had you not been forbidden to?"

"Probably not." Bryce looked away. "At least not at once. I needed time to make sense of things, to accept the enormous revelation I'd been handed." He swallowed. "Finding out I'd been lied to for ten years was quite a blow—one I had to contend with, and recover from, on my own."

"I didn't sleep for weeks, worrying over your reaction," Hermione added softly.

"I got over it." Bryce drew a sharp breath, determined to bring this conversation to an immediate halt. "In any case, you have nothing to apologize for. Certainly not for Whitshire, who committed his sins of his own accord. What's more, he's dead. Therefore he's no longer a threat to either of us. So why are we discussing him?"

"Why indeed." Hermione studied Bryce's expression thoughtfully.

"Let's get back to your note. Affection notwithstanding, it didn't sound to me as if you were inviting me to a reunion. Your tone was terse, strained. So why don't you tell me what's on your mind."

Hermione smoothed her hair in a light, fluttering gesture. "Goodness, but you're formidable. I wouldn't want to face you in a court of law."

A corner of Bryce's mouth lifted. "That's as it should be, given the enormity of your investment. You ensured me the finest education and training—Eton, Oxford, the Inns of Court."

"I paid only for you to attend. The fact that you flourished at each of those fine institutions was your feat and your feat alone." Rising, Hermione glided slowly across the library, in that majestic way Bryce remembered marveling at during her visits to the secluded cottage she'd established as the Lyndleys' home—*his* home.

The first and last home he'd known.

Fetching a volume from the bookshelf, Hermione opened it, smoothing out the pages of what appeared to be a scrapbook of sorts. "You finished at the top of your class, year after year," she cited aloud, flipping through the pages, caressing each one as if it were a precious jewel. "These are letters of commendation from the headmaster at Eton and from countless tutors at Oxford and the Inns of Court. You became thoroughly versed in both law French and law Latin. You were one of the youngest and most avid students to sit at Westminster Hall, and are now perhaps the most eloquent barrister to address the Chancery, King's Bench, and the Common Pleas Courts."

Again she turned the page, pointing at a newspaper clipping. "You're working toward establishing a General School of Law, which would teach both those reading for the bar and articled clerks alike. You're also making astonishing headway in the area of married women's property law, which would afford women rights they once never dreamed possible." Hermione looked up, proud tears glistening in her eyes. "And I have it on the finest authority that you are not only sought after by every respected solicitor in England but that, if the benchers at Lincoln's Inn have their way, you will one day be the youngest barrister ever to become Queen's Counsel—an incredible feat, given your humble origins." A half smile. "Shall I continue?"

"That scrapbook is a history of my life?" Bryce managed, stunned beyond comprehension. "You've actually kept records of every step of my schooling and my career?"

"Indeed I have. And not only through letters from the schools you attended and newspaper clippings extolling your fine legal accomplishments. My investigators have been quite thorough, informing me of all those things *not* covered by newspaper clippings and letters: your financial security, your connections to all the right people. So, yes, Bryce. I took—*take*—great pride in your accomplishments. And I follow your life with the utmost care."

"I see." His throat felt oddly tight.

"Did you think my only contact with you was through the occasional letter I dashed off?"

"In truth? Yes. Why in the name of heaven would you want to . . .?"

"Because my investment, as you call it, delves far deeper than you realize; it was more emotional than financial. Yes, I paid for your schooling. Yes, I bought your clothing, books, everything you needed to get by. But you're forgetting why I did all that, why I sequestered you in my late husband's obscure little Bedford cottage, selected my trusted servants the Lyndleys to fill the role of your parents while making sure Richard never knew. I did that, Bryce, because I cared about you—as I care about you still. You're my nephew, the closest thing I have to a child of my own. Were it not for Richard's coldhearted stubbornness . . ." Abruptly she swayed, clutching the bookshelf for support.

"Hermione, what is it?" Bryce was by her side in an instant, seizing her elbow and leading her back to the settee. "Are you ill?"

"Not ill. Old." A tired smile curved her lips. "Old and very, very weary."

"Nonsense." A muscle flexed in Bryce's jaw as he settled her in her seat, perched on the settee beside her. "I've never met anyone with more energy than you."

"You haven't seen me since you were eight, Bryce. Twenty-three years is a long time. I've aged—a lot." She patted his hand. "Which brings me to the reason why I summoned you. I need your help, if you'll agree to offer it."

"Consider it yours. How can I assist you?"

Another smile. "You're as gallant as you are intelligent and honest. I've chosen well."

"Chosen . . . for what?"

"To begin with, to revise my will. I have changes to make, things I want to secure, people I want to provide for. 'Tis imperative that all my papers and affairs be put in order. I'm asking you to take care of that for me."

"Of course. But what about your customary solicitor?"

"He's perfectly adequate. In this case, however, I need someone superior, someone I trust implicitly to effect these changes. I need you."

"I'm flattered." Bryce crossed one long leg over the other. "Very well, Hermione, I'd be pleased to lend my services."

"Good. Then you'll stay a few days."

"A few days?" His brows drew together in puzzlement.

"Certainly. It will take at least that long to review the details. I'll have Chaunce gather up all the household accounts and we can go through them together."

Bryce studied Hermione's earnest expression closely. If he hadn't known better, he'd have sworn he was being manipulated. But why? What could she hope to gain—unless it was company? Could she truly be lonely, frightened by her weakened condition? If that was the case, Bryce had no intention of denying her what she wished.

"All right," he agreed. "A few days, then. We'll revise your will and get your affairs in order."

"Excellent." She beamed, a bit of color returning to her cheeks as she lifted her cup to her lips. "That takes care of my immediate dilemma. Once we've addressed those issues, we can discuss the rest of your duties—those associated with your inheritance of my estate, your overseeing of my home and loved ones." Grandly she gestured toward the plate of cinnamon cakes. "Please have another."

"What did you say?" Bryce demanded, his every muscle going rigid.

"I merely urged you to—"

"Not about the cakes. Before that."

"Before that . . ." Hermione pursed her lips as she contemplated Bryce's question. "I believe I said we can discuss the remainder of your duties later. Is there some problem with that?"

"Hermione." Bryce gripped his knees. "Let's stop playing games. Did you just imply you'll be appointing *me* as beneficiary to your estate?"

"I didn't imply it. I stated it. Why—is that so surprising? As I said, you *are* my nephew, whether anyone else is aware of it or not. You're also a brilliant, accomplished, and compassionate man. Knowing you'll be inheriting my home, looking out for those I care for, will grant me peace of mind as my time draws near."

"So that's what this visit is all about."

"Whatever do you mean?"

Bryce tamped down on his exasperation, his trained legal mind striking out in a pragmatic direction. "Whitshire's son, Thane—he's your nephew, too. And were he your beneficiary, your estate could pass down without a shred of scandal. Surely you've considered that?"

"Of course I have. And you're quite right—as my legitimate nephew, Thane is, in the eyes of the world, the obvious choice. Up till Richard's death, he was my *only* choice. But that's no longer true, I'm relieved to say."

"Relieved? Why? Is Whitshire's son untrustworthy?"

"Oh, no, anything but. Thane is honest, decisive, and intelligent—a most remarkable man. Unfortunately, he's also overburdened with all the obligations associated with the management of Richard's empire, which was evidently more vast than any of us realized. The last thing he needs is another estate—and its residents—to oversee."

"That doesn't explain your relief that he's no longer the only possible choice of beneficiaries. If he's such a fine man, I would think you'd be eager to turn everything over to him—and terribly disappointed that his other commitments preclude him from accepting."

"That's why you're the barrister and I'm the wise old matron," Hermione replied, sipping at her coffee. "You think with your mind, and I with my heart. And what my heart tells me—what it's always told me—is that you're the best, the only, choice."

The *only* choice?

That prompted another thought.

"Your heart seems to have forgotten your niece," Bryce inserted dryly. "Even if, for whatever reason, you've deemed Thane unsuitable as your heir, that still leaves her."

Now it was Hermione's turn to look surprised. "My niece?"

"Yes. I met her a short while ago as my phaeton rounded the drive. Gaby, I believe she said her name was. I distinctly heard her refer to you as Aunt Hermione."

Hermione chuckled. "I should have known better than to think Gaby could wait to meet you when the others did. She has an abundance of curiosity—it's twice the size she is."

"Actually, she didn't intend to meet me. She was pursuing a rabbit and rushed into my path. She specifically asked that we not make our introduction a formal one so she wouldn't disappoint you."

"She could never disappoint me," Hermione amended warmly. "Gaby is the most precious person in my life—with the exception of you."

"Is she related to you through your late husband?"

"No. She's not related to me at all—at least not by blood. But as you yourself just said, blood ties are not always the most meaningful. I love Gaby every bit as much as if she were my daughter. In fact, I've raised her for thirteen years, ever since she was orphaned at five."

"I see." Actually, Bryce saw very little. Something was going on here, something quite odd. The problem was, he had no idea what it was. All he knew was that his head was reeling, both from what he *had* been told and from what he *hadn't*. He needed time to ponder this entire arrangement as well as to consider Hermione's implications and her motivations.

"You're troubled," she determined, scrutinizing Bryce's brooding expression.

"No, I'm taken aback. I'd like a chance to digest everything we've just discussed."

"I assumed you might." Hermione set down her coffee cup, dabbing delicately at each corner of her mouth with her napkin. "So I took the liberty of having your chambers made up. Chaunce can show you to them as soon as you've met the staff." A warm smile. "'Tis the one favor I ask of you before you retire to contemplate our chat. The servants are all terribly excited about meeting you, having heard years of praise regarding your achievements. I think you'll find my staff equally as exceptional as I do. As for your chambers, I think you'll be pleased with those as well. The wardrobe and chest have been stocked with every article of clothing you'll require, sized and styled to your precise needs and tastes, of course. As for the adjoining sitting room, it's been furnished with your most frequently consulted legal texts as well as a desk full of quills with which to pen your ideas, and paper upon which to pen them. In addition, the kitchen contains all your favorite foods, which Cook has been advised to prepare in whatever order you prefer. The wines—"

"Stop." Bryce rose from the settee, eyeing Hermione with equal amounts of wonder and disbelief. "You went to all this trouble for a few days' stay—and its intended outcome?"

"No, I went to all this trouble because pleasing you pleases me. As for the rest . . ." Hermione spread her hands with an optimistic sweep. "I can only pray that, once you've met my little family, pondered my request, you won't refuse what I'm asking of you."

"Family? What family?" Bryce was beginning to think he'd lost his mind.

"Why, the staff, of course." With that, she rang the bell beside her. "You will agree to meet them, won't you? Of course you will," she decided for him, gazing expectantly at the door, her expression brightening as she heard approaching footsteps. "Ah, Chaunce." She beamed as the butler entered the library.

"Yes, madam?"

"You've assembled everyone?"

"Indeed I have."

"Excellent. Then show them in."

"Certainly, madam."

Watching his retreating back, Hermione clapped her hands together, looking for the moment like an excited schoolgirl. "At last. All those I love will finally have the opportunity to meet one another."

Bryce remained silent, wondering at Hermione's choice of words as well as her enthusiasm. Obviously

23

her staff meant far more to her than mere employees. That shouldn't astound him; after all, she'd always treated the Lyndleys as if they were dear friends rather than a housekeeper and a valet. Still, he'd always assumed that was a special affinity reserved just for his parents. It had never occurred to him that Hermione felt the same fierce commitment and affection for every member of her staff.

Perhaps that was because he'd never imagined so much love could exist inside one person.

Bryce's attention snapped to the doorway as a flurry of footsteps sounded from the hall, accompanied by a profusion of excited voices and an occasional "ssh" when the din got too loud.

An instant later Chaunce reentered the room, a dozen pair of curious eyes peering around him. "We're all accounted for, my lady."

"Then by all means come in." Hermione gave a regal wave. "Everyone—come in."

Chapter 2

Bryce had no idea what he'd expected.

But whatever it was, it hadn't been this.

Hands clasped behind him, he stood beside the settee, keeping his expression carefully nondescript as the most curious and widely varied array of people one could envision traipsed, tripped, and stumbled into the room.

There were about thirty in all, men and women alike, ranging in age from six to sixty. The younger ones—three boys and two girls—wore trousers and day dresses rather than uniforms, looking more like children of the manor than like servants. In contrast to their polished attire, however, they seemed excessively timid, clustering together and hanging behind the adults to peek surreptitiously at Bryce with wide, awed gazes. Only one of them, a curly-haired lad of about eight, stood off to one side, leaning stiffly against the wall and occasionally shifting his weight as if he were in discomfort.

The cook, a heavyset woman with a crisp white

apron and eyes that crinkled when she smiled, marched straight over to the curly-haired lad, bending to say something soothing, nearly suffocating the boy with her bosom in the process. The lad averted his head in order to breathe, but despite whatever difficulty that entailed, he was clearly eased by the cook's gentle words, for he stood a bit taller when she ruffled his hair and turned away.

The ten or twelve footmen, whom Bryce recognized from their frantic efforts when he arrived, wore red uniforms with gleaming buttons. One of them, a stout man of middle years, kept frowning at a spot on his chest where a button was missing, muttering something unintelligible under his breath as he did. And another, a gaunt fellow with thinning gray hair, kept squinting in Bryce's direction, pausing occasionally to grope in his pockets and mumble about his missing spectacles.

The sturdy woman standing at the head of the female servants was clearly the housekeeper. She had wiry hair—strands of which stuck out of her bun like small, broken twigs—and a no-nonsense demeanor that reminded Bryce of a British general. Twice she whipped about to reprimand a round-faced maid in the rear who kept tripping on the Oriental rug and toppling forward onto an elderly maid just in front of her. The elderly maid looked oblivious to the fact that she was being flung about, smiling sweetly and chatting with the gnarled and wrinkled maid beside her, who Bryce was certain couldn't remain upright without benefit of the walking stick upon which she leaned.

Behind the maids came the serving girls, most of whom were painfully skinny and pale, two of whom had oddly vacant looks in their eyes, as if they weren't quite certain where they were and why.

In the rear, three men stood just inside the door: to the far left, a lanky fellow whose wheat-colored hair and spindly build made him look for all the world like a straw of hay and who clutched a garden shovel tightly in his hands; to the right, a leathery old chap who winced each time he shifted his weight; and between them, chatting incessantly first to the gardener then to the elderly servant, neither of whom replied, stood a ruddy-faced man with a wide mouth and an insufficient number of teeth, clad in an improperly buttoned driver's uniform.

Bryce had never seen such an unusual collection of servants in all his life.

"Now then, let's all settle down," Hermione began, clapping her hands, her tone gentle and commanding all at once.

Instant silence settled over the room.

"I'd like you all to meet . . ."

The library door jolted open, and rustling layers of green muslin tumbled in. "Forgive me," the girl named Gaby proclaimed, gazing anxiously about. "I'm late, aren't I?"

Hermione had no chance to respond.

"Miss Gaby—at last!" The awkward maid who'd been tripping over the Oriental rug stumbled forward, her round face lined with worry. "By now I'm sure you discovered the shattered pieces that are all that's left of that lovely vase you kept on your nightstand. I can't tell you how sorry I am for breaking it. You see, I was rewinding your music box when the edge of it accidentally bumped against the vase. I tried to save it, but I couldn't catch it in time and—"

"Marion," Gaby interrupted, clasping the distraught maid's hands and soothing her with the kind of wisdom and insight Bryce seldom beheld, much less perceived in one so young. "You did absolutely the right thing. In order to rescue the vase, you would have needed two hands and your full attention. And where would that have left my music box? I shudder to think. Given a choice between the two—you know very well where my heart lies. As always, you recognized precisely what to do. Your quick thinking saved my greatest treasure. And your honesty in relaying the truth to me proves yet again what a remarkable person you are."

The maid's eyes filled with grateful tears. "I'm so glad you feel that way."

"I do." Gaby gave her a conspiratorial wink. "Besides, that vase was big and unwieldy and took up far too much of my nightstand. Now my music box can stand alone, as it should."

"Miss Gaby?" The gnarled, elderly maid captured her attention, her tone as tentative as her stance. "Did you happen to have a chance—"

"I received confirmation this morning, Dora. Your new walking stick is on its way. It will be delivered tomorrow afternoon. According to the merchant who crafted it, it's twice as sturdy as the one you've been using." Gaby gestured toward Dora's cane—which, so far as Bryce could see, appeared to be in perfect condition.

"Wonderful." A smile softened the maid's wrinkled face. "Thank you."

"You're quite welcome." Gaby's gaze fell on the squinting footman, who was still groping through his coat pockets and muttering. "Bowrick, your spectacles are way down at the bottom of your left pocket," she supplied helpfully. "There you go—you've got them."

With a warm nod in his direction, she weaved her way through the crowd, hurrying forward to where her aunt stood. "I apologize for being late, Aunt Hermione," she resumed, a worried pucker reforming between her brows. " 'Tis just all these petticoats . . ." She broke off, blushing. "In any case, I'm here."

"Splendid, my dear." Hermione seemed not at all troubled by the unconventional entrance or the scandalous mention of undergarments. "Please." She beckoned the girl closer. "Come here. Before you dash out of the manor to go scampering through the woods with your animals, I'd like you to meet Bryce. Bryce, this is my niece, Gabrielle Denning. Gaby . . . Bryce Lyndley"—the barest heartbeat of a pause—"my dear friend and business adviser."

Bryce stepped forward to acknowledge the introduction, noting that the enchanting young woman before him bore little resemblance to the rumpled girl he'd met an hour ago—with the exception of her vitality and those bottomless cornflower-blue eyes. Her chestnut hair, no longer tousled, was now neatly arranged in shining curls that cascaded down her back, and her face, scrubbed free of smudges, was exquisitely delicate and incredibly lovely.

"Gabrielle," he addressed her, fully intending to make believe their earlier meeting had never occurred. "'Tis a pleasure." Smiling politely, he brought her fingers to his lips.

Gaby inclined her head, her eyes veiled with uncertainty. "Mr. Lyndley and I have met, Aunt Hermione," she blurted. "I never intended for it to happen. I was truly going to wait this time, I promise. But you see, Crumpet dashed in front of Mr. Lyndley's phaeton, and I had no choice—"

"It's all right, Gaby," Hermione interjected. "Running into someone can be described only as an accident of fate, not a formal presentation. Thus, we'll consider this to be the first time you and Bryce have met."

"Oh, thank you," Gaby breathed, her entire face lighting up. "In that case, I'm delighted to meet you, Mr. Lyndley. And I apologize for being late."

A grin tugged at Bryce's lips. "Think nothing of it. However, if you'd like, I could lend you a pocket watch. It might help both you and Crumpet."

Gaby dissolved into spontaneous laughter. "That would be greatly appreciated—by both of us."

From the corner of his eye, Bryce saw one of the youngsters, a little girl with a solemn expression, inch forward, tugging on Chaunce's sleeve until the butler leaned over, after which she cupped her hand over his ear and whispered something into it.

"Ah, thank you, Lily. I'm sure Miss Gaby will be quite relieved." He straightened, looking over at Gaby. "It seems Lily came upon Crumpet during her morning stroll. He had invaded the garden yet again."

"What'd he eat this time?" the hay-straw fellow piped up from the rear, sounding more resigned than angry. "Just tell me, so I'll know where my shovel and I will be spendin' the afternoon."

"Actually, your garden is intact, Wilson," Chaunce assured him. "As good fortune would have it, Lily arrived just moments after Crumpet. She thwarted his intended eating binge, scooped him up, and took him to her room, where he is currently awaiting punishment."

"Good girl, Lily," Wilson praised. "Hear that?" he murmured to his shovel. "Thanks to Lily's quick thinkin', we can work on that section of primroses, just like we planned."

"Oh, Lily, you're wonderful! Thank you." Evidently unperturbed by Wilson's chat with an inanimate object, Gaby rushed over and hugged the little girl, whose solemn face erupted into a heartwarming—and Bryce suspected rare—smile. "I was frantic about Crumpet's whereabouts, especially since I hadn't time to search all his favorite hiding places. And even if I'd had the time, I'd never have thought to look in the garden, not after he was banished from it last week. How clever of you to find him!"

"Shall I bring him to you?" the child asked in a whisper.

"I have a better idea. After we've all met Mr. Lyndley, you and I can go to your chambers and deal with him together."

"New curtains will have to be ordered," Chaunce said with a tolerant sigh. "Master Crumpet so likes the frilled curtains in Lily's room—I suspect that, by now, they're quite ragged at the edges."

"I suspect you're right, Chaunce." Gaby grinned. "Sometimes I think Crumpet is part goat. In any case, fear not. I myself shall take Lily to the village and select material for her new curtains. We'll sew them together. How would that be, Lily?" She gazed lovingly down at the child.

A vigorous nod was her reply.

"Excellent." Gaby cast another rueful glance at Hermione. "I've disrupted your introductions again, haven't I?"

"To the contrary, you've made them that much more memorable," Hermione countered. "You've helped show Mr. Lyndley precisely what makes our family so special." She cleared her throat. "Bryce, the charming young lady beside Gaby who rescued Crumpet from an even sterner punishment is Lily."

"Hello, Lily," Bryce responded.

Lily dropped her gaze, scraping her shoe along the rug, obviously uncomfortable at being the center of attention.

"Lily is a bit shy," Hermione continued, "as is her sister, Jane, the little moppet over there." She pointed at a blond child whose legs were so reed-thin that Bryce wondered how they could support her. "Lily is seven, Jane six. They, along with the boys—Peter, Henry, and Charles—help Gaby take care of her animals—or rather, her menagerie. Gaby has dozens of pets, and they're all mischief-makers, just like Crumpet." Hermione gestured the boys forward. "Come, boys. Say hello to Mr. Lyndley."

Henry and Charles, two sturdy boys with dark hair and eyes, came forward with only a tad more ease than the girls, murmuring their how-do-you-do's as quick as a wink, then rushing back to their places, pausing only to toss Gaby a grin. Peter, the lad who'd been leaning against the wall, followed after, limping forward and dragging his right leg in his wake. He halted at the settee, studying Bryce's face with a clear, intelligent gaze. "How do you do?" he said aloud.

"Very well." Bryce shook the boy's hand, his chest tight with compassion.

"Peter is Cook's son," Hermione explained. "When I hired Cook, I was blessed to get him as well."

"I'm extremely pleased to meet you, Peter," Bryce told the lad. "You *and* Henry, Charles, Jane, and Lily. Gabrielle is lucky to have five such capable helpers to assist her with her pets."

"You needn't pretend," Peter inserted calmly. "I know I'm not nearly as capable as the others. I also know why: it's because I'm lame. But that's okay. I do the best I can. The truth is, my lameness makes other people more uncomfortable than it makes me."

"I wasn't pretending. Yes, I can see your leg gives you some trouble. But I can also see that you have a keen mind and a generous heart. Not to mention the fact that you're straightforward and honest. Those traits, Peter, will more than make up for a reluctant limb."

Interest flickered in Peter's eyes. "How do you know I'm all those things?"

"Because part of my job is figuring out people's natures when I meet them. And, like you, I'm very good at my job."

"Lady Nevon says you're a barrister."

"That's true."

"It will be harder for me when my time comes," Peter stated candidly. "I'll have to take exams—and pass them. You probably became a barrister before that rule started. Not that it would have mattered. You would have passed those exams without even trying. Lady Nevon says you're the smartest barrister in England."

Bryce blinked, startled by the lad's implication, as well as by the realization of just how quick his mind was. "Are you saying you want to become a barrister, Peter?"

"Yes, sir. I know I'm not a nobleman—"

"Neither am I," Bryce interrupted. He squatted down, meeting the lad's gaze head-on. "How old are you, Peter?"

"Nine."

"Nine." Bryce shook his head in amazement. "Peter, I have a distinct feeling that you are not only going to become a barrister but that, in twenty years or so, you're going to unseat me in Lady Nevon's estimation as the smartest barrister in England. In fact, I'm sure of it."

Pride emanated from every inch of Peter's frame. "Thank you, sir." He hesitated. "Is it true you have legal texts in your chambers?"

"From what I understand, yes. Would you like to see them?"

"May I?" It was as if the lad had been promised the world. "I know I won't be able to read many of the words, but just looking at them would be enough."

"Consider it done." Bryce glanced at the clock on the mantel. "Why don't we check with your mother, then set a time after lunch. How would that be?"

"Splendid, sir."

Bryce looked past Peter, searching the crowd until he spied Cook. He was stunned to see tears gathered in her eyes. "Is that acceptable?" he asked.

"You're very kind, Mr. Lyndley. Thank you."

"You're more than welcome, Mrs. . . . ." He paused in question.

"Hayzeldenton," the buxom woman supplied, dashing the moisture from her eyes and giving Bryce a warm smile. "Which is far too long and much too difficult to pronounce. So please call me Cook. Everyone at Nevon Manor does." She sank into a curtsy, her bowed head disappearing into the pillow of her own bosom. "I'm honored to meet you, sir," she declared as she rose.

"I'm please to meet you as well, Cook." Bryce was relieved to see that she was still breathing.

"Excellent. Now you've met Cook," Hermione said with a nod of approval. "Mrs. Gordon?" She gestured toward the housekeeper. "It's your turn."

The stout woman with the twigs for hair marched forward. "How do you do, Mr. Lyndley?" she barked. "I trust your shoes are clean."

Bryce blinked. "Pardon me?"

"Mrs. Gordon keeps an immaculate house," Hermione supplied. "She believes in cleanliness . . ."

"And discipline," the housekeeper added.

"Of course. And discipline," Hermione amended. Lowering her gaze, she studied Bryce's shoes intently. "I don't think you need concern yourself, Mrs. Gordon," she pronounced. "Mr. Lyndley is clearly neat as a pin."

With a suspicious glance at Bryce's feet, the housekeeper gave a wary sniff. "I'm glad to hear that. I have enough trouble keeping things in order as it is. Take that rabbit for example. Why, I'm sure by now he's covered Lily's room with his tracks."

"I sympathize with your plight, Mrs. Gordon." Bryce found himself studying his own shoes, grateful to see they were devoid of any offensive specks of dirt. "I'll do my best not to contribute to your dilemma."

"See that you do." With that, the housekeeper turned and strode back to her place.

"Mrs. Gordon has been with me for one and thirty years," Hermione explained to Bryce, showing not a trace of discomfort at her servant's sharp tongue. "Ever since your mother left her position here in order to oversee my Bedford cottage and, of course, to raise you. I was so dependent on Mrs. Lyndley—I'd never have survived losing her had it not been for Mrs. Gordon's ability to step right in and take charge. She's been a lifesaver all these years." Pausing, Hermione glanced over at Bryce, a flicker of amusement twinkling in her eyes. "You needn't look so terrified," she murmured for his ears alone. "Her bark is worse than her bite."

"I'll try to remember that," Bryce returned dryly.

"Now then," Hermione continued in a normal tone. "For the rest of the family. Wilson, as you've probably guessed, is our incomparable gardener. Over there"—she gestured toward the leathery fellow on the right—"is Reaney, who runs the stables as if they were Ascot, acting as groom, trainer, and stableman all in one . . . and that's despite his advanced case of gout. Standing between Wilson and Reaney"—a wave toward the babbling fellow with the misbuttoned uniform—"is Goodsmith, the finest driver *and* storyteller in all of England. Say hello to Mr. Lyndley, gentlemen."

All three men complied.

Before Bryce could catch his breath, Hermione launched onward, introducing a long line of footmen, maids, and serving girls whose names Bryce couldn't retain but all of whom had two things in common: their unswerving loyalty—both to Hermione and to each other—and their obvious and assorted oddities, the essence of which clearly diminished their effectiveness as employees.

And yet Hermione had hired them. No, she'd more than hired them. She'd retained, nurtured, and treasured them, not only in spite of their oddities but, as Bryce's heart and instincts concurred, because of them.

He couldn't remember the last time he'd felt so moved or the last time he'd seen such selfless generosity.

Then again, maybe he could.

He cast a swift, tender look at his hostess. Once again Hermione Nevon had rendered her magic, this time not with a bastard infant but with a group of lost souls, wresting them from a questionable fate, taking them in and transforming them into a family.

A family she wanted to bequeath to him, to entrust to his care when she was no longer there to offer them hers.

Lord, the magnitude of that responsibility was overwhelming.

To accept it would be arduous.

To refuse it, unforgivable.

Which left him—where?

"You're exhausted, Bryce," Hermione said quickly, as if reading her nephew's thoughts. "To be frank, so am I." She sighed, sinking back against the cushions of the settee.

"Are you all right?" Bryce asked at once.

"Yes, of course." A faint smile. "Just fatigued. Besides, 'tis you, not I, I'm concerned about. We've bombarded you with enough excitement for one morning." Her weary gaze swept the room. "You can all return to your chores now," she instructed the staff, forcing a reassuring smile to her lips. "We'll meet again at lunch, at which time we can continue our visit with Mr. Lyndley."

On cue, the servants began milling—and in some cases stumbling—out of the library, leaving only Chaunce, Gabrielle, and the little ones in their wake, all of whom hung back, their expressions anxious.

Hermione's lashes fluttered. "Bryce, Chaunce will take you to your chambers so you can rest."

"Forgive me, madam," Chaunce inserted, clearing his throat. "But it is time for your medicine. Shall I fetch it before escorting Mr. Lyndley to his room?"

"No. It can wait until you've returned."

"It most assuredly cannot." Startled and troubled by the knowledge that Hermione required medication, Bryce bit back his concern—and his questions—about what she was taking and why. "I'm perfectly capable of locating my own room. Let Chaunce see to your medicine."

"I won't hear of it," Hermione demurred.

"I'll fetch your medicine, Aunt Hermione," Gaby offered, concern furrowing her brow as she hastened to her aunt's side. "Lily," she asked, giving the child a meaningful look, "you won't mind entertaining Crumpet a few minutes longer, will you?"

Lily shook her head at once, her distressed gaze fixed on Hermione.

"Good." Pride and tenderness laced Gaby's tone. "Go on, then, you and the others. I'll come to your room in a little while." With that, she turned back to Hermione. "Where can I find your medicine? You've never actually told me where you keep it."

"It's in the pantry," Hermione murmured. "On the very top shelf—far too high for you to reach. Chaunce keeps it there so none of the children can mistake it for refreshment and accidentally drink it." A contemplative frown. "I don't see how we can manage this."

"Might I suggest that Miss Gaby show Mr. Lyndley to his quarters?" Chaunce proposed. "In that way, you'll feel reassured that our guest is settled, and he in turn will feel reassured that you're receiving the proper care."

"Of course," Hermione said, relief flooding her face. "Whatever would I do without you, Chaunce? That's a wonderful idea." She inclined her head at Gaby. "Would you mind, dear? You know which room Mrs. Gordon readied for Mr. Lyndley."

"Of course I don't mind," Gaby replied, looking as relieved as her aunt. "Come, Mr. Lyndley. I'll show you the best route to your quarters."

Brushing a quick kiss to the top of Hermione's head, Gaby led Bryce from the room.

"This really isn't necessary," he said once they were in the hallway. "As I told your aunt, I'm perfectly capable of finding my own quarters."

"That's what you think," Gaby apprised him. "You'll soon see otherwise. Nevon Manor is huge, its halls more winding than a maze. Why, some of the servants still have trouble finding their way around, and they've lived here for years. Trust me, Mr. Lyndley, without the proper guidance, one could get dreadfully lost."

A corner of Bryce's mouth lifted. "Just as Alice did in Wonderland?"

Gaby's laughter spilled forth like sunshine. "Precisely so."

"In that case, I'll retract my claim and accept your guidance with the utmost humility."

"A wise choice." Gaby gestured toward the stairway. "Come." Gathering up her skirts, she led him up to the second floor landing, then along a series of corridors that twined to and fro until Bryce began to feel grateful for the escort.

"Who on earth designed this manor?" he muttered.

"Lord Nevon did," Gaby supplied, slowing down until she could walk beside Bryce. "He was a great fan of mazes, so he fashioned Nevon Manor as one. It's wonderful fun, especially for the children. They conduct their races right here in the hallways."

"'Tis a wonder they ever emerge." Bryce glanced about him, noting the stark contrast of decorations—oddly shaped vases atop elegant mahogany side tables, unusual paintings adorning traditionally textured walls. "Is there nothing ordinary about this house?" he asked aloud.

"Not a thing. How could there be? There's nothing ordinary about Aunt Hermione." Gaby followed Bryce's gaze and smiled. "What you're seeing is a bit of everyone's taste. As a family, we're all permitted to provide little touches of our own. Hence an unusual blend of decorations, not only in our individual rooms but throughout the manor."

"The residents are unique as well."

"True." Gaby tucked a strand of hair behind her ear, angling her head to study Bryce's expression. "You're puzzled. I suppose I would be, too." She pointed down the hall, where their path curved off to the right. "Your room is just around that bend. If you'd like, I can answer your questions—at least a few of them—while I acquaint you with your surroundings. I'd answer them all, but I did promise Lily I'd fetch Crumpet as soon as possible. So the rest of our discussion will have to wait until later."

"Thank you." Bryce fell silent, his mind racing over the myriad questions he wanted answers to, trying to decide which ones were the most pressing.

His concern decided for him.

"Hermione," he announced the instant Gaby led him through the door to his chambers. "I want to know about Hermione. Is she ill? What medicine does she require and how long has she been taking it? Is her condition serious?"

Gaby paused at the mahogany chest, her fingers skimming its gilded handles. "I don't know how serious Aunt Hermione's condition is," she said quietly. "According to her, she's just tired and still recovering from her brother's death. She summoned our physician, Dr. Briers, just after word of His Grace's passing reached her. It was on that visit that Dr. Briers insisted Aunt Hermione begin taking medicine."

"On *that* visit?" Bryce repeated. "Were there others?"

"Yes." Gaby swallowed. "One other that I know of—about a month before the duke's death. Aunt Hermione is very private about her health, so I haven't an inkling what was discussed, nor do I know what condition her medicine treats. All I know is that most times she's her usual vital self; but every once in a while—especially this past week—she becomes terribly tired and weak. Then we're all excused from the room except Chaunce, who's the only person she'll turn to for help, and we don't see her for hours. Presumably she's resting. At least that's what I tell myself. Ofttimes I stand outside her door, aching to burst in and insist that she accept my support. But I understand how proud she is, how important it is for her to feel independent. So I force myself not to intrude."

A poignant pause before Gaby added, "My intentions are not entirely noble, I'm afraid. There's a part of me that doesn't want to hear anything dire, doesn't want to face the possibility that Aunt Hermione isn't well. Instead, I pray. Every night I ask God to leave her with us, to understand that we need her far more than he possibly could. I realize that's selfish. But in truth, I don't know what we'd do without her." Gaby's voice broke, and she bowed her head, fighting for control. "Forgive me. I'm sure you didn't want to hear all that."

The knot in Bryce's gut had intensified with each passing word. No, he hadn't wanted to hear Gaby's fervent explanation. But not for the reason she suspected. She thought him a detached stranger, one who was drifting through their lives like a passing cloud, only to vanish as quickly as he'd arrived; that, as a result, he'd feel uncomfortable, maybe even irritated by hearing so intimate a recounting. In truth, just the opposite was true. What he felt was a combination of wonder and trepidation; trepidation over the possibility that Hermione's health might be failing, wonder over Gaby's ardent, genuine anguish. Clearly, the young woman standing before him loved Hermione with all her heart.

It was humbling to realize that Hermione was capable not only of feeling such love but also of inspiring it in others.

Grappling with a barrage of unexpected sentiments, Bryce walked over, handed Gaby his handkerchief. "I'm the one who should apologize," he countered, staring at her crown of shining hair and experiencing a sudden and insistent need to comfort her *and* to make her understand whatever fragments of his state of mind he felt able to share. "I didn't mean to upset you or to besiege you with questions. It's just that, in my own way, I care a great deal about Hermione. I've always thought of her as—inexhaustible, I suppose, perhaps even invincible. It's hard to imagine her as ill or weak."

"I agree." Gaby dried her cheeks, raising her chin to regard Bryce thoughtfully. "You've known Aunt Hermione your whole life, haven't you? Your mother was once her housekeeper."

Warning bells. "Yes. Hermione had been widowed but a few short years when I was born. With her customary generosity, she allowed my family the use of her late husband's small Bedford cottage. To hear her describe it, it was *they* who were doing *her* the colossal favor by agreeing to change residence just to oversee Lord Nevon's neglected estate. But my parents knew the truth—and they blessed Hermione for it every day of their lives."

"The truth?"

"Um-hum. My father, you see, had served as Lord Nevon's valet, and with his lordship gone, there was no dignified position at Nevon Manor for my father to fill."

"Leaving him with a new babe and no job," Gaby supplied.

"Something like that," Bryce hedged. "In any case, thanks to Hermione's typical show of kindness, Father acquired both."

"I see." Gaby never averted her gaze. "She obviously cared deeply for your parents, just as she does for you. She speaks of you with such pride, such love. All these years I tried to envision what you'd be like, if you'd really be as wonderful as Aunt Hermione claimed. Frankly, I doubted it. I'm so glad I was wrong."

Bryce started, taken aback by the blunt, contradictory assessment—an overt insult followed by a charmingly candid retraction. "Now you've sparked my curiosity. Why did you doubt your aunt's faith in me and what makes you think your doubts were misplaced?"

"My doubts were rooted in one simple fact: I couldn't accept that a man as remarkable as Aunt Hermione described would elect never to see her, that not one time in all these years have you visited Nevon Manor."

Everything inside Bryce went cold. "Did you put that question to Hermione?"

"Yes. Only once, because it seemed to upset her greatly."

"And what did she say?"

"She said it was her fault, that she'd severed all direct ties with you a lifetime ago, that her motives were sound and unable to be discussed."

"And you didn't believe her?"

Gaby's tongue wet her lips. "Of course I believed her. But knowing *why* you never came here shed little light on *how* you could discipline yourself not to do so. I don't care how definitively Aunt Hermione ordered you to stay away or what her motives were for doing so. I just couldn't understand your willingness to comply, to remain absent all this time. Not when we all saw firsthand how much Aunt Hermione missed you, how incredibly proud of you she was. Why, rarely a day went by that she didn't boast of your intelligence, your accomplishments, your compassion. I'm sure you had your reasons, but I just couldn't fathom what they were. I still can't. Nor have I the right to ask."

Guilt reared its ugly head as Gaby's accusation sank in, along with the memory of Hermione showing him her scrapbook, proudly recalling all the highlights of his life, not to mention announcing she'd chosen him to inherit hers. Until today he'd never so much as imagined Hermione thinking of him, much less praising him, following his career, and—as Gaby had just suggested—missing him.

By Gaby's portrayal, he sounded like a scoundrel.

Feeling her eyes upon him, Bryce shelved his guilt for the moment, realizing that his immediate dilemma was responding to her unspoken question. He rubbed his palms together, weighing her words and his reply. He should have come prepared for this sort of confrontation, but he hadn't. Then again, he hadn't anticipated conversing with anyone at Nevon Manor other than its mistress. By his original estimations, he'd be on his way back to London by now, having completed his business—*and* his unwanted brush with the past.

Lord, had he been wrong.

"What your aunt told you is true," he began, determined to absolve Hermione while skirting the same painful truth she herself had avoided. "Except the part about our separation being her fault. She wasn't the villainess here; if anything, she was the heroine. I'm afraid that's all I can say."

Gaby nodded, twisting the handkerchief in her hands. "I understand this matter is a private one and that Aunt Hermione wishes for it to stay that way. Still, I thank you for your candor. It makes me all the more certain of my response to your question—the one about why I believe my doubts of you were misplaced. *I* didn't change my mind about you, Mr. Lyndley. *You* did."

"You've lost me."

Tenderness softened her bright blue eyes. "I watched you today, not only with Aunt Hermione but with everyone. From Lily to Mrs. Gordon, from Wilson to Reaney—you accepted them all, not with judgment but with the very compassion Aunt Hermione boasts you possess. And then there's Peter. What you did for him was more valuable than all the Queen's jewels combined. Oh, everyone discerns Peter's intelligence, but few take the time to delve deeper, to see beyond the surface to the extraordinary boy beneath. In your case, it took scarcely a minute before you recognized just how special he is, how desperately he wants to be a barrister, to apply his mind in a way that will help others. Did you see his face when you promised to show him your legal texts? He's was positively glowing, ready to explode with excitement. I've never seen him so elated. He's always rather quiet and inward, resigned to the fact that he can't keep up with the others. You felt his yearning, Mr. Lyndley. That's not done with the mind, no matter how much you profess otherwise. That, sir, is done with the heart."

Gaby paused, drew a slow breath. "And speaking of the heart, let's discuss your concern for Aunt Hermione, your keen sense of loyalty and respect for her." Another pause, as if there was so much to say and insufficient words, or time, in which to say it. "Thank you for caring," she finished in a small voice. "Regardless of your reasons for staying away, I'm glad that, at last, you've come to Nevon Manor. I believe it will make all the difference in the world—to Aunt Hermione, to all of us." She held out Bryce's handkerchief, dispelling her solemn mood with a tiny speculative smile. "And now, I'd best get to Lily. Heaven only knows what havoc Crumpet has wreaked by this time."

Automatically, Bryce took the folded square of linen, his fingers brushing Gaby's, his gaze flitting over her delicate, fine-boned features with more than a flicker of amazement. Never had he encountered someone who demonstrated such natural and open expressions of emotion, who said what she thought and displayed what she felt without hesitation or censure. An open book—how incredibly refreshing in a world of self-containment and false veneers.

A world to which he himself subscribed.

"Mr. Lyndley?"

Gaby's questioning tone told Bryce he'd been staring. "Yes?" Recovering himself, he found he was curiously loath to let her leave, despite the fact that his mind was screaming its need to properly digest the morning's events. Did his reticence stem from the dozen questions he wanted answered, or was it a simple reaction to how very much he was enjoying her company?

"I really must be on my way," Gaby repeated, her expression uncertain and a trifle apologetic. "Can the remainder of your questions wait until later?"

"That depends," Bryce heard himself say. "Will I see you later?"

"Of course." Gaby's nod was definitive. "At lunch."

"And may I ask my horde of questions then?"

"By all means."

"In that case, go to Lily." He stepped back, making a wide sweep with his arm and watching as she gathered up her skirts and walked toward the doorway. "Gabrielle?"

She turned, brows raised in question.

"Thank you for showing me to my room."

Warm color tinged her cheeks. "Welcome to Nevon Manor, Mr. Lyndley."

Quick as the white rabbit, she was gone.

Downstairs, Chaunce reentered the library, shutting the door and placing a tray on the side table. "Your medicine, my lady," he announced.

Hermione sighed, leaning back against the cushions of the settee. "Thank you, Chaunce," she managed in a whisper.

"The others have returned to their chores," he advised her, "and the library door is locked."

One eye cracked open, and she peeked up at him from beneath her lashes. "We're alone?"

"Quite alone, madam."

"Excellent." Leaping lightly to her feet, Hermione smoothed her hair into place, facing Chaunce with a glow in her eyes. "Splendidly done, my friend. A fine onset."

"Thank you, my lady." Deliberately, Chaunce poured a measure of liquid into a cold glass of water. "Your medicine," he reminded her.

"Oh, yes, of course." Beaming, Hermione hurried forward and took the glass, drinking it down with great enthusiasm. "Thank you, Chaunce. You do make the most delicious lemon water."

"I try, my lady." Replacing the refreshment on its tray, he clasped his hands behind his back, inclining his head in question. "How did it go?"

"Better than even *I* expected—worth every dreadful moment of the past week's feigned infirmity." She interlaced her fingers, her cheeks flushed with pleasure. "Did you hear them laughing together in the hallway?"

"I did indeed. Their banter accompanied me all the way to the pantry." A satisfied smile. "So their first meeting was a success."

"A huge success. According to my sources, Bryce rarely laughs and never lets down his aura of reserve, especially with that *woman* he's been escorting about Town."

Chaunce's lips twitched. "That *woman,* as you refer to her, is a well-bred young lady from a fine family."

"I don't care. She's all wrong for Bryce. *I* know it, *you* know it, and soon *Bryce* will know it, too. I intend to make quick work of Lucinda Talbot."

"I'm sure you will. But getting back to the immediate issue, how did today's meeting with Mr. Lyndley go? How did you fare?"

Hermione's smile faded a bit. "As well as could be expected, given the circumstances. At least he heard me out. I was half afraid he'd bolt before I'd finished."

"You told him about the guardianship?"

"No, Chaunce, I didn't dare mention that—yet. 'Twas enough that I asked him to inherit Nevon Manor and all it entails. That in itself was a shock. I shudder to contemplate what his reaction would have

46

been had I proclaimed the rest in the very same breath."

"So that's all you discussed—inheriting Nevon Manor?"

"That and revising my will. He had a dozen questions about Thane and my motives."

"We knew he would."

"Yes, we did. In any case, I've given him a great deal to mull over. He's met the staff. Knowing Bryce's level of compassion, he understands what I need of him—and why."

"But not all of it."

"No, not all of it."

Chaunce pursed his lips. "Still, I do believe I can discard our original plan, devised before the duke's passing. His Grace is no longer a threat, and Mr. Lyndley is very much here. So no creative methods will be necessary."

"True." Hermione sighed. "Such a stubborn man, Richard was. He could have reveled in the splendid man his son has become. And instead . . ." She broke off with a shrug. "What's done is done. Richard is gone, along with all the pain he inflicted on Bryce's life. Now 'tis time for me to change the course of things, to rectify the future. I'd undo the past if I could, but I fear such a feat is beyond even *my* capabilities. But the future . . . ah, now, that is another matter entirely." She paced about, tapping her chin thoughtfully. "We'll continue our strategy with arrangements for lunch. Chaunce, make sure Gaby is seated next to Bryce."

"It's already been arranged, my lady. Also, with regard to Miss Gaby, you'll be pleased to learn that she has yet to return from showing Mr. Lyndley to his quarters."

"Wonderful!" Hermione clapped her hands together. "That was an excellent touch, Chaunce, arranging for Gaby to show Bryce to his room. You're becoming quite adept as a matchmaker."

"You're a fine instructor, madam."

"I've had years of self-tutoring in preparation for orchestrating Bryce and Gaby's future. I mean for this plan to succeed. Thus far we've confronted and conquered step one. Nevertheless, we have a long way to go. Tonight, after Bryce feels a bit more settled in, I'll proceed to step two: elaborating on my earlier request that he oversee the estate after my death. I'll ask you to fetch your meticulously kept household accounts for the three of us to review together. Once that's been done, I'll explain to Bryce the provisions I've made for my staff—provisions I want him to ensure. Finally, and most crucially, I'll reveal to him the single most significant part of my bequest."

"The guardianship?"

An exhilarated nod. "The guardianship. At which point, Chaunce, you and I must hold our breath, gauge Bryce's reaction, and await his decision—a decision I pray will be the one we seek."

Delicately, Chaunce cleared his throat. "And if it's not?"

Hermione's smile was the essence of confidence. "Then we'll simply have to change his mind."

Chapter 3

GABY'S FINGERS DANCED OVER THE KEYBOARD, HER EYES
sliding shut as the melody seeped inside her, pervading the room along with the late afternoon sunlight.
She'd come here straight from Crumpet's warren,
where she'd lingered only long enough to verify that
he'd stayed put, as commanded, since just before
lunch. Reassured that no further escape attempts had
been made, she'd headed directly to her beloved
piano, somehow needing the peace and beauty only
Beethoven could provide.

Some of her happiest hours were spent here, in the
richly decorated green velvet music room that
brought her closer to her feelings, her thoughts . . .
and her memories.

Today it was the present rather than the past that
prevailed, her thoughts scrambling over one another
in their efforts to be heard.

Having shared two introductions, one chat, and an
afternoon meal with Bryce Lyndley, Gaby had determined that he was everything and nothing she'd
expected.

He'd been an absent yet exalted presence at Nevon Manor since the day she'd come to live here, the pride of Aunt Hermione's life and an example to them all. How many stories had she heard of the boy whose intelligence and compassion had propelled him into a success that far surpassed anything expected of a commoner? How many times had she watched Aunt Hermione pore over newspaper clippings describing Bryce Lyndley's latest legal accomplishments or most recent social appearance?

Part of her had been in awe, inspired by the reality that decency and commitment truly could prevail.

And part of her had wondered just how decent Bryce Lyndley really was—how someone so benevolent could neglect a woman like Aunt Hermione, a rare and remarkable woman who loved him like a son.

Clearly there was more here than met the eye.

But the one time she'd broached the subject, asking Aunt Hermione why Mr. Lyndley never visited, her aunt had become visibly shaken, offering a swift, vague answer before turning away, eyes brimming with tears.

At that moment Gaby had actually hated the man.

Later she'd calmed down, reminding herself that she knew little of the truth and could therefore not assign blame.

And now that she'd met and talked with him, she was more confused than ever. For the extraordinarily handsome man with the infectious smile, the uncanny gift for understanding and relating to people, and the probing forest-green eyes was very much the person Aunt Hermione had depicted.

With one variation—the pain Gaby saw reflected in those eyes.

Pain that was all too similar to what she'd read on Aunt Hermione's face the day she'd questioned her, a deep-seated suffering Gaby was willing to bet was integrally tied to whatever secrets her aunt and Mr. Lyndley shared . . . and guarded.

On that notion, Gaby's fingers paused, caressing the piano keys as she thought. True, what was between her aunt and Bryce Lyndley was none of her concern. Still, anything that hurt Aunt Hermione hurt her as well. The enormous-hearted woman was everything to her—her guardian, her friend, the head of her family . . . not merely the mistress of the household but, in all ways that mattered, her mother.

Gaby's memories of her real mother and father hadn't faded. They were always there, warm and vivid, wrapped in an eternal cocoon that was tucked away in her mind and heart, to be called upon at will. But the agony of losing them had slowly diminished over the years, and *that* she owed to Aunt Hermione, who had taken a traumatized five-year-old into her home, held her while she cried, then patiently coaxed her from her grief into a world of nurturing and love.

Slowly, and without Gaby ever feeling it happen, Hermione Nevon's devotion had worked its magic, and suddenly, one reassuring day, Gaby had realized that her loss had become bearable.

Although not even her aunt's love could erase the unshakable, nightmarish memory of how her parents had died . . .

No, Gaby castigated herself, throwing back her shoulders and staring fixedly at the ivory keys. Now wasn't the time to think about that. Now was the time for getting to know Bryce Lyndley.

At least as much of him as he would share. He'd been as guarded at the dining room table as he'd been when she'd shown him to his chambers, making polite conversation with everyone, listening intently yet offering nothing of his own life in return. Immediately following the meal, he'd excused himself, returning to his chambers yet again, sending for no one but Peter.

Gaby smiled, remembering how Peter had glowed when he emerged an hour later, a thick legal volume clutched in his hands. Why, his limp had been nearly indiscernible. And all because of the enigmatic Bryce Lyndley.

With a sigh, she resumed playing.

"Pardon me, am I intruding?"

The object of Gaby's thoughts addressed her from the music room doorway, and her head came up, her gaze darting over to meet his. "No, of course not." She eased back on the bench, dropping her hands to her sides. "Come in."

"Please don't stop," Bryce requested quietly, crossing over to stand beside her. "You play beautifully."

His compliment sent a surge of pleasure coursing through her. "Thank you. I love the piano. I've played since I was six. Aunt Hermione arranged for me to have lessons the instant she saw how enthralled I became every time I touched the keys."

"You're fond of Beethoven's works?"

"Very," Gaby answered fervently. "I enjoy the works of many composers, but there's something hauntingly beautiful about Beethoven's musical pieces—at least to me. My sentiments are a little difficult to explain."

"You don't have to explain." To Gaby's surprise, Bryce sank down beside her on the piano bench. "Music is one of the few things that must be felt rather than defined. Some people are capable of doing that, others are not."

Gaby studied him with solemn insight. "And you're one of those who are."

A corner of his mouth lifted. "How would you know that?"

"I just do." A glimmer of humor shone through her gravity, sparkled in her eyes. "Let's say it's instinct—another of those things that must be felt rather than defined."

Bryce chuckled, a deep, husky sound. "A point well-taken." He gestured toward the piano. "Please, continue. I'm enjoying your recital immensely. "Moonlight Sonata" is one of my favorites."

"Mine as well," Gaby agreed. "Beethoven was a perfect example of one who felt his music. Even though he was deaf, he was able to create his masterpieces. 'Tis as if the symphonies just echoed inside him, needing no discernible ear to affirm their beauty." With that, she fell silent, her fingers repositioning themselves, flowing over the exquisite notes.

All else vanished, and Gaby sank into the music, totally absorbed until the final notes of the piece reverberated through the room.

"Magnificent." The sound of Bryce's quiet praise yanked her back to awareness. "And precisely what I needed. Thank you."

"My pleasure." Gaby inclined her head quizzically. "Although, if I remember correctly, what you needed was rest. I assumed you were still in your chambers getting some."

"I tried—all day, in fact. It's no use. My mind is racing and refuses to cooperate. So I took a stroll, hoping it would accomplish what hours in my room could not. Your music drifted out to me through the open window. It seemed to offer me the peace I craved. I hope you don't mind."

"I don't."

"Good." Bryce leaned forward, gripping his knees and idly rubbing his forefinger over the fine woolen twill of his dark trousers. "I felt a bit self-conscious about entering the room when I did. You play with such emotion—it almost made me feel that I was intruding on something intensely personal. I didn't want to invade your privacy." A rueful smile. "But I suppose I did anyway, didn't I?"

"Not at all." Gaby shook her head, sending a few stray tendrils of hair tumbling onto her cheeks. "I don't mind company when I play, especially when that company is someone who appreciates Beethoven's works as I do. In truth, I forget everyone's presence, including my own, once my fingers touch the keys."

"I can tell. Are you equally enthralled when others play?"

"Others?"

"I was referring to the symphony. Do you attend concerts often? I would think you'd revel in orchestral music."

"I'm sure I would." Anticipation shimmered through Gaby, an anticipation she had learned to squelch. "I often try to imagine what it would be like, hearing the collective beauty of the piano, the strings, the wind instruments."

"You've never been to a concert?" Bryce's brows shot up in surprise. "Why? Do you prefer the ballet?"

"I've never been to the ballet, either."

At this point Bryce looked thoroughly stunned. "Why in heaven's name not? London is only a few hours' carriage ride from here."

"That's what Aunt Hermione says. She keeps insisting that we go. But thus far I've managed to discourage her."

"Why would you discourage her?"

Silence.

"Is it because of her weakness?" Concern tightened Bryce's hard masculine features. "Is Hermione so depleted that a mere trip to the ballet or the symphony would exhaust her?"

"No." Hastily Gaby dispelled his worry. "It's not that." She hesitated, trying to find the most tactful way to explain. "Aunt Hermione is needed here. Many of the staff members become . . . upset when she disappears for too many hours at a time. She's the foundation of our family, a family that thrives on constancy."

"Are you implying that Nevon Manor's residents never leave the estate?"

A small smile played about Gaby's lips. "It's not nearly as ominous as you make it sound, Mr. Lyndley. The truth is, they don't choose to leave, when every-

54

thing that's dear and familiar—and safe—is right here."

"Safe," Bryce repeated reflectively. "Odd, neither you nor Hermione strikes me as someone who would be intimidated by venturing into the world. In fact, I'd have guessed quite the opposite."

His perceptiveness is uncanny, Gaby thought, studying his keen, appraising expression.

"Your presence here is necessary." He verified her assessment by supplying his own answer, and Gaby felt a peculiar tightening in her chest.

"Yes," she whispered. "Not only *my* presence but, more importantly, Aunt Hermione's. Although she does make occasional visits to Whitshire," Gaby added quickly, lest Mr. Lyndley think they were totally reclusive. "That's Aunt Hermione's brother's estate—pardon me, her *late* brother. The duke recently passed away. Whitshire now belongs to his son, Aunt Hermione's nephew, Thane. She's always made periodic visits there, so the staff is used to it. Besides, Whitshire is a mere five or six miles ride from Nevon Manor. So her jaunts there take her away from us for only a few hours at a time."

"'Us'—don't you go with her?"

A more familiar tightening, this time in Gaby's stomach. "No. I haven't been able to bring myself to—at least not yet."

Realizing how odd her answer sounded, Gaby half expected Bryce to grill her further. But he surprised her, merely studying her pensively and murmuring, "I see," before clearing his throat and addressing the original subject: "Perhaps I can conjure up a way for you to attend a concert without upsetting the staff. Let me mull it over for a while and see if I can devise an acceptable solution."

Gaby felt a wave of gratitude—and a surge of hope. "Thank you, Mr. Lyndley. With your brilliant legal mind, I haven't a doubt you'll find a way. I can practically hear the first strains of the music."

"'My brilliant legal mind'?" Amusement laced Bryce's tone. "That sounds like one of Hermione's biased assessments. Let's just say I'm resourceful." He adjusted his frock coat, stretching out his long legs and crossing them at the ankles before turning back to Gaby. "Hermione says you've lived at Nevon Manor for thirteen years."

"I have." Gaby recognized that he was again trying to understand her, and she resolved that this time she would not attempt to evade him. After all, he had no way of knowing how painful the incident was that had brought her to Nevon Manor. Besides, he'd been so kind; she owed him her honesty. Very well, she'd merely answer his question, then put the subject to rest. "My parents were killed in a fire when I was five," she stated, keeping her voice even, her gaze fixed on Bryce's silk necktie. "The fire occurred at Whitshire, destroying the servants' quarters and everyone in them. My father was the duke's head groom; he and my mother were trapped in their quarters when the blaze tore through. Its cause was never determined. It could have been anything: an overturned lantern, a smoldering cheroot—Lord only knows. I haven't returned to Whitshire since the day my parents died—which is why I've never visited the estate with Aunt Hermione."

"Dear God." Bryce's voice sounded strangled, and Gaby could feel her composure slip.

She pushed on, determined to have done with it. "The important thing is, Aunt Hermione took me in, gave me a whole new life and a deluge of love. When I first arrived at Nevon Manor, I was devastated; I had no one and nothing. Now I have a family. Despite my loss, I feel incredibly blessed."

There, she'd said it.

"I'm so terribly sorry." Sympathy—and something more—rumbled through Bryce's deep voice. "Hermione told me you were orphaned, but she never mentioned how . . . or where." He sucked in his breath, jumping to his feet and pacing restlessly about, surprising Gaby with the intensity of his reaction. "I didn't mean to pry or to make you recall difficult memories." He came to an abrupt halt, shoving his hands in his pockets and staring broodingly down at her.

To Gaby's mortification, hot tears sprang to her eyes. "You didn't pry; you asked. Nor did you make me recall difficult memories. I think about Mama and Papa all the time, with no instigation from anyone." Self-consciously, she brushed the tears from her cheeks. "But after all these years I generally think about them with a full heart and dry eyes. I haven't a clue as to why I'm crying now. I suppose pondering something and giving voice to it are two different things." She inhaled, brought herself under control. "Honestly, I'm quite recovered, thanks to Aunt Hermione."

"There are some things from which one never fully recovers."

Startled by his fervent proclamation, Gaby raised her chin, her gaze darting back to his as a glimmer of realization sparked. "You're right," she replied softly. "What's more, you're speaking from firsthand experience, aren't you?"

"Yes. I am."

"You were orphaned at a young age as well, were you not?"

"When I was ten, yes. But my situation was far less traumatic than yours. My parents, like so many other people, died of influenza. I mourned their loss— deeply—but it didn't destroy my life. I wasn't even living at home when they died. I was at Eton."

"Being on one's own and being alone are two entirely different things," Gaby inserted quietly. "Before your parents' death, you'd been on your own. Afterward you were alone."

Silently Bryce ingested her words, a veiled expression crossing his face. "You're right," he agreed at length. "I was alone."

"Then why didn't Aunt Hermione—" Gaby bit her lip to silence the unwelcome question. "Never mind. I won't ask."

"Thank you."

She inclined her head. "You're an intriguing man, Mr. Lyndley. I know so much about you and, at the same time, so little."

"You're far less in the dark than I," he reminded her, resting his elbow atop the piano. "And you did promise to answer all my questions."

"Yes, I did, didn't I?" Gaby's smile returned, impish and teasing. "And I shall—*if* you'll do the same for me."

Bryce's lips twitched, although his expression became guarded. "What is it you'd like to know?"

"Everything. Your experiences at school, in court, in society—everything but the secrets you clearly choose not to discuss."

To her surprise, he began to laugh. "I've never met anyone quite as direct as you, Gabrielle."

"Does my candor offend you?"

"Not in the least. I find it incredibly refreshing. Very well, I'll accept your terms. Your revelations in exchange for mine. Now, who shall begin?"

"I shall," Gaby said at once. "After all, my answers to your questions are far more essential than yours to mine. I'm suffering only from an excessive bout of curiosity, while you're suffering from a lack of information that will obviously affect your life, given the inner peace you're seeking." She folded her hands in her lap. "Therefore, Mr. Lyndley, what would you like to know?"

An odd light flickered in his eyes. "You're very insightful. And before we begin, please call me Bryce. After all, we're practically related, if only through our love for Hermione."

"I'd like that . . . Bryce." Gaby rather liked the sound of his name as she spoke it. "Shall I begin by explaining the makeup of our little family?"

"That would be ideal. It's unmistakable that Hermione cares deeply for everyone at Nevon Manor. It's also clear that . . ." He broke off, seeking a subtle choice of words.

"That everyone is in some way impaired?" Gaby supplied. "That's equally true, although I don't think any of us notices the others' limitations anymore. We simply see the person within."

"That's as it should be." Bryce frowned. "I don't want you to misunderstand my concerns. It's not an issue of judgment; if anything I was extremely impressed by the loyalty and unity I witnessed in the library this morning. I'm simply trying to assess the situation. Suffice it to say I have a decision to make—a decision that will affect not only me but all the residents of Nevon Manor. In order to make the right determination, I need to know all I can about the staff. Their limitations—and my abilities to handle them correctly—will have a direct impact on what I decide."

"Aunt Hermione wants to leave Nevon Manor to you," Gaby realized aloud. "Of course. It makes perfect sense. You have just the right combination of strength, insight, compassion, and, of course, humor, without which life, here or anywhere else, would be unbearable. Bequeathing Nevon Manor to you is the only way for Aunt Hermione to ensure that things stay as they are."

Bryce didn't even attempt to deny it. "Why? Why is it the only way to ensure things stay as they are?"

"The very fact that you're asking me that is answer enough." Gaby watched his brows knit in puzzlement. "Mr. Lynd . . . Bryce," she amended, "how many people do you know who would keep on a stable manager who can scarcely walk? A maid who's too unsteady to carry a tray? A footman who can scarcely hear or scarcely see? A gardener who views his shovel as a dear friend? Not to mention children who are far too skinny and weak to do a significant number of chores?"

"Only one," Bryce replied. "Hermione Nevon."

"Two," Gaby corrected. "Aunt Hermione—and you." She leaned forward, unconsciously gripping Bryce's forearm. "Here, those fine people are accepted, loved, given a sense of purpose and belonging. Out there, in the real world, they'd be scorned, discarded like broken playthings. Aunt Hermione won't allow that to happen. Neither will you."

"Nevon Manor seems to be running very smoothly, limitations or not." A gentle note crept into Bryce's tone. "Then again, I have a feeling you, Chaunce, and Hermione are always on hand to smooth out any wrinkles that might occur."

"They don't occur that often. It's amazing how effective people become when someone believes in them. Just look at Peter. His limp was all but gone when he left your quarters today. Why? Because his soul had been nourished. I'm willing to bet there was nothing he wouldn't have been able to accomplish at that moment, lame or not."

"I agree." Bryce shifted, making Gaby aware of her grasp on his forearm.

Awkwardly she released him, interlacing her fingers in her lap. "If you'd like, I can provide you with the background of each and every servant at Nevon Manor. Most of them were discharged from other jobs by dissatisfied employers who demanded perfection and refused to accept less. As for the children, Peter, of course, is Cook's son. The others are orphans like me. No," she amended softly. "Their circumstances when Aunt Hermione took them in were far more dire than mine. Their mothers were unwed, cast into the streets where they died of starvation or illness, leaving behind children who were little more than infants. Lily, Jane, Henry, Charles—they have no memories to sustain them, nothing to hold on to at night to help keep their parents alive. I, thankfully, have both—memories and my music box."

"Music box?"

Gaby nodded. "Mama told me that Papa gave it to her the day I was born. He used nearly all his savings to purchase it—as you can guess, head grooms didn't make very much money. Anyway, she'd admired the box in a shop window, and Papa was determined that she should have it. So he had the shopkeeper put it aside until I arrived, and that very day he rushed down and bought it. I vividly recall how deeply Mama cherished that box; she kept it nearby all the time, sitting on her nightstand. Except on those nights when I had a bad dream. Then she'd bring the box to my room and open it, letting me listen to its beautiful melody—'Für Elise,' my very first taste of Beethoven. Sometimes Mama would leave the box beside me when she tiptoed back to bed. Those times were my favorites. I could listen until the melody lulled me to sleep." Gaby swallowed past the lump in her throat. "It's the only possession of theirs that wasn't lost in the fire."

This time it was Bryce who reached out, gently squeezing her shoulder. "The music box sounds lovely."

"It is. It's made entirely of mother-of-pearl with gilt trim and a delicate stone in the center." Feeling the reassuring pressure of his hand, Gaby gave Bryce a tentative look. "Perhaps, if you have time during your stay, I could show it to you."

"I'd be honored." Bryce withdrew his palm, his expression pensive. "You've certainly given me a great deal to contemplate."

"Does that mean it's time for *you* to answer *my* questions?" Gaby saw the perfect opportunity to lighten the mood—and to accomplish her goal, that being to learn more about Bryce Lyndley.

He grinned, making a wide sweep with his arm.

"Ask away. Where shall we begin, with my experiences in school or in court?"

"What about in society?"

A shrug. "Those are distinctly unexciting."

Gaby's eyes widened in surprise. "I should think just the opposite would be true, especially of late."

"Of late?"

"Yes. Oh, please don't misunderstand. I thought your previous companions sounded charming," Gaby hurriedly clarified. "But judging from the glowing accounts we've received, Miss Talbot is uncommonly poised and intelligent, not to mention incredibly beautiful. Why, one newspaper description likened her to a golden-haired fairy-tale princess. She's always on hand to herald your accomplishments and to share your pastimes. You've escorted her all about London—to the theater, the balls, and of course the symphonies we just discussed. Then there are those carriage rides through the park, the sailing jaunts along the Thames. . . . Your courtship sounds exhilarating."

Bryce's jaw dropped. "I don't recall seeing such a comprehensive portrayal of my activities recounted in the papers. Who have you been talking to? What's more, why in the name of heaven have you been collecting information on my friendship with Lucinda? Wait—never mind." He shook his head in disbelief. "I needn't ask: Hermione. Lord, is there *anything* about my life she hasn't delved into?"

"I've upset you." Gaby felt more puzzled than remorseful. "But why? And why would Aunt Hermione's knowledge of your courtship suggest to you that she'd pried? You've hardly kept your relationship with Miss Talbot a secret. Let the truth be known, Aunt Hermione's investigators provided her with very little information she hadn't already gleaned from Chaunce. Or rather from his butler associates, most of whom work for prominent members of society and are therefore privy to all the latest gossip, most particularly during the Season, when the gossip flows so freely. Why, nearly every butler in Hertford passes tidbits on to Chaunce, and you'd be stunned to learn how many of those tidbits have, of late, pertained to you and Miss Talbot. You obviously don't read the newspapers too carefully; items about you two have appeared regularly, complete with details and descriptions. Just as they appeared when you were seeing Miss Chatham, Miss Dods, Miss Wells, Miss—"

"You've made your point," Bryce interrupted, his expression growing more and more incredulous with each passing word of Gaby's elaborate explanation. "And I'm sure all those 'items' you're referring to line the pages of Hermione's scrapbook. Given that fact, together with the findings provided by Hermione's investigators and the reports provided by Chaunce's contacts, I don't know what possible questions I can answer. Clearly you know more about me than I do."

"I know this particular courtship has gone on much longer than the others." Gaby ignored Bryce's wry assessment, seeking something far more crucial. "Are you in love?" she demanded eagerly.

Bryce blinked. "In love?"

"Yes—with Miss Talbot. And if so, is it everything the poets claim it to be?" Even as she asked the question, Gaby could actually feel Bryce withdraw, retreat behind his earlier wall of reserve.

"I'm afraid you're asking the wrong person," he replied, sounding more dispassionate than angry. "I'm not a big believer in what you're describing."

It was Gaby's turn to blink. "What I'm describing is what you and I have just spent the past hour discussing—love."

"We were discussing compassion, not love."

"We were discussing both. You yourself used the word 'love' when you spoke of our feelings for Aunt Hermione."

"That's hardly the same emotion you're referring to

now." Folding his arms across his chest, Bryce challenged her words, delivering his argument as if he were in court. "Love, as in the ability to feel benevolence or devotion, and love, as in the ability to lose oneself in a fantasy, are two entirely different things. One is simple decency or regard. The other is consuming, romantic, involving far more than mere respect and affection. That kind of emotion is one I can't understand, much less subscribe to, for no poet has yet to explain it in a way I can fathom."

"Explain it? Aren't you the one who said some things must be felt rather than defined?" Gaby paused, waiting for Bryce to reply. When he didn't, she softly added, "A man who can make such an evaluation, who can feel the beauty of music, is also a man who can love, both affectionately and romantically."

"Gabrielle, you're very young."

"And you're very jaded. Did one of the women I mentioned earlier hurt you? Is that why you're averse to falling in love?"

Bryce stared in utter disbelief. "Hurt me? Of course not. They were delightful companions."

"So is Crumpet. That doesn't answer my question." Gaby studied Bryce's baffled frown, a dawning knowledge kindling inside her. "Perhaps I'm wrong. Perhaps it does." Slowly she rose from the piano bench. "You're a very complex man, Bryce Lyndley. But I don't think you're nearly as removed and analytical as you believe—at least not in all matters. I won't press you about the secrets you're guarding. But whatever they are, I suspect they must be quite painful— painful enough for you to erect a wall around your heart that's as unnatural as it is self-imposed. I hope for your sake you decide to lower that wall, at least long enough for someone like Miss Talbot to enter. From what I understand, love—like music—is magic. Don't deny yourself that magic. It would be an enormous mistake." A sudden thought struck Gaby, and she smiled, marveling at what could be a wonderful and ironic twist of fate. "Earlier I told you how glad I was that you'd come to Nevon Manor, how much I believe you can offer our family. Now that I consider it, I believe we can offer you equally as much in return. Perhaps you should consider staying here for a while. Perhaps it would be the best thing not only for us but for you as well."

Bryce opened his mouth to reply, but whatever he intended to say was cut off by a knock at the partially open music room door.

"Yes?" Gaby called.

"Pardon me, Miss Gaby," Chaunce said politely, stepping into the room. "I hope I haven't interrupted your conversation at an inopportune moment. But Lady Nevon wishes to speak with Mr. Lyndley. Now—before the family gathers for dinner."

"Is Aunt Hermione all right?" Gaby asked anxiously.

"Yes, the medicine did her a world of good, as did her afternoon nap," Chaunce confirmed. "However, she is still a bit peaked. Thus Mrs. Gordon and I persuaded her to remain in her chambers, if not abed, until the time comes to dress for dinner. She's there now, awaiting Mr. Lyndley in her sitting room."

"I'll see her immediately." Bryce was still staring at Gaby, his expression unreadable. Abruptly he looked away, walking automatically toward the doorway. "Hermione and I still have a great deal to discuss."

"Yes, sir," Chaunce concurred, hands clasped behind his back. "A great deal." He turned to follow Bryce, his gaze flickering over Gaby in the process.

She could have sworn she saw satisfaction gleaming in his eyes.

Chapter 4

"AH, BRYCE. PLEASE COME IN." HERMIONE GESTURED for Bryce to enter. Nestled on the velvet settee, her dark skirts billowing out around her, she looked small, wan, and far more frail than Bryce would have liked.

Renewed pangs of worry assailed him, supplanting the brooding humor that had accompanied him from the music room and his unsettling conversation with Gabrielle.

"How are you feeling?" he asked, eyeing Hermione's pallor and trying to keep his tone light, unconcerned.

"Years younger, now that you're here." She smiled, patting the cushion beside her. "Sit with me." Tipping her chin up, she glanced beyond Bryce, giving Chaunce a businesslike nod. "You may fetch the books now, Chaunce. While you're gathering them, I'll finish my chat with Mr. Lyndley."

"Very good, madam." With a half bow, the butler took his leave, shutting the door behind him.

Bryce crossed over and lowered himself onto the settee. "You're still somewhat pale. Did you rest?"

Hermione waved away his concern. "You sound like Dr. Briers. I'll answer you as I do him: I've done nothing *but* rest all day." A sigh as she rubbed the fine silk of her gown between her fingers. "As for being pale, I only look that way because of these drab colors I've been wearing since Richard's death. In truth, I loathe them. I much prefer bright hues, especially on a woman my age whose wrinkles already make her look dreary enough. But for the next few months at least . . ." She paused. "I realize you can't possibly fathom this, Bryce, but Richard was, for the most part, a dutiful brother. And even those times when I thought him unfeeling, he was still my brother—the only brother I had. If I failed to show some display of mourning, I'd feel as if I were dishonoring him. I suppose in your eyes that makes me a dreadful hypocrite."

"No, it makes you a devoted sister—in anyone's eyes."

Warmth suffused Hermione's face. "Thank you. You're a kindhearted man. And not only on my behalf. Cook spent a quarter hour in my chambers going on and on about the miracle you wrought with Peter. She's never seen the lad this enthusiastic—*or* this self-confident. Whatever did you say to him?"

"Nothing magical," Bryce assured her, crossing one long leg over the other. "I showed him some of the legal texts you provided me. We chatted about the Inns of Court. I read him the outlines of a few interesting cases. He took one of the books to his room." A faint reminiscent smile. "He won't be able to read much of it, but I don't think it will matter. It didn't to me. The first time I held a legal text in my hands, I was at Eton and not much older than Peter. I hadn't anywhere near a full understanding of what was in that book, but I knew that when I held it I felt like an authentic barrister, necessary skills or not."

"Well, evidently Peter feels the same way. And you're the person responsible for his sense of well-being. Just as you're responsible for his mother's. Not to mention the other children, who hung on to your every word at lunch; Wilson, who's been boasting all day that you admired his primroses; my devoted lady's maid, Dora, who glowingly informed me that you aided her on the staircase when her walking stick faltered; and even Mrs. Gordon, who claims you've not left a single track of dirt in the manor—not even after returning from your walk on the grounds."

Wry amusement lifted Bryce's brows. "Those were simple courtesies, Hermione, not heroic acts."

"I beg to differ with you. Why, I understand from Bowrick that you even took time to help him find his spectacles."

"I passed Bowrick in the hall. The spectacles were in his pocket. The entire exchange took less than two minutes." Amusement vanished as Bryce's instincts clamored to life once more. It wasn't his imagination. He was being fattened like a lamb for slaughter. The ironic thing was that the entire performance was for naught, given that flattery would have as little effect on his decision as would the abundance of attention with which he was being lavished. The answer he eventually gave Hermione would be rooted in something far deeper than his popularity among the staff.

"Hermione, is this deluge of praise meant to influence my decision as to whether or not I'll agree to act as your beneficiary?" he asked. "Because if it is . . ."

"I understand Chaunce found you in the music room with Gaby. Doesn't she play beautifully?"

Bryce considered pressing his point, then changed his mind. For whatever reason, Hermione wanted no part of his explanation, nor was she ready to address the issue of her earlier request head-on. Rather, she seemed set on her own course—a course that included presenting every member of her household in the most favorable light. Very well, he would play this game her way. "Yes, she plays exquisitely."

"And did the two of you have a nice chat?"

Casually, Bryce draped his arm over the back of the settee, tilting his head and meeting Hermione's inquisitive gaze. "Indeed we did. We discussed music, the servants, and you. We also discussed Gabrielle herself: her background, her interests, her opinions."

"She's a remarkable girl, isn't she?"

"She most certainly is."

"Her background—did she tell you about her parents? How they died?"

"How *and* where." Some of Bryce's earlier pensiveness returned at the memory of what he'd learned, the unexpected link between Gabrielle's past and his own.

"Then you know how vulnerable she is." Ignoring Bryce's reference to Whitshire, Hermione bent forward and massaged her temples, her voice wavering as she spoke. "More than any of the others, I worry about Gaby, about what will become of her when I'm gone. She's like a beautiful butterfly, Bryce—rare and delicate. And so trusting. It troubles me more than you can imagine."

"Why?" Bryce blinked, taken aback by the unanticipated course of Hermione's conversation. He'd expected a citing of Gabrielle's virtues, not an expression of anxiety over her future. "Why would you worry about Gabrielle's fate? Everyone at Nevon Manor adores her. None of your staff would ever hurt her."

"No, they wouldn't. But can you make the same claim about the outside world?"

"Forgive me, Hermione, but I'm lost. According to Gabrielle, the residents of Nevon Manor are a very sequestered group who rarely venture from the estate."

"True. But unlike the others, Gaby cannot remain sequestered for much longer. She's eighteen, Bryce, a grown woman—one who has so very much to give. She needs a life, a husband, a family of her own. And that means leaving Nevon Manor, joining the real and ofttimes unkind world outside our gates. Gaby is totally unprepared for that—which is my fault for keeping her so sheltered. But because she endured what she had, and at so young an age, I wanted her to feel safe, to have a home, security. Now I wonder if I did her a disservice. For despite Gaby's innate joy of life, despite the limitless strength she finds for others, she's very innocent and very fragile. It would take only the wrong situation, the wrong man, to shatter her. And if I'm not here to protect her . . ."

Bryce scowled, unable to refute a word of Hermione's fervent reasoning. His talk with Gabrielle had revealed her to be precisely the young woman Hermione was describing. And without Hermione as her guardian . . .

"You're right," he inserted quietly, his mind racing to explore possible solutions. "I understand your trepidation. In fact, I'd go so far as to suggest we act upon it."

Hermione's head came up. "Act upon it? How?"

"By making provisions for Gabrielle's future in the will you'll be amending."

"That's precisely the route I was contemplating. It's also the reason I wanted to chat with you tonight, before Chaunce returns with the household accounts."

"Do you have a specific proposal you wish to discuss?"

"Yes. I'd like to appoint a legal guardian for Gaby—one who would be responsible for seeing to her future in the event of my death."

Bryce looked surprised. "Naturally that would be the ideal solution. However, I got the distinct impression there was no one you trusted to fill that role."

"On the contrary, there is indeed someone—*if* you'll agree to do it."

70

Bryce jerked upright. *"I?* You want *me* to act as Gabrielle's guardian?"

"I don't *want* you to. I *plead* with you to." Hermione inhaled slowly, clasping her trembling hands together. "Please, Bryce. I implore you to accept. I have no one else to turn to, not even Thane. He and Gaby have met only a dozen times, and they're such entirely different people; Thane wouldn't have a clue how best to pave Gaby's future. Whereas you, having dealt in a much more diverse environment, having experienced so much of your own suffering . . ."

Hermione pressed her fingers to her lips as if seeking the right words to convince him. "It would be no more than a minor inconvenience. As my beneficiary, you'd be living at Nevon Manor anyway. And you wouldn't have to invest a shilling of your own money; I'd leave a sizable trust fund for Gaby, which you would oversee, of course. You could make certain she met the right people, shield her from cruelty and ugliness. The entire staff would help you; as you said, they love Gaby dearly. But they alone are not strong enough, steady enough, to manage this all-important responsibility on their own. I need to leave someone strong at the helm, someone intelligent and insightful who can look out for Gaby, protect her, guide her along the right path. That someone, Bryce, is you. Please—you mustn't say no."

Coming to his feet, Bryce stalked the room, hands clasped behind his back. He was numb with shock, overcome by the enormity of what Hermione was asking of him, a request that had escalated from the weighty to the ponderous. To agree to oversee her unorthodox staff would be a massive enough responsibility, necessitating his changing his residence, his priorities, his entire way of life. But this? Taking on a young woman as his ward, introducing her to society, securing her future? For this he had no experience, no preparation, no inclination.

How the hell could Hermione ask this of him?

Because there was no one else. No one to care for Hermione's staff, no one to see to Gabrielle's future. No friends, no family. No one.

Being alone, fending for oneself—these were prospects Bryce understood only too well, for he himself had confronted them years ago, the day he'd received Hermione's letter, learned the Lyndleys were gone, and faced the sickening fact that he was without a foundation upon which to stand, without a supportive hand to grasp.

The pain that had accompanied that realization was not something he'd want anyone else to endure, certainly not one as tenderhearted as Gabrielle.

"You're sure that Thane . . .?" he began.

"I'm sure." Watching the play of emotions on Bryce's face, Hermione leaned forward, adding gently, "Bryce, this favor I'm asking is quite possibly a mere formality. As you're well aware, I consider Gaby my own. Bearing that in mind, I fully intend to bring her out next Season, to carefully initiate her emergence into society." A resigned sigh. "I'd originally intended to do so this Season, but because of Richard's illness I deferred my plans. Which gives me the better part of a year to persuade Gaby that Nevon Manor can survive without us for several days here and there. She worries so about our family's ability to cope with change, although I'm more than confident that Chaunce can keep things running with reassuring familiarity during Gaby's and my occasional forays into Town. I would never desert my family for long intervals. But, I do not intend to neglect Gaby's future. Given that by next spring my mourning period will be very much over, Gaby will be brought out then, at which time I expect a dozen eager suitors to be contending for her hand. Why, she'll probably be married and a mother before I pass on. Still, I must take the necessary precautions, just in case. Surely, being a barrister, you understand the prudence of my plan."

"Yes, Hermione, I understand," Bryce muttered, wishing he could find one bloody flaw in her logic. Unfortunately, there was none. Not with regard to her plea for Gabrielle or her plea for her staff. She loved these people, she was desperate to protect them, and she fully believed he was the sole person to secure their future.

Perhaps he was.

Which incited a most baffling question.

Abruptly Bryce halted, squaring off to meet Hermione's gaze. "What would you have done had Whitshire not died when he did?"

Hermione drew an unsteady breath. "The truth? I'd been grappling with the idea of contacting you anyway, begging you to come—under an assumed name, if need be, pretending you were my business adviser, my solicitor, anything—and praying you wouldn't refuse and Richard wouldn't suspect who you really were. *That's* how desperate I was becoming. Then God intervened. He saw a way to bring you to me. I never wished for any harm to befall my brother"—a shadow darted across her face—"except when he cast you aside, at which time I actually wished him in hell. Nevertheless, my anguish went unanswered and Richard's fate was ultimately decided by a higher being. Still, the timing—his death, my deterioration—I don't believe it was mere coincidence. In my heart I believe God concurred with my wish for you to come back into my life, guide the paths of those I love, and fulfill the role you were never able to claim while Richard lived."

At the last, Bryce went rigid. "What does that mean?"

Silence.

"Hermione, what else haven't you told me?"

Hermione's lashes drifted to her cheeks. "With regard to what?"

"You know full well with regard to what." Bryce strode forward, stood directly over Hermione, where he intended to remain until he got some answers. "Let's dispense with the games. I much prefer truth to pretense, as your investigators have doubtless advised you. Well-meaning or not, you have quite a thorough plan mapped out, a plan that puts me at its center but which you've neglected to clearly define aloud. Initially you said you wanted me to draw up your will, look over your household accounts, and—as you announced to your staff—act as your business adviser. Then, as an afterthought, you added that you've selected me to inherit your home and take on your staff. A few minutes ago you beseeched me to oversee Gabrielle's future. Now you're alluding to some other—and I suspect thoroughly inconceivable—role you wish me to play. So I repeat, what else do you intend to ask of me?"

Hermione wet her lips, her pale blue gaze steady on his. "Very well, Bryce, if you want me to be direct, so be it. There is one more facet of my request."

"Which is . . .?"

"To meet your brother."

"My brother," Bryce echoed, the word tasting bitter and foreign on his tongue.

"Yes—Thane. As I said, he's a fine man. Different from you, different from Gaby, but decent and kind nonetheless. Richard was the only obstacle standing between you. Now he's gone. And I want the two of you to meet. Soon—before my time comes."

There it was again. Hermione's obscure reference to her failing health.

Deferring the adamant refusal to meet Whitshire's son that hovered on his lips, Bryce confronted this more important subject head-on. "Before we say another word, I want to understand precisely what the status of your health is. You just implied that your life could be nearing an end. Yet a moment ago you reassured me you'd be here next spring for Gabrielle's coming-out. Which is it, Hermione? Are you ill? If not, why do you keep referring to your demise as if it's imminent? And while we're on the subject, what is that medicine you've been taking?"

A pulse fluttered at Hermione's throat, a clear indication that she was unnerved. Seeing that, Bryce frowned, accosted by the distressing possibility that perhaps Hermione's illness was indeed serious, that her entire plan had been devised in an attempt to protect those she loved—providing for their future while shielding them from the truth for as long as it was feasible to do so.

Squelching his concern, he awaited her reply.

When it came, it was with a quavering lift of her shoulders. "To my knowledge, I'm not ill, only weak. According to Dr. Briers, the medicine is a tonic that will help sustain my strength. Whether that's the truth or simply his kindhearted attempt to placate an old woman, I'm not sure. Nor does it matter. To be blunt, my intentions and fate's might not concur—at least not with regard to my health."

Hermione paused, resting a moment to recapture her strength. "I'm not *planning* to succumb overnight," she continued. "However, I must be practical. At my age, how much remaining time could there be? I can't ignore the fact that I've been feeling increasingly peaked these past few weeks. It's almost as if I'm being prepared. I'm a fighter, Bryce; I intend to hold on to life with every fiber of my being. But Richard's death made me realize we're all mortal—even I. Fighter or not, I can't stop the passage of time or change the course of nature. I've lived a long, full life. With a modicum of luck, my pluck and my medicine will help sustain me a few years longer. Nevertheless, I want my affairs to be in order, and, more important, I want those I love to be provided for, physically *and* emotionally. And that, my dear boy, includes you." Hermione's hands dropped to her lap. "Have I sufficiently answered your question?"

Bryce rubbed the back of his neck, his head pounding with conflicting emotions. "You have."

"Good. Then perhaps you'll answer mine. Will you give me the peace of mind I seek?"

How in God's name could he say no? "You seek a great deal," he heard himself say.

"Very well," Hermione responded. "Then let's address each of my requests separately. You've already agreed to revise my will and look over my accounts. So it seems to me my requests are down to three." She counted them off with quiet dignity. "One, will you allow me to appoint you my beneficiary? Two, will you agree to act as Gaby's guardian in the event of my death? And three, will you meet with your brother, forge a relationship that should have begun thirty-one years ago?" A whisper of a smile curved her lips. "Since you don't want me to die, why not give me something to live for?"

Bryce sucked in his breath. "Your requests are bloody unconscionable, do you know that? Fine. I'll serve as your beneficiary *and* as Gabrielle's guardian, should that prove necessary. Which I fully intend that it won't be."

"And Thane?" Weak or not, Hermione wasn't backing down an inch. She raised her chin, determination etched into the fine lines of her face. "Will you meet him?"

Years of denial refused to be silenced. "I know you mean well, Hermione, but I harbor no secret yearning for acknowledgment, not at this point in my life. To the contrary, I'm quite comfortable with who I am, and I neither want nor need acceptance from Whitshire's son to validate my sense of self-worth."

"Self-worth is not the issue. Family is." Slowly Hermione rose, clutching the arm of the settee as she steadied herself on her feet. "Bryce, the man is your brother. Aren't you the least bit curious about him? His stature, his mannerisms, his beliefs? I've just told you he's a good, decent man, one who's nothing like his sire. Given your probing, inquisitive mind, wouldn't you like to see for yourself that I'm telling the truth?" She reached up, touched Bryce's jaw. "He has your coloring, you know. Also your hard, bold features, your height and build. I've seen you in him so many times, and each time my heart cried out at the injustice of you two never having met."

Bryce swallowed hard. "I doubt he'd want to meet me, his father's bastard son."

"You're wrong. Knowing Thane, he would have sought you out on his own, had he known of your existence."

"With Whitshire alive? That I doubt. Your brother would have had his head."

"That wouldn't have stopped Thane. Like you, he doesn't compromise his principles—not even for his father."

Bryce's curiosity and his commitment to Hermione were fast outpacing his stubbornness. "When did you want this meeting to take place?"

"Tomorrow night." Hermione smiled, sensing victory. "I've already written to Thane, asked if we might hold a small dinner at Whitshire despite the fact that we're all in mourning. I explained that my legal adviser is visiting and that I'd like him to speak with Mr. Averley, the Whitshire steward, in order that he might discuss my business affairs. As you know, Chaunce handles my household accounts, but for anything more complicated, I, like Richard, consult with Mr. Averley, who has advised my family in matters of business for years. Thane, of course, agreed. I received Thane's confirming note while you were in the music room chatting with Gaby. We're expected at Whitshire tomorrow evening at seven o'clock."

Bryce's jaw dropped. "You've already arranged this?"

"I kept your true identity a secret, but yes. I couldn't afford to waste time. Time would give you the opportunity to change your mind."

"I hadn't even made up my mind!"

"Well, now you have." A sunny smile. "Besides, you'd be doing a great service to Gaby."

"To Gaby." Once again, Bryce felt as if he were being dragged under by a great muddling wave. "Where does Gabrielle fit into this?"

"She hasn't been back to Whitshire since the fire."

"Yes, she told me."

"It's time she confronted her past. The best way to do that is by convincing her that she's needed, that she'd be visiting Whitshire as a favor to someone other than herself."

"And that someone is me." Bryce shook his head in amazement. "You think Gabrielle's protective instincts will rush forward if she thinks I need emotional support on my first excursion to Whitshire." A frown. "Does she know my true parentage?"

"No. That is something no one knows." Hermione hesitated. "With the exception of Chaunce."

"Now, why doesn't that surprise me?"

"The point is, we needn't hide the facts any longer, need we?"

That brought Bryce up short. "Hermione, don't even consider making a public announcement." He clenched his fists at his sides, a gesture as totally unyielding as his demand. "The reality might be that Whitshire died last week, but to me he's been dead all my life. Nothing's changed, nor do I choose that it should. I am Bryce *Lyndley*. Were I to agree to meet Whitshire's son, it would be a concession to you, not a bid to alter my status. Is that clear? I mean it, Hermione. No newspaper tidbits, no gossip whispered among servants—nothing. If any of those things should occur—"

"I would never reveal anything that was solely your right to tell," Hermione interrupted. "Nor have I the slightest inclination to proclaim the truth to the world. This isn't about status, Bryce; it's about family. Rest assured, the only people I was suggesting we confide in were Gaby and Thane, both of whom would be directly affected by your announcement and both of whom are thoroughly discreet. Why, if you consider it, you'd be doing Gaby a great service and bringing me an abundance of joy—and all without relinquishing one iota of Bryce Lyndley." A twinkle. "Surely that wouldn't pose a threat to someone with as strong a sense of self-worth as you?"

Bryce opened his mouth, then promptly shut it. "And *you* wouldn't want to face *me* in court?" he muttered.

A serene smile was his only reply.

"All right. All right." Bryce shook his head in exasperated disbelief. "But I must say that my life was singularly uncomplicated before today."

"That's what family does. It complicates your life, turns it upside down, and brings you more fulfillment than you could possibly imagine." Hermione gazed up at him, her eyes growing damp. "I mean to give you a family, Bryce. If not for your sake, then for mine."

As if on cue, a crisp knock sounded at the door, and an instant later Chaunce entered, crossing the sitting room while gingerly balancing a pile of six or seven books. "Our ledgers, sir," he pronounced, placing the books on the end table.

"Oh, Chaunce, I'm glad you're back!" Hermione exclaimed, easing herself onto the settee. "I have wonderful news. Bryce and Gaby will be joining me when I ride to Whitshire for dinner tomorrow night."

"That's splendid, madam." A polite smile touched the butler's lips. "His Lordship . . . Forgive me, His Grace will be pleased."

"His Grace," Bryce reminded Chaunce dryly, "is expecting Lady Nevon's legal adviser."

"Which, among other things, is precisely what he shall get." Chaunce tapped the pile of books. "These are the most current household accounts, covering the past few years. The items listed range from staff wages to the cost of food and supplies to specific extras required by individual staff members. As you'll see, the entries have undergone very little change from year to year. However, in the ledgers we'll be compiling for the current year, we must provide for several additional items with regard to Miss Gaby's first London Season: namely, an extensive new wardrobe—gowns, accessories, and whatever else a lady requires for her debut—plus the commencement of dance lessons, coupled with her customary pianoforte lessons, of course."

Chaunce paused in his explanation, indicating the three thicker books on the bottom of the pile. "To continue. These three sets of ledgers contain information that is more complex than those I've just described to you. Rather than the day-to-day workings of Nevon Manor, they itemize the incomes received from Lady Nevon's various properties, as well as the expenses necessary to run those properties. The estates concerned are extensive—including everything from Nevon Manor to the small Bedford cottage in which you were raised—and were, for the most part, willed to Lady Nevon by her late husband. The majority of them house tenants as well as servants. My suggestion with regard to these books is that you take them to your room and review them tonight, after which you can discuss the details with Mr. Averley when you visit Whitshire tomorrow. As the late duke's steward, he's handled the entire Rowland family's more intricate household accounts for decades."

"Rowland," Hermione interrupted, "is your . . . pardon me, is *Thane's* family name."

"I'm aware of that," Bryce returned stiffly, lifting the top four books from the pile and setting them aside so he could gather up the heavier ledgers beneath. "Very well, Chaunce. I'll go over these three volumes in detail, first on my own, then with Mr. Averley." Raising his head, he glanced at Hermione. "I want to understand the full extent of income derived from all your estates, including the rent you receive from your tenants. The more knowledge I have of your assets, the better able I'll be to advise you, both on amending your will and on setting up Gabrielle's trust."

"Excellent." Hermione smoothed a strand of silvery hair from her cheek. "And speaking of Gaby, when do you intend to speak with her? Not about the trust, of course—I don't want to cause her any additional worry over my health—but about our visit to Whitshire tomorrow and its purpose."

Bryce frowned, contemplating how he was going to relay a past he'd never before shared with anyone. "I suppose the sooner I confront this the better." He set his jaw. "Let's review the household accounts now. We can probably do a fairly thorough job before dinnertime. Immediately following dessert, I'll take Gabrielle for a stroll. I'll explain the whole ugly situation to her then."

"Don't sound so grim," Hermione appeased him gently. "The facts aren't changed by being uttered aloud, any more than you're changed by uttering them. You are as you are, Bryce: an extraordinary man who is willing to reopen his own wounds in order to help others heal theirs."

Bryce shot her a look, pulling up a chair and lowering himself to it. "I'm not nearly as self-sacrificing as you choose to believe, Hermione. Had anyone but you made these particular requests, my compassion alone would not have been enough to convince me. I would have long since been gone from Nevon Manor, my refusal echoing in your ears."

With that, he shoved aside the heavier ledgers and opened the first book of household accounts.

"Spring is my favorite time of year." Gaby paused at a budding oak, gently touching one of its newborn blossoms. " 'Tis as if everything comes alive all at once."

"Hmm? Yes, I suppose you're right." Bryce's reply was vague, his mind preoccupied with the conversation he was about to commence.

He shoved his hands in his pockets, the brooding humor that had clung to him all evening heightening as he contemplated the untenable subject he was on the verge of broaching. Opening up this particular chapter of his life was both an unforeseen and an unpleasant step, one he'd never before considered taking, and he wondered why in the name of heaven he'd allowed Hermione to talk him into it.

One glance at Gabrielle, now caressing the oak's blossom as if it were a priceless gem, provided him with his answer. In truth, his revelation would cost him nothing more than a few moments' discomfort while, for Gabrielle, it could provide an opportunity to make peace with her past.

And who better than he knew how important that was? He, who had faced that very challenge himself.

Well, that challenge was behind him now. The facts surrounding his true lineage had long since been put to rest, relegated to a place where they lay dormant, tangible but unable to cause him pain. So if sharing the truth with Gabrielle would help silence her own ghosts, the effort would be worth the discomfort.

Sucking in his breath, he turned his attention back to Gabrielle, frowning as he noted her continued fascination with the oak. "Is this the first time you've walked this particular path?" he demanded.

Gabrielle looked surprised. "Of course not. I go by here every day, often at a dead run. This grove of trees leads directly to Crumpet's warren. Why do you ask?"

"Because clearly that oak has been standing here for years. Yet you're acting as if you're seeing it for the first time."

"In a way I am." She stroked the delicate blossom, then released it. "This bud wasn't here yesterday. Nor will it look exactly the same tomorrow." She turned her gaze to Bryce, her cornflower-blue eyes bright with insight. "A great deal depends upon the way one views life, I suppose. It can either be very mundane, or exciting, new, like . . ."

"Wonderland?" Bryce suggested, amusement lacing his tone.

"Only those aspects of Wonderland that are truly remarkable," Gaby replied, as solemn as Bryce had been teasing. "The other aspects—the loneliness, the confusion, the turmoil—those we have right here on earth. But then, you know that already, don't you?"

His amusement faded. "I'll say it again. For one so young, so isolated from life, you're surprisingly astute."

"Perhaps." She leaned back against the tree trunk. "I'm certainly astute enough to deduce there was a reason you asked me to go strolling."

"You're right." Bryce cleared his throat, realizing for the first time that his whisking her away from the manor might have proved disconcerting. Unlike Lucinda and the other sophisticated women of his acquaintance, Gabrielle hadn't endured years of instruction on how to properly conduct herself with a gentleman. Quite the opposite, in fact. She was not only entirely unexposed to the subject, she was unaccustomed even to visiting with a man, much less taking a solitary stroll with one. And here he'd rushed her from the dining room into the evening and into a secluded grove of trees without so much as an explanation.

"I apologize for ushering you away so quickly," he said, determined to put her at ease. "Not to mention without benefit of a chaperon. But what I need to speak with you about is both pressing and private. Please believe me when I say that my motives are entirely honorable, and Hermione is fully aware of our whereabouts."

Astonishment flashed across Gaby's face. "I never imagined otherwise. From all I know of you, and from all I'm learning firsthand, it never occurred to me that your intentions would be anything but honorable. Besides," she added, an impish grin curving her lips, "even if they weren't, I'm perfectly safe and well protected right here where we stand."

"By whom?"

"Screech and Brick."

With a quick glance about, Bryce asked, "Who?"

Gaby patted the tree trunk behind her, raising her eyes upward. "Two of my animal friends. Screech is hovering in the hollow just over our heads, and Brick, the last time I spied him, was scurrying along the branch of a sycamore tree several yards down."

Bryce followed her gesture, tilting back his head and examining the lowest hollow of the oak.

A sharp-billed woodpecker peered down at him, its black eyes piercing and alert.

"Screech is not at all shy," Gaby assured Bryce. "If he felt I was in danger, he wouldn't hesitate to shriek the leaves off the trees, then swoop down and hammer my assailant until he fled. And Brick"—she glanced off to the left, indicating a sleek red squirrel poised in the branch of a sycamore several trees down, a half-eaten nut clasped between his paws—"his color alone isn't responsible for his name. Do you see that nut he's clutching? When Brick decides to pelt people, they bear the scars for days."

Laughter rumbled from Bryce's chest. "Formidable adversaries, indeed. Please assure Screech and Brick that I have no intention of harming you."

"They know that." Gaby turned her attention back to him, folding her arms across her breasts and rubbing the silken sleeves of her rose-colored gown. "Animals have extraordinary instincts. They must in order to survive. My two escorts are merely standing guard, just in case."

Bryce watched the movement of Gabrielle's delicate hands, remembering the exquisite music they'd created earlier that day. He could well understand why Hermione wanted to protect her. There was something rare and fine about Gabrielle, something that inspired one's protective instincts, brought them clamoring to life.

"What was it you wanted to discuss?" Gaby prompted, inclining her head in question. "Have you decided to accept Aunt Hermione's offer, to allow her to bequeath Nevon Manor to you?"

"Yes. But that in itself is not what I want to discuss with you." Bryce cleared his throat again. "I want to discuss the reason Hermione chose me as her beneficiary."

"I already know why. You're a knowledgeable barrister. You're also kind, compassionate, and a dear family friend."

"What I am is Hermione's nephew—not only in heart but in fact."

Gaby's eyes narrowed in puzzlement. "I don't understand."

With a heavy sigh, Bryce stared downward, examining the plush grass beneath his feet. "Neither do I, but I'll do my best to explain." A weighted pause. "This is going to be even more difficult than I expected. You see, I've never spoken of this before. Not to anyone."

"The subject is painful."

"Once, yes. Not anymore. Now the subject is just awkward, like an old indiscretion I'd prefer to forget. Only in this case, the indiscretion wasn't mine. I was, however, its result."

"An indiscretion—does this involve a relative of Lord Nevon's?"

"No. It involves a relative of *Lady* Nevon's. The Duke of Whitshire, to be exact—pardon me, the *late* Duke of Whitshire." Bryce spoke the words dispassionately, as if they told the story of someone other than he.

"Thirty-two years ago His Grace enjoyed a brief liaison with a very young and reputedly beautiful actress named Anne Parks. Neither of them planned on Miss Parks conceiving the duke's child. But conceive she did. The question of paternity was a nonissue; apparently, Whitshire was Miss Parks's first and only lover. In any case, when her pregnancy was discovered, she found herself out of work and out of money. She was frantic. She went to Whitshire's estate, told him of her dilemma. He had her thrown out, barred from the grounds. She then tried writing to him—several times—pleading for his help. He wrote back, vowing he'd have her jailed if she dared claim him as the child's father. Evidently she didn't know where to turn, a dilemma that was greatly eased by a decided lack of maternal instinct. She gave birth to the child, then shifted her problem to the capable shoulders of the duke's older sister, Hermione, whose benevolent nature was well known to nobility and commoners alike.

"In short, Miss Parks left the newborn babe on Hermione's doorstep, along with the letters to and from Whitshire as proof that he was the boy's sire. Hermione was moved—and furious with her brother for abandoning his own flesh and blood. She confronted him. They had a fierce argument, during which he admitted the truth but refused to acknowledge the babe, even in secret, demanding that it be returned to its mother and forgotten. That, however, was no longer an option. The chit had already taken off, soon after to die in a brothel. Upon discovering that fact, Hermione decided to adopt the child and announced this decision to her brother. He became crazed with rage. He swore he'd kill her and the babe if she dared threaten his marriage and his legitimate son by keeping . . . let's see . . . if I recall correctly, his exact written words in describing the child were 'the coarse urchin bastard.' He demanded that it be thrown into the gutter or left on the steps of a workhouse, any place where it would remain anonymous or die.

"Needless to say, Hermione wouldn't allow that,

even though she was terrified by her brother's threats and helpless to prevent them. Lord Nevon had passed away several years earlier, leaving her without an ally powerful enough to combat Whitshire. So she arranged for Lyndley, her late husband's valet, and his wife, her trusted housekeeper, to move to Lord Nevon's small Bedford cottage and raise Whitshire's son as their own. This would enable him to have a home, a normal life, two fine parents, and ultimately the best education and future that Hermione's money could buy."

"Why do you keep referring to this child as 'it' or 'him'?" Gaby demanded, her voice choked with emotion. "This is not some intangible being you're describing. It's you."

Taken aback by the fervor of Gabrielle's response, Bryce glanced swiftly at her face—and was stunned to see tears gathered in her eyes. "Very well, then: 'I.' And please don't cry. My scars were minimal, and have long since faded."

"I don't believe that," Gabrielle surprised him by saying. "Neither do you. Just this afternoon you claimed there are some things from which one never fully recovers. Now I understand what prompted you to say it—*and* why you reacted so fiercely to my mention of Whitshire." She dashed the moisture from her cheeks. "Have you always known the truth about your parentage? Did Aunt Hermione tell you?"

"Eventually. But not until I was ten. When my parents—When the Lyndleys died of influenza, Hermione wrote to me. She told me everything, sent me the letters that had been left in the basket with me. But she also warned me to stay away from the duke—for my own good. She said that, much as she wanted to see me, it would be a fatal mistake for me to visit her. And she was right. If Whitshire had learned of my existence, he *would* have destroyed me. Worse, he would have destroyed Hermione. *That* I couldn't allow, after all she'd done for me.

"Besides, if I'm to be honest, staying away posed no real sacrifice on my part. My true parents, those who had raised me, were dead, severing whatever connection I had to my past. What point would there be in coming forward? I had no desire even to lay eyes on Whitshire, much less acknowledge him. The only Rowland I felt an allegiance to was Hermione, and that allegiance meant keeping her safe and her life intact. Despite all their differences, she cared about her brother, but she feared him as well. I understood that, and I accepted it. I heeded her advice so that my life and Hermione's could go on as they were. As for Hermione's feelings for me . . ." Bryce swallowed, finally uttering something that had the power to affect him: "I had no idea how strong those were. I knew only that she'd saved my life, given me a future. But I truly believed that she did so out of kindness and charity, not out of any personal attachment. The deep emotional ties she feels for me—the ones you and I discussed earlier—those I learned of only today. I was shocked, and more moved than I can describe. I owe that woman everything. Which is why I've agreed to do something that prompted me to reveal all this to you."

"And what is that?"

"To meet the late duke's son."

Incredulity widened Gaby's eyes—incredulity that was instantly eclipsed by a spark of understanding. "Of course! Aunt Hermione would want you and Thane to become acquainted. That makes a world of sense."

"Perhaps to you. I, on the other hand, see little point in our meeting, other than to please Hermione. Whitshire's son has no idea of my existence, and I have no interest in his."

"Oh, but Bryce, you must." Gaby moved away from the tree, took the few steps that separated her from Bryce, and gazed fervently up at him. "He's your brother."

"That fact is as meaningless as the one which states that Whitshire is my father."

"No, it's not." Gaby shook her head, sending waves of chestnut hair spilling over her shoulders. "It's entirely different. The late duke was every bit as unworthy as you just described. Thane, on the other hand, is a brother you can be proud of."

She paused, wetting her lips with the tip of her tongue, her delicate features drawn as she sought the right words. "I'm not merely saying that in response to your story. My own instincts recognized Aunt Hermione's brother as a cold and unfeeling man years ago. True, I seldom came in contact with him— certainly not when I lived at his estate. He rarely mingled with the servants, and when he did, it was only to issue orders. But during the thirteen years in which I've lived at Nevon Manor, I've had ample opportunity to study him. And though I hate to speak ill of the dead, I must confess that the entire household became nervous and unsettled each time he visited—which, thankfully, wasn't too often. He was impatient, biting, especially to those of our family who were physically incapable of doing his bidding as fast and as well as he liked.

"But the most difficult part was watching the change that came over Aunt Hermione whenever her brother was here. She went from proud and regal to quiet and apprehensive, like a beautiful bird whose song had been silenced. He was never actually cruel to her, but . . . let's just say I heaved a sigh of relief each time His Grace's coach disappeared around our drive."

A muscle flexed in Bryce's jaw. "Why are you telling me this?"

"Because I want you to understand the differences between Aunt Hermione's late brother and Thane. I'd never have encouraged you to seek out Richard Rowland; your assessment of him was totally accurate. But Thane is another story entirely. Unlike his father,

Thane is considerate and gracious. I don't think there's a mean or condescending bone in his body."

"He sounds noble indeed."

"Indeed and in fact," Gaby replied softly. "Whereas his father used to blatantly shun Lily, Jane, and the boys, avoiding any contact with them as if they carried some repugnant disease, Thane always arrived with a smile and a few sweets to dispense. And whereas his father constantly snapped at the servants, shoved his way past them as if they were dirt, Thane made certain to slow his pace, to follow their lead so as not to deprive them of their dignity."

"If Thane is so bloody noble, why does Hermione claim he's wrong for Nevon Manor and different from you and me?"

"Because he is," Gaby answered calmly, in immediate accord with her aunt. "Thane is like the first notes of a sonata. He lacks the fullness, the richness, of the entire piece, without which the onset is merely a prelude, one that brushes the surface, but never really penetrates the heart and soul. Thane has so much potential. Unfortunately, he has no idea how to realize that potential. He isn't shallow. He's simply never had reason to unfold, never had occasion to call upon anything more profound than a practiced smile or a brilliant business maneuver. Remember, Bryce, your life has been much richer in experience, much deeper for the pain you've withstood—and overcome. Now that I think about it, you have an enormous amount to offer Thane. Why, you could be the very person to inspire him to flourish. Contemplate that prospect. If you were to help Thane grow, to become all he's capable of being, you'd be enhancing more than just Aunt Hermione's life. You'd be enhancing your brother's life as well."

Bryce sucked in his breath. "I can't think of him in that capacity."

"Perhaps one day you will."

"Have you any idea how difficult—"

"Yes." Gaby laid a gentle hand on his forearm. "When are the two of you to meet?"

"Tomorrow evening. At Whitshire, given that Thane's period of mourning has just commenced. Hermione asked him if she might bring her legal adviser to dinner to discuss her affairs with Mr. Averley, the Whitshire steward."

"And you're that legal adviser."

"Exactly." Bryce covered Gaby's hand with his, bluntly stating his purpose. "I want you to come with me."

He could feel her fingers tense. "To do what?"

"That's the reason I confided the truth to you about my past. Gabrielle, I have an enormous step to take. You have a similar step. For different reasons, we both have ghosts to confront at Whitshire. Hermione would like us to confront those ghosts together." Bryce's fingers tightened about Gabrielle's, and with a jolt of surprise, he realized he meant every word he was saying. "I know your loss was excruciating. And if you truly believe that visiting the estate where your parents died is more than you can stand, I won't press you. Just know that it would mean a great deal to me if you'd accompany me, to ease my way with Thane. As I told you earlier, you're the most refreshing person I've met in ages. I'm hoping that your warmth, your exuberance, will make an otherwise unbearable situation bearable."

Gaby swallowed, visibly moved by his words and, it would appear, weighing her decision.

Her reply, when it came, startled him.

"This is a critical and poignant moment in your life, Bryce. Wouldn't you rather Miss Talbot accompany you?"

"Lucinda?" He shook his head, baffled by the unexpected question. "Definitely not. Lucinda knows nothing about my past or my true parentage. What's more, I have no intention of enlightening her."

It was Gaby's turn to look perplexed. "Why not?

Surely having her emotional support would make things easier."

"Emotional support is not something I turn to Lucinda for."

"I see." Gaby pondered that for a moment, her expression intense, those startlingly blue eyes searching his face. "Yet you turned to me. Which leads me to wonder if you honestly believe I can help or if you are making this request entirely for my benefit—a cloaked attempt, courtesy of you and Aunt Hermione, to ease *my* dilemma?"

A half hour ago Bryce's answer would have been different. But now he had no trouble uttering the truth: "Both."

Relief flooded Gabrielle's face, and her palm relaxed beneath his. "Very well. In that case, I'll go."

"Thank you." Bryce was stunned to find he was as relieved as she.

"Bryce." Her tone was solemn, fervent. "What you did tonight—confiding in me about the true circumstances of your birth—must have been extraordinarily difficult. Even if your lineage means nothing to you, sharing yourself is obviously not something you do often or readily. I'd like to thank you by offering you the same." She withdrew her hand, gathering up her skirts and taking two steps away. "Wait here. I'll be right back."

She darted off before Bryce could reply, and he watched her go, lounging against the tree and wondering what she was about.

He hadn't long to wait.

A scant five minutes later, Gaby reappeared, breathlessly making her way through the trees to where Bryce stood. "Here," she announced. "The most precious thing I have to share."

Bryce glanced down, slivers of moonlight illuminating the delicately crafted object that Gaby proffered, its mother-of-pearl surface gleaming like the finest porcelain, its gilt trim shimmering like spun gold.

"It's Mama's music box," she whispered, caressing the tiny stone atop the lid before opening it, releasing the tinkling strains of Beethoven "Für Elise." "Isn't it beautiful?"

An uncustomary knot tightened Bryce's chest. "Yes, Gabrielle, it is." He reached out, gently caressing her cheek with his forefinger. "And so are you. Thank you for sharing your music box with me."

Gaby smiled, utterly aglow at his reaction to her treasure. "You're welcome."

"Chaunce . . . listen." Hermione sat upright at her dressing table, putting down the face powder she'd been applying to create the chalklike skin pallor she'd worn all week.

"I hear it, madam." Chaunce crossed over to the slightly open window, throwing it wider and giving a self-satisfied nod. "So that *was* what Miss Gaby dashed to her room to collect. I thought it might be."

"You do realize whom she's playing it for—that she's still with Bryce." Hermione jumped to her feet, joining Chaunce and peering into the night sky.

"I do indeed, my lady. And if my sense of direction remains accurate, I'd say they were standing amid the grove of sycamores where Miss Gaby's woodpecker makes his home. A most private spot for a chat."

"Not just any chat, but an intensely crucial and personal one," Hermione added, leaning forward against the sill, eyes sparkling as the music box melody continued to play. "Oh, Chaunce, this is going even better than I dared hope!"

"I quite agree." The butler straightened, smoothing his mustache before clasping his hands behind his back. "And I must say, I'm delighted. Not only for Miss Gaby and your nephew, but for myself as well." A haughty sniff. "I don't mind mixing dose after dose of lemon water each day, but sneaking into your chambers in order to refill your cosmetic pot with that odious white mixture—really, my lady, that's too undignified for words. Were it being done for anyone but you . . ."

"But it is for me, Chaunce," Hermione interceded with a winsome smile. "And you know why I can't ask Dora to do it. No one must suspect that my illness is anything but genuine—not yet."

"I understand. Still, I do hate to see you mask your radiant complexion with that . . . substance." He glanced at the dressing table, giving a repugnant shudder. "No, madam, as far as I'm concerned, our plan cannot come to fruition quickly enough to suit me."

"I quite agree." Hermione patted Chaunce's arm, her gaze returning to the direction from which the music emanated. "Don't despair, my dear friend. I have a feeling I'll soon be making a sudden and miraculous recovery."

Chapter 5

GABY PUSHED THE FOOD AROUND ON HER PLATE, WILLING her uncooperative stomach to settle.

She had agreed to come to Whitshire for Bryce's sake, but in the two hours since they arrived, he seemed to have adapted far better than she. True, he had yet to tell Thane his real identity, but the two men had taken to each other at once—effortlessly on Thane's part, more reservedly on Bryce's. They'd exchanged niceties, shared a brandy, then escorted the ladies in to dinner, where Mr. Averley joined them, with the understanding that Lady Nevon would require some private time after dinner with her new legal adviser and Thane. For the past hour and a half the discussion had centered around business, investments, and legal estates.

In a way, Gaby was relieved. True, she felt like a fish out of water, but at least she wasn't expected to participate in the conversation. That gave her the opportunity to confront the unsettled feelings she was experiencing being back here—feelings that were far

95

more intense than she'd anticipated, given that she'd never so much as set foot in Whitshire's dining or drawing rooms. In fact, during the five years she'd lived here, she had entered the main house solely for meals and even then had come in through the rear, her movements restricted to the kitchen and the servants' dining quarters. To her recollection, she'd never even seen the elegant rooms she was frequenting tonight. She would not have forgotten plush Oriental rugs, opulent furnishings, and glittering chandeliers such as these. So why were her insides tied in knots?

Perhaps it was the painfully remembered faces of those servants who had been at Whitshire thirteen years ago and had escaped the fire: Couling, the solemn butler, Mrs. Fife, the cook, and Mrs. Darcey, the kindly housekeeper who'd found Gaby's unconscious body and who'd rocked her in her arms during those first horrifying moments when Gaby had realized her parents were gone. Odd, how these three servants—together with Mr. Averley and one or two familiar-looking footmen and maids—no longer resembled the towering giants her five-year-old eyes had perceived them to be. Now they were mere mortals with slowing steps and graying temples, greeting her with a touch of uncertainty and a reserve that was typical of people who hadn't seen each other in years. Unsure of Gaby's status, they bowed hesitantly, murmured about what a lovely, mature young woman she'd become, then scurried off to resume their duties.

God forgive her, but all Gaby could think about was how lucky these people were—how lucky *she* was—to be alive. Why couldn't her parents have been equally lucky—had the evening off on that fateful night or been anywhere other than in their chambers when the fire blazed through to claim their lives?

Bile rose in her throat.

"Is the mutton not to your liking, Gabrielle?"

Thane's voice interrupted her rampaging emotions, his blue-gray eyes filled with concern.

"Pardon me?" Gaby had no idea what he'd asked her. "I'm sorry. I was thinking."

"We're boring you." A smile curved his lips, and Gaby was struck at that moment by how very much Thane and Bryce resembled each other. The hard aristocratic features, the dark coloring, the disarming smiles—yes, there was a definite family likeness. Even their builds were similar: both men were tall with broad shoulders and powerful stances. But their eyes were different, not only in hue but in intensity as well. While Bryce's eyes were deep and probing, Thane's were more aloof, less enigmatic.

Brothers, yes. But different men with different backgrounds.

"No, of course you're not boring me," she replied. "Please, go ahead and talk. I'm concentrating on my dinner."

"Which you've scarcely touched," Hermione said gently. She leaned over, squeezing Gaby's hand. "Are you all right?"

"Yes. I'm fine." Gaby suddenly found herself the center of attention, which was the last thing she wanted.

"Forgive us, Gabrielle. Of course you're bored." It was Bryce who came to her rescue, his penetrating gaze appraising her from across the table. "A discussion of my legal accomplishments hardly makes for fascinating dinnertime conversation."

"The fault is mine." Averley, the stout, ruddy-cheeked Whitshire steward, laid down his fork with a cordial smile. "I'm the one who has kept Mr. Lyndley talking about himself. It's just that I'm extraordinarily impressed with his obvious business acumen and his outstanding credentials."

"You sound surprised, Averley," Hermione noted aloud. "I know you're protective of my interests, but certainly Bryce's reputation precedes him. Delmore and Banks, and Newsham and Satterley—two of London's most prestigious soliciting firms, both of whose names are undoubtedly familiar to you—are constantly clamoring for his services. Articles verifying that fact have been written up in all the newspapers, as have many of Bryce's court appearances, not to mention the superb advancements he's made in married women's property law—"

"Hermione," Bryce interrupted, his lips twitching with amusement, "perhaps Mr. Averley doesn't commit small newspaper articles to memory. I respect the man for worrying over your financial well-being. If he has concerns, let him voice them. After which"—he inclined his head in Gaby's direction—"we'll change the subject to something more interesting than business."

With a terse nod, Hermione resumed eating, her every motion conveying disapproval of Averley's tactics.

Averley was far from oblivious to that disapproval. Shifting uncomfortably, he refilled his wineglass, casting a rueful glance at Bryce. "I believe I owe you an apology, Mr. Lyndley. My intention was not to make you feel as if you were being interrogated or judged. Of course I've read of your fine contacts and your legal achievements. I also know what an excellent judge of character Lady Nevon is. I'm just a very cautious man."

"No apology is necessary," Bryce assured him.

"Still, I'd like to offer you an explanation. A very frank one, if you don't mind."

"Not at all. I prefer candor to evasion."

"Good." Averley lowered his glass to the table. "Then I'll be blunt. The truth is, I've known Lady Nevon for many years. Yes, she's a fine judge of character. However, she's also incomparably loyal to those who work for her. One of the responsibilities assigned to me by the late duke was to ensure that his sister's compassion didn't compromise her business interests. Thus, when her message arrived at Whitshire yesterday, stating the surname of her new business and legal adviser, I was plagued by the possibility that her commitment to you stemmed not from her awareness of your credentials but from her longstanding ties to your parents. I'm delighted to learn just how wrong I was."

Bryce's eyebrows rose in surprise. "I didn't realize you knew my parents."

"I didn't. Not personally, that is. But I am quite familiar with them as a result of Lady Nevon's glowing descriptions. According to her, your father was an exemplary valet, indispensable to Lord Nevon until the day he died. And your mother was a highly respected, extraordinarily efficient housekeeper. I recall what a difficult task it was to replace her when she and your father moved to the cottage where you were born. In any case, Lady Nevon made it no secret that she held your parents in the highest regard. It stood to reason she'd feel the same way about their son. Hence my concern." Averley cleared his throat, feeling Hermione's less than subtle glowering stare. "Nevertheless, I've exceeded my bounds and upset Lady Nevon with my overprotectiveness."

"Your commitment to Hermione is admirable," Bryce replied, in an obvious effort to diffuse Hermione's annoyance. "No offense was taken." He swallowed the last bite of his mutton. "Now that we've cleared that up, let's move on to another topic."

"I think we should defer dessert," Hermione announced suddenly, easing back her chair. "I'd like to have that chat with Thane and Bryce now."

Gaby blinked at the abruptness of Hermione's decision, although she well understood its cause. Clearly Mr. Averley's choice of topics had provoked her aunt further, making her all the more determined to get on with a reunion she believed would permanently obliterate any doubts about Bryce's place in her life.

Very well, Gaby concluded. *'Tis time to make my exit.* "If you'll excuse me," she began, laying her napkin on the table. "I'll use this time to stroll the grounds."

"No." Bryce came to his feet, shaking his head as he did. "I'd prefer you join us."

Slowly Gaby raised her head, met his gaze. *For whose sake?* she wanted to cry out. *Yours or mine?*

Perception registered on Bryce's handsome features. "It would ease my mind if you didn't go off on your own. After all, the grounds of Whitshire span countless acres, and it is getting dark So, for both your sake and mine, please stay."

"I spent many childhood hours dashing about the grounds of Whitshire; I won't get lost," she assured him, her legs already trembling at the prospect of wandering back to the spot where she knew they would take her. What's more, she was sure Bryce had guessed her destination and was attempting to spare her the pain that would result from going there alone. She swallowed. Perhaps he was right.

"Your dashing about Whitshire's grounds—now *that* is something I do recall," Averley remarked with a faint reminiscent smile. "You were a tiny slip of a child, Gabrielle, but you caused the rest of the staff immense anguish on a daily basis by disappearing from your quarters time and again, only to be found tending to one animal or another somewhere on the estate, usually in the woods, the barn, or the stables."

An answering smile touched Gaby's lips. "Your memory is accurate, sir. And I needn't ask why, at least not with regard to me. I can remember at least three occasions when the servants had to abandon their chores for a full day to comb the grounds of Whitshire in the hopes of recovering me. While I, in turn, unaware and unbothered by the havoc I was wreaking, was blissfully chasing after a rabbit, a fawn, or a bird. I can't imagine I made your job easy."

He chuckled. "No, you didn't. But your antics

weren't intentional. The fact was that your affinity for animals overshadowed your sense of judgment."

"It still does," she admitted.

"In that case, I'd take Mr. Lyndley's suggestion and accompany him, Lady Nevon, and His Grace to the sitting room. I'm not nearly as young as I once was, nor are the other servants. We wouldn't want to have to organize a search party to retrieve you from parts unknown."

"I wholeheartedly agree." Hermione smoothed her skirts, giving Averley his first approving look of the evening. "In the interim, Averley, I'd appreciate your fetching whichever business records of mine you deem important. Once my conversation with Thane is concluded, I'd like you to fill Bryce in on everything he needs to know in order to put my legal affairs in order."

"Of course." Averley nodded. "Where shall I bring the records?"

"Is the music room convenient?" Bryce broke in to inquire.

Gaby's chin came up, simultaneous with Averley's puzzled "Pardon me?"

"I assume an estate this size has a music room," Bryce repeated smoothly, his questioning glance on Hermione. "I was merely asking if that would be a convenient place for us to reconvene."

A heartbeat of silent communication passed between them, so brief in duration that no one even noticed it.

No one but Gaby.

"What a splendid idea, Bryce," Hermione concurred at once, satisfaction lacing her tone. "Whitshire's music room, which is just down the hall from the sitting room, is warm and comfortable. In addition, it boasts a magnificent Broadwood grand piano, one I'm sure Gaby would enjoy seeing. Indeed, that is precisely where we'll review the records. Averley, give us an hour. Then join us there."

"Very good, my lady." Averley took his leave.

Gaby swallowed, touched by the generosity of Bryce's gesture. Regardless of how subtle he thought he'd been, she knew precisely why—and for whom—he'd suggested the music room. By securing her in an environment that, by her own definition, she deemed a warm haven, he was hoping to put her at ease, to alleviate the heartache she was experiencing as she confronted the demons of her past. Given the difficult reunion he himself was about to face, his display of concern was more than admirable—yet another clear indicator of what kind of man Bryce Lyndley really was.

In contrast, however, he neither expected nor accepted anything in return. Not from her, not from anyone. Of that, Gaby was certain. In fact, she was willing to bet that, with the exception of Aunt Hermione, whose financial support had served as his very lifeline from boyhood to manhood, Bryce had never accepted anything from anyone in his life. Not materially and not emotionally. Gaby was more sure of that with each passing moment in his company, and now that she'd heard the full details of his background, her conviction had strengthened tenfold, as had her determination to teach him the beauty of accepting in return, to allow him a taste of the give-and-take that defined caring.

The kind of caring in which she'd been enveloped at Nevon Manor, thanks to Aunt Hermione and the extraordinary staff that had become her family.

With that, Gaby lowered her lashes, studying Bryce as inconspicuously as possible, trying to decide how best to offer him the same comfort he was offering her.

Oblivious to Gaby's thoughts, Thane had risen and was addressing Hermione with undisguised curiosity. "Now that that's settled, shall we adjourn to the sitting room? Whatever this discussion is about, it's obviously important."

"*Very* important," Hermione said with quiet emphasis.

Given that Gaby was scrutinizing Bryce so closely, she could actually discern the ever-so-subtle change in his demeanor effected by Thane's words. His jaw set as he steeled himself, and his shoulders went rigid, a veritable soldier preparing to do battle.

Or preparing to defend himself in one.

Without further deliberation, Gaby acted. Casually she made her way around to the other side of the table, pausing before Bryce and giving his arm an indiscernible squeeze.

He looked startled, his chin snapping down until his gaze settled on her hand, then lifted to meet her eyes.

She gave him a soft, reassuring smile. "Have faith," she whispered, wishing she could reach up and erase the grim lines of tension from about his mouth. "You're not alone. Music rooms are but one type of haven. Solace comes in all forms, as do those who offer it." With that, she released him, following her aunt and Thane into the sitting room, holding her breath until she heard Bryce's purposeful strides behind her.

Once they were all inside, Thane shut the door, rubbing his palms together and assessing the others. "We'll forgo brandy and the like and get to the point. What is this private discussion about?"

Bryce stood at the window, staring across the grounds, hands clasped behind his back.

With a sigh, Hermione lowered herself onto the settee, gesturing for Gaby to join her. "Bryce," she said, addressing his profile, "the armchair is unclaimed."

"I'll stand."

With a baffled expression, Thane gazed at Bryce's unyielding back. "Lyndley," he stated flatly, "like you, I pride myself on being a frank and intuitive man. So before we begin, I'm going to be as blunt as

Averley was. It's apparent that you resent me, despite the fact that we've gotten on quite well since your arrival. Why? Have I done something to offend you?"

"I don't resent you, Your Grace." Bryce pivoted slowly. "I'm just bloody uncomfortable about meeting you."

"Why?"

Silence.

Hermione wet her lips. "Bryce . . . may I?"

A shrug. "Feel free."

She nodded, clearing her throat. "Thane, we both know your father was a stubborn and difficult man. Sometimes difficult to the point of brutality. We don't speak of it aloud, but we know it to be true."

Thane looked incredulous. "I hardly think this is the time to discuss Father's flaws."

"I beg to differ with you. It is precisely the time. Because your father is at the core of this discussion *and* at the core of Bryce's resentment." Folding her hands in her lap, Hermione lifted her chin, speaking with the regal dignity that was hers and hers alone. "What I'm about to reveal to you is going to come as quite a shock. I trust you to receive it with a full heart and the realization that it was entirely my idea that you be told. Bryce was against it. And, given that he's been privy to this information for over two decades, I think you'll agree he's had more than sufficient time to divulge the truth, *if* he had chosen to. Which he didn't, for many reasons. Some of those reasons I concurred with, others I did not. Well, those that I concurred with died along with your father. Bryce has his own private reasons for remaining silent, which I understand but cannot accept. Out of respect for me, he's agreed to forgo his own reservations and share the truth with you. It wasn't an easy decision for him to make, nor will it be an easy truth for you to hear. Nevertheless, I fervently believe you must and should be told."

By this time, Thane had gone pale. "For God's sake, Hermione, what is it?"

"Bryce is your brother."

"What?"

"I said, Bryce is your brother. Your half brother, to be exact." With that, she proceeded to relate the entire story of Bryce's birth and the controversy surrounding it, from Anne Parks's futile attempts to elicit the late duke's help to Richard's brutal rejection of his child to the drastic abandonment that brought Bryce to Nevon Manor and, ultimately, to Hermione's Bedford cottage and the Lyndleys. Without pause, Hermione explained how she'd provided for Bryce's future, her tone firm and without the slightest hint of an apology for the actions she'd taken. She didn't stop until she had disclosed every detail, right down to her summoning Bryce after Richard's death. "So," she concluded, watching Thane sink down on the sofa, his face chalk-white. "That is why we're here tonight—at my insistence. For your sake and for Bryce's. 'Tis time you met your brother—and he you."

A hush settled over the sitting room, and only Gaby, sitting beside her aunt, could see by the trembling of Hermione's fingers how much that speech had cost her.

Worriedly, she leaned forward, clasping Hermione's hands in hers, terrified that this had all been too much for her aunt's failing health. At the same time she sneaked a peak at Bryce, trying to assess his reaction to the events as they'd unfolded thus far.

Bryce hadn't moved a muscle. His posture remained as stiff and unyielding—and self-protective—as it had been before.

"Thane?" Hermione pressed gently, looking from Thane to Bryce and back again. "You must have questions."

Thane rested his elbows on his knees, clearly attempting to assimilate all he'd just learned. "Yes, I must. At the moment, however, I'm too stunned to think what those questions might be." He inhaled sharply, struggling for the control he'd been trained always to display. "Forgive me. I seem to be at a loss. I . . ." He rose, raking his hand through his hair and prowling the room.

"Is it confirmation you seek?" Hermione asked cautiously. "Do you doubt what I've told you?"

"Confirmation?" Thane halted. "No, Hermione, what I seek is a way to make sense of all this. I hardly think you'd lie to me about something of this magnitude. On the other hand, Father did, didn't he? Then again, the two of you are as alike as night and day." A bitter laugh. "Of course I knew Father was a ruthless man. Still, I never imagined he was capable of something so monstrous. To cast his own flesh and blood into the gutter. . . . Even if he wanted to keep his bloody indiscretion a secret *and* to deny his child, why wouldn't he allow you or some other trustworthy family to adopt him? How could he condemn a newborn babe to the streets or to a workhouse—or worse?"

"For many reasons. First, Richard didn't believe that his indiscretion, as you put it, could remain hidden if Bryce was provided for—by anyone. A trustworthy family? Richard didn't believe such a thing existed. He was convinced that those who adopted the babe would delve until they'd unearthed the facts surrounding the child's lineage, at which point they would bleed Richard dry. And even if they were unable to learn the truth, someone else would—someone with the cunning and the wealth to do so and with the power to ruin the Rowlands. Why, in Richard's estimation, the instant the *ton* caught wind of the fact that a newborn babe of unknown origin had been adopted, his secret was as good as out. Whispers would become speculation; speculation would broaden into prying. Eventually someone somewhere would piece it all together. The result? A scandal, something your father would never tolerate—for himself or for any member of his family.

"Which brings us to me. The very idea of *my* providing for Bryce, Richard considered to be not only the riskiest choice imaginable, but a flagrant slap in his face. He nearly exploded when I suggested it." Hermione frowned, remembering. "And, Thane, in addition to your father's obsession with averting a scandal, he was also convinced that your opinion of him would be tainted were you to learn that he'd been stupid enough not only to bed a green girl who was also a common actress but to allow her to conceive his child, to boot." A disgusted sniff. "As if your opinion of him isn't tainted knowing what he intended for Bryce. And with regard to his *allowing* Miss Parks to become pregnant, I don't think she managed that particular feat alone, nor do I believe my brother was coerced into providing his cooperation. The fact is that neither he nor Miss Parks considered the possible outcome of their actions until it was too late."

Another sniff. "And the last, but most significant, of Richard's so-called reasons for disposing of Bryce was his supreme possession: his title. Given that Richard believed everyone's values were as shallow as his own, he assumed that, were Bryce nurtured into manhood, were there the slightest chance he'd discover who his sire was, he would doubtless have challenged you for the exalted title Duke of Whitshire. It didn't appease Richard to hear my reminders that you were his sole legitimate son, nor that you were nearly a year Bryce's senior, both of which rendered you the indisputable heir to the dukedom. No, my arguments fell on deaf ears. Richard was convinced that Bryce would fight you to the death in order to get what he wanted."

Hermione shook her head, her gaze shifting to Bryce, her expression and tone growing warm with pride. "My brother was a cruel and arrogant fool. If he'd only allowed himself the pleasure of getting to know his second son, he would have realized that titles, fortunes, glittering jewels, and elegant estates— all of those are of very little value to Bryce. What Bryce values are the very traits he himself possesses: decency, compassion, and honor, all of which are inborn and can neither be inherited nor measured in pounds. Your father was a hard-hearted scoundrel who cheated himself out of far more than that which he deprived Bryce of."

"And you're an incredibly brave woman." A bit of Thane's composure and color had returned, along with a semblance of clearheadedness. "To brazenly ignore Father's instructions, take on this quest yourself . . ." He jammed his hands into his pockets. "Why didn't you tell me? I could have helped."

"Impossible. The risk was too great. Can you imagine the enormity of Richard's fury if he'd learned you were privy to my deception? He'd not only have destroyed Bryce and me, he'd have lashed out at you as well. I didn't dare consider it."

"I deserved to know." Thane sounded more remorseful than accusing.

"Yes, you did. But you also deserved to be protected. I opted for the latter, for both our sakes. So if you're angry with me, I understand."

"Angry with *you?*" Thane's brows shot up. "No, Hermione, to the contrary, I'm touched and amazed by you, by what you've managed single-handedly all these years. It's my father I'm angry with. I realize one shouldn't speak ill of the dead. Nevertheless, I cannot forgive him for this. God . . . a brother." He turned slowly, focusing his full attention on Bryce, assessing him from an entirely new perspective. "We resemble each other," he noted after careful scrutiny.

Gaby's glance followed Thane's, and she was relieved to see that sometime over the past few minutes the grim lines about Bryce's mouth had softened and a hint of compassion had warmed the chill from his eyes.

"Yes," he returned in a measured tone, "I suppose we do."

Without further hesitation, Thane walked forward, withdrawing his hand from his pocket, and extending it to his brother. "Bryce, I'm not sure what to say. So I'll just welcome you and apologize that the welcome is coming thirty-one years too late."

Bryce clasped Thane's hand, looking astonished and, for the first time since Gaby had met him, totally off-balance. "I'm less certain than you what to say," he admitted. "Other than to accept your gracious welcome. Hermione was right about you. I'm glad I gave in to her request and came to Whitshire tonight."

Thane's lips twitched. "You'll find Hermione has a way of getting what she wants."

"So I've noticed."

The two men shared their first comfortable chuckle since entering the sitting room.

"Before we go any further, I want something understood." Bryce abruptly withdrew his hand and held his arms rigid at his sides. "I agreed to come here to tell you the truth, and as I said, I'm glad I did, but that doesn't mean I want anything in my life to change. I want no announcements, no acknowledgments, no attempts by you to make amends for your father's actions. As I told Hermione, what's done is done, and the results are a fait accompli. I like my life, and I don't intend to alter it. I want this point clarified for both our sakes," he added in a milder tone, "so that both our lives can continue without upheaval. You're not responsible for what Whitshire did to me any more than you're responsible for his being the kind of man he was. In many ways the conversation that just took place here was more difficult for you than it was for me. I've had over twenty years to adjust to the truth. You're first being burdened with it. The point is, I want nothing from you—not your assets or your feelings of guilt and obligation. I simply want things to go on as they are."

"I understand," Thane replied, pursing his lips, "and I respect your decision as well as your attempt to absolve me of any responsibility or obligation. Now let me tell you where I stand." He drew a sharp breath, an earnest expression tightening his features. "With regard to my father—*our* father—you're right. I cannot answer for his contemptible behavior, nor, even if I tried, could I begin to make up for his renunciation of you and whatever hardships that caused. I won't insult you by saying otherwise. Nor will I insult you with an offer of monetary compensation, which I presume is what you were referring to when you said you wanted nothing of my assets. Let it be known, however, that anything you ever need or want is yours—and I'm *not* making that offer out of guilt."

Thane's gaze was unwavering, his stance as uncompromising as Bryce's. "We don't know each other, Bryce. I want to change that. The first thing you'll discover about me is that I'm nothing like our father. I don't view wealth and titles as life's ultimate achievements. I understand honor, decency, and integrity as well as you do. And based on that fact . . . no, I cannot promise you I'll feel no sense of obligation or commitment toward you. If I could make that promise, I'd be no better than Father, and you'd have no respect for me as a human being. You're my brother, a reality I cannot simply dismiss as if it were inconsequential. What's more, I'm hoping you'll not only understand that fact but also agree with it, and that, despite your adamant stipulations, you're as eager as I to become acquainted—without any announcement being made," he added hastily, holding up his palm to ward off Bryce's objections. "In public we'll present ourselves as business associates and friends, neither of which, I'm beginning to suspect, will be a fabrication. As for our relationship as brothers—*that* we will acknowledge only in private and only among those who are privy to the facts. Would that be acceptable?"

A flicker of something—wary relief, perhaps—registered on Bryce's face. "It would."

"Good." Thane looked equally relieved. "Then suppose you tell me who else knows our secret."

"Only those in this room."

"And Chaunce." Clearly Thane considered that to be a certainty.

"Ah, yes. And Chaunce." A corner of Bryce's mouth lifted. "I think I'm going to enjoy the opportunity to further our acquaintance, Your Gr . . . Thane."

"As am I."

"Thank God," Hermione murmured. She stirred on the sofa, excitement bringing a tinge of color to her ashen complexion. "I believe a toast is in order. Thane, retrieve your brandy and sherry immediately. We still have a few minutes before we're to meet Averley in the music room. Let's secure your new relationship with Bryce with a proper flourish."

"Right away." With a mock salute at his aunt, Thane crossed over to the sideboard, and poured sherry for Hermione and Gabrielle, and brandy for himself and Bryce. "Shall I make the toast?" he asked Hermione as he finished distributing the drinks.

"No, I claim that honor." She looked thoroughly smug and elated. "To my two nephews," she pronounced, raising her glass high. "May you forge the kind of brotherhood you both deserve, and may all I wish for you come to pass."

"Uh-oh," Gaby heard Bryce mutter into his brandy. "All you wish for us? Lord only knows what *that* means."

"I heard that, Bryce," Hermione admonished.

"Did you?" His eyes were twinkling as he swirled

the contents of his snifter about. "Then I don't suppose you'd care to divulge whatever it is your clever mind is dreaming up this time?"

"Why, I have no idea what you're implying."

"You never do."

Listening to their good-natured banter, seeing Bryce's earlier tension rapidly ebb, Gaby felt a warming combination of comfort and delight. She knew how terribly difficult this discussion had been for him—both anticipating it and enduring it—and while she'd been certain of Thane's ultimate acceptance of his brother, she was still very glad the entire ordeal was over.

Now if they could only skip over the rest of the evening and head straight home to Nevon Manor, perhaps her own disquiet could ease.

Even as that fleeting thought wafted through her, the anxiety she'd experienced earlier—temporarily held at bay by her concern for Bryce—resurged. Rational or not, being back at Whitshire was proving to be far more distressing than she'd envisioned. In truth, all she wanted to do was bolt.

Several timeless minutes passed—minutes that seemed more like an eternity.

Glancing at the mantel clock, Gaby was dismayed to see that it was only half after nine. She'd been certain it was nearing eleven by now. Still, even half after nine was late for Aunt Hermione, given her weakened state—wasn't it?

She opened her mouth to say just that—and was interrupted by a knock at the door.

"Yes?" Thane called.

"Pardon me, Your Grace." Couling hovered in the doorway, his eyes widening in astonishment as he surveyed the occupants of the room, who were engaged in what was obviously a small celebration, hardly what he'd expected given the recency of the late duke's passing. "Averley asked me to inquire if you were ready for him yet." The butler awaited

Thane's reply, his curious gaze wandering from the new duke to Bryce to Hermione and finally settling on Gaby, where it lingered.

Gaby could just imagine what Couling was thinking. He was probably wondering how she, the orphaned child of Whitshire's late head groom, came to be part of this seemingly momentous discussion.

She was wondering the same thing herself, not because she doubted her place by Aunt Hermione's side nor because she regretted having been able to offer Bryce her support, but because now that she was no longer needed, her own dilemma was thrusting its way into the forefront, making it increasingly evident that the peace she sought was not forthcoming—at least not tonight.

"Tell Averley we're on our way," Thane was instructing Couling. "We're about finished here. We'll meet him, as planned, in the music hall."

"Very good, sir." With a final quizzical look, the butler turned and retraced his steps.

Gaby seized her chance posthaste.

"Aunt Hermione," she blurted, placing her glass on the side table. "Perhaps we should postpone whatever legal matters need evaluating for another time. It's getting late and—"

"Nonsense." Hermione shattered Gaby's plan to bits without ever realizing she was doing it. Shaking her head, she rose slowly from the settee, intent on her own course of action. "I want Bryce to spend the better part of an hour with Averley—*and* a bit of private time with Thane. Don't worry, darling, we'll still be home long before midnight."

"But your medicine . . ."

"Chaunce will leave it at my bedside. I'll take it the instant I return." Hermione smoothed her snowy hair into place, regarding first Thane, then Bryce with an expression of profound joy. "Truly, Gaby, I'm feeling more myself tonight than I have in ages."

"Of course you are." Guilt knotted Gaby's stomach. Here she was, encouraging her jubilant aunt to leave Whitshire under false pretenses, when it was really she herself who wanted to leave. Shame mingled with guilt, reminding her what a pivotal occasion this was for her aunt. Hermione had waited all these years for Bryce and Thane to meet, and now that they had, now that they even seemed to *like* each other, Hermione was positively elated. She deserved to be here to bask in the glory of her family being united at last. Gaby would simply have to overcome her own unease—this instant. Even if it meant remaining at Whitshire for hours. She owed that much, and more, to her aunt.

"Darling, are you all right?" Hermione was asking, concern lining her forehead as she studied Gaby's face. "You're as white as a sheet. Are you not feeling well? Then perhaps we *should* go."

"No." With a bright smile, Gaby gathered up her skirts and made to rise. "I'm feeling fine, truly."

"Wait." Bryce halted Gaby's motion with a wave of his arm. Purposefully, he crossed over to the settee, goblet in hand. "Sip at this," he instructed quietly, pressing the brandy snifter to her lips. "It will restore your color—and your reserves."

Gaby's lashes lifted, and she met Bryce's gaze. "Thank you," she murmured, referring to far more than just the brandy.

"You're welcome." He waited until she'd complied, watching as the spirits did their job. "Better?"

"Yes." Gaby felt the chill that had pervaded her subside a bit, more from Bryce's solid presence than from his brandy, she suspected.

"Let's not keep Averley waiting," Bryce suggested, when it was clear Gaby felt more herself. Casually he set down his goblet and guided Gaby to her feet, seizing her elbow in a firm, steadying grip that belied his seeming nonchalance. "I'll make sure you reach the music room without incident."

"Excellent." On the heels of Bryce's declaration,

Hermione made her way to Thane's side and slipped her arm through his. "Then my other handsome nephew shall be my escort."

"My pleasure," Thane agreed with a smile.

"The music room is two doors down on your right," Hermione called over her shoulder, already urging Thane toward the hallway.

"Are you able to do this?" Bryce asked Gaby the moment his aunt and brother were out of hearing range.

Her indrawn breath was shaky. "I *must* do this. It means so much to Aunt Hermione." She balled her hands into tight fists of frustration. "I don't understand it, Bryce. I was doing much better while you and Thane were talking. Then suddenly, when I contemplated the rest of the evening, that dreadful apprehensive feeling returned. Why? It's not as if I've encountered anything since we arrived that would incite my uneasiness. Even the rooms we've been in tonight hold no memories for me; I've never so much as seen them before. When I lived at Whitshire, the only sections of the manor I was permitted to enter were the kitchen and the servants' hall. So why am I reacting like this? I expected this visit to be trying, but I also assumed it would ease, not worsen, as the night wore on. I'm baffled, but more important, I'm determined not to let these misgivings interfere with Aunt Hermione's joy."

Reflexively, Bryce brushed a strand of hair off Gaby's face. "Maybe your distress will ease in the music room. You yourself claimed you lose yourself while playing the piano."

"So I did." Gaby's train of thought shifted abruptly as she recalled Bryce's earlier insight and sensitivity. "You remembered our conversation about Beethoven—that's why you suggested meeting Averley in the music room." She inclined her head, studying Bryce with open wonder. "Aunt Hermione is right. You *are* an extraordinary man. I don't know what astounds me more, your ability to see inside people or your ability to soothe them."

Amusement curved Bryce's lips. "I know quite a few people who would take exception to *that* description of me. Soothing? My colleagues would laugh themselves silly. As for my being able to read your mind, it hardly takes a visionary to do so. You're not exactly adept at disguising your feelings. Trepidation was written all over your face."

"Thane didn't detect it," Gaby pointed out. "Do you remember what I told you—about Thane being the first notes of a sonata? Well, you're the entire concert—richly textured and deep. Music, as we discussed, must be felt. Emotions, even blatant ones, must be perceived. Perhaps mine were written all over my face, but it took you to read them."

A heartbeat of silence.

"While we're on the subject of emotions," Gaby continued, deliberately steering the conversation in a direction Bryce would find less disturbing. "I'm so happy things went well for you and Thane."

"So am I. I think." Absently, Bryce rubbed his chin. "I didn't expect tonight to result in an alliance with Whitshire's son. I'm having a bit of trouble with all this, trying to determine who I am, at least with regard to Thane. We're total strangers, yet we're brothers. It's damned disconcerting."

"The lack of a defined rapport between you and Thane will amend itself. As for who you are, you know the answer to that. The situation may be unsettling, but the man beneath is unchanged. You're Bryce Lyndley. You have a challenging new maze to navigate, but you'll find your way, both here and at Nevon Manor. And who knows? You just might grow a bit in the process." Gaby's gravity vanished, twin dimples appearing in her cheeks. "Just as Alice did in Wonderland—and I don't only mean in the physical sense, when she gobbled up the cake that said 'eat me.'"

Laughter warmed Bryce's eyes to a velvety green. "Or when she nibbled on the proper side of a mushroom?"

"Precisely."

"You're a lot like Wonderland yourself, you know. A beautiful and carefree fairy tale with an inner core of wisdom that one must perceive in order to benefit from. Has anyone ever told you that?"

Wordlessly, Gaby shook her head, a peculiar knot tightening her chest. "No," she admitted. "Never."

"A flagrant oversight." Bryce's knuckles caressed her cheek. "Consider it remedied." An odd expression crossed his face, and he dropped his hand to his side. "We'd best get going or Hermione will march down here and drag us to the music room so that Averley can teach me all I need to know."

"And so you can spend time with Thane," Gaby reminded him, the reality of the evening ahead eclipsing the warmth of the past few moments.

"That too." Bryce paused, assessing Gaby carefully, then tucking her arm through his. "Remember, you're not alone. If the uneasiness persists, we'll leave. All right?"

"All right." With a sharp inhalation, Gaby followed Bryce's lead, walking beside him to the hallway. As they veered toward their destination, she reassured herself that his encouragement and Whitshire's music hall would provide enough magic to keep her trepidation at bay.

She knew at once she was wrong.

The instant she crossed the threshold, entered the richly decorated music hall, Gaby felt her insides clench—despite the encouraging smile bestowed upon her by Aunt Hermione, the pleasant greetings offered by Averley and Thane.

Her troubled gaze took in her surroundings, trying to fathom the cause for her excessive distress. Whitshire's music hall was twice the size of the one at Nevon Manor, but it was also as unfamiliar as it was grand. She'd never set foot in here before, of that she was certain. So why was her heart pounding like a drum?

She continued her scrutiny.

The room, which overlooked the southern portion of the estate, boasted gilded moldings and arches, and huge trefoil mirrors divided the long row of windows on the far side of the room. The windows were adorned with gold brocade drapes, tied back with matching sashes so as to allow onlookers an unobstructed view of the grounds. Beyond the glass, acres of greenery stretched out, blanketed by darkness, black velvet broken only by the outline of the stables and the lights dotting the rooms of the servants' quarters.

The servants quarters. Gaby's mouth went dry as she realized what her subconscious had already known: that she was staring through a window to her childhood—and to the terrifying nightmare that had ended it. No wonder she was reacting so intensely. Why in the name of heaven did the music room have to overlook this particular section of Whitshire?

Avoiding her ghosts was no longer an option.

Walking away from Bryce, she perched on the edge of a mahogany chair, steeling herself to confront what she must. Stiff-backed, she stared outside, vaguely aware of Thane and Averley summoning Bryce to the far corner of the room, equally aware of Bryce complying, albeit with reluctant concern. After that, everything became a vague, faraway blur: the droning of the three men's voices as they pored over documents, Hermione's occasional suggestions as she ensured that Bryce's every question was addressed.

The only thing that was screamingly vivid in Gaby's mind was her own increasing distress.

Pressing her damp palms together, she focused on the quarters before her, realizing why she hadn't recognized her whereabouts right away. This entire wing of Whitshire was foreign—an observation that struck her like a blow, even though she knew she should have expected it. Of course the buildings had been redesigned. After all, the fire had destroyed everything, burned to ashes all the structures from Whitshire's rear entrance to its coach house. Only the stables had been spared, given that they'd been set apart and a great enough distance away, and the wind had blown the fire in the opposite direction.

Tragically, that direction had blazed a straight line to the servants' quarters, where dozens of innocent people had been devoured by flames, dying before they had a chance of escape.

With a will of its own, Gaby's gaze combed the darkness, fixed on what now looked to be a section of the coach house, but what had thirteen years ago been the storage room in which she'd slept that fateful night, lulled by her music box, content in the knowledge that the baby robins she'd wandered out to inspect slept, too.

While in the meantime, the blaze had robbed her of everything, everyone, she loved.

She squeezed her eyes shut, attempting to blot out the suddenly vivid images that sprang to mind. The unnatural light that had blinded her upon awakening. The smoke curling slowly beneath the door. The musky smell of burning timber and scorching blossoms. The terrifying feeling that she would never escape—and the blast of fresh air when she had.

The sickening realization of where that wall of flame was headed.

Dear God. This wasn't difficult, it was unbearable.

Drawing a deep, supposedly calming breath, Gaby was seized by a wave of panic so acute she nearly cried out. Rising unsteadily to her feet, she moved restlessly about the room, trying to appear as natural as she could, all the while taking slow, soothing breaths, feeling sicker with each passing second, and more and more as if she were being engulfed by some frightening wave. The harder she struggled, the worse it got.

"Gabrielle, why don't you play for us?"

It was Bryce's voice, penetrating her turmoil and bringing her head up. "Pardon me?"

He put down his quill, a troubled frown knitting his brows as he indicated the exquisite Broadwood grand in the center of the room. "I've only once had the pleasure of hearing you play. I'd be delighted if you'd do so now; it would add some spirit to the otherwise dry task of assessing tenant records." He inclined his head in the direction of the piano, giving Gaby an encouraging nod to assure her he knew, at least to some degree, what was going on inside her. "Beethoven would be my preference," he added gently.

"As I'm sure it would be Gaby's," Hermione agreed, her pained expression indisputable proof that she'd completely forgotten what section of grounds Whitshire's music hall overlooked—an oversight for which she was now berating herself. Her anguished gaze narrowed on Gaby as she attempted to discern whether or not her niece was capable of seeing the evening through or whether they should abandon this initial and unexpectedly glaring attempt to face her past. "Please, darling, do as Bryce suggests," she said at length. "It would give me something captivating to listen to while these gentlemen do their tedious legal reviews. If the Broadwood doesn't lighten your heart, we'll end our visit and head directly back to Nevon Manor."

"All right." Relieved that her aunt had deduced the situation and was willing to leave if need be, Gaby walked over to the bench and sat. Her heart was still slamming against her ribs, but she forced her mind away from it, resting her unsteady fingertips on the keys. The cool ivory felt like an old friend, and her eyes slid shut as she closed out the rest of the world and sank into that peaceful place where only she and the musical tones resided.

A place even the panic couldn't penetrate.

She began with Beethoven's Minuet in G, partly because it was Aunt Hermione's favorite, partly so she could lighten the tension that pervaded the room. After that, she switched to sonatas, playing movements from two or three of Beethoven's most beautiful compositions, including "Moonlight Sonata" for Bryce.

With a will of their own, her fingers shifted, finding and producing the initial strains of "Für Elise," bowing her head as she immersed herself in the melody that brought back her parents, her childhood, her memories.

Abruptly she pulled away, her hands shaking as she pressed them to her cheeks, felt the wetness of the tears she hadn't remembered shedding.

"Gaby." Aunt Hermione was beside her, gently stroking her hair.

"I'm sorry," Gaby whispered. "I just—"

"No, *I'm* sorry." Hermione wrapped a fiercely protective arm about her shoulders. "We'll go home now." She half turned, murmuring, "Couling, would you ask Goodsmith to bring my carriage around?"

"Of course, my lady."

Surprised at the proximity of Couling's voice, Gaby raised her head, pivoting about to find out where he was and when he'd entered the room. Her question died before ever emerging.

Couling, Mrs. Fife, Mrs. Darcey, and several other servants hovered just inside the doorway, staring at her with awed expressions. Mrs. Darcey had tears glistening on her lashes, tears she dabbed away with a handkerchief.

"That was beautiful," she said fervently. "You play like an angel. And forgive me for crying. It's just that it's been a long time since I heard that particular melody."

Gaby swallowed. "You remember?"

"Your mother's music box? Of course I do. It was

her prized possession—and yours. You were clutching it so tightly that night, I couldn't pry it from your fingers. Any more than I could stop your sobs."

"Mrs. Darcey," Hermione commanded quietly.

The housekeeper looked positively mortified. "I'm sorry. I didn't mean—"

"I know you didn't."

"You play exquisitely, Gabrielle," Averley inserted, clearing his throat and speaking in an even tone that strove to take the edge off everyone's rampaging emotions. "Lady Nevon was right. You are an accomplished musician."

"Indeed." Couling was regarding her intently. "I feel as if I've just attended a recital."

"Thank you." Gaby rose, relieved when Bryce crossed over to assist her, he and Hermione flanking her. "Now if you'll all excuse me, I really would like to go home."

"Yes," Couling agreed. "I'm sure you would." He gestured to the other servants. "Resume your duties. I'll summon Goodsmith and fetch the coats."

"I appreciate your compassion," Gaby managed, glancing out the windows with a shudder. "I'm sure I'll be fine once I reach Nevon Manor. Yes, I'm quite sure of it," she reiterated, giving everyone a bright, reassuring smile.

Somehow no one looked convinced.

Least of all, she.

Chapter 6

BRYCE PROWLED ABOUT HIS BEDCHAMBER, SIPPING AT A glass of Madeira and grappling with all that had happened tonight—all that had happened during the past few days—the sum total of which gnawed at him, refused to let him sleep.

Gabrielle had been silent on the carriage ride home, a silence that had disturbed Hermione as much as it had him. He'd wanted to discuss the situation with his aunt, but she'd been thoroughly exhausted herself and he'd restrained himself from keeping her awake to further upset her. Besides, Chaunce and Dora had ushered her directly to bed, although privately Bryce wondered if, in Dora's case, it wasn't Hermione doing the guiding rather than the other way around. Regardless, the conversation would have to wait until morning.

Morning—his third day at Nevon Manor.

Bryce scowled into his goblet. He hadn't intended to be here so long. He had people awaiting him in London, depending on his return, both professionally and personally.

123

Personally. That brought his musings to Lucinda.

It was the first time he'd thought about her since he'd left London, a fact that sparked a tad of guilt. Not that she'd protested his making this trip. In fact, she'd applauded it, given who Bryce was going to see the highborn and eminently charitable, not to mention well connected, Lady Hermione Nevon. Lucinda's eyes had sparkled with pleasure at the thought of such a woman summoning Bryce to her home to discuss the handling of her legal matters. A challenge and a coup, was how she'd described it. Certainly worth sacrificing a few parties for, regardless of how much she enjoyed the London Season.

Imagine how delighted Lucinda would be if she knew the full and actual basis for this visit, what Hermione wanted of Bryce, and what their blood ties truly were.

With a sigh, Bryce made his way to the bedchamber window, rolling the glass of Madeira between his palms. He harbored no illusions about Lucinda's motives. She yearned for his professional success as fervently as he did, but her motivations were entirely different. It wasn't that she lacked compassion, only that her compassion took second place to her desire for position and monetary comfort. Bryce couldn't fault her for that, not given the background from which she hailed. Unlike him, Lucinda had grown up in a sheltered and affluent home, with devoted parents who had groomed her to marry someone of the same ilk, someone who could take care of her. She was accustomed to the finer things in life, and while she wasn't cold or greedy, she was ambitious about Bryce's future, although her ambition never extended to asking Bryce to compromise his principles. To Lucinda's way of thinking, the proper planning could result in his establishing a legal practice that would challenge him, make him feel worthwhile, and at the same time benefit them both socially and financially.

If he acquired clients like Hermione Nevon.

A corner of Bryce's mouth lifted. Ever practical, that was Lucinda. More than practical, actually. She had a place and a degree of importance assigned to everything in her life. And while her priorities often differed from his, her pragmatism was one of the things that made their association so agreeable. They shared the same organized thought process, the same clearheaded thinking, the same respect for each other's individual interests. And since those individual interests often took them in different directions, neither intruded on the other's privacy or demanded an overabundance of the other's time.

It was a sufficiently undemanding relationship, one that would inevitably lead to a satisfactory future.

Undemanding or not, however, even Lucinda had her limits. And he had told her he'd be back in a day—two at the most.

Well, two was about to become three. And with the magnitude of his commitment to Hermione, three would doubtless become four, five, or six. Hell, he'd be lucky if he saw his town house again before next week.

Yet how could he leave Nevon Manor when so much was still unsettled, when so many people were relying upon his decisions, his help? Especially Hermione, who was leaning on him, counting on him to take care of her assets, her family, her life.

He'd promised to thoroughly review all the books Chaunce had given him, to make sure Nevon Manor was in good running order. He'd also agreed to look over Averley's notes and suggestions as well as familiarize himself with the accounts of all Hermione's other properties.

And that only covered the less important concern of her monetary assets. Then there was her biggest worry: her family. He'd vowed to her that he would take the time to get to know them.

Staring into the darkness, Bryce contemplated the endearing residents of Nevon Manor, for whom he was already developing an affinity, people who understood the meaning of devotion, cooperation, and family. With an ironic shake of his head, Bryce wondered who the true misfits were—the denizens of the manor or the foolish people who shunned them.

The question was moot. He already knew the answer.

With a fond smile, Bryce recalled his return from Whitshire two hours ago. Goodsmith had followed him from the carriage, finishing his colorful yarn about the time he'd been rushing to Town to visit his sister who was ill, and wouldn't you know it? He'd sped past the carriage of none other than Queen Victoria, who not only acknowledged his apologetic tip of the hat but, upon seeing his agitated state of mind, gestured for him to pass. Bryce had to agree that Her Majesty was a most gracious lady. Still grinning, he'd turned to find Chaunce hovering in the entranceway, wearing a look of unspoken but nonetheless evident concern over the evening's outcome with Thane, his astute gaze darting from Bryce to Hermione in an attempt to assess what had transpired. And then came the culmination—and in some ways, the high point—of the evening: Bryce had climbed the stairs to his bedchamber only to discover Peter asleep in the hallway outside, huddled so contented and still that Bryce had nearly tripped over him *and* the legal text that lay beside him. Upon being awakened, Peter had rubbed his eyes and hobbled to his feet, stammering that he'd come to return the volume he'd borrowed, but that he'd marked a dozen legal phrases he'd tried hard to understand, but couldn't—and could Mr. Lyndley possibly take a few minutes to shed some light on them for him?

Bryce had sent him off to bed, along with the assurance that tomorrow right after breakfast they would have a professional chat.

And those were but a few of the fine staff members with whom Bryce had vowed to become acquainted.

Also, after tonight he had another welcome responsibility—that of getting to know his half brother, an objective that could potentially enrich not only Hermione's life but his own and Thane's as well.

In addition, he had yet to begin working on the other two aspects of Hermione's request: revising her will and establishing a trust for Gabrielle.

Gabrielle.

Even her name elicited a smile. Softhearted, frank, and fiercely loyal, Gabrielle was an enchanting entity unto herself, a charming combination of wisdom and innocence. She'd endured an evening of hell just to ease his way with Thane, and Bryce would be forever indebted to her for that unprecedented show of support.

Now it was *his* turn to help *her*.

His smile vanished, as he considered Gabrielle's precarious state of mind. She'd been as white as a sheet when she went up to bed, her brilliant blue eyes shrouded with frightened memories. She'd been in torment at Whitshire, a torment that, Bryce knew, had embedded itself deep inside her, accompanying her from the estate and remaining excruciatingly present despite the fact that they'd left behind the spot where the tragedy had occurred. Her reaction had been too powerful, too emotional, to be fleeting. Clearly she'd been carrying this pain around for years. It was only now emerging, prompted by her visit to the place where her parents had died.

And during that hour in the music room the look on her face had been devastating, the dread of reliving the past too much for her. What had she seen when she stared out those windows? What ugly picture had surfaced in her mind? Was it the fire swallowing up the servants' quarters, destroying those she loved? And what in the name of heaven was Bryce to do? He had no experience at helping someone through this kind of trauma. His own emotional hurdles had been difficult enough to overcome, and they paled in comparison with Gaby's. How in the name of heaven did one recover from something of this magnitude?

Leaning against the window frame, Bryce set down his goblet and rubbed his eyes. He knew what he had to do—what he wanted to do. He would send Lucinda a note, telling her he was detained at Nevon Manor on pressing business. She would accept it with her customary grace and breeding, and await his return with her customary patience and composure. They'd been apart before, when a particularly compelling case kept him working long hours or when she traveled abroad with her family. The separations never seemed to hamper the compatibility that marked their relationship.

And it had to be done.

Bryce folded his arms across his chest, dismissing Lucinda from his mind, his thoughtful gaze sweeping the grounds of Nevon Manor. He wasn't sure what was troubling him more at the moment, the enormity of his own challenges or the enormity of Gabrielle's.

As if in answer, a flash of white caught his eye, making him blink and focus more intently on the cluster of trees just outside. Something was darting about, a stark figure that was not nearly small enough to be Crumpet but that was frantically making its way across the grounds.

That something was a person.

Straining his eyes, Bryce stared more closely, watching the jerky movements of the ethereal creature that was maneuvering rapidly between the trees.

Gabrielle.

The instant he recognized her, Bryce was on the move. Snatching up his coat, he raced down the stairs and out the door, heading directly toward the area in which he'd spied her.

He stopped, his breath coming in short pants as he

scanned the grounds, searching and listening all at once.

A twig snapped in the distance, and Bryce's head jerked toward the sound.

She was pushing away from an oak about thirty yards away, regaining her balance, and stumbling on with a muffled cry.

"Gabrielle!"

If she heard him, she gave no sign, just continued to shove her way forward, her linen nightgown catching on branch after branch.

Bryce reached her in seconds. "Gabrielle." He seized her arm, but she yanked it free, her slender body trembling with cold, shaking with sobs.

"No!" she gasped, shaking her head wildly from side to side. "Oh, no." She pressed on.

"Wait." Bryce reached for her again, only to hear her cry out in pain as she tumbled to the ground.

"Gaby." He knelt beside her, genuine fear knotting his chest. Tousled waves of hair draped over her shoulders like a dark curtain, shielding her face from view. But the reason for her cry was obvious: her feet were bare and badly cut by the twigs and acorns that covered the ground. "You're bleeding," he murmured, smoothing her hair away as sobs racked her body. "Why in God's name are you—" He broke off as she stumbled to her feet again.

"Mama . . . Papa . . . No!" Her words were garbled, but chillingly recognizable.

"Gaby." He caught her by the waist, dragging her against him.

She was clutching an object to her chest. The glistening alabaster color, the size, the shape—Bryce knew immediately it was her music box.

"Mama . . ." she whispered brokenly.

Gazing into her face, the vacant look in her eyes, Bryce realized with a sickening sensation that she was asleep. "Gabrielle." He touched her cheek tentatively,

129

unsure how to calm her, less sure how to awaken her. "Sweetheart, wake up."

"Please, no . . ." she choked out, striking his shoulder with her small fist in an attempt to free herself. "Papa . . ."

"Gabrielle, wake up." Abandoning his experimental attempts, Bryce shook her—hard—gripping her arms and holding her firmly against him. "It's Bryce. Open your eyes, please."

She gasped, then blinked, the emptiness in her eyes replaced by bewilderment. Like a lost child, she stared up at him, trying to establish her whereabouts, to regain control of reality. "Bryce?" she asked, her teeth beginning to chatter.

"Yes." He sat back on his haunches, cradling her against him while he tugged off his coat, wrapped it around her quaking shoulders. "It's all right. You're all right."

"Where are we?" She gazed about the grounds. Abruptly, her head snapped down and she took note of her attire, the music box she clutched. "Oh, God," she choked out before Bryce could even begin to formulate a credible and soothing explanation for the past few minutes. "I was walking in my sleep. Again. After all these years. Oh, no." She bowed her head, tears streaming down her cheeks, drenching his shirt.

It had happened before, he realized with a start. Not recently but a long time ago. And it didn't take a scholar to guess when—or why.

"You were reliving the fire," Bryce said softly. "Trying to save your parents."

Mutely she nodded.

"Was this the first time this has happened since just after they died?"

"No. I walked in my sleep over and over for months after I came to Nevon Manor." She drew a shuddering breath. "Aunt Hermione and Chaunce used to take turns keeping vigil outside my room, stopping me before I could run outside and hurt myself.

Finally, after nearly a year, the sleepwalking stopped. It never happened again. Until now." More broken weeping.

"Shhh." Bryce stroked her hair, wrapped the coat more securely about her. "It was the visit to Whitshire. You never should have gone." He gritted his teeth, berating himself for persuading her to accompany him. "You're shaking. We've got to get you into the manor."

"No." Gaby sat upright, her quivering mouth set in determined lines. "Please. Don't let Aunt Hermione see me like this. Not when she's been so weak. It will destroy her."

"You're scarcely clothed. You're also freezing. And your feet are badly cut. They need attention." Bryce rose, taking Gaby with him, walking purposefully toward the house. "I don't want to upset Hermione either, but it can't be helped. We're going to your chambers."

"Bryce, wait." Gaby gripped his shirtfront. "Listen to me. If you insist on taking me inside, please use the servants' entrance. It's around back. No one ever uses it other than delivery men, since no one here is considered a servant. Everyone will be asleep. We can use one of the other staircases in this maze Lord Nevon built; I'm familiar with them all. Please."

"All right." Bryce relented. "You direct me."

"I can walk."

"No, you can't. And don't bother arguing—I'm carrying you."

A shaky sigh. "Very well. Follow that path over there." She pointed.

Five uneventful minutes later Bryce carried Gaby into her room and placed her carefully in the center of the bed, setting the music box just as carefully on her nightstand. Then he turned, seeking and finding a basin, crossing over to fill it with water. Scooping up a towel, he returned to the bed. "I'd suggest immersing your feet, but I'm afraid the sting would be unbearable. So I'll wash the cuts with this." He frowned, seeing the stream of blood that trickled on both feet, one on her toes and ankle, the other along the entire length of her instep. "I'll be as swift as I can."

Gaby winced at the first contact, but she bit her lip, silencing any cries that might awaken someone. Bryce worked quickly and efficiently, finally completing his task, pleased to see the bleeding had stopped.

"Good. Now let's get you warm." He glanced uncomfortably around the room. "Where do you keep your nightgowns?"

"In there." Gaby pointed at the chest. "I can fetch one myself."

"Stay off those feet. I'll get it." Bryce opened the chest and removed a clean nightgown, which he placed in Gaby's hands. "I'm going to start a fire. My back will be to you. Change."

She nodded, her cornflower-blue eyes still wide with trauma. "All right."

A quarter hour later the fire was blazing and Gaby was tucked beneath the bedcovers.

Bryce stood beside her, rubbing his palms together and watching her worriedly. "Would you like to sleep?"

"No." She looked positively stricken. "Please stay with me for a while."

"Very well." Normally he would never have agreed to such a scandalous suggestion. But how could he leave her when she'd just endured such a harrowing experience and when she still looked so utterly terrified? "Would you like to talk?" he asked, pulling up a chair and lowering himself to it.

"About what just happened?"

"Not if it upsets you. We could discuss any topic you choose."

The fear in Gaby's eyes banked. Settling herself beneath the blanket, she studied Bryce from beneath wet, spiky lashes. "You and Thane truly liked each other."

He took her cue, relaxing in the chair and crossing one long leg over the other. "Yes, we did."

"When do you intend to visit him again?"

Not "if" Bryce noted with an inner smile, but "when." "Soon. After I've had a chance to review Hermione's papers and get to know her staff a bit."

"You've already won most of them over. The rest should take no more than a few hours."

Bryce chuckled. "I appreciate your faith in my congeniality."

"It isn't your congeniality," Gaby said softly. "It's your heart."

The absolute conviction in her claim was humbling. "It doesn't take heart to care for such fine people, Gabrielle. In fact, it would take effort not to."

"I agree. But then, I love them. They're my family; the only family I . . ." Her voice broke, her own words triggering a painful resurgence of the past. "Whenever I relive that night, I can't help thinking that I should have yelled louder," she confessed abruptly. "I should have gotten help. I should have found a way to stop the flames from spreading." Tears gathered in her eyes, slid down her cheeks. "But it all happened too fast. By the time I got out of the shed, it was already too late. There was nothing I could do . . . nothing to save them."

Bryce moved across to Gaby's bedside, gathered her gently in his arms. "You were a child," he murmured, his fingers sifting through her hair. "And even if you'd been grown, you would have had no way to combat such a rampaging fire."

She pressed her wet cheek to his shirt. "I know. Truly I do. It's just that . . ." An aching pause, filled with the fear and uncertainty of someone poised at the edge of an unknown and menacing abyss.

But why? It wasn't as if she'd never spoken of this before.

Realization struck Bryce like a blow: she hadn't.

"Gaby, you've relived this night countless times in

your mind, but have you ever discussed it with anyone, expressed your feelings aloud?" Bryce asked, knowing what her answer would be, simultaneously recognizing how he could help her.

For a long moment she didn't reply, and when she did, it was in a thin, watery voice. "There was nothing to discuss. No matter what I said, it wouldn't bring back Mama and Papa. Besides, I didn't want to upset Aunt Hermione any more than she already was. My sleepwalking, my agonized state of mind—she'd acquired both of those along with the little orphan girl she'd taken in. I couldn't add to her burden."

"Hermione's a strong woman."

"I know." Gaby swallowed. "The truth is, I didn't restrain myself only for Aunt Hermione's sake. I did it for my own sake as well. And not because I couldn't give voice to my feelings; the pain was there whether or not I spoke of it. But because I was terrified of the consequences. Even though Aunt Hermione never complained, I knew what an emotional burden I was. If I upset her any more, pushed her any further, she might . . . I was afraid she would . . ."

"You were afraid she'd turn you out." Bryce completed the thought flatly. This was one fear he could not only sympathize with but relate to—from first-hand experience. "I understand." His palm slid beneath her hair, caressed the nape of her neck in slow, soothing motions. "I know what it feels like to live in constant dread that whatever little security you have left might be snatched away at any time. I felt that way when I got Hermione's letter at Eton—that if I dared do anything, albeit minor and inadvertent, which resulted in the discovery of my true identity, Whitshire would have me thrown into the streets, where I would doubtless perish. You had that same fear to contend with, plus the emotional scars from the fire. You must have been scared to death."

"I was—which only made me worry more," Gaby

whispered. "After all, the way I was acting . . . what could Aunt Hermione have thought? Here she was, welcoming me into her home, and instead of accepting my good fortune with joy and gratitude, I was withdrawn, consumed by anguish and worry."

"Gabrielle, you were five years old. The entire foundation of your life had been destroyed. You were totally alone. Many people couldn't have survived that kind of trauma."

"You did."

"No." He shook his head, his chin brushing the dark crown of her hair. "I never endured so devastating a loss. My parents, the Lyndleys, didn't die until after I was away at school and living on my own. The rest was but an ugly story written on a piece of paper. Yes, I had my ghosts to confront. But I never had to survive the nightmare you did, certainly not when I was little more than a babe."

Bryce's embrace tightened. "You were extraordinarily strong. You still are. A minute ago you said you would have been able to talk about the fire right after it occurred. That's far more than I've ever done, at least until last night when I confided in you. My initial pain and anger upon receiving Hermione's letter were so acute that I could barely ponder her revelations, much less speak them aloud. After that, I buried the truth inside me until time dulled the pain into indifference. So you see, you're far stronger than I. You could address your loss then, *and* you can address it now. Talk to me. Tell me about the night your parents died. Where were you when the servants' quarters caught fire?"

"In the storage shed." She hesitated—and then the words seemed to spill forth with a will of their own. "I couldn't sleep. Even the music box didn't help, although Mama left it on my nightstand to serenade me into slumber. But it didn't work. I was too worried about the robins."

"Robins?"

"Yes. There was a nest down the way from our chambers. All the animals congregated in that area; it was just across from the stables. The way that section of Whitshire used to be arranged, there were the stables, separate and apart, followed by a long service wing beginning with the coach house, then the wood and coal rooms, and then the storage shed. On the other side of the shed were the servants' entrance and hall and, of course, our quarters, followed by another entrance leading to the steward's and butler's rooms. After that, the wing ended, and a small garden separated it from the main manor."

"And the fire destroyed that entire wing?"

"Everything from the coach house to Averley's and Couling's quarters, yes. Fortunately Couling was still manning his station at the entranceway door and Averley was walking back from the tenants' quarters at the time the fire struck. So neither of them was hurt. Averley was the first to spot the flames and run for help. Thank God he did, or the rest of the manor might have caught next, and everything would have burned to the ground. As it was, the losses were staggering. The only servants who were equally as lucky as Couling, Averley, and me were those who had the evening off and those who were working late shifts in the manor's main living quarters."

"I don't understand," Bryce inserted, frowning. "You just said you were in the shed, where I assume you went to keep an eye on the robins. If so, how did you escape the fire?"

"Fate willed me to survive, I suppose. Because you're right, I *was* in the shed when the fire started. And you're also right that I left my bed to go check on the robins. They had just hatched that morning, and the May night was unusually cold. So I took my music box and crept outside to ensure their well-being and to soothe them with Beethoven."

Tenderness relaxed Bryce's frown as he pictured a

small Gaby, fiercely guarding her baby birds and gifting them with "Für Elise." "Then what?"

"I sat with them for some time, until my shivering became severe. As I said, it was terribly cold, and I was wearing nothing but a nightgown. I knew I needed to go inside, not only to avoid catching influenza but also to avoid discovery. There were still a few servants about, like Whitshire's head gardener, Dowell, and two or three stable hands. Each time one of them passed by, I hid in the grassy hollow beneath the oak. But I couldn't stay there forever, nor could I stop the sound of my chattering teeth. Eventually someone would have spied me and alerted my parents to my whereabouts. And I so hated to upset them—again." Gaby gave a sad little shrug. "As you heard Mr. Averley say earlier, my disappearances were not uncommon. And they worried my parents terribly."

"Why didn't you go back to bed?" Bryce asked, puzzled by her behavior yet altogether grateful for its outcome.

"Because I wanted to check on the robins again later that night, to make sure they hadn't been harmed by the cold. So I crept into the shed and curled up in a pile of blankets. I waited until I couldn't hear any more footsteps or voices. Then I opened the music box and let it play. I must have fallen asleep. When I awakened, the entire room was in flames. I fought my way out—I remember thinking over and over again that I didn't want to die. But once I escaped, realized where the flames were headed"—a choked sob—"I wished I could change my mind. I tried to get to the servants' quarters, but the fire was like a blazing wall. I called out Mama's and Papa's names, and I fought so hard to get through that wall. But I couldn't . . . I couldn't.

"I don't remember anything else until I opened my eyes and found myself clasped in Mrs. Darcey's arms. I was on the ground, and everything smelled funny—smoky and sweet all at once—I'll never forget that smell. Nor will I forget how brown and barren every-thing looked. I knew something was very wrong. At first I thought it was that my music box was gone. But when I asked Mrs. Darcey for it, she gave it to me. She was crying, and then she began rocking me back and forth in her arms. All of a sudden I remembered. I started crying, kicking to free myself, and begging for my parents. But even as I did, I knew they were gone, that I'd never see them again. I knew."

Gaby's whole body was shaking with painful sobs. "Aunt Hermione took me away that very night. She never even let me go back inside—not that there was anything for me to go to. And she didn't bring me to the main manor. Afterward I realized it was because her brother would never have permitted it." Gaby turned her face into Bryce's shirt. "You know the rest."

"Yes, I know the rest." Bryce's chest was so tight he could scarcely speak. "And that's what you were seeing tonight, when you were looking out the music hall windows? You were reliving the fire?"

A tremulous nod. "I don't know how much of Whitshire's servants' wing you could make out in the darkness. But that's the section of the estate that's visible from the music hall windows. It's been rebuilt, of course. Only the stables remain unchanged; they were untouched by the flames. But I wasn't seeing the wing as it is now; I was seeing it the way it was then—the night Mama and Papa died."

Bryce had never felt such a fierce need to absorb someone else's pain as he did at that moment. He closed his eyes, his palm warm against Gaby's neck. He could feel the pounding of her heart, the an-guished shivers of memory still trembling through her as she rested her forehead against him, absorbing whatever fragments of strength and compassion he had to offer.

"Thank you," she whispered after a time. "Thank you for listening." She eased away from him, her eyes huge and emotion-filled. "I didn't realize how much I needed to talk about what happened. You're very insightful."

"I spoke from experience, not insight. And I'm glad I could help."

"You did more than help. You warmed away the pain." Gaby's fingertips brushed his jaw. "Just as a magnificent symphony would."

An odd emotion constricted Bryce's throat—one that had little to do with compassion.

Abruptly he looked about the room, realizing for the first time in too many minutes how inappropriate this whole situation was.

"What is it?" Gaby asked, her head tilted quizzically. "What's wrong?"

Bryce eased her back against the pillows, then rose swiftly to his feet. "I apologize for this less than proper situation," he said, more disconcerted than sorry. "I'm not in the habit of visiting women in their bedchambers or of taking advantage of their distress by holding them in so intimate a manner, much less when they're clad in their nightgowns."

To his amazement, Gaby began to laugh.

"What's so funny?"

"I just survived a devastating experience, thanks to you. I walked in my sleep, relived the worst nightmare of my life, and, in the process, cut my feet to ribbons. You rescued me, awakened me, and nursed my wounds. You carried me to my bed so I wouldn't have to walk, soothed me when I cried, and did it all silently and alone so as not to alert Aunt Hermione and risk upsetting her. You then persuaded me to give voice to memories I'd buried inside me for years and which desperately needed to be said. And now you're apologizing for being in my room, sitting on my bed, and catching a glimpse of me in a nightgown?"

Bryce's lips curved. "I see your point."

"Do you?" Gaby sat up, raising her knees and wrapping her arms about them, regarding Bryce with that innocent wisdom of hers. "I think not. And while I welcome this unexpected humor for helping to make an otherwise unbearable situation bearable, I have to wonder—do you *ever* challenge protocol?"

"Pardon me?" Bryce was thrown completely off-balance by the unexpected question.

Gaby dashed away her tears. "I asked if you ever challenge protocol."

"I heard you. What I meant was, what exactly does your question mean?"

"Precisely what it sounds like it means. I realize you're a man who prides himself on his principles and on his clearheaded, pragmatic approach to life. Nevertheless, surely this was not the only time your feelings have ever compelled you to do something that would otherwise be considered improper."

Bryce considered the question. "Actually, until I came to Nevon Manor, I was a fairly stable, predictable fellow."

"What about Miss Talbot?"

"What about her?"

"Don't you ever behave unpredictably around her?"

"No."

Gaby looked amused. "No? What about when you're alone together? Surely there are times *then* when your heart rules your head. I can only imagine how extraordinary a feeling that must be." She leaned forward. "I know this question is *truly* improper and certainly none of my business to ask, but given how frank you've been with me about everything else, I'm going to risk offending you and blurt it out nonetheless. Where do you and Miss Talbot go for privacy? Not specifically, of course, but in general—you know, unoccupied anterooms that you slip away to during grand balls, moonlit parks that you stroll through only to lose yourselves among the trees, that sort of thing. Or is there perhaps a specific spot—a quiet embankment along the Thames, for example—where lovers can be alone. I've always wondered about that with regard to courting. Your world is much more vast than mine, so I'm sure you can answer me. Where is it permissible for a man and a woman to express their affection for each other?"

Bryce's jaw had dropped, and it took him a full moment to recover. "I don't believe this," he muttered.

"That's not an answer."

"Gabrielle." Bryce sank back down into the chair, reminding himself that he might someday be called upon to oversee this young woman's future. "I don't know where you get your ideas, but I'd better set you straight right now. It's *never* proper for a woman . . . that is, it's wrong for a well-bred young lady to express affection—*real* affection . . ." He broke off, raking a hand through his hair.

"You're referring to passion?" Gaby supplied helpfully.

His eyes narrowed. "What do you know of passion?"

"I'm not a dolt, Bryce. I have eyes and ears. I read. I ask questions. I see glances exchanged right here at Nevon Manor—blushes, heated looks, flirtatious smiles. I've even seen animals mate. I know what intimacy is all about. What I don't know is where people display it. Oh, I have a pretty good idea where the residents of Nevon Manor go, but our family is hardly typical of the rest of the world."

"Damn." Bryce exhaled sharply, praying that Hermione would live forever. The very thought of being guardian to Gabrielle was beginning to send chills down his spine. "First of all, the mating of animals has little to do with the passions of human beings. Second, I'm not the one you should be addressing this type of question to—Who?" he interrupted himself. "Who have you seen those romantic interactions between? And where is it you think they . . . go . . . to be affectionate with each other?"

A secret smile. "I've seen several people. You'll see it for yourself when you've been here long enough. For one, Goodsmith is dreadfully infatuated with Marion. She's that warmhearted maid who's a bit unsteady on her feet. Marion is sweet and amusing, and she's willing to listen to Goodsmith's stories for hours on end. Why, on some afternoons when the carriage has been polished until it gleams and there are no other chores for either of them to do, Goodsmith and Marion disappear for an hour or more, and very little of that time, I suspect, is devoted to Goodsmith's storytelling. The carriage house," Gaby added, "is delightfully deserted at that time.

"Then there's Wilson, who can scarcely take his eyes off Ruth, that refreshing young serving girl with the enchanting smile. Oh, I know she's somewhat dizzy, and often seems a bit vague, but she's not bothered by the fact that Wilson's best friend is his shovel. So it all evens out." Gaby leaned forward conspiratorially. "Whenever Ruth takes a stroll in the garden, Wilson stops what he's doing to stare at her with a lopsided grin and a besotted expression. Occasionally he joins her, at which point they make their way around to the far side of the stables, supposedly, according to Wilson, to inspect the shrubs he planted there, shrubs I have yet to notice. Afterward he sighs for an hour as he ambles about the garden doing not a stitch of work. Why, he doesn't even address his shovel during that time. And there are"—a reflective pause—"others at Nevon Manor who are deeply taken by each other."

"Others," Bryce repeated woodenly. "And do you know where these *others* meet, as well?"

Gaby grinned, her first broad grin all night. "Of course. What I *don't* know is the procedure for those outside Nevon Manor."

"Nor should you," Bryce returned, making a mental note to speak to Hermione first thing tomorrow about this inappropriate exposure of Gabrielle's, however limited, to the romantic interludes of the staff. "No proper young lady needs that kind of information."

"Isn't Miss Talbot a proper young lady?"

"Of course."

"I see." Gaby cocked her head quizzically. "So the two of you are never alone?"

"Exactly."

"Nor were you ever alone with any of the other women you courted?"

"Never."

Gaby's face fell. "Then you know as little as I do about passion."

"No. Yes. I mean—that's not what we were discussing."

"What isn't?"

"Passion. We were discussing the appropriate mode of behavior for well-bred young women."

A glimmer of understanding lit Gaby's eyes. "As opposed to ill-bred young women."

"Precisely."

"What about men? Are they divided into similar categories?"

Bryce wondered why he'd ever found arguing at court difficult. He also wondered when in God's name Hermione had intended to teach Gaby what the world was about, given she was to be brought out next Season. "No. Men are not subjected to the same rules of conduct as women are."

"I see." Gaby rested her chin atop her knees, digesting this new information.

"Do you?"

"Yes."

Bryce nearly sagged with relief. "Good. Then we can drop the subject."

"You're telling me you escort well-bred women about Town, but it's courtesans you visit when you want to express affection."

Bryce's relief vanished. "Gabrielle, I—"

"That's all right, Bryce. I asked." Gaby shook her head in baffled amazement. "Although I can't understand such absurd rules. Wouldn't you rather be intimate with the woman you love than with a stranger?"

"It doesn't work that way," Bryce managed. "As for love, you and I have already held this conversation. You know my opinion on the subject."

"Yes. You don't believe in love, only in compassion. And, as I told you, I'm hoping our family can change your mind." She wet her lips with the tip of her tongue. "Let me ask you something else."

"I can hardly wait."

"You said I was the first person with whom you'd shared the truth about your lineage, that you don't turn to Miss Talbot for such things. What *do* you turn to Miss Talbot for? Exactly what do the two of you share? Not physical intimacy, not emotional intimacy. What, then, is left?"

"Many things." Frowning, Bryce stared at the toes of his shoes. "We share a number of interests: theater, sailing, the opera. We share a circle of mutual friends. We share similar outlooks, goals, priorities."

"Isn't honesty one of your priorities?"

"You know it is."

"Yet Miss Talbot knows nothing about your past, about what shaped you into the man you are."

"She knows all that's important."

"I don't understand you, Bryce," Gaby murmured. "Unless the newspapers have exaggerated, you're on the verge of proposing marriage to this woman. Don't you owe her the truth? Further, don't you *want* to give it to her?"

Bryce's frown deepened. "I don't feel I'm being dishonest by relegating my past to the place where it belongs. The details surrounding my birth have no impact on my future, nor would they affect Lucinda's. So honesty isn't the issue here. Privacy is. Married or not, I'm entitled to retain some. To my way of thinking, a commitment doesn't necessitate baring your soul."

"In other words, you join your lives but not your hearts, your minds, or your spirits."

Silence.

"You do intend to marry her, don't you?"

"The subject has come up."

"You don't sound very enthusiastic."

Bryce rubbed his palms together. "Marriage is a partnership, Gabrielle, not an exhilarating romp or a magnificent symphony. Lucinda is a lovely, sensible woman. She's also past twenty. Marriage is the prudent, logical step for us to take."

Gaby looked positively incredulous. "How can you speak of marriage with such detachment?"

"Not detachment—practicality." Bryce rose. "I think it's time for you to sleep."

"And for you to avoid the subject."

"I believe we've said all there is to say."

"Have we?" Gaby traced the quilted edge of the bedcovers with her forefinger. "If you say so. I happen to disagree." She tensed as Bryce walked toward the door. "Wait."

Bryce turned, on the verge of curtly informing her that their conversation was at an end. Seeing the panicked expression on her face, he changed his mind. "What is it? Are you afraid to go to sleep?"

"What if it happens again?" she whispered. "What if I sleepwalk?"

Pressing his lips together, Bryce contemplated that prospect. "Gabrielle, our wisest course of action would be to—"

"Please don't suggest telling Aunt Hermione," she broke in, reading his thoughts. "Please. Bryce, have you seen how weak she is? If she learned of tonight's incident, she'd be worried sick. I can't and won't do that to her."

"Very well." Bryce leaned back against the closed door, his determination crumpling beneath the pleading look in Gaby's eyes. "I'll make a deal with you," he heard himself say. "I'll stay in your chambers tonight, serve as your sentry. I'll pull the armchair over to the door and make it my bed. That way, should you sleepwalk again, try to leave the room, you'll encounter an immovable object: me. I will then awaken you and send you back to bed. How would that be?"

Gaby's slender shoulders sagged with relief. "And you won't breathe a word to Aunt Hermione?"

"Not this time. However," Bryce added firmly, "should this incident recur—tonight or any night—Hermione must be told. For your safety and for my peace of mind. Gaby," he said in a gentler tone, detecting the fine tension that had reclaimed her. "I won't be remaining at Nevon Manor forever, at least not at this point in my life. Nor can I leave knowing you might conceivably hurt yourself—a distinct possibility, should the sleepwalking recur without Hermione having been alerted and given the chance to take the necessary precautions. I know you worry about her; so do I. But remember, she might be physically weak, but emotionally she's strong. She'd be able to take in her stride what's happened, as well as to understand its cause."

"You don't think it's over, do you?" Gaby asked in a small, frightened voice. "You think I'll sleepwalk again."

"Not necessarily, no." Bryce shook his head. "I'm trained to consider every angle of a situation, and that's what I'm doing. But that doesn't mean I expect the sleepwalking to continue. It's quite possible, now that you've put your first visit to Whitshire behind you and spoken of the night of the fire for the first time, that you've quieted your ghosts enough for you to sleep peacefully and undisturbed by memories."

"I hope you're right," she murmured.

"So we're agreed, then." Bryce walked around the armchair and shoved it across the room until it blocked the door. "I'll sleep here and make sure you stay put until morning."

"Will you awaken me before you leave?"

"Yes. I'll leave at dawn, before the rest of the house is up and about. I'll awaken you first."

"All right." Gaby nodded. "We're agreed." She slid down beneath the covers, snuggling into the pillows like a relieved child. "Thank you, Bryce."

"You're welcome." He cleared his throat. "Shall I wind your music box for you?"

She shook her head, her voice muffled by the pillows. "It's not necessary. With you here, I'll be able to fall asleep without it. After all, I'm just trading one soothing melody for another."

Bryce lowered himself into the chair.

But long after Gaby's even breathing told him she was asleep, he lay awake, staring at the ceiling and pondering the conversation that had just taken place—a conversation that, despite his show of indifference, had struck a profound chord inside him.

A chord that was part of an unfamiliar and strangely disturbing melody.

Chapter 7

"I REALIZE IT'S BARELY PAST SEVEN O'CLOCK, BUT Chaunce said you were up and about. He told me to just knock and come in. I hope that's all right." Bryce wasn't really waiting to find out. He strode into his aunt's sitting room and perched on the edge of a chair.

Hermione looked up from the settee upon which she'd been reclining, appraising Bryce's tense stance with some degree of concern. "Of course it's all right. My door is always open to you. But you looked upset. Is something amiss?"

"In my opinion, yes. Quite amiss."

"Pardon me, my lady." Chaunce hovered in the doorway, carrying a tray. "I took the liberty of bringing up a pot of coffee and a small plate of cinnamon cakes with a jar of raspberry jelly. This way, should your conversation with Mr. Lyndley take longer than expected, you'll have some nourishment prior to breakfast."

"How thoughtful of you, Chaunce." Hermione managed a weak smile as her butler crossed over and set down the tray. "And what an excellent idea. Tell the others to begin eating without us. Bryce and I will join them as soon as possible."

"It's already been done, madam," he replied.

"You're indispensable, my friend." Her smile strengthened a bit. "Thank you."

"My pleasure." He turned to Bryce. "That pressing message you wanted me to send has been dispatched. Miss Talbot should have it alongside her breakfast plate."

"With time to spare," Bryce commented dryly. "Lucinda doesn't awaken until close to noon, especially during the Season. Nonetheless, I appreciate your taking care of the matter so promptly. Lucinda needs to know I've been detained. She was doubtless expecting me home by now." Pursing his lips, he looked away, dismissing Lucinda as he considered the all-important issue he was about to address with his aunt.

"Indeed." Chaunce's glance flickered over Bryce's head to meet Hermione's. "If there's nothing else . . ."

"There is," Bryce interrupted suddenly, his chin coming up. "Chaunce, if you're not needed at breakfast, would you mind staying for this conversation? I'd like your opinion—a man's opinion—of the subject I'm about to broach."

Chaunce's eyebrows rose fractionally, but he nodded, posting himself beside Hermione's settee. "As you wish."

Clearing his throat, Bryce glanced back to Hermione. "This pertains to Gabrielle. She and I had an interesting chat, out of which emerged a rather disturbing fact."

"Really?" Hermione looked more curious than worried. "And what might that be?"

"Are you aware that several of your staff members are"—Bryce sought the right words, finally choosing the ones Gaby herself had used—"taken with each other?"

"Ah. You mean Goodsmith and Marion."

"Among others, yes. You are aware of these relationships?"

"I am."

"Well, so is Gabrielle. One thing I'm sure you're *not* aware of, however, is that Gabrielle has witnessed, and continues to witness, these couples disappearing for what she describes as private displays of affection."

Hermione leaned forward, taking up the pot of coffee and calmly pouring three cups. "Chaunce, just a touch of cream. Bryce, black. Me, some sugar for energy I should think," she murmured.

"Hermione, did you hear me?" Bryce demanded.

"Certainly." She handed him his cup, along with a plate containing two cinnamon cakes. "Help yourself to the jelly," she suggested. With that, she turned to Chaunce, waving away his protest and offering him his refreshment. "You wait on me all the time. It feels good to reciprocate once in a while."

"Hermione . . ." Bryce began again.

"Let's get back to your concern over Gaby," his aunt responded quickly. "What is it, precisely, that she's seen?"

"Several couples continually slipping off to . . ."

"To what? Has she actually witnessed any of these sordid displays you're envisioning? Have these couples been seen in compromising positions— unclothed or groping tastelessly at each other?"

Bryce's jaw dropped. "I—I doubt it."

"Then what exactly is your worry?"

"I don't think you understand. Because of your staff's actions, Gaby believes that physical intimacy is a wonderful, enviable activity, something to dream about and aspire to."

"And you don't?"

This time Bryce nearly dropped his cup. "Pardon me?"

Delicately, Hermione bit into one of the cakes. "Mmm, delicious, as always. Cook has outdone herself, hasn't she?"

"Indeed, madam," Chaunce agreed, having already finished his first cake.

With that, Hermione resumed speaking to Bryce. "I merely asked if your opinion of physical intimacy differed from Gaby's."

"What has my opinion got to do with Gabrielle?" Bryce burst out in frustration. "I'm a thirty-one-year-old man who's been out in the world for an eternity and knows all its rules. Gaby's an eighteen-year-old woman who's about to be introduced to that world—in less than a year, may I remind you—and who knows absolutely nothing about those rules and how they could affect her life, her future. Surely you understand the possible ramifications of her misconceptions about physical intimacy?"

"I think that's where our difference of opinion lies, Bryce." Hermione set down her cup and saucer, folded her hands primly in her lap. "I don't think Gaby has any misconceptions about physical intimacy. She believes that two people who care deeply for each other want to be close in every way possible—their minds, their hearts, and their bodies. I happen to share her belief. The key here—and what you're failing to see—is the inexorable link that Gaby recognizes between love and intimacy, a link that precludes the kind of ramifications to which you're referring. Gaby would never allow a man with whom she wasn't in love to touch her or to take any liberties whatsoever. In fact, I think she would find the whole idea reprehensible."

"But what if she falls in love with a cad?"

Tinkling laughter. "That will never happen."

"How can you be so sure?"

"Because we'll make certain of it." Hermione leaned forward, patted Bryce's arm. "Whichever one of us oversees Gaby's future will carefully select the gentlemen to whom she's introduced."

"We can do that only to a certain extent, Hermione. As you well know, not every scoundrel is instantly detectable as such. Most are too clever to allow their true colors to show. They conceal them beneath flattery and charm. What if Gaby inadvertently meets someone like that?"

"I have faith in our ability to see through such rogues. And ultimately, despite her innocence, I have faith in Gaby. Don't you, Chaunce?"

"Without question, my lady."

Bryce whipped about to face Chaunce. "You *agree* with all this?"

"Every word, Mr. Lyndley." Chaunce folded his napkin in one smooth gesture. "Miss Gaby is sensitive, bright, and intuitive. She'll choose the right man upon whom to bestow her heart. Our job is only to ensure that she meets him. Miss Gaby herself will do the rest."

"Are you both aware of just how sheltered Gabrielle has been?" Bryce demanded.

"You know the answer to that. It's the reason I asked you to act as Gaby's guardian, if need be." Hermione resumed drinking her coffee. "Still, Bryce, I think your particular concerns are unfounded. Gaby is innocent, yes, but she's not quite as naive as you seem to think. She understands the significance of physical intimacy. She just doesn't harbor the same inherent misgivings about others and their motives as you do. The reasons for that are obvious. She's led a very different life than you have. Trust and love come easily to her."

"That's what I'm afraid of," Bryce muttered.

"Well, don't be afraid. As Chaunce said, Gaby is bright and intuitive. With a bit of guidance from us, she'll know when the right man comes along. Until then, her virtue will remain her own, regardless of what she sees. And on that subject, am I to take it you disapprove of the relationships within our little family?"

Bryce frowned, beginning to feel like a cad himself. The way Hermione phrased it made him sound like a coldhearted bastard who would deny her staff even a modicum of emotional fulfillment. "Of course I don't disapprove. I think it's splendid that your residents are happy. It's only that I—"

"They *are* happy, Bryce," Hermione interjected quietly. "They're also not carrying on as you suspect. Let me put your mind at ease. First, little that transpires at Nevon Manor escapes my notice. So rest assured, if there were improper goings-on here, I would know it. Second, my family might be unusual, but they're highly moral. As a result, nothing inappropriate is occurring. The only couple on the verge of serious involvement are Goodsmith and Marion. And, if you promise to keep a secret, I'll tell you that Goodsmith has already sought me out and asked for Marion's hand. He's a good man. Just as all the other men at Nevon Manor are. None of them would take advantage of women—most particularly women they cared for. Nor would they permit Gaby to witness anything indecent. The displays to which you refer are merely long strolls and occasional embraces. Is that too indelicate for your taste?"

Hermione's eyes twinkled. "I think not, given the tidbits I've inadvertently overheard Chaunce's friends passing along to him regarding your liaisons—and I don't mean the innocent calls on Miss Talbot, but rather the less virtuous, albeit discreet, visits to those whose seasoned reputations make it possible for Miss Talbot to keep hers."

"Damn," Bryce hissed, indignity eclipsed by amazement. "Why do I ever think I can spar with you and win?" A corner of his mouth lifted. " 'Inadvertently overheard'? That I doubt. Nothing you do is inadvertent, Hermione. When am I going to learn that?"

A beatific smile. "As I said, little that transpires here escapes my attention. But that's not the point. The point is that you're a worldly man who understands a person's need for companionship. What occurs here is nothing more than that: men and women enjoying each other's company, in the purest sense of the word. Now, does that pose a problem for you?"

"All right, Hermione, you've accomplished your goal," Bryce muttered, giving it up. "You've made me feel like a snake."

"Good." A self-satisfied nod. "And have I also alleviated your concerns?"

"Indeed you have." Now that Bryce's fervor had diminished, he found himself wondering at the intensity of his reaction to this whole matter. It was thoroughly unlike him to be so irrational, not to mention judgmental and prudish. What the hell had possessed him to swoop down on Hermione like some sort of avenging angel?

"Don't look so distressed, sir," Chaunce advised, smoothing his mustache. "Your reaction is both understandable and natural. Miss Gaby has a way of kindling one's protective instincts. There's an unspoiled beauty about her that one yearns to preserve."

"There certainly is," Bryce concurred, his unsettled mood intensifying. Abruptly he pushed away his refreshment and rose. "On that note, I'll take my leave. I promised Peter I'd explain some legal terms to him after breakfast. Also, I want to begin drawing up the various documents we discussed. I've already been away from London too long. My plan is to finish up here in a day or two, then head back to Town."

"So soon?" Hermione asked, inclining her head in surprise.

"I can't stay here indefinitely, Hermione. I have obligations awaiting me." Bryce drew a slow breath.

"And a great deal to ponder—a whole bloody life to sort out." With that, he turned and left the sitting room.

"He's overwhelmed," Hermione murmured, her lips pursed with concern.

"Indeed. Overwhelmed and confused," Chaunce agreed.

"I don't blame him, with all that's happened—all that's still happening. It's no wonder he's eager to leave."

"He'll be back—sooner than he imagines, I suspect."

New lines of worry creased Hermione's forehead. "You don't think the allure in London is too great?"

Chaunce sniffed. "Certainly not. I don't even deem it an issue. Nor should you."

"I don't." Hermione's lips curved. "I just needed reassurance from you." She leaned forward, her eyes dancing like a young girl's. "He's begun calling her Gaby—have you noticed?"

"Twice," Chaunce confirmed. "And the depth of his outrage is clearly not something one would expect from someone who is no more than a casual acquaintance or, at best, a benevolent friend and potential guardian."

"I couldn't agree more." Hermione's expression grew wistful. "They need each other, Chaunce. More than even I realized."

"They've found each other, my lady," Chaunce assured her, rising to gather the dishes. "We have only to make them realize it."

Downstairs in the music room, Gaby wandered about, unable to concentrate on anything, Beethoven included, other than the fact that Bryce and Aunt Hermione had been glaringly absent from breakfast. Where were they? What were they discussing? Was Bryce advising Aunt Hermione of last night's sleep-walking incident?

No. Gaby shook her head, sinking down on the piano bench and clasping her hands in her lap. He'd promised he wouldn't. And breaking his word was something Bryce would never do.

But the incident had happened. And Gaby was terrified it would happen again.

There had been no recurrence last night, she consoled herself. She'd slept peacefully until dawn, when Bryce had awakened her before he returned to his own quarters. But whether her uninterrupted slumber was due to mere coincidence, sheer exhaustion, or Bryce's comforting presence in her room, Gaby wasn't certain. She could only pray that the episode had been a onetime event, triggered by her upsetting visit to Whitshire.

Tracing the piano keys with the tip of her finger, Gaby found her thoughts returning to Bryce. He'd said nothing about his intention to skip breakfast, but then again, he hadn't said much of anything this morning. He'd merely awakened her, looking tired and rumpled from his uncomfortable—and, Gaby suspected, sleepless—night in the armchair, verified that she was all right, then stiffly excused himself and left.

Why was he suddenly so uncomfortable in her presence? Was this all because he'd broken his cardinal rule of protocol? Or was he angry with her for wreaking such havoc on his life, then insisting he take on the responsibility of not only hearing but keeping her secret?

If he was angry, she couldn't blame him. He'd arrived at Nevon Manor a virtual stranger and had, in a matter of days, been besieged with emotional obligations. Taking on Aunt Hermione's burdens was one thing. Taking on hers was quite another.

Troubled, Gaby chewed her lower lip, feeling guilty for adding to Bryce's strain and sad at the tension that had sprung up between them. They'd shared such a warm and wonderful rapport, an almost instant affinity. Yet, after last night, Gaby instinctively knew that Bryce wanted nothing more than to finish his business here as quickly as possible and be on his way.

Was that what he and Aunt Hermione were discussing? Was he trying to wrap up her aunt's legal affairs and put everything in order so he could return to London?

And if so, was his eagerness spawned by what he was escaping from or what he was returning to?

For the dozenth time, Gaby reflected on Bryce's description of his relationship with Lucinda Talbot, a description he seemed to apply to all his past courtships. Baffled, she tried to imagine existing in such an ordered, emotionless world. She couldn't. And it made no sense for Bryce to do so, either. Beneath his composed veneer, he was a passionate man—passionate about his beliefs, his commitments, his work. Surely that passion had to extend to something more.

What, she wondered, was Bryce's life like—*truly* like? Oh, she knew the details of his activities, thanks to Hermione's newspaper clippings. But newspaper clippings couldn't describe joy or introspection, restlessness or contentment. Nor could they describe fervor. It was clear that Bryce was intense about his work, but was he equally intense about anything else? Clearly not about Miss Talbot, whom he spoke of with all the detached regard one would grant a respected business associate. What about his home, his rituals, his diversions? Did he savor the open waters when he sailed? Gaze out his office window, reveling in the sounds of busy London carriages as they passed? Did he unlock his door at night and feel a gratifying sense of belonging as he crossed the threshold?

Somehow she thought not. And if not, how very many of life's offerings Bryce Lyndley was missing.

Odd, she mused. London is so vast, and Nevon Manor so small. How is it that I've been exposed to so much more of what matters than he has?

"Gaby?" Bryce's voice interrupted her unanswerable question. "Are you all right?"

Her head came up, and she jumped to her feet, crossing over to him at once. "I'm fine." She minced no words. "Where were you during breakfast?"

He frowned, reflexively reaching out to trace the dark circles beneath her eyes. Gone was the tousled man who'd awakened her, Gaby noted. He'd vanished along with his rumpled clothing and shadow of a beard. In his place was the impeccably groomed, strikingly handsome barrister she'd met in Nevon Manor's drive, a man who hid his vulnerability so well that even he himself couldn't perceive it.

"I was speaking with Hermione," Bryce replied, his fingertips brushing her skin. "I didn't expect our conversation to last so long. Peter is probably wondering where I am; we were to meet directly after breakfast. But I wanted to check on you before I went off to find him. Now I'm glad I did. You look exhausted. I think you should go upstairs and rest."

Gaby caught Bryce's wrist. "You didn't tell Aunt Hermione, did you? About the sleepwalking?"

"I told you I wouldn't. Did you doubt me?"

Her lashes drifted downward. "No. Not really. It's just that neither of you were at the table, and my imagination took over."

"Well, don't let it. I said nothing."

"Thank you. And not just for remaining silent. For everything." Gaby's chin came up. "You're planning to leave Nevon Manor, aren't you?"

Conflict warred on Bryce's face. "Not today. But soon, yes."

She nodded, trying to conceal her disappointment. "I hope you won't stay away too long. Our family needs you." *And you need them,* she added silently.

"I'll do my best." His arm dropped to his side. "I'd best get to Peter."

"Bryce." She caught his sleeve, staying his retreat. "What about Thane?"

"What about him?"

"Promise me you'll see him before you leave for London. You two need to spend more time together—time I deprived you of last night."

"You deprived us of nothing. You had a devastating experience, one that required cutting the evening short."

"Nevertheless, you and Thane have a great deal to resolve and much time to make up for. And while I realize Hertford is only twenty-five miles from London, I also realize it's all too easy to lose sight of things once they're removed from our immediate vision, after which, no matter how good our intentions, more current priorities take over. Time passes. And before you know it . . ."

"Gaby," Bryce interrupted, laying his forefinger across her lips, "I will see Thane. I give you my word."

"Today," she pressed. "Promise me you'll see him today—before time has a chance to erode the initial strides you two have made toward a friendship. Once you've strengthened yesterday's tenuous bond, a few weeks of distance won't matter."

Bryce studied her intently, his eyes softening to a velvety green. "You're astounding. So sheltered, yet so wise."

"Will you give me your word? If so, I promise to go upstairs and rest while you visit with Peter."

Amusement tugged at Bryce's lips. "Negotiating, are we?"

"Are my terms acceptable?"

He inclined his head, thoughtfulness supplanting amusement. "What if I were to ask Thane to come here? Given the circumstances, I doubt he'd refuse me, mourning period or not. And the truth is, I do need to see both him and Averley, to conclude our review of Hermione's records. I'll ask Chaunce to send them an invitation to tea. That way I can spend most of the day working on Hermione's will and the provisions she wants outlined for the residents of Nevon Manor. Then I can turn my attention to her other estates once Thane and Averley arrive in the late afternoon."

"While ensuring that I'm not left alone or excluded from the pleasantries," Gaby added with quiet insight. She sighed, feeling utterly ashamed at her weakness. "I'd love to be part of your gathering. But don't alter your plans because I'm a coward—too afraid to return to Whitshire."

"First of all, I'm not altering my plans. Having Thane travel here allows me more time to concentrate solely on those of Hermione's legal affairs that pertain to Nevon Manor. And second, you're not a coward. You'd be a fool to willfully repeat the agonizing experience you endured last night." Bryce folded his arms across his chest, giving her an expectant look. "So . . . are *my* terms acceptable? I'll see Thane this afternoon, but at Nevon Manor, not Whitshire."

Gaby smiled, tenderness unfurling inside her like warm mists of smoke. This was the way it had been between them before last night had intruded, an affinity as natural as it was right. "Perfectly acceptable. Better than acceptable—wonderful. Thank you, Bryce, for understanding—and for caring."

Their gazes locked.

Abruptly Bryce stiffened, an odd expression crossing his face. He took a reflexive step backward, something akin to confusion and astonishment mirrored in his eyes. Then shutters descended, and Gaby could actually feel him erect an invisible wall between them. But why? What had she done to prompt him to withdraw from her again?

"Bryce?" she questioned hesitantly.

He cut her off with a slight shake of his head. "I'll be leaving for London tomorrow, Gaby," he announced, his tone strained.

"Tomorrow?" She could no longer hide her distress. The suddenness of his announcement, the severity of his reaction . . . What had just happened that she had missed? "I don't understand. You said—"

"I said I'd be leaving Nevon Manor soon."

"Soon, yes. But tomorrow? Why?"

A muscle worked in his jaw. "I must. For many reasons. Now, if you'll excuse me, I'll go find Peter. Get some rest. I'll see you at tea."

With that, he was gone.

Teatime came later than expected for Gaby.

Troubled by Bryce's unexpected decision and stymied by its cause, she spent a good portion of the day trying to rest, only to find she was unable to do so. At last she gave up her pondering and her attempts at slumber, instead donning her gown and leaving the manor for a long stroll about the grounds, hoping that the fresh air would clear her mind and the walk would allow her to expend some energy.

Both the air and the walk failed miserably.

As a last resort, she headed off to Crumpet's warren, certain that frolicking with her pet would provide the welcome balm she needed.

That attempt yielded far more than she bargained for.

Delighted to be released from confinement, Crumpet exploded into freedom, leading Gaby on a merry chase, first across the gardens, where he promptly destroyed Wilson's primroses, then into the woods, where he disappeared among the trees.

It took ages to find him, much less catch him. And now . . . Gaby frowned at the grass stains on her tattered gown, gathering up her skirts and sprinting toward the manor. Now it was ten minutes before five, nearly an hour past the time she'd been expected for tea. And she had yet to change her clothes—a necessity, given her soiled and sorry state. Mentally she chastised Crumpet, more for his poor timing than for the shambles he'd made of her gown. Why did he always pick the most inopportune moments to perform his antics?

Scarcely turning the door handle, Gaby eased her way into the house, praying that Aunt Hermione was having refreshments served in the blue salon, way at the far end of the corridor and well past the flight of steps she was about to dash up. Their guests were here; she'd seen Thane's carriage round the drive a full hour ago when she'd been crawling through the trees, groping for her mischievous, elusive rabbit.

Gaby tiptoed inside the entrance hall, turning to shut the door behind her, grateful to notice that the area was deserted.

A light tap on her shoulder made her jump and whirl about. "Chaunce," she gasped, nearly sagging with relief when she saw who her discoverer was. "You startled me." She glanced swiftly about. "Thank goodness it's only you. I was afraid one of our guests had come upon me, someone less apt to fathom how a grown woman would willingly take part in a diversion that resulted in her looking like an unkempt waif."

"'One of our guests'—ah, you're referring to Mr. Lyndley." Chaunce's tone said he harbored not a shred of doubt over which guest Gaby was referring to. "Need I remind you that you two met after you'd taken a similar romp and that Mr. Lyndley was hardly offended by your refreshing and unaffected appearance?"

"Refreshing?" Gaby couldn't stifle a giggle as she pointed at the shredded hem of her gown, the huge stains that decorated her skirts. "Perhaps then, but certainly not now. I wouldn't call this refreshing, Chaunce; I'd called it filth."

"I see your point." The butler's lips twitched. "Well, fear not. It was only I who heard you enter the manor—I who am quite used to seeing you in this informal though no less lovely state." He kept his voice hushed. "I was waiting to tell you that Marion laid out your lemon-yellow day dress and prepared a basin of warm water for your use. I suggested she let you dress unassisted, because—despite your customary practice of allotting extra time for her to trip over your skirts and spill your hairpins—I'm afraid Crumpet has depleted whatever extra time Marion might have had, and then some. Also, I made certain to show our guests to the blue salon, so no one need see you rush upstairs." With that, Chaunce clasped his hands behind his back.

"Oh, thank you." Gaby stood on tiptoe, kissed his cheek. "What would I do without you?"

"I shudder to think. Now hurry and get dressed. By the way," he added in a whisper, "Mr. Lyndley and His Grace are getting on famously. They're in the process of disagreeing over gaming techniques and arguing over political views."

Gaby frowned. "That's getting on famously?"

A profound sniff. "For gentlemen? Without a doubt."

"I see. Very well, thank you for telling me, Chaunce. I'll go change now."

"Excellent. And I'll fetch tea."

Twenty minutes later Gaby made her way downstairs, tucking one last tendril of hair into her yellow satin ribbon, wondering what kind of reception to expect. She still hadn't figured out the cause of the baffling change in Bryce's behavior. And while he had asked her to join them for tea, that was before his abrupt emotional withdrawal. Perhaps she should leave well enough alone and stay away, she mused, slowing her steps as she neared the blue salon. The amiable murmur of voices emanating from inside seemed to indicate that all was going well. Perhaps her appearance would only complicate matters.

She stopped, then turned away.

"They're awaiting you, and the tea is getting cold," Chaunce informed her, blocking her path.

Gaby blinked. "This is the second time you've emerged out of nowhere. Have you discovered a splendid new hiding place?"

"Really, Miss Gaby," Chaunce responded with an offended frown. "You know better than to think I'd resort to covert scrutiny of our family. I simply do my job, overseeing the household from my customary post by the entranceway door or wherever else I happen to be at the moment. And what I witnessed this time was your step faltering as you neared the blue salon. As a result, I hurried down to suggest you dismiss any foolish notion of vanishing. Mr. Lyndley's business with His Grace and Mr. Averley is about to conclude. That means it's time for refreshments; I delivered the tray while you were changing clothes. What's more, your aunt is becoming increasingly more concerned over your absence. I've reassured her time and again that you're fine and on your way, but she needs to see that fact for herself. If not . . ." Chaunce's voice trailed off, as if leaving the upsetting prospects to Gaby's imagination.

"Oh, dear. Then of course I'll go." Gaby chewed her lip, gazing anxiously up at Chaunce. "Did you explain what detained me?"

"I mentioned something about Crumpet being lost. The details I left for you to provide."

"Wonderful," Gaby muttered. "I feel like a fool."

"You *look* absolutely lovely."

Gaby eyed him skeptically, her lips curving into an impish grin. "That helped fortify my courage—truthful or not."

"It's very much the truth," Chaunce assured her. "One would never know that the beautiful young woman standing before me was a half hour ago, to quote your words, an unkempt waif."

Laughter spilled from Gaby's lips. "You are quite the charmer, Chaunce. Also quite convincing." So saying, she pivoted. "Wish me luck," she requested.

Squaring her shoulders, she took the remaining steps to her destination.

Chaunce smoothed his mustache, staring after Gaby with a frustrated frown. "Luck is not what you need, Miss Gaby," he murmured to himself. "What you need is opportunity. Our job is to provide it. Yours is to seize it."

Unaware of Chaunce's reflections, Gaby paused outside the blue salon.

"Have Averley and I answered all your questions?" she heard Thane asking.

"Absolutely." It was Bryce's voice. "I'll take the notes I've jotted down, and of course Averley's ledgers, with me to London."

"You shouldn't have any problem determining what each of my entries represents," Averley assured him. "The books are in perfect order. The late duke insisted that they be clear and precise."

"Yes, Father was nothing if not insistent about things being done his way," Thane muttered dryly, more than a trace of irony in his tone.

"What could be keeping Gaby?" Aunt Hermione chimed in, her anxious voice implying she'd asked the question several times already.

That was Gaby's cue.

Walking into the room, she glanced at her aunt with a rueful smile. "Crumpet kept me, Aunt Hermione. He was missing for hours. I had to find him before dark. Please forgive me."

All three gentlemen rose to their feet.

"It *was* Crumpet. Then Chaunce wasn't just trying to placate me." Aunt Hermione sagged with relief. "I suppose my aged mind is beginning to play tricks on me, conjuring up nonexistent possibilities over which to worry."

"Your mind is as sharp as a tack," Gaby declared loyally, crossing over and seating herself on the Chippendale sofa beside her aunt. "Crumpet *was* gone an exceptionally long time today. He covered far more territory than usual: the garden, the woods—everywhere but his warren. I only just recovered him a short while ago." She squeezed her aunt's hand, then looked from one gentleman to the next, acutely conscious of Bryce's commanding presence where he stood at the far end of the adjacent settee. "I apologize for delaying your tea. If it's cold, I myself will prepare another pot."

"Nonsense," Thane chuckled, reseating himself in the chair closest to Aunt Hermione, propping his elbow on the chair's cushioned arm. "Your timing is perfect. We just concluded our business. As for the tea being cold, you needn't worry. Chaunce only brought it in five minutes ago."

"Besides," Averley added, settling himself in a walnut side chair and rolling a half-filled goblet between his palms. "We've contented ourselves with a brandy in the interim. I, for one, intend to forgo my tea in favor of another."

"As do I," Bryce concurred quietly.

Gaby's gaze slid over, finally meeting Bryce's. He was clasping an open ledger, watching her with an intent, unreadable expression.

"How did Peter fare with his morning's lesson?" Gaby asked carefully.

"Brilliantly." Bryce closed the ledger, depositing it atop the others on the end table. A look of genuine pride crossed his face. "The lad is a born barrister. His mind is lightning quick, and his grasp of legal theories is so keen it astounds me. I have to keep reminding myself he's only nine years old, else I might be tempted to take him on as a partner."

"Someday, perhaps," Aunt Hermione suggested brightly as she poured tea for the ladies.

"Perhaps." Bryce nodded, moving to fetch the bottle of brandy from the sideboard in order to refill the gentlemen's glasses. "I'd be very fortunate. It isn't often one finds Peter's level of intelligence *and* compassion in one person, much less one so young."

"It is rare," Hermione agreed. "But it can be found, ofttimes in one who has had great obstacles to overcome."

Bryce's jaw tightened, a clear sign that he was aware of Hermione's affectionate, pointed analogy—and that he had no intention of acknowledging it. "Peter's lameness doesn't hinder him," he responded, his attention fixed on replenishing his drink. "He simply accepts it as a given and presses on in spite of it."

"Or *because* of it," Hermione amended softly, undeterred by her nephew's reaction. "Obstacles have a way of inspiring people—the right people."

This time there was no ignoring her obvious reference to Bryce. Only Averley looked puzzled, rubbing his chin and inclining his head in Hermione's direction.

"I agree." Thane nodded his thanks as Bryce refilled his goblet. He cleared his throat, studying his brother's face. "Speaking of formidable obstacles, Hermione mentioned at dinner the other night that you're heavily involved in the area of married women's property law. I recall reading in the newspapers that you're working on an amendment that would afford women greater rights. Is that correct?"

"It is." Bryce replenished Averley's drink, then set down the bottle with a determined thud, lifting his chin to meet Thane's gaze. "It troubles me that women are required to turn over all their assets to their husbands when they wed—actually, even before they wed. No one should be reduced to living as another person's chattel. It strips people of their dignity, makes them feel like victims."

Thane's blue-gray eyes grew thoughtful. "Your point is well taken, but unfortunately, I doubt many husbands support your theory. And given that most women rely on their spouses for income, I suspect you receive little or no compensation for your time and services in this area."

Bryce shrugged. "That's often true, yes. My interest in this matter doesn't stem from a desire for monetary gain, however, nor is it spawned by altruism. It arises from firsthand knowledge of what it's like to be vulnerable, to be at the mercy of circumstance and to realize that, but for your own guardian angel, you'd be penniless and cast into the streets. If I can offer that same security to others, I consider it my duty to do so."

"You've aroused my curiosity, Lyndley," Averley said, finally giving in to his urge to seek answers. "So if I might be so bold as to ask, who is this guardian angel of yours?"

Unhesitatingly Bryce replied, in a straightforward manner that made Gaby realize he'd rehearsed his explanation: "Lady Nevon—as I'm sure you already suspected." Bryce turned briefly toward Hermione, raising his glass in tribute before turning back to Averley. "You yourself voiced concern over Lady Nevon's tender heart and the vulnerable position in which it placed her. And as I reassured you the other night, I don't blame you for your concern. After all, you're the one who's handled her finances all these years; you must be aware that large amounts of her money have been allocated to her servants—those at Nevon Manor as well as those who reside at her other estates. I'm one of the lucky recipients. When my parents died, it was Lady Nevon who ensured that the rest of my education was paid for, that the right doors were open to me. Her loyalty to her staff and their children was and is unparalleled."

"Bryce, please, you're embarrassing me." A becoming flush stained Hermione's cheeks.

"I don't mean to embarrass you; I mean to praise you." Bryce took a deep swallow of brandy. "Heaven only knows you deserve it."

"In truth, I did suspect something of this nature,"

Averley admitted, "especially given how costly your education was and how limited was your parents' income. Still, I was never formally advised of Lady Nevon's contributions, to you or any of her staff. I was told only that she was donating funds to various charities, and it was never my place to ask for details. Now that I realize the full extent of her generosity, I quite agree with you, Lyndley. Lady Nevon's actions were inspiring. More than inspiring; extraordinary. No wonder you feel so indebted to her."

"Bryce has more than repaid any assistance I granted him," Hermione clarified at once. "And not only by agreeing to manage my legal affairs. Nothing is better evidence of my sound judgment in electing to help Bryce than seeing the good he's done, and continues to do, for others. Why, he has more clients than he can handle. In fact, I'm fortunate he was able to grant me these past few days, so busy is his legal practice."

"Is that the reason you're hurrying back to London?" Thane asked Bryce. "Pressing business matters?"

"Among other things, yes." Bryce cleared his throat, leveling his gaze on Hermione. "Which brings me to a favor I must request. Given that I'll be leaving at first light, would you mind if I spoke with Thane in private for a few minutes? We have a few personal matters to finish discussing."

"Of course not," Hermione burst out almost before Bryce had finished speaking. "Gaby and I will entertain Mr. Averley. You two step outside onto the terrace. It's a lovely evening. Take as much time as you need."

Bryce nodded his thanks, his eyes flickering over Gaby before shifting to Thane.

Gaby watched the two men leave the room, shutting the terrace doors in their wake. Studying them through the glass panes, she wondered just what it was that Bryce was so eager to convey to Thane.

"Gaby, would you like more tea?" Aunt Hermione asked. "You look a bit peaked from your romp with Crumpet."

"That would be lovely. Thank you, Aunt Hermione." Gaby proffered her cup.

"Now that I think of it, you also looked exhausted earlier today. Didn't you sleep well, dear?"

"No." Gaby stared into her cup, offering as much of the truth as she could without upsetting her aunt. "The trip to Whitshire obviously upset me even more than I realized. I had a fitful night."

Averley gave an uncomfortable cough, as if deciding whether or not to speak. "Mrs. Darcey was terribly worried about you," he offered at last. "She reminded me six times to ensure your well-being while I was here and to offer you her good wishes. So did Mrs. Fife. Even Couling followed me out to the carriage tonight, requesting that I send his regards."

A small smile touched Gaby's lips. "Goodness. He *must* be anxious. The Couling I recall would never have lowered his reserve enough to display worry. I'm touched."

Averley smiled back at her accurate assessment of the Whitshire butler. "You were always a particular favorite of the staff's, Gabrielle—despite the upheaval you caused. Which, incidentally, was not that dissimilar to what your friend Crumpet provoked today."

Amusement danced in Gaby's eyes. "I see now why you were all so exasperated with me, and why Mama and Papa continually chastised me for my disappearances."

"They would be grateful that one of those disappearances saved your life."

All semblance of humor vanished, raw emotion tightening Gaby's throat. "But not theirs."

"Forgive me," Averley murmured, a flush staining his already ruddy complexion. "I've overstepped my bounds. I apologize. I certainly didn't mean to make things worse. I only wanted to remind you how very much your parents loved you, in the hope that it would ease the painful memories that made last night so difficult for you to bear."

"Thank you, Mr. Averley." Gaby inhaled deeply, feeling horrible to have incited his guilt, yet unable to dispel her anguish, which seemed to be intensifying rather than abating. "It isn't your fault," she assured him. "It's just something I must overcome on my own. Please don't apologize. I appreciate your concern, and the rest of the staff's as well. Please thank them for me." Another shaky breath. "Perhaps someday I'll feel strong enough to visit Whitshire again and thank them myself."

"But not for a long while," Aunt Hermione said, taking Gaby's hand in hers. "For now you'll remain at Nevon Manor with those who love you and with a lifetime of happy memories—those already made and those yet to come."

Gaby clung to her aunt's words like a lifeline. "Yes," she concurred in a fervent whisper. "I'll stay right here at Nevon Manor, where I'm safe."

Chapter 8

THE GRANDFATHER CLOCK CHIMED THREE, A SURE INDICA-
tor that Bryce should be asleep rather than prowling
about his chambers, contemplating the dawn.

A dawn that would sweep him back to the comfort
of his familiar life and away from the bewildering
emotions he'd encountered these past three days at
Nevon Manor.

His second talk with Thane had gone well. He
hadn't known what sort of reaction to expect when
Thane learned that Hermione had bequeathed her
entire home to her illegitimate nephew—a man she
hadn't seen in years. He'd only known that, given how
much she'd already revealed at Whitshire last night,
Thane had a right to know this key piece of information about his newly acknowledged brother, as well as
how Bryce's future would, at least peripherally, touch
his. *And* he had a right to know now, before Bryce left
for London.

So Bryce had told him.

Thane's reaction was surprising, rooted not in the

shock or resentment Bryce had anticipated but in genuine concern.

Leaning against the terrace railing, he'd let out a long, low whistle. "Beneficiary to Nevon Manor—that's quite a responsibility Hermione's handed you. Is it what you want?"

Bryce had stared out over the grounds of Nevon Manor, an estate that would one day be his. "I don't know what I want, Thane. Needless to say, I have a great deal to think about. That's part of the reason I must leave Hertford so abruptly."

"To consider your decision?"

"No." Bryce shook his head. "I've already agreed to Hermione's request. And it *is* a request—I want you to know that. I have no designs on Hermione's home or her assets, nor, quite frankly, do I need the income associated with either one."

Thane's brows arched. "That possibility never occurred to me."

"It should have. You don't know me very well. You have every reason to question my motives. Therefore I'm elaborating more than I ordinarily would in the hope of easing any doubts that might creep into your mind. The basis for my decision has nothing to do with money. It has everything to do with the fact that I owe Hermione my life. She's never asked for anything in return . . . until now. Consequently, I couldn't—wouldn't—refuse her." A pause. "If I'm to be completely honest, that's not the only reason I chose to honor Hermione's request. Having spent these past few days with the residents of Nevon Manor, I find I've developed a great deal of respect and admiration for them. Given that fact, it's very likely I would have agreed to Hermione's request of my own accord."

"I'm sure she counted on that fact," Thane remarked dryly.

Bryce shot him a wary look, uncertain whether

Thane intended the comment to be an observation or a barb. "Knowing Hermione, I don't doubt it," he'd carefully replied. "In any case, I felt you should be told about the situation. I also wanted to make it clear that Hermione did not overlook you as a probable beneficiary. Her concern was that you might be over-burdened managing your father's holdings, and she was loath to add such an enormous obligation to that burden."

"Bryce, stop," Thane had interrupted, holding up his palm. "I don't require this prolonged explanation. What's more," he added, putting an end to Bryce's doubts and surprising him with the depth of his insight. "I understand Hermione's motives better than you think. I believe she made a wise choice, the best choice, for reasons far more crucial than my taxing responsibilities. Nevon Manor requires some-one special at its helm, someone who can continue what Hermione began. Our two meetings and my fine instincts tell me you're that person."

Relief, more vast than Bryce had imagined feeling, surged through him, along with a strong wave of respect. "I'm glad you feel that way. I was half afraid you'd think I was trying to divest our aunt of her funds."

"Hardly. First of all, I'm aware that you're far from financially needy. I do read the newspapers, you know. In addition to which I also have, as I just mentioned, fine instincts, instincts that tell me you're much too ethical even to consider what you're de-scribing." Thane folded his arms across his chest, giving an unequivocal shrug. "After all, only an ethical man would have thought to initiate this con-versation."

"Or a guilty one who was anxious to cover his tracks."

"Spoken like a true barrister." Thane's lips curved. "I'm beginning to enjoy this sparring of ours. Unfortunately, the next round will have to wait. Before I left Whitshire, Couling placed a huge stack of papers on my desk, all of which need my immediate attention. So I must be getting back. Suffice it to say I'm delighted with Hermione's choice of beneficiaries and can scarcely wait to continue our heated debates on politics, gaming tactics, and moral ethics the instant you return to Hertford." A pause. "Whenever that will be. You never did say what unresolved issues are driving you to London—or should I say, away from Hertford? Or how long it will take you to resolve them."

Bryce's gaze had flitted toward the window, and he was assessing Gaby's delicate features with a brooding expression. "No," he'd replied, besieged by a multifaceted conflict that ranged from consternation over her nightmares to doubt as to whether he was the right choice to serve as her guardian. "I never did."

Now, ambling about his quarters, Bryce reexamined that conflict, wondering if it had been a mistake to agree to that portion of Hermione's request. True, the guardianship would probably never come to pass, given that next year's Season was less than a year away. But still, what had he gotten himself into?

The truth was that he and Gaby had a unique affinity for each other that he found both unsettling and unfamiliar. She inspired an odd protective instinct in him that was getting out of hand, partly because it was so unlike anything he'd ever experienced before, and partly because he feared Gaby was misreading it as something far more serious. All those questions about Lucinda, about being in love, about private moments, intimate moments, between a man and a woman . . . Gaby was so very young and such an unwavering romantic; Lord only knew how she interpreted his regard for her well-being. But whatever was transpiring in that lovely head of hers, it wasn't good. It was time to put things in perspective—for both their sakes. And the only way to do that was to place some distance between himself and Gaby's imaginary Wonderland. Now. Because the longer he stayed at Nevon Manor, the worse things were going to get.

A muffled sound from the hallway brought his head up, and he tensed, straining to hear the noise again. A sense of foreboding knotted the pit of his stomach—although why, he hadn't a clue. One of Gaby's house pets was probably out there—maybe one of the kittens who slept in Lily's and Jane's rooms. They often wandered about the manor getting into mischief.

A thud, closer to his quarters this time, followed by a choked whimper and the sound of padding feet. Human feet.

Bryce crossed over and yanked open his door, stepping into the hall in time to see Gaby round the corner, her nightgown billowing about her slight form, her music box clutched to her chest.

She was asleep.

He reached her in a half dozen strides, tugging her into an alcove and out of sight. "Gaby." He shook her, anxiously searching her face, awaiting some kind of response.

Her exquisite eyes were vague, obscured by sleep, her hair tumbling in waves about her shoulders. "Fire . . ." she gasped, her entire body trembling with fear. "Flames . . . high . . . too high . . . I can't—"

"Gaby." Bryce's voice was hushed but insistent, his fingers digging into her arms. "Sweetheart, you've got to wake up." Another hard shake.

"What . . . ?" Awareness jolted through Gaby's limbs, crept into her eyes, and she gazed up at him, pressing the music box against her as if it could ward off oncoming pain. "Bryce?" she asked blankly.

"You were sleepwalking," he told her, struggling to keep his voice calm. Then, seeing her anguish, feeling tension grip her, he relented, drawing her to him and enfolding her in his arms. "You're all right," he murmured, stroking her hair. "You're inside the manor, down the hall from my quarters. I stopped you on your way to the stairs."

"It's not over, then," she whispered, clearly fighting back tears. "Last night was only the onset."

"You don't know that," Bryce heard himself saying—he who never diluted the truth. "It could be the aftermath, like echoing rumbles of thunder. If so, it will fade."

"When, Bryce? When will it fade?"

With a harsh sigh, Bryce rested his chin atop her head. "I don't know."

"Gaby?" Hermione's voice reached their ears, hushed but audible—and filled with worry. "Dear, are you out here?"

"It's Aunt Hermione." Gaby tensed, her fingers digging into Bryce's shirt. "She must have heard the commotion and checked my room, only to find it empty." A choked sound. "Force of habit from the past."

Bryce nodded, knowing what had to be done, wondering if Gaby was going to fight him.

She answered his question before he asked it.

Drawing back, she gazed up at him, her eyes bright with unshed tears. "We have to tell her. We have no choice." Her lips trembled. "Oh, Bryce, what if she's too weak to take this? What if I make her illness worse?"

"Stop it." Bryce framed Gaby's face between his palms. "Hermione is stronger than all of us combined. She'll cope splendidly. And she'll help you, be there for you since I . . ." His voice trailed off.

"Since you can't?"

Guilt surged inside him. "Gaby." His thumbs caressed her cheeks. "I want to be here, to offer you the strength you need. But I . . . It's just that . . .

dammit," he muttered as Hermione called out again, this time more urgently. "We can't talk about this now."

"No, we can't. I don't want Aunt Hermione to think I've disappeared into the dead of night." Gaby gave him a long, searching look. "I just wish I understood why you continually withdraw from me, erect a wall between us. Perhaps you can explain it to me when you return to Nevon Manor."

With that she stepped away from him, squaring her shoulders and walking into view. "I'm here, Aunt Hermione," she called softly, beckoning to her aunt. "Please don't worry. I'm well, truly." She glanced behind her as Bryce emerged from the alcove. "Thanks to Bryce," she added, indicating his presence.

Even across the ten yards of hallway that separated them, Bryce could perceive Hermione's absolute sweeping relief. She halted in her tracks, obviously having been contemplating the worst, and sagged weakly against the wall. Her face was drawn, her stance unsteady, and her fingers fluttered over the belt of her dressing robe, tightening it reflexively.

An instant later her inner strength prevailed, and she steadied herself on her feet, making her way toward them even as Gaby rushed to her side.

"Aunt Hermione," she demanded anxiously, clutching her aunt's hands. "Are you all right?"

"I'm more than all right, now that I know you are." Hermione enfolded Gaby against her, her lips trembling with emotion. "Thank God," she murmured, her gaze sweeping the heavens. Drawing back, she smoothed a gentle palm across Gaby's cheek. "What happened?"

"It's the sleepwalking again." Gaby minced no words. "This is the second time it's recurred. The first time was last night, after returning from Whitshire. I . . ." She wet her lips with the tip of her tongue. "I'm sorry."

"It's I who am sorry," Hermione replied. Her troubled gaze flickered up and down the deserted hallway, then settled on Bryce. "Let's the three of us go to my sitting room and talk."

Bryce nodded his understanding. There was no point in awakening any of the others and alerting them to the situation.

He cupped the women's elbows and led them to Hermione's quarters.

Once there, Hermione insisted Gaby lie down on the settee, where she covered her with a blanket. Minutes later Bryce saw why, as Gaby's teeth began to chatter uncontrollably.

"This used to happen sometimes," Hermione explained quietly to Bryce, her own face ashen. "After a particularly upsetting bout of sleepwalking. Dr. Briers described it as an emotional reaction, not a chill." She pointed at a small cabinet beside the settee. "You'll find a bottle of sherry in there. I'd appreciate your pouring Gaby a glass."

"I'll pour you both a glass—*after* you sit down," Bryce replied.

This time Hermione didn't argue, merely nodding and accepting his arm as he escorted her over to one of the sitting room's plush chairs.

Once she was seated, Bryce crossed to the cabinet and filled two glasses, handing one to Gaby, the other to Hermione. He stood silently for a moment, watching Gaby sip at her drink, relaxing a bit as her shivering began to subside. "Hermione," he resumed, turning to his aunt, "based upon the explanation you just gave me, I assume your personal physician knows of these incidents."

"Yes." Hermione raised her glass to her lips, her anxious stare still fixed on Gaby. "I had no choice but to seek his help. When Gaby first moved here, the sleepwalking episodes were frequent and severe, recurring nearly every night. I had no idea how best to handle the situation. But I was determined to ease poor Gaby's suffering and help her heal as quickly as possible. Dr. Briers was a godsend. He suggested ways I could make Gaby feel more secure, including guarding her door, letting her know she was protected. Chaunce and I took turns doing that each and every night. Thanks to Dr. Briers's guidance, the sleepwalking eventually ceased. It hasn't returned since—until now."

A tremor crept into Hermione's voice. "I blame myself for suggesting Gaby return to Whitshire. It never occurred to me that the scars were still fresh enough to trigger this entire ordeal once again." She swallowed. "And this time without my knowledge and, therefore, without my protection. Oh, Gaby, you could have hurt yourself so badly."

"No, I couldn't have," Gaby refuted softly, rubbing the blanket between her fingertips. "Bryce saw to that—on both occasions. Last night he found me outside, struggling my way through the woods. My feet were cut and bleeding. He took me to my room, tended to my cuts, and posted himself inside my door for the duration of the night, just in case I had a second episode. And tonight he stopped me before I even reached the staircase. I was very fortunate, and I have Bryce to thank."

"We both have Bryce to thank," Hermione echoed fervently, giving him a tender smile. "I'm more grateful than you can imagine." Her smile faded. "Now the question is, why didn't either of you tell me immediately after the first episode? And don't bother saying there wasn't time. Bryce, you spent over an hour in my chambers this morning discussing other matters. Surely you could have found a minute to disclose last night's events?"

"That was my fault, not Bryce's," Gaby intervened at once. "I begged him not to tell you, not until— unless—the situation recurred. I was praying it was a onetime incident. Then you never would have had to know." Gaby frowned into her glass. "But after what just happened, I had no choice. You had to be told. It's clear that this situation is not going to correct itself, at least not right away."

"You don't know that," Bryce reiterated. "As I said, this could very well be the aftermath of last night's visit. Don't assume it will turn into months of sleepwalking episodes."

"I hope you're right, Bryce," Gaby answered softly, lashes lowered. "Because I refuse to allow Aunt Hermione to play the part of sentry. Thirteen years is a long time. Circumstances change. Physical strength alters, as well."

"If you're implying I'm incapable of taking care of you, you're completely wrong," Hermione countered, raising her head in that regal way Bryce recalled and admired. "I'm surprised at you, Gaby. You, better than anyone, know how much my family means to me. When it comes to protecting you, I find renewed strength and unfailing determination. Besides," she added in a gentler tone. "We have Chaunce. He's every bit as spry as he used to be. The instant I alert him to the situation, he'll be a devoted ally. We'll divide the watch so that each of us gets enough sleep." A peppery spark lit her eyes. "Need I remind you that you don't exactly sleep a long night. Four hours, if we're lucky. It takes until well after midnight for you to settle your various pets down for slumber. And most of them are up before dawn, especially Screech, who welcomes each day with that incessant hammering against the oak outside your window."

"That's true." A bit of the tension eased from Gaby's face.

"I, on the other hand," Hermione continued, "have been retiring early these days. So Chaunce will take the midnight watch, then awaken me when he tires. If either of us feels fatigued, we can nap during the day. It's as simple as that." She leaned forward, her expression reassuring. "And it won't be forever. You'll see, darling. In no time, this relapse will be behind you and life will resume as always."

Gaby pressed her lips together and nodded. "I pray you're right."

"I usually am." Hermione tilted back her head, assessing Bryce thoughtfully. "You'll be leaving at daybreak?"

"Unless you need me—yes." Bryce paused, meeting his aunt's gaze and awaiting her response. One word, one gesture, that warned him she was physically or emotionally in need of his presence, and he would abandon his departure plans. He knew it. More importantly, Hermione knew it.

An unreadable spark flickered in her eyes, then vanished. "We'll fare splendidly here, just as we always have. Don't worry about us, Bryce. Do what you must."

Hermione's words nagged at him long after he returned to his chambers, long after he'd relinquished all thoughts of slumber and simply gone downstairs to await the fast-approaching dawn.

Alone in the sitting room, Bryce jabbed his hands in his pockets, staring out the window where the first rays of sunlight were drizzling through its panes. "Do what you must," she'd said, giving him that inscrutable look of hers. It was almost as if she perceived his turmoil. Well, perhaps she did. After all, she'd been its onset, if not its cause.

"Pardon me, sir, would you like your coffee served in here?" Chaunce inquired from the sitting room doorway.

Bryce turned to see the butler waiting expectantly, a steaming silver tray in his hands. "Thank you, Chaunce. That would be greatly appreciated."

"I assumed you'd want to be on your way early," Chaunce continued, crossing over and placing the tray on the table. "So I prepared a light breakfast for you.

This way you needn't delay your journey a moment longer than necessary. Incidentally, shall I say your good-byes for you?"

Halfway to the table, Bryce halted, scowling darkly at the butler. "No, Chaunce. I intend to say my own good-byes. And by the way, dispensing guilt doesn't become you. I'd suggest another tactic."

"Tactic, sir?" Chaunce smoothed his mustache. "That wasn't a tactic, it was a suggestion. Although I must say I'm pleased that you intend to see the family before taking your leave."

"I'll be back, Chaunce."

"Of course you will, sir." The butler clasped his hands behind his back. "Incidentally, don't worry about Miss Gaby. Her ladyship and I will ensure her safety."

"You know about Gabrielle's relapse? Hermione talked to you?"

"She generally does, sir."

Bryce's lips twitched. "Yes, I suppose she does." Amusement faded. "Chaunce, take care of them. *Both* of them."

"You have no worries on that score, sir." A pause. "On that note, I'll leave you to your breakfast. I'll arrange for your carriage to be brought around and your bags loaded. By that time the family should be up and about. You can bid them farewell and be on your way."

"Thank you, Chaunce."

Three-quarters of an hour later Bryce stood beside his carriage, stunned by the swell of people hovering about him. Every resident of Nevon Manor—from serving girls to chambermaids, from footmen to kitchen staff—had come to see him off.

It was the most humbling display of affection he'd ever witnessed, much less been the recipient of.

"Here, Mr. Lyndley." Cook came forward first, her plump face beaming as she handed him a picnic basket filled with cinnamon cakes and a fat jar of raspberry jelly. "Take this. I hope there's enough to last you until you come back to us."

"Thank you," Bryce murmured, staring down at the basket for a long minute before placing it carefully on the carriage floor. "That was very thoughtful."

"I have something for you, too, Mr. Lyndley," Peter declared, leaning past his mother and handing Bryce a small parcel. "It's a leather-bound writing pad, small enough to fit in your pocket. This way you can jot down whatever legal points are on your mind without waiting to get back to your office." A grin. "I filled the first page with questions about the Elementary Education Act. I figured you could answer them whenever you have time and bring the answers with you when you come back."

Bryce glanced from the painstakingly wrapped package to Peter's eager face. "It will be a privilege. And thank you. I don't know how you knew, but this is precisely what I needed."

He had no time to recover before the unexpected showering of gifts continued. Mrs. Gordon gave him a fresh cloth so his shoes might remain spotless. Goodsmith gave him the very cap he'd tipped at Queen Victoria. Wilson gave him a new shovel that closely resembled his own, and the children collectively thrust a squirming yellow kitten at him, stammering that Sunburst had volunteered to keep Bryce company so that he wouldn't be lonely in London.

By the time Chaunce bowed his good-bye—having added two bottles of Bryce's favorite brandy to the pile of gifts—and Hermione kissed his cheek, Bryce was more moved than he could describe.

"Hurry home," Hermione instructed, squeezing his arm. "You'll be missed."

Abruptly Bryce realized that one of Nevon Manor's residents was missing. "Where's Gaby?"

Hermione shaded her eyes from the rapidly rising sun, squinting as she intently scanned the grounds. "Why, out there somewhere, I imagine. She hasn't returned from her early morning romp with Crumpet." A delicate pause. "Can you wait? Or shall I give her a message?"

"Neither." Bryce shook his head, scrutinizing the vast grounds about him. "I'll find her myself."

Watching him stalk off, Hermione pursed her lips, gesturing for the staff to reenter the manor. "I wonder if he'll succeed in finding her," she murmured to Chaunce.

"Oh, I rather expect he will." A sideways glance. "I don't suppose it's an accident that Miss Gaby isn't here."

Hermione's expression remained utterly serene. "It's possible she's waiting for one of the children to fetch her. I might have inadvertently implied that I'd arrange for her to be summoned when it came time for Bryce's departure."

"Ah. What a pity that it slipped your mind."

"Yes. Isn't it."

With that, she patted Chaunce's arm, gathered up her skirts, and made her way into the house.

It took Bryce a quarter hour to locate the splotch of color that told him he'd found the person he sought.

Gaby.

Weaving his way through the line of trees that separated him from his goal, he rounded the garden and walked over to the broad flat rock where Gaby sat, quietly stroking Crumpet's ears.

She obviously heard his approach, because she swiveled about, a questioning look in her eyes. "Bryce. Is everything all right?"

"Why wouldn't it be?" He studied her face, wondering why she'd chosen to avoid him this morning. Did she find good-byes difficult, or was she angry with him for what she perceived as desertion, not only of her but of Hermione and all of Nevon Manor's residents as well?

He was about to find out.

"I merely came looking for you to say good-bye."

"Is it time already?" Gaby surprised him by asking, her slender brows arching upward. "I had no idea. Lily was supposed to fetch me when your carriage was brought around."

"Ah." Realizing she'd had every intention of seeing him off, Bryce relaxed. "That explains it. Lily probably couldn't get away. She had her hands full until now."

An understanding grin. "Sunburst, yes. He is quite a handful. Not nearly as unruly as this scamp"— Gaby shot Crumpet a reproving look, which he promptly ignored, continuing to nibble at the skirts of Gaby's yellow-and-white day dress—"nor as destructive. Sunburst is just an intelligent, inquisitive fellow with a quick step and an excess of curiosity." Gaby's grin turned impish. "Actually I thought he was a wise choice on the girls' part. All the kittens are wonderful, but Sunburst reminds me a great deal of you."

"How so?"

"Oh, many things. His mind is keen, but he would fare better if he occasionally gave that brilliant mind a rest. His heart is good, but he refuses to acknowledge that it's also tender. And he's still at the point where he believes that independence is ideal, for he hasn't yet learned that needing others is a virtue and a strength."

Bryce sighed, staring out across the grounds. "Ah, Gaby, sometimes I wish I could view life as you do, if only for a little while. But each of us is born with certain qualities that, together with the sum total of our life experiences, make us the person we become. I know you hope to reform me, but that's not going to happen. First, I have no desire to change. Second, I'm thirty-one years old—hardly a tender enough age to undergo this major transformation you seek. Nonetheless, thank you for your kind intentions."

"Please don't patronize me, Bryce," she replied, her grasp on Crumpet tightening as the rabbit made to dash off. "I don't want to reform you. You're a wonderful man. I only want to coax forth qualities you have yet to perceive." She paused, her shoulders tensing as she visibly grappled with whether or not to continue. Ultimately her candor overcame her caution, and her voice when she spoke was as quiet as it was intense—more intense than Bryce had ever heard it. "What's more, I have something to say to you, something I wish I'd said days ago."

Feeling as taken aback as he did curious, Bryce urged, "Go on."

Gaby rose, turning around and lifting her chin to meet Bryce's gaze. "To be blunt, I'm growing tired of your assessment of me. Yes, I love life—and animals and the miracles of each new day, but I'm not a frolicking child who's steeped in fairy tales and silly fantasies. I am, as you just put it, the sum total of *my* experiences, one of which was the most tragic I can imagine anyone enduring. But the way one copes with adversity is as significant to one's character as the adversity itself. Losing someone doesn't preclude caring again, abandonment doesn't preclude the forming of new ties. And nothing, nothing, should prevent someone from dreaming and hoping and, most of all, from loving. You think those are the qualities that define a child? To the contrary, barrister, I believe those are the qualities that define a person."

Bryce felt a bit as if he'd been punched. Not because he found Gaby's argument logical, because it wasn't—given that it was based entirely in feeling rather than fact. No, his reaction was rooted in the fact that he'd never imagined this fiery side to her nature, a realization that only served to confirm her claim about his perception of her. She was right—or rather, partially right. He *did* view her as a child—sometimes. Other times he viewed her as the most courageous woman he'd ever met. And now he was viewing her in a whole new light—strong-willed and definite, as unyielding about her beliefs as he was about his. She was the most unique blend of contradictions he'd ever seen.

"I know you disagree," Gaby continued when the silence had stretched on for long minutes. "And I'm sorry about it—not for me but for you."

"Gaby . . ." he began, his thoughts still in turmoil.

She gave a hard shake of her head, sending chestnut waves cascading down her back. "I think we've said enough. Besides, your carriage is waiting." She gathered Crumpet closer. "Have a safe trip. And again, thank you for everything you've done, for me and for Aunt Hermione. You've filled a void in her heart that has gnawed at her for three decades—a healing that will last long beyond your visit."

"Stop it." Bryce heard his own sharp retort, feeling inexplicably angered by the finality in Gaby's tone. "I'm not vanishing. I'll be back."

"I hope so. For Aunt Hermione. For me and everyone else at Nevon Manor. But most of all, Bryce, for you." Gaby studied him for an instant, that inherent wisdom vividly present in her cornflower-blue eyes— as if she knew something about him that he didn't.

Perhaps she did.

Abruptly she stood on tiptoe and brushed a kiss to his cheek. "Godspeed," she whispered, her fervor softening to gentleness. "Whatever answers you're seeking, I hope you find them."

Bryce never knew what made him turn his head, whether it was a conscious decision or just an accident of fate. But turn it he did—just the few inches it took to bring his mouth close to hers.

Their lips touched, brushed, touched again. Bryce saw Gaby's eyes widen in astonishment, felt his own rush of disbelief.

He acted on pure instinct.

Catching Gaby's face between his palms, he lowered his head, covering her mouth in a deep, binding kiss that was as shattering as it was brief, a heated melding that obliterated time, space, and reality.

And which ended as quickly as it had begun.

Bryce wasn't sure who broke away first. All he knew was that he was staring into Gaby's startled face, his own incredulity reflected in her eyes.

"Gaby," he managed, "I'm sorry . . . I—" He broke off, wondering what the hell to say, his mind for the first time utterly, totally blank.

To his amazement, Gaby smiled, not a besotted smile but a radiant one. "I'm not. I've been trying for days to coax you into performing a single impulsive, irrational act. I believe I just succeeded." Her nod was the essence of satisfaction, her step light as she backed away from him, moving toward Crumpet's warren. "Perhaps Nevon Manor has worked its magic after all. Perhaps that's why you're reluctant to leave us, yet equally reluctant to remain. If so, I hope you find it impossible to stay away, that you're back before the magic has a chance to fade."

Five miles away the worried figure prowling about Whitshire's pantry was hoping just the opposite.

Why doesn't Bryce Lyndley leave? He's the last complication I need. And what the hell did Gabrielle remember the other night? Why was she so over-wrought? What is it she knows? I've got to find out. Damn. How can this be happening? Now—after all these years. How?

It can't. It won't.

I won't let it.

Chapter 9

MIDMORNING SUNLIGHT WASHED THE HALLS OF NEVON Manor, the smell of fresh flowers wafting through the open windows, heralding spring and celebrating the wonders of life. Creating a beautifully deceptive illusion, a direct contrast to the adversity of the past seven days.

Hermione made her way down the stairs, the lines of fatigue about her eyes no longer feigned but very real despite the long morning naps she'd been taking. Even Chaunce, who never wore physical evidence of his personal trials had begun looking a bit haggard. How could he not, given the arduous week they'd just endured? Much strain, little rest, and an overabundance of frustration.

And it seemed to be getting worse, not better.

Reaching the ground floor, Hermione peered down the hall, frowning when she saw that Chaunce was absent from his customary post at the entranceway door. True, he was exhausted. Lord knew he had reason to be. He'd kept vigil outside Gaby's chambers for seven nights now, halting her sleepwalking attempts, gently awakening her, persuading her to go back to sleep—only to have the entire process repeat itself again hours later. Still, nothing, not even bodily depletion, would be enough to drag Chaunce from his station.

Unless he was needed elsewhere.

An anxious tremor ran through Hermione's fragile frame, and ignoring the protest of her aching muscles, she quickened her pace, determined to discover Chaunce's whereabouts—and Gaby's too, for that matter. Her niece wasn't in her chambers; Hermione had just come from there. Then again, that was hardly unusual for this time of day. By now Gaby was normally outside, playing with the children or gallivanting about with her pets.

Still, with both Chaunce and Gaby absent . . .

Hermione neared the entranceway, fully intending to begin her search outdoors.

Abruptly her eye was caught by a motion off to her right, just inside, though several yards askew of, the towering wooden doors of Nevon Manor. Upon closer inspection, she realized it was Bowrick, perched on a chair near where he perceived the entranceway to be, muttering under his breath and frantically polishing his spectacles.

"Bowrick," Hermione called to him as she approached, "where is Chaunce?"

The elderly footman shoved his spectacles back on his nose and jumped to his feet, blinking in the direction from which his ear told him Lady Nevon was approaching. "Chaunce had to tend to somethin' outdoors, m'lady," he said to a potted plant that stood next to Hermione. "He asked me to assume his post till he returned. I was just makin' sure my spectacles were really clean so I wouldn't mistake one visitor for another. I wanna do as good a job as Chaunce, make him proud."

A soft smile touched Hermione's lips. "You always make us proud, Bowrick—Chaunce *and* me."

Bowrick's stooped shoulders straightened. "I'm glad, m'lady."

"Did Chaunce mention *where* outside he was going?" Hermione inquired, knowing it was useless to ask which direction he'd headed in, given that Bowrick couldn't see a foot in front of him.

"Uh, I think he said somethin' about a problem near the warren, m'lady."

Gaby—just as Hermione had suspected. A problem near the warren could mean nothing else. But was Chaunce merely assuring himself of Gaby's well-being or had something else happened to cause him concern?

She intended to find out.

"Thank you, Bowrick." Gathering up her skirts, Hermione pressed on, patting the footman's arm as she let herself out. "You've been very helpful. No, don't bother with the door," she added hastily, already through it and on the other side. "Dr. Briers wants me to get a bit of exercise each day. Opening this stubborn plank of wood will serve my purposes nicely—that and a nice stroll about the grounds. I'll be back shortly. Keep up the fine work, Bowrick."

With that, she veered in the direction of Crumpet's warren, wishing she were just a bit younger and more spry. The past week had taken its toll on her strength, and between that and her advanced years, rushing across the grounds was no longer an option.

She came upon Chaunce a quarter hour later. He was standing discreetly behind a tree, watching Gaby, who, unaware she was being observed, was sitting on a lawn chair, staring intently into the distance, her attention captured by something that seemed to fascinate her.

"Has something happened?" Hermione demanded, quietly making her way to Chaunce's side.

He shook his head, thoroughly unsurprised by Hermione's presence. "No. She was just in a very agitated state when she left the house. After a while, I thought it best to check up on her."

"Has she been out here long?"

"For over an hour. I thought for certain she'd sleep the morning away after the difficult night she just spent. It was the worst one thus far."

Hermione sighed, clasping her hands together in distress. "Three sleepwalking episodes in one night. That is not only unprecedented, it's debilitating, even for one as energetic as Gaby. I'm afraid for her, Chaunce. I'm not certain how much more her body can take."

"Her body *or* her mind," Chaunce reflected, his mouth set in grim lines. "She's becoming more despondent by the day. I think she's losing hope that these incidents will ever cease. Just look at her, staring aimlessly across the grounds, not even seeking her pets for comfort."

That particular observation elicited a completely different reaction from Hermione. A flicker of insight lit her eyes, and she craned her neck, trying to ensure that her suspicions were correct. "I agree that Gaby is devastated by her inability to break free of her past," she murmured. "However . . ." A pause, followed by a nod of satisfaction as Hermione found what she sought. "I believe the preoccupation you're witnessing is prompted by something entirely different. Different and far more encouraging."

Chaunce blinked. "Which is?"

"Look." Hermione pointed in the distance, indicating two forms—a brawny man wearing a cap and a stout woman who was tripping every third step—ambling side by side, hands clasped, toward the stables. "It's Marion and Goodsmith. They make the most charming couple, don't they? What's more, he intends to propose marriage this morning."

"Really?" Chaunce looked inordinately pleased. "How do you know today is the big day?"

"Because Goodsmith came to my sitting room yesterday to ask my opinion of the crimson-and-white checked hair ribbon he'd selected as Marion's betrothal gift. He wanted to choose something beautiful and properly binding."

"And you told him . . . ?"

"That the ribbon was lovely, of course."

Chaunce shot her a sideways look. "Nothing more? You merely admired the ribbon and sent him on his way?"

Hermione patted her hair in a flurry of motion. "Perhaps I offered him a trinket from my jewel case around which he could tie the ribbon. If so, it was only to bolster his confidence. He was so terribly nervous about the proposal."

"The ruby you've been polishing so dutifully each night?" Chaunce suggested.

A faint smile. "Am I that transparent, then?"

"Only to me, my lady."

"Good." Hermione squeezed his arm fondly. "The important thing is that we'll soon have a wedding in the family. And"—again she indicated the retreating couple and Gaby's perusal of them—"I think Gaby finds the prospect of love, and all its resulting nuances, much more intriguing than she would have a month ago."

"Ah, I see your point." A spark of satisfaction glinted in Chaunce's eyes. "By the way, did I mention to you that during your morning nap I received word from my source in London? Evidently Mr. Lyndley is quite restless these days, not at all himself. Why, he's spent more time pacing the banks of the Thames than he's spent working in his office. And it seems he cut short three of his social engagements with Miss Talbot—the most glaring one being two nights ago when they attended the symphony. Why, he escorted Miss Talbot home less than an hour into the concert. Apparently he didn't care for the music."

"Or the company," Hermione suggested wickedly, looking utterly elated by the news. "Thank you for sharing that bit of information with me. It makes my stroll out here even more crucial."

"Meaning?"

"Chaunce, I came to Crumpet's warren for several reasons. Obviously the first was to find you and Gaby, to satisfy myself that you've both managed to"—she studied her friend's face, renewed worry surging through her as she evaluated his signs of fatigue—"weather the strain of the past week." An aching pause. "Chaunce, you and I are no longer blessed with the precious ally of youth. What I've asked of you this week is more than I had the right. 'Tis just that I rely upon you so heavily. I don't know what I'd do if . . ."

"You won't." The lines about Chaunce's mouth softened, and he leaned forward ever so slightly. "Continue to rely upon me, my lady. I wouldn't have it any other way. As for my capabilities, I assure you that age hasn't marred my resilience, only enhanced my wisdom. It would take far more than a few sleepless nights to thwart me."

Tears glistened on Hermione's lashes. "Good," she replied, trying to keep her voice steady, knowing she was failing miserably. "In any case," she continued, blinking away the moisture and bringing herself under control, "my second reason for coming out here is that I want to talk to Gaby. I've kept my tactful silence long enough. I believe it's time she was offered an understanding ear and perhaps a word or two of advice on matters of the heart."

"Say no more. I wholeheartedly agree."

"And last, I wanted to tell you that I've sent for Dr. Briers." At that, Hermione's voice strengthened, determination supplanting tenderness. "I've refrained from summoning him all week, hoping that you and I together could see Gaby through this ordeal. But we've succeeded only in preventing her from harming herself by awakening her the instant she tries to leave her chambers. That is a balm, not a cure. It's time to seek help. Dr. Briers will be here within the hour."

Chaunce nodded. "I think that's wise. Perhaps the doctor can think of something we've overlooked, something that would help put Miss Gaby's mind at ease." He glanced from Hermione to the manor and back. "Given Dr. Briers's imminent arrival, I'd best resume my post." A thoughtful frown. "Actually, I believe I'll ask for Bowrick's assistance. With him beside me at the entranceway door, there will be two of us to look out for the doctor's carriage."

Affection warmed Hermione's heart. Chaunce no more needed assistance greeting guests than the sun needed assistance in rising—certainly not from an elderly footman whose eyesight was all but gone. But in his typically generous manner, Chaunce was seeking Bowrick's aid so that a worthwhile human being could retain his dignity. "You, my dear friend, are an incredible fraud," she said softly. "You're also the finest man I've ever known. Thank God you're with me."

"That, my lady, is a certainty you need never question," Chaunce replied, his own voice a bit rough. "Always remember that." Swiftly he cleared his throat. "Good luck with Miss Gaby. I'll send for you when Dr. Briers arrives."

Hermione stared after Chaunce's retreating form, the exacting stance and ageless strength, for a long time. Then she turned and walked stiffly into the clearing and toward Gaby's side.

Gaby's head pivoted, her brows arching in surprise when she saw her aunt. "Aunt Hermione." She sprang to her feet. "I had no idea you were coming out here. Are you looking for me?"

"I wanted to check on you, and perhaps to have a little talk." Hermione leaned against a tree, resting a moment to recoup her strength.

"Here." Gaby sprang into motion, grasping her

196

aunt's elbow and leading her to the lawn chair. "Sit down. You just took an exceptionally long walk—after a wretched, sleepless night. Rest."

"Thank you, darling." Hermione sank gratefully into the chair.

"What did you want to talk about—or need I ask?" Gaby questioned, anguish tightening her features. "I don't know why the sleepwalking has been recurring more and more often. I thought by now it would be improving, if not gone, but I certainly never expected it to worsen." She knelt before her aunt, clutching her hands. "Aunt Hermione, look at you. You're paler than ever, and the circles beneath your eyes are growing more pronounced. I'm so frightened you'll become seriously ill. We can't go on as we have been. I've been thinking . . ." Her voice quavered, then recovered, conviction underlying every word. "Perhaps I should leave Nevon Manor for a time. I could go to an inn, hire a discreet companion who would be advised of my circumstances and whose job it would be to ensure my well-being. That way, you and Chaunce would be able to recover your strength and distance yourself from my problem. Life here could resume as usual without my—"

"Stop it!" Hermione nearly bolted from her seat, her fingers gripping Gaby's with trembling intensity. "How could you even suggest such a thing? We're a family. Families don't turn away from each other in times of hardship. They pull together, devise solutions, and that is precisely what we're going to do."

"What if there are no solutions?" Gaby appealed. "Then what?"

"There are *always* solutions, Gaby. Sometimes they're just harder to find than we anticipate. So we keep searching." Hermione laid a palm against Gaby's cheek. "Which is why I've sent for Dr. Briers. You're too young to remember how committed he was to resolving your problem the first time we faced it. He provided hope and a sensible, ultimately successful solution. I truly believe he can do that again. He'll help us, Gaby; I know he will." A pause, as Hermione took in Gaby's skeptical expression. "I hope you don't feel I've betrayed your confidence by sending for him."

"Of course not. It's just that I don't see how Dr. Briers's advice can apply this time. The circumstances are so very different. I was a child last time; now I'm a grown woman. We're no longer dealing with a five-year-old's feelings of loneliness and abandonment. I know I have a home, people who love me. But for whatever reason, my memories of Mama and Papa's death are obviously deep and painful—too painful to obliterate with the simple reassurance that my family is there for me."

"Which is why we must seek the wisdom of someone better trained to alleviate pain."

Gaby pressed her lips together, a ray of hope penetrating her despair. "Do you really think the doctor is our answer?"

"Yes," Hermione replied thoughtfully. "Somehow I do."

"Very well, then." Gaby sighed. "I'm willing to try anything. And if Dr. Briers is the one to restore our lives to the way they were before . . ."

"Now, *that* I didn't say."

Gaby started. "But you just said—"

"I said I believe Dr. Briers can help end your bouts of sleepwalking. I didn't say he'd restore you to the girl you once were. No one can do that, Gaby, nor would you want them to."

"I don't understand."

"Don't you?" Hermione glanced nonchalantly over her shoulder. "I noticed you watching Goodsmith and Marion."

A self-conscious smile. "I suppose I was. I just think it's so glorious, the way they feel about each other. Don't you?"

"Indeed I do. In fact, as I just told Chaunce"— Hermione leaned forward conspiratorially—"I do believe Goodsmith is asking for Marion's hand even as we speak."

"Really?" Gaby's eyes grew as round as saucers. "Oh, how wonderful!"

"Love *is* wonderful, Gaby. You'll know for yourself one day soon."

At that, Gaby's lashes drifted downward. "Will I? Sometimes I wonder."

"Wonder what?"

A brief hesitation, then Gaby's head shot back up. "When you fell in love with Lord Nevon, did you know it right away? Did he? Did it happen the instant you met? Or did it strike you suddenly like a lightning bolt?"

Hermione chuckled. "So many questions all at once. Tell me, is anything in particular prompting this sudden and timely curiosity? Or should I say any*one?*"

Wide blue eyes searched Hermione's face. "You know, don't you?"

"That depends. What is it you think I know?"

"What I'm feeling. Who I'm feeling it for. What happened between us just before he left Nevon Manor."

"Wait." Hermione held up her palm. "The first two points I'm fairly confident about. But the third— you'll have to be a bit more specific."

Gaby wet her lips with the tip of her tongue. "Are you *sure* you realize who it is I'm referring to?"

"Bryce."

"And you're not mortified?"

"Why would I be? You, of all people, know what I think of my nephew. He's a fine, compassionate, wonderful man."

"Who's practically betrothed to another woman," Gaby burst out.

A twinkle. "When one grows to be my age, one learns that there is an enormous distinction between 'practically' and 'actually.' Now, would you care to tell me what happened between the two of you before Bryce left Nevon Manor?"

"He came looking for me. He wanted to say good-bye." Gaby swallowed. "I said some things I shouldn't have, accused him of regarding me as a child. Then I wished him a safe trip and kissed his cheek."

"And that's what's plaguing you? I'm sure Bryce won't hold a grudge about your outburst; he's quite forthright himself."

"My outburst is not what's plaguing me. What's plaguing me is what happened next."

"Which is . . . ?"

"Bryce kissed me." A flush stained Gaby's cheeks as she recalled those breathless, unexpected moments. "Or, to be honest, we kissed each other. Oh, I'm not sure who kissed whom. Or why. I only know that one minute we were talking and the next minute . . . we weren't." Gaby rose and paced about the clearing. "It lasted only a few seconds. Afterward Bryce was utterly bewildered—and furious with himself for feeling that way. I could see it in his eyes, that refusal to understand why he'd acted on impulse rather than logic. It took every shred of my self-control to make light of the whole occurrence. But I did make light of it—for Bryce's sake and for mine. That way, he could dismiss the incident as inconsequential, and I could escape without making a total, utter fool of myself." A self-deprecating laugh. "If I'd given in to the dictates of my body, my knees would have buckled under me and I would have fallen to the ground. The result? I would have died of embarrassment and shown myself to be the very child Bryce perceives me to be."

Gaby paused, her fingers brushing her lips. "But, oh, Aunt Hermione, I never imagined such extraordinary feelings—certainly not out of the blue, with no warning, no prelude. And not with a man who views me as a tenderhearted—albeit wise, considering I'm so sheltered—child, a man who's totally committed to a far more sophisticated woman."

"'Wise, considering you're so sheltered,'" Hermione repeated offhandedly. "Is that how Bryce described you?"

"Yes." Gaby gazed helplessly at her aunt. "Would you please shed some light on what's happened? Or, at the very least, comment upon it?"

"What would you like me to say?"

"Are you shocked?"

"That you kissed a man? Hardly." Hermione's eyes twinkled. "As you yourself pointed out a few minutes ago, you're a grown woman now. 'Twas only a matter of time before you enjoyed your first kiss. That you kissed Bryce Lyndley? No. He's an extraordinarily handsome, charismatic man. That he kissed you? Now, that surprises me least of all. Bryce is desperately in need of a specific kind of sustenance—that of the soul—something he himself doesn't understand. You are the very embodiment of that sustenance. He seeks you as a flower seeks sunshine. So no, Gaby, nothing you've said surprises me."

"Did you fall in love with Lord Nevon right away?" Gaby persisted, returning to her original question.

A soft smile touched Hermione's lips. "I suppose I did. John was dashing, warmhearted, and relentless in his pursuit. He bombarded me with gifts and visits, declared his intention to wed me within a fortnight— to me, my parents, the world—vowing he'd spend the rest of his days making me happy. And he kept his promise. Our time together was shorter than I would have liked—he was a great deal older than I—but it was no less joyful for its brevity. My memories are wonderful ones, filled with laughter and excitement and passion. I wouldn't trade them for the world."

"You must miss him dreadfully," Gaby said softly.

Hermione studied her folded hands, considering her answer carefully before offering it. "John's been gone for many years. At first the loss seemed unbearable. Then time wrapped the pain in a soothing cocoon and tucked it away, allowing the happy memories to surge forth. Now I feel only tenderness and nostalgic pleasure." She raised her head. "I've learned something else since then, Gaby. There are many different types of love. None is better or more precious than another, nor does the luster of one dim the radiance of its predecessor. Each is unique and must be cherished as the blessing it's intended to be. The same is true of you, my dear. You're a once-in-a-lifetime treasure waiting to be discovered—discovered and reveled in. The right man will do that, Gaby. You'll see. I'm as sure of that as I am of the happiness that man will bring you."

Gaby's eyes were misty, filled with emotion and uncertainty. "How will I know when I find him?"

"You won't. Not right away. You'll suspect, but you won't be sure. You'll ask yourself questions, wonder about your feelings—and his. But later, when it truly matters, you'll know. Just as I did." A rueful grin. "Hindsight is a wondrous thing, Gaby. It holds little room for error. Unfortunately, it's not around when we need it most, which is before the event occurs. If it were, our decisions would be that much easier."

"So what do you suggest I do about Bryce? Dismiss what happened as a chance incident?"

"Can you do that?"

"No." Gaby gave an adamant shake of her head. "I've been reliving our kiss all week long. Every waking moment. And not only the kiss—everything. Things I gave no special credence to until that magical moment, but which suddenly took on a whole new light."

"Such as?"

Gaby fingered the folds of her gown, contemplating her response. "This is very difficult to explain, but I'll try. It's as if Bryce and I understand each other in some fundamental way that has no name or explanation. When we talk, it's like two musical notes blending in perfect harmony. The tones are entirely different, yet when combined, the melody is that much richer, the strains that much fuller, for resounding together. Does that make any sense?"

Despite her best intentions, Hermione felt her lips quiver. "Perfect sense."

"Bryce seems to know precisely when I need him, and somehow he always manages to come to my rescue. Even more significant is the fact that he allows me to do the same for him, even if he doesn't realize he's allowing it." Gaby released her skirts, found Hermione's gaze with her own. "Such as when he told me about his past. I realize you asked him to do that so I'd accompany him to Whitshire. But I don't believe your request alone would have induced him to reveal all the details he shared with me. He told me not only the facts but also his feelings, his fears. He's never discussed any of that with anyone, not even Miss Talbot. She doesn't know the truth about his heritage, nor does he intend to tell her. I've pressed him on the subject, but he immediately shuts me out. Bryce is complex; there are layers I have yet to reach, let alone to completely fathom. Sometimes he's a reserved stranger who's intent on keeping his distance. But other times he's warm, open, tender, not only with me but with everyone at Nevon Manor. It's as if he's afraid to care."

"He is," Hermione replied softly. "Surely you can understand why."

"Of course I can. His childhood, his entire life, he's been alone. Caring involves risk, risk Bryce is not willing to take. What I can't understand is his anger. Not at the others but at me. Whenever he feels most vulnerable, he reacts. With the others he pulls back. But with me he becomes coldly detached, almost biting. Why?"

"Experience has taught me that acute feelings incite acute reactions."

Gaby sucked in her breath. "You think it's because he cares for me—maybe more than he wants to?"

Hermione shrugged. "It's possible, given your description of his behavior."

"So what should I do?" Gaby spread her arms helplessly. "He's committed to another woman, a woman who's probably far better suited to him than I. And while I refuse to interfere in that relationship, my heart refuses to heed the dictates of my mind. The result is that I can't act—and I can't not act."

"Then you have your answer," Hermione concluded.

"What answer?" Gaby asked in bewilderment. "Aunt Hermione, what if I'm falling in love with—"

"Gaby," Hermione interrupted, "stop. Don't inundate yourself with questions or rack your brain for solutions that are still out of reach. Wait. See what happens, what the future holds in store. Your answers will come to you—I promise."

"Will they?"

"Yes." *And so will Bryce,* Hermione added silently, making a mental note to seek Chaunce out the instant Dr. Briers had finished talking to Gaby.

Given these exhilarating circumstances, it was time to expedite Bryce's return to Nevon Manor.

"Physically, you're fine, except for a clear case of exhaustion," Dr. Briers announced, rising from the edge of Gaby's bed and giving his diagnosis to both her and Hermione. "However, we knew this problem wasn't a medical one, which makes it even more difficult to treat, given there's no medicine you can swallow to alleviate your symptoms."

Gaby pushed herself up on her elbows. "Are you saying the situation is hopeless?"

"Not at all." The physician scowled, stroking the coarse whiskers that had once been black but were now gray. "I'm saying that we must seek an emotional remedy to your condition."

"We know what prompted Gaby's relapse," Hermione inserted, leaning forward in the tufted chair. "Our trip to Whitshire and the memories it evoked. The question is, how do we reverse the damage that was done that night?"

"How indeed?" Dr. Briers murmured. "Gabrielle is correct in saying that the method which worked when she was five is obviously no longer effective. Nightly vigils are a mere safety precaution now, not a cure."

"Not to mention that I refuse to have Aunt Hermione and Chaunce sitting up all night overseeing me," Gaby insisted, swinging her legs over the side of the bed and rising. "Aunt Hermione is weak enough as it is. Which reminds me . . ." She turned to Dr. Briers. "Aunt Hermione needs a fresh supply of medicine. When Chaunce took down the bottle this morning, I noticed it was almost empty. Please leave a fresh supply with him before you go."

"Hmm?" Dr. Briers's forehead wrinkled. "Medicine?"

"Yes, Henry, my medicine," Hermione prompted swiftly.

"Ah, yes, your medicine. Of course." Realization erupted on his face, and Dr. Briers nodded emphatically. "Forgive me, I'm just preoccupied with Gabrielle's dilemma. Certainly I'll leave another bottle with Chaunce. Continue taking it as I directed."

"I will." Hermione folded her hands in her lap. "But my weakness is not what we're here to discuss. Gaby's sleepwalking is. Now, what do you suggest we do about it?"

"Something that might surprise you." The physician paused, pursing his lips as he contemplated the advice he was about to offer. "I suggest that Gabrielle return to Whitshire as soon as possible."

"What?" Gaby paled.

"Hear me out." Dr. Briers held up his palm, warding off her protest. "I think you should go back—but under different circumstances. In my opinion, the mistake you made was not in returning but in how and when you did so, under conditions too apt to elicit the wrong kind of memories."

"I don't understand."

"Think about it, Gabrielle. Except for that final horrible day, your experience at Whitshire was a warm and loving one among your parents and their friends. Some of those friends are still working at the estate, are they not?"

"Yes. A small number of the staff survived the fire and remained on."

"Excellent. Then I suggest that you plan a visit with them—and not at night but during the day. Even under optimum conditions, the darkness tends to bring with it a sense of foreboding that, for most of us, is absent during the day. This is especially true in your case, when you equate the night with pain and loss. Therefore, schedule a visit to Whitshire during the late morning or early afternoon. Seek out as much that is familiar and good in your old home as possible. Duplicate the pleasant situations you enjoyed there. Meet with your old friends. Stroll with them across sections of the grounds on which you romped as a girl. Don't, under any circumstances, return to the servants' quarters or any part of the wing that stands where the fire took place. Perhaps by reliving your happier memories, you can help counter the effects of your last visit."

Hermione's eyes were gleaming. "It's worth a try, Gaby. I can alert Thane, tell him what we intend to do—if you'll allow me to discuss your dilemma with him. I'm sure he'll be more than sympathetic. I know he'll agree to involve the entire staff, especially those servants who were employed at Whitshire thirteen years ago." She rose, walked over to clasp Gaby's cold hands. "I realize how frightening the idea of returning to Whitshire is for you," she said quietly, studying her niece's bowed head. "Lord knows, I myself was dead set against it. But after hearing what Dr. Briers just had to say, I now believe it does make sense. If you still feel you can't put yourself through the ordeal, I won't press you. We'll simply find some other way."

"But this could be our answer," Gaby replied, raising her chin.

"Yes. It could."

"On the other hand," Gaby continued, "revisiting Whitshire could make things worse." A humorless laugh. "What an absurd statement. Three sleepwalking attempts in one night—how much worse could the situation get?"

Hermione glanced from Gaby to Dr. Briers and back to Gaby. "Going back will take a great deal of courage on your part—courage that only you can muster. So the decision must be yours. Shall we give it a try?"

For a long moment Gaby remained silent, her expression veiled. Then she nodded. "Yes. Let's follow Dr. Briers's advice. And let's pray that it works."

Chapter 10

Whoever claimed that time and distance brought all things into focus was a bloody fool.

Tossing back his drink, Bryce slammed his glass down on the balcony railing and stared broodingly into the night sky, only minimally aware of the sounds of the ball commencing behind him, instead wondering if he had lost his sense of reason.

He'd been back in London for a week. Everything was precisely as he'd left it, yet nothing was the same. He'd come back to gain some perspective, to immerse himself once again in his life, his work.

Instead all he'd done was worry about Nevon Manor—Hermione's weakness, the staff's ability to function if she fell ill, and, most of all, Gaby's sleepwalking.

Why had he become so irrationally and personally involved with these people? In comparison with his long-standing day-to-day existence, the three days at Nevon Manor had been an isolated speck of unreality, a deluge that had carried him into a wealth of unfamiliar circumstances amid a multitude of unfamiliar people. A lot like poor fictitious Alice when she'd been carried off by a river of her own tears, Bryce thought, his own analogy eliciting a wry grin. Hell, three days at Nevon Manor and he might as well have toppled down that rabbit hole to Wonderland with Alice.

Still, the "wonder" part of it was undeniable, he mused, rolling his empty goblet between his palms. Wonder permeated Nevon Manor, right down to the smallest detail.

The contrast had struck him full force the instant he arrived at his London town house and mounted the stairs to his bedchamber. Standing in the doorway, he'd scrutinized the room, seeing it as if for the first time—a pleasant blend of color and texture, rich walnut and tasteful decoration.

But a room; nothing more.

Conversely, he recalled the loving care and attention to detail that had been given to his chambers at Nevon Manor—the legal texts and other personal touches, even clothing that was designed just to his liking. All right, he admitted to himself. He'd become attached to the quarters and everything in them. True, it wasn't like him to find comfort in possessions, yet those possessions were different, just as Nevon Manor, its owner, and its residents were different. As for the uncharacteristic nature of his response, that shouldn't have surprised him. His visit to Hermione's estate had resulted in his experiencing a wealth of peculiar responses—all foreign, some of which he was having a difficult time understanding.

Some of which he didn't want to understand, only to dispel.

Those involving Gaby.

He hadn't forgotten the unexpectedly startling way they'd said good-bye.

Forgotten it? Unlikely. The truth was, he'd dwelled on it incessantly from the minute he'd driven away from Nevon Manor.

And he was dwelling on it still.

What in God's name had he been thinking of, kissing her like that? Had he been insane? And his self-censure didn't only stem from the fact that he had a commitment to Lucinda, although Lord knew he felt guilty as hell on that score. More importantly, it stemmed from the decision he'd made about Gaby herself. One of his intentions in leaving Hertford was to discourage any romantic illusions Gaby might be harboring about the two of them. Instead he'd heightened them by giving in to a demented, inexcusable impulse.

And the most ironic part was that, after all his worry over Gaby's potential daydreams, he'd been more deeply affected by the kiss than she. He had spent all week worrying over it, whereas she had strolled off, secure in the belief that she'd opened some new door between him and his true self.

So much for protecting Gaby. Evidently she was less fragile than he'd realized. And she'd certainly minced no words in her blatant assessment of his weaknesses and all that Nevon Manor could do to eliminate them.

That memory stirred up an oddly bereft feeling in his gut, a hollow ache he couldn't fathom much less explain. Why did he feel as if he'd lost something far more precious than a mere kiss when he drove away from Nevon Manor? It wasn't as if he had gone away forever, nor, for that matter, had he been there that long. He had a life to return to, one that had been established years before he ever journeyed to Hermione's home. Conversely, he had no intention of disappointing any of them—Gaby, Hermione, or the others. He *was* going back, as soon as his work, his thoughts, and his reality allowed. Nonetheless, he continued to feel a strange sense of emptiness that transcended his affinity for Gaby. Why?

"There you are." Lucinda glided onto the balcony,

gloved hand outstretched. "I thought perhaps you'd been swallowed up by the crowd inside."

With more than a twinge of guilt, Bryce turned, dutifully capturing Lucinda's fingers and bringing her to stand beside him. "Nothing so exciting as that. I merely needed some air—although one could easily drown in that crowd. There must be six hundred people in that ballroom."

Lucinda laughed, a light, sparkling sound that suited her perfectly. "Not quite that many, although I do believe five hundred were invited. I rather enjoy Lord and Lady Wilcox's elaborate parties. Each year they add at least one extra touch to outdo themselves. This year it's the three additional musicians and a second roomful of refreshments. I suppose the two correspond—one must do a considerable amount of extra dancing in order to make up for consuming that amount of food."

"I suppose." Bryce's smile was automatic, his concentration shifting from Nevon Manor's residents to Lucinda, although not to capture the details of her idle chatter. For the first time he studied Lucinda as an objective observer might, scrutinizing the woman the newspapers referred to as "a fairy-tale princess."

It was easy to see why. Everything about her was lovely—her golden hair upswept and adorned by a coronet of flowers, her elegant peau de soie ball gown the very height of fashion, its blue hue the perfect contrast to her ethereal features. She was flawless, like a priceless painting captured on canvas—refined, tasteful, and above all else, consistent.

Why did that consistency suddenly seem like a shortcoming rather than an asset? What the hell had come over him this past week?

"Bryce?" A worried frown creased Lucinda's brow. "You really do seem out of sorts. Actually, you haven't been yourself all week. Is something wrong?"

"No. Nothing's wrong." Bryce shifted restlessly,

staring into his empty glass and massaging his temples. "I suppose I'm just tired. I had more work piled up on my desk than I expected when I returned from Hertford."

"I'm not surprised. No one—myself included—expected you to be away for so long." Lucinda smoothed her skirts. "Lady Nevon obviously had a great many legal matters to discuss."

"She did. But that wasn't all that kept me away. Her staff . . . the people who live there . . ." He broke off, uncertain how to explain—or, more to the point, how much he *could* explain. He'd already tried, several times, to convey his ambivalence toward Hermione's staff—his concern over their future, his admiration for their commitment to one another—but he'd been met only by a sympathetic nod and a distressed murmur, Lucinda's customary manner of placating him.

Normally it didn't matter. His causes were his own. It wasn't necessary that Lucinda share them, only that she not deter him from doing what he must.

But this time was different. This time he wanted to shake some sense into her, to shout out his pride in these people's accomplishments, to make her see that, inside Nevon Manor, what she viewed as impairments weren't impairments at all.

Thus far he'd been unsuccessful.

And Lucinda's next comment reinforced that fact all the more. "From what I've gleaned from you thus far, Lady Nevon's staff sounds like an eccentric little group, to say the least. Were I you, I'd stick to my dealings with their mistress and leave them to their own devices."

"Why?" Bryce bit out.

"Why?" Lucinda gave him an odd look. "Because they're Lady Nevon's responsibility, not yours. In addition, she's clearly the only one who's equipped to handle their special needs. As for my regarding them as eccentric, how else would you describe people who give parting gifts to a man they hardly know—and such peculiar parting gifts: a shovel, a cap, and a cloth with which to dust your shoes?"

"I'd describe them as caring."

"I don't doubt their motives, Bryce," Lucinda replied in that calm, sensible voice of hers. "Only their clearheadedness." Gently she touched his sleeve. "I wasn't suggesting you treat them unkindly. However, in the future, I don't think you should allow them to become quite so attached to you—or you to them, for that matter. It's not healthy, the amount of time you've spent worrying over them this week. Objectively consider what I'm saying, and you'll see that I'm right. They are, after all, Lady Nevon's charges. And you are her legal adviser, not a companion for her staff."

"That's not terribly charitable of you, Lucinda," Bryce returned coolly. "And I'm afraid I'm not as adept as you are at relegating people to neat little niches. These are individuals, not some generally labeled group. Each of them is different and unique. Take Peter, for example. At nine years of age, the lad already has the potential to be a brilliant barrister, and he *will* be, with the right encouragement. If I can provide him with that encouragement, and perhaps some knowledge and opportunity, how can I not?"

A sigh. "I'm not a monster, Bryce. I heard your colorful descriptions of Nevon Manor's residents. Certainly I'm not suggesting that you scorn them, only that you moderate this fierce sense of personal duty you brought home with you. Help the lad, of course. Give him some of your books. Put in a word or two at Eton, if that would help. But you needn't appoint yourself his personal champion."

Silence.

Lucinda gave a helpless shrug, glancing behind her as the music in the ballroom resumed. "Please, Bryce, let's not argue. Everything I'm saying is for your own good. I realize you feel a deep sense of compassion for

Lady Nevon's servants, and you know how much I admire your commitment to those less fortunate than we. But I don't like to see you so distressed. Remember, Nevon Manor functioned just fine before your arrival. I'm certain it's sustaining itself equally well since your departure." Her fingertips brushed Bryce's forearm, her smile coaxing. "Now let's go back inside. I believe the musicians are striking up a waltz."

With a terse nod, Bryce complied, fully aware that this discussion was going nowhere and deciding that dancing, which required no conversation, was preferable. Wordlessly he led Lucinda past the glass doors and back into her world: the ballroom.

The music had indeed resumed, and despite his lack of enthusiasm for the ball itself, Bryce found the melody oddly comforting after the tension of the past few minutes—harmony on the heels of discord. Concentrating on the lively cadence of the waltz, he swept Lucinda about the crowded floor amid the throng of laughing, chatting people.

Oblivious of the crowd, Bryce stared off into space, his gaze settling on the pianist. Idly, he wondered what Gaby would think of his performance. The gentleman was quite impressive, as was the gleaming pianoforte on which he played. But, skill notwithstanding, the music lacked the emotion, the intensity of feeling, that Gaby exuded when her fingers touched the keys. And the lighthearted waltz he was playing—Bryce grinned inwardly—was definitely not Beethoven.

The concert he and Lucinda had attended the other night had featured several of Beethoven's symphonies. Those Gaby would have adored, as she would have the entire musical experience. The richness of the symphonies, the full-bodied sound of all the instruments playing as one—each its own entity, yet together so unified—Gaby would have blossomed like one of the springtime buds she so treasured.

As he whirled Lucinda about, Bryce's thoughts

214

converged on his promise to find a way for Gaby to attend a concert. He'd already given it a great deal of thought and had resolved at least one of the problems: that of Gaby's chaperon, given that Hermione was presumably too weak to travel. He'd considered the limitations of the various residents of Nevon Manor and had decided upon Marion. She would be ideal. Not only was she steady enough, both physically and mentally, to spend an evening away from the estate and in London, but she would relish the opportunity to ride alongside her beloved Goodsmith in the carriage. It would provide them with one of those miraculous opportunities for privacy that Gaby had alluded to.

Bryce's grin faded as he realized whom he'd instinctively chosen for the role of Gaby's escort: himself. The idea was inadvisable, potential guardianship or not. If he walked into that concert hall with Gaby by his side, if not on his arm, the wrong conclusions would be drawn. He could ask Lucinda to join them, of course, but given her reaction to his entire Nevon Manor experience, she would doubtless balk at the notion of entertaining Hermione's adopted niece.

A niece, he reminded himself, who'd been mentioned only briefly in the descriptions he'd provided Lucinda of Hermione's residents.

He didn't dare contemplate the reasons why.

Bryce jerked his thoughts back to the matter at hand: the dilemma of getting Gaby to the symphony. The only way he could see of accomplishing this was for Hermione to attend. And if she was too ill . . . Bryce frowned. There had to be another course of action. For Gaby's sake and for his. The truth was, he didn't want anyone else escorting her to her first concert. Quite simply, he wanted to be the one to see the look on her face, to share her exhilaration as she immersed herself in the experience.

That unsettling voice inside his head—the one that had been assailing him all week—chimed in once again, dryly proclaiming that, should he manage to accomplish his goal, he doubtless wouldn't have the same problem he'd had the other night. He'd found the concert to be surprisingly flat and uninteresting, and he couldn't leave soon enough to suit him. In fact, the entire event had seemed irritating rather than enticing, the music devoid of its customary resonance.

And he knew bloody well why.

Damn.

"Where did you get those scratches?" Lucinda murmured as the waltz came to an end.

"Pardon me?"

"Your face." One gloved finger grazed his jaw. "You have scratches on your chin and along your jawline. Did you injure yourself?"

"Ah, those." A faint smile touched Bryce's lips as he recalled the tussle that had resulted in those scratches. "No, I didn't injure myself, at least not in the way you mean. The children at Nevon Manor conspired and granted me their own farewell gift: a cat. Actually, a kitten—an unruly little scamp named Sunburst, who thinks he's a tiger. He's accustomed to making himself at home when and where he chooses. As of now, he's chosen my bedchamber as his lair. He's taken it over and is most reluctant to share it. We had a small disagreement over the use of the bed this morning. Thus the scratches."

Rather than smiling, Lucinda looked concerned. "Perhaps you should put him out, before his attacks really hurt you."

"I think I can hold my own against a kitten," Bryce returned dryly. "Besides, I would hardly call a few scratches an attack. Don't worry; I'm fine."

"Surely there are families with children who would be delighted to give your cat a home."

Abruptly, Bryce wasn't smiling. "He doesn't need a home," he said, feeling an irrational surge of annoyance. "He has one. Furthermore, I would never give him away; he was a gift. If I simply handed him off to another family, it would hurt Lily, Jane, and the boys terribly."

A flicker of surprise widened Lucinda's eyes—one that was quickly extinguished, supplanted by comprehension. "Of course. I understand. If you hurt the children's feelings, it would upset Lady Nevon, something you cannot risk doing. She is, after all, a very important client. She's also well known for her benevolence. Now that I consider it, your strategy—the empathy you're showing her staff—is a sound one. Heartfelt, I know, but also quite sound."

"My strategy," Bryce repeated in a wooden tone. He drew a slow, tired breath. "Lucinda, I think it's time we took our leave. It's late, and I have an early morning appointment."

"Of course." Ever the consummate lady, Lucinda hid her disappointment. With one swift, baffled look at Bryce, she gathered up her skirts and glanced about the room. "The ball will be winding down soon anyway. Why don't you arrange for the carriage to be brought around? I'll find Lady Wilcox and say good night."

"Fine." Bryce turned, surveying the crowd and steeling himself for a push toward the hallway.

For one brief instant the full impact of his surroundings struck home. An opulent party, lavish gems, unspeakable affluence, notable guests.

So many people, so little purpose.

Abruptly Bryce had to get out of there. Immediately.

"Welcome back, Gabrielle." Thane came out to greet Hermione's carriage personally, extending his hand to assist Gaby in alighting.

"Thank you, Thane—and not just for the welcome," she murmured when she stood beside him. "For everything."

"My pleasure." He leaned forward to help his aunt

217

down, giving her a reassuring nod as he did. "You're looking stronger today, Hermione. And you're soon to look stronger still. Mrs. Fife has prepared an enormous lunch for us, one that might just cause the dining room table to collapse. Afterward the staff has an exhausting afternoon planned for Gabrielle—and for us, if we can manage to keep up. Mrs. Darcey has arranged for a long stroll about the grounds, stopping at all the hiding places she and Averley assure me were Gabrielle's favorites. Following that, one of the fillies Gabrielle adored as a child—Maiden, I believe Mrs. Darcey said—will be saddled and brought around for a ride."

"Oh . . . Maiden!" Gaby exclaimed, her mind flooded with fond memories. "She was my absolute favorite, all long-limbed and gangly, but with a hint of grace and a wealth of energy. Papa put me on her back when I was two—probably just so I'd stop nagging him to do so."

Thane shot Gaby a grin. "Well, Maiden's awkward youthful phase is over. Like you, she's grown to adulthood. Her gangly limbs are now swift and strong, her grace fully developed. Her energy level remains unchanged, though. She's now a thoroughly spirited mare who races like the wind. I guarantee she'll tire you out. However, if your eyelids have yet to droop after your ride and your stroll, the staff has organized a late afternoon game of croquet, to be followed by a much needed tea party in the garden." A chuckle. "You'll probably sleep through the entire carriage ride home, and certainly throughout the night."

Gaby's throat tightened with gratitude. "It sounds wonderful," she managed. "I can hardly wait."

"Good. Then let's not delay Mrs. Fife's banquet."

Lunch was all Thane had promised and more. Served by a half dozen familiar faces and overseen by Mrs. Fife herself, the meal consisted of roast mutton with browned potatoes and carrots—which Gaby instantly recognized as her most clamored-for meal as a child—followed by apple pastries, her all-time favorite. Biting into one of the warm confections, she smiled to herself, recalling how many times she'd wandered into the kitchen and tugged on Mrs. Fife's skirts to get her attention, and all for the purpose of receiving the first pastry hot from the oven.

She'd usually accomplished her goal.

Gaby's memories warmed still further during the stroll Mrs. Darcey had arranged. Accompanied by the housekeeper herself—and several younger maids who took over when Mrs. Darcey's strength ran out— Gaby walked the grounds of Whitshire, encountering one delightful reminder after another. Each stopping point triggered another filament of recall: The massive rock at the edge of the woods, the thick cluster of trees, the grassy hollow alongside the stream—they all brought to mind a curious little girl who'd been discovering new and interesting places to explore.

Then came the highlight of the afternoon: her reunion with Maiden.

The mare was as splendid as Gaby remembered, maturity having only enhanced her beauty and spirit. Having been led by a groom to Whitshire's course— clearly to avoid Gaby's having to visit the stables and nearby servants' quarters—the magnificent mare was saddled and ready to be mounted, tossing her golden brown head and eyeing Gaby as she approached.

Gaby paused beside her, stroking her mane and her silky muzzle. The way her ears perked up when Gaby said her name made it clear that Maiden remembered her.

"Is that really you, Gaby?" The groom, who had stood silently by during this reunion, now spoke up, sounding—and looking—utterly amazed as he uttered his question.

Shifting her attention, Gaby studied the man's face, her eyes narrowed quizzically as she tried to place him. He was in his late twenties, she should say, with a ruddy complexion and a ready smile. Something about him was familiar, but she just couldn't place it.

Noting Gaby's puzzlement, the man grinned, and the twinkle that lit his dark eyes brought his identity back in a rush.

"Thomas?" she gasped, trying to liken the fifteen-year-old stable boy who'd fed and watered the horses to the muscular man now gazing back at her with amused disbelief. "Is that you?"

"I'm easier to recognize than you are," he retorted, politely trying not to stare. "When His Grace said you'd be visiting, I assumed you'd look different than I remembered—taller, older. After all, I haven't seen you since you were five. But I didn't expect a fully grown, beautiful . . ." He broke off, flushing as he realized he'd overstepped his bounds. "Sorry. It's just that I've always pictured you the way you were: the little imp who was forever underfoot when your father was trying to get his work done." A rueful sigh. "It certainly makes me feel old."

A smile touched Gaby's lips. "We've all changed, Thomas. Not old, just older."

Thomas nodded, the toe of his boot scraping the dirt. "Denning would be real proud of you. You've got his way with horses. You also look a whole lot like your mother." His head came up, and he watched her, his expression distinctly uncomfortable. "I hope I didn't upset you by saying that."

"Not at all," Gaby assured him, feeling choked, but in a profound and tender way rather than a pained one. "In fact, I can't think of a lovelier compliment."

Nodding again, Thomas shifted awkwardly, gesturing toward Maiden. "Can I help you up?"

"Yes, thanks." Gaby moved to Maiden's left side, accepting Thomas's assistance and easing into the sidesaddle. "Is it all right if I take her over the course alone?"

"Yeah, I guess it can't hurt, given you're not riding

astride. You can't let Maiden take control. If she thinks she's boss, she'll take off like a bullet. Before you know it, you'll be sailing over her head and landing on your—" He cleared his throat. "You know what I mean."

"Indeed I do." Gaby bit back her laughter, giving Maiden an affectionate pat. "Thank you, Thomas. I promise not to become overzealous."

Sidesaddle or not, the ride was exquisite, a ballet without music. Gaby guided Maiden across the grounds, taking in the familiar sights that mere strolling had circumvented: the manicured length of the course, the twists and turns she remembered so vividly, having followed her father countless times as he cooled down the horses for the day.

The recollection brought with it a reassuring sense of peace, solace rather than pain.

She missed her parents still, but they were alive in a cherished place inside her heart.

Perhaps Dr. Briers had been right. Perhaps this visit was precisely what she'd needed.

By the time Gaby had restored Maiden to Thomas's side, she felt wonderfully renewed. Waving as horse and groom headed off to the stables, she had scarcely caught her breath when Mrs. Darcey reappeared to escort her to a rousing game of croquet on the front lawn.

At the game's conclusion, Gaby sank gratefully into a garden chair, just as Thane had predicted. She was exhausted, probably more from the emotional intensity that had accompanied her to Whitshire than from actual physical exertion. Nevertheless, she was content to settle herself among the flowers, inhaling the late afternoon fragrances and sipping tea with family and friends. Thane had kindly and insightfully invited Mrs. Darcey, Mrs. Fife, and Averley to join him, Gaby, and Hermione for refreshment, knowing that Gaby's childhood meals had been taken with the staff, not the family.

"These scones are delicious," Gaby proclaimed, taking a bite. "And the afternoon was perfect—just what I needed." Her gaze swept everyone around her. "Thank you. Thank you all. You've helped bring back so many happy memories—memories I'd lost sight of."

"We're glad," Mrs. Darcey replied earnestly, "because you gave us joyful memories as well. You were a bright spot in our lives, Gaby."

"Unruly and unmanageable," Mrs. Fife qualified with gruff affection, "but a bright spot nonetheless."

Gaby's lips curved. "I did cause a great deal of trouble, didn't I?"

"Indeed you did," Averley confirmed. "I can't recall how many search parties were organized to find you."

Thane grinned over the rim of his cup. "I wish I'd been here to see these amazing antics. In contrast, my life at Oxford seems dull and uneventful."

"Uneventfulness can sometimes be a blessing," Gaby returned quietly, more introspective than despondent. "That's something I've learned since childhood."

"More tea, Gaby . . . pardon me, Miss Gaby?" Couling inquired, appearing at her side.

"Yes, thank you, Couling." She held out her cup, nodding her appreciation as he refilled it. "I suppose that discovery is a natural result of growing up," she continued, staring at her saucer but not really seeing it. "We learn that consistency, being safe and loved, is far more inspiring than any unknown adventure. Or perhaps we discover that fact only when—*if*—our foundation is torn away and we're lucky enough to find someone who helps us build a new one."

Silence hung heavy in the air.

With a guilty start, Gaby snapped back to reality, feeling a wave of remorse as she noted all the concerned expressions surrounding her. "Forgive me," she murmured. Inhaling sharply, she berated herself for sounding so dismal. "I didn't mean to go on like that."

"Don't apologize." Aunt Hermione rushed to her defense instantly. "Every word you just said was true. We are all fortunate, each of us who's lucky enough to love and be loved. We must never forget to count our blessings. And you, Gaby, are an incomparable one of those blessings—to me and to all who know you." She reached out, took Gaby's hand in hers.

"As are you," Gaby whispered, her fingers tightening around her aunt's.

"On that note I think we should return to Nevon Manor," Hermione announced, as if some sixth sense had advised her of such. "It's getting late, and Chaunce will worry if dusk arrives without us."

Dusk? Gaby's head came up, and everything inside her tightened as she assessed the first wisps of shadows that danced across Whitshire's lawns.

"Chaunce's worry notwithstanding," Aunt Hermione went on, unaware of Gaby's surge of dread, "we have you to consider, Thane. We've kept you the entire afternoon. You must have a hundred business matters to attend to."

"Not at all," Thane countered. "Actually, other than some correspondence I need to address, I'm free until morning. At which time I do have an appointment—right after breakfast, in fact." He inclined his head in Hermione's direction. "That appointment, incidentally, is with William Delmore of Delmore and Banks."

"The soliciting firm?"

"One and the same."

"You sound surprised. Is it unusual for you to do business with them?"

"Not especially." Thane shrugged. "However, this time I haven't a clue what this business pertains to. According to the initial correspondence I received from Delmore, he and Father were in the midst of a business transaction at the time of Father's death. As a result, my signature is required on some final papers. What that transaction was, I haven't a notion. I suppose I'll have to temper my curiosity until tomorrow. In any case"—Thane changed the subject, waving away the preliminary issue—"I brought it up because when I wrote back to Delmore, agreeing to see him at Whitshire, I mentioned that I'd had occasion to meet and conduct business with a colleague."

Aunt Hermione leaned forward, her eyes glinting with interest. "Bryce?"

A grin. "Bryce. Delmore's response was enthusiastic. In his confirming note he praised Bryce effusively, both his legal skills and his character."

"I'm not surprised," Hermione declared, pride lacing her tone. "Pleased, but not surprised." Her gaze met Thane's. "Thank you for telling me."

With a meaningful look only Gaby and Hermione could understand, Thane replied, "Thank *you* for introducing us. Bryce is indeed an exceptional man."

"Yes, he is," Gaby agreed, struggling to avert her gaze from the setting sun. "I—that is, everyone at Nevon Manor misses him a great deal."

"He'll be back soon," Hermione said with the utmost confidence. "Of that I'm certain." With that, she rose. "Come, Gaby, let's start for home."

Thane helped his aunt to her feet while Averley walked around to assist Gaby. "Your day was enjoyable, then?" he asked her politely.

"Yes. Very. You've all been wonderful."

"I hope we accomplished our goal," Averley added. "As of now I pray all your ghosts have been laid to rest."

"As do I." She gathered up her skirts and drew an unsteady breath, inhaling the cool scents of dusk.

The constriction in her chest intensified.

Would nighttime at Whitshire always affect her so badly? she wondered, fighting off the panic that threatened to obliterate the day's pleasure.

"Is something wrong?" Evidently Averley perceived her tension, and he gripped her elbow as if to offer her support.

"No. I'm just tired. And it's getting late . . ." She broke off, knowing she couldn't begin to explain her increasing dread.

"I'll see that your carriage is brought around at once." It was Couling who spoke, and Gaby looked up in time to see him studying her intently.

"Thank you, Couling. I'd appreciate that."

Ten minutes later, amid a flurry of good-byes, Hermione and a much relieved Gaby climbed into the carriage and were on their way.

A lone figure watched their carriage disappear around the drive. Brow dotted with sweat, the observer retreated into the safety of the trees, mind racing.

Dammit, I didn't learn a bloody thing except that, whatever the hell the brat remembers, it's still inside her head. Even after this whole day, it's still there. But what is it? It can't be insignificant. If it were just memories of the fire, today would have helped. But it didn't. So what's provoking this sleepwalking I'm first hearing about—sleepwalking that apparently started after her last visit here? What is she remembering? Why now? And why is she still drawn to that bloody music box tune?

Stop it, came the silent command. *Gabrielle Denning is secondary—at least for now. I've got a more pressing problem: Delmore. He's coming here, to Whitshire. Why? What does he want?*

A bitter laugh. *That's a stupid question. There's only one reason he'd be coming to see the new duke. Well, that meeting can't take place. I can't allow it. Everything would blow up in my face. I've got to stop him. William Delmore can never reach Whitshire.*

Chapter 11

"DON'T BE DISCOURAGED, MY LADY," CHAUNCE SAID gently, handing Hermione a soothing cup of tea. "It may take time for yesterday's positive effects to show themselves."

With a weariness that was as sweeping as it was unfeigned, Hermione sighed, leaning back against the settee and sipping at the fortifying brew. "Do you really believe that's possible?" she asked, giving Chaunce a hopeful look.

"Of course." Glancing swiftly at the sitting room door to ensure that it was shut, Chaunce placed a comforting hand on Hermione's shoulder. "Miss Gaby had a wonderful time at Whitshire. She spoke of it all evening long. Perhaps she was overtired. Perhaps she had too much excitement for one day. Perhaps one visit is not enough to counter the pain that's causing her to sleepwalk. Any or all of those circumstances could be responsible for last night's episode. We mustn't give up."

Hermione smiled, patting Chaunce's hand. "You know me better than that, my friend. I never give up."

"I'm glad to hear that remains unchanged." Satisfaction laced Chaunce's tone. "In any case, Miss Gaby is sleeping now—restfully. I checked on her a quarter hour ago."

"That blasted woodpecker had best not awaken her," Hermione grumbled, eyeing the clock on the mantel. "It's scarcely eight o'clock. It was half after five when Gaby finally settled down enough to sleep. She needs her rest. With any luck, Screech has given up waiting for her and gone off to cause mischief elsewhere."

"He has," Chaunce assured her. "I personally ousted him from his perch near Miss Gaby's window at six o'clock. He wasn't pleased, but he did comply."

At that, Hermione chuckled—her first real chuckle since the hour preceding dawn, when an inner voice had roused her from slumber and urged her from her bed. And with good reason. She'd slipped into her wrapper and made her way down the hall only to see Chaunce guiding a disoriented and thoroughly distraught Gaby back to her chambers.

Another sleepwalking episode. And after the delightful afternoon they'd spent at Whitshire. It made absolutely no sense.

There had to be a way to end this madness. Something had to help Gaby put this agony behind her.

Something . . . or someone.

"Was there any word from Bryce yesterday?" Hermione demanded abruptly. "Gaby and I were at Whitshire most of the afternoon. Did he make any attempt to contact us?"

Chaunce cleared his throat. "Not directly, no. However, my sources tell me he canceled all his appointments for the latter part of this week, beginning the day after tomorrow. Which leads me to believe—"

"That he's coming home to us," Hermione finished for him. "Oh, Chaunce, that would be the best medicine of all for Gaby. She needs him—even more than she realizes. Even more than *I* realized, until Gaby and I had that little chat the other day. She's falling in love with him, just as I prayed. And he—"

"Is experiencing similar emotions," Chaunce reported triumphantly. "Oh, he's fighting them, to be sure. But without much success. Why, the Wilcox butler tells me that Lord and Lady Wilcox's ball was but halfway over when Mr. Lyndley made a hasty retreat, and that was after spending a good portion of the evening out on the balcony, gazing off into space. Alone, I might add."

"And what of Miss Talbot?" Hermione asked, anticipation dancing in her eyes.

"Delivered to her parents' home unfashionably early. Just as she was on the nights of the ballet, the theater, and, of course, the symphony."

"Excellent." Satisfaction laced Hermione's tone. "Why, I'm feeling stronger already." Her smile faded. "I just wish I knew what was causing these dreadful episodes of Gaby's. Last night was heartbreaking. It took your efforts *and* mine to stop her tears and calm her down enough to sleep. It was as if she were driven by demons, determined to rush from the manor and undo the horrors of that fire. Oh, Chaunce, what if Dr. Briers is wrong? What if the visit to Whitshire didn't help? What will we do?"

"We mustn't think that way, my lady. It's far too soon to reach such a conclusion. Besides, even if Dr. Briers is wrong, we still have our prayers. We also have a splendid hero about to ride to Miss Gaby's rescue."

Hermione nodded, interlacing her fingers and pressing them to her lips. "You're right. I truly believe that." Her gaze drifted toward the window. "I only wish Bryce would hurry."

Bryce couldn't shake the feeling that he was needed.

Frowning, he paused before the offices that bore the sign "Delmore & Banks," instinctively glancing up and down the street as if he'd been verbally summoned.

All that greeted his perusal was the customary stream of businessmen who strolled up and down this busy section of Fleet Street.

Straightening his waistcoat, Bryce continued on his way, veering up the path to the solicitors' office door. It had to be his imagination—a feeling aroused by his unending worry over the residents of Nevon Manor. Well, that would soon cease to be an issue. After today's meeting with Banks, and the next day and a half's frenzied schedule of appointments—all of which added up to four days of work condensed into less than two—he would leave London and return to Nevon Manor.

For more reasons than he cared to ponder.

Stepping inside the waiting area, Bryce turned to approach the clerk's desk, intending to announce himself and ask if Mr. Banks was ready to begin. Abruptly he halted.

Something was very wrong.

An air of panic permeated the room, although the waiting area itself was devoid of people—unnaturally deserted, given that it was nearing one o'clock. Just beyond the outer office, however, rumbled a blend of distraught voices punctuated by a flurry of motion, which Bryce identified as coming from Mr. Banks's office.

He turned his head for a closer look.

Hovering in the doorway, grim-faced and intense, were two men whose uniforms clearly proclaimed them members of the London Metropolitan Police. One of them was writing rapidly in a notebook while the other directed a series of questions, obviously of a grave nature, at Banks and his clerk, both of whom were white-faced and visibly shaken, the clerk looking all the world as if he might swoon.

Whatever was transpiring, it was serious.

"Frederick?" Bryce addressed Banks quietly. "May I be of assistance?"

The bald solicitor caught sight of Bryce and beckoned him forward. "It's William," he announced tersely, his voice trembling as he spoke the given name of his partner, William Delmore. "He's been murdered."

"Murdered?" Bryce recoiled as if he'd been struck. "When?"

"Sometime this morning. The police found his body. They just arrived—" Banks broke off, pulling out a handkerchief and mopping at his forehead.

"May I ask who you are, sir?" one of the policemen asked Bryce.

"My name is Bryce Lyndley. I'm a barrister. Mr. Banks and I had an appointment at one o'clock." Bryce's mind was racing. "How did this happen? Who would do such a thing?"

"It looks like the work of a highwayman, sir. There was evidence of a robbery; Mr. Delmore's timepiece and pound notes were missing."

"A highwayman—in broad daylight? Where did this occur?"

"A passerby found Mr. Delmore's carriage abandoned about twenty miles from here, in Hertford, where he'd driven for an early morning meeting. The local constable was summoned and began a search. He found Mr. Delmore's body in a section of woods not far from the roadside. He'd been shot, then apparently dragged into the trees, divested of his valuables, and abandoned."

"Hertford," Bryce repeated. A sudden inexplicable sense of foreboding clenched his gut, and he turned to Banks. "Who was Delmore going to see?"

"The Duke of Whitshire," Banks replied, naming one of the two estates Bryce had hoped not to hear. "This nightmare occurred about two miles from the duke's manor."

"Dammit." Bryce sucked in his breath. "Does Thane know about this?"

"I don't know. I suppose so. Word must have spread through half of Hertford by now." Banks continued to mop his brow, babbling on in a vague, disoriented manner. "That's right. You're acquainted with Whitshire. I remember that the duke mentioned you in his last note to William. Something about conducting business together."

"Yes," Bryce confirmed tersely. "Frederick, was William carrying an unusually large sum of money?"

A pause. "Not to my knowledge, no."

"This makes no sense." Bryce turned toward the older police officer. "Mr. Delmore's carriage is modest, with no family crest that would lead someone to mistakenly believe he was a nobleman. Why would a highwayman choose to rob him when the Duke of Whitshire lived just down the way? Surely it would be more prudent to wait for the duke's carriage to pass and be assured of a more profitable haul."

The officer frowned. "That's what we're trying to determine, Mr. Lyndley." He folded his arms across his chest. "You say you know the duke?"

"Yes. As Mr. Banks just mentioned, I've had occasion to work with His Grace. I also handle the legal affairs of his aunt, Lady Hermione Nevon." Bryce's mind was racing, an inner voice screaming that something didn't fit. "Frederick, what business did William have with Thane?"

Banks pressed his damp palms together. "It pertained to the late duke's estate. You know I can't divulge specifics without Whitshire's permission. But I will tell you the matter involved only the signing of documents and not the exchange of money, at least not at this point."

"Where are the documents William was conveying to Whitshire?"

"I have them," Banks responded. "They were retrieved by the police, along with William's personal effects—" His voice cracked, and he looked away, damp-eyed.

"Would you object if I took those papers to Thane?" Bryce pressed. "I give you my word that I will place them directly in his hands without opening them."

"We intend to do that, Mr. Lyndley," the younger police officer inserted. "I'm as interested as you in hearing what the duke has to say about those documents."

Bryce's head whipped about, and he regarded the two policemen intently. "I'm sure you are," he conceded, recognizing that a different tactic was needed. "Let me ask you this—would you object to my accompanying you to Whitshire? Given that I'm well acquainted with both the duke and Mr. Delmore, I might be able to help you determine if there is a connection between Mr. Delmore's death and whatever business he meant to conduct with His Grace."

The younger fellow glanced at his partner.

The older man shrugged. "It's fine with me, although I personally think it's a waste of your time. With the missing pocket watch and money, this looks like a clear case of theft. Still, it can't hurt to investigate every angle. The only problem is, your schedule might not make it possible for you to leave London on such short notice; we mean to be on our way to Hertford within the hour. We have a few more questions for Mr. Banks and his clerk, after which we'll be heading for the railroad station."

"I have an idea," Bryce interjected quickly. "I'll cancel my appointments, pack a few things, and be back here in an hour. I had plans to visit Whitshire and Nevon Manor for several days at week's end; I'll simply rearrange those plans and leave today. This way I can escort you to Whitshire in my carriage and you'll only have to take the railroad one way."

"Sounds good to me."

"Fine." Bryce glanced at Banks. "You'll give those papers to these officers?"

"Of course." Banks clasped Bryce's hand, his unfocused gaze a clear indication he was still in shock. "Thank you, Bryce. I don't seem to be able to think straight." An unsteady pause. "William and I have been partners for over twenty-five years, and I just can't believe . . ." His voice trailed off.

"I understand." Bryce felt pretty shaken himself. "I'll do everything I can to help."

He went back to his office just long enough to dispatch messages canceling his next two days' appointments—and to send a brief note of explanation to Lucinda. He told her only that Delmore had been murdered and that, as a result of this sudden and unexpected tragedy, Lady Nevon required his counsel, as did her nephew.

As he sealed the note, Bryce's lips twisted into a wry grin. He wasn't worried about Lucinda's reaction. Nothing, he mused, would heighten her satisfaction over the fact that he'd been retained by Lady Hermione Nevon more than the prospect of his being retained by the Duke of Whitshire. Consequently any inconvenience spawned by this unexpected trip to Hertford would be viewed by Lucinda as being well worth the nuisance.

Making a brief stop at his residence, Bryce tossed a few things into a bag—including the two pages of answers he'd provided to Peter's questions—scooped up Sunburst, and left.

Fifty minutes later, he arrived back at Delmore & Banks, and ten minutes after that, he, the officers, and the documents were on their way to Hertford.

Couling's eyes widened when he opened Whitshire's front door late that afternoon to find two uniformed police officers on the threshold, flanking Bryce.

Quickly the butler recovered himself, admitting the three gentlemen. "Mr. Lyndley, is His Grace expecting you?"

"No, Couling, he isn't." Bryce indicated his companions. "But this is a matter of some urgency, so would you please advise the duke that we're here?"

"Certainly." Without another word, Couling turned on his heel and complied.

Not three minutes later Thane himself came striding down the hall. "Bryce." His greeting was strained, his ashen expression suggesting that he had indeed heard the news about Delmore. "Come in." His gaze shifted to the police, his question terse and to the point. "Is this about the murder of Mr. Delmore?"

"Yes, Your Grace, it is." The older man cleared his throat.

"Thane, this is Officer Dawes," Bryce said, offering the names he had learned en route to Whitshire. "And this is Officer Webster. They're investigating Delmore's death. I had an appointment with Banks earlier this afternoon. That's how I learned what had happened—and who Delmore was en route to see when he was killed. I took the liberty of accompanying Dawes and Webster to Whitshire. I hope you don't mind."

"Mind? I'm relieved." Thane looked visibly so. "Gentlemen, we can talk in my study." He led the way, closing the door firmly behind them. "Can I offer you anything?"

"No, sir." Dawes shook his head and extracted his notebook. "We apologize for bothering you. From what we can see, this was a clear case of robbery. Still, we have to make sure, so would you mind telling us what Delmore wanted to see you about?"

Thane frowned. "I'm not sure I can help you much on that score. All Delmore's note said was that it concerned a business transaction my father had initiated before his death and that my signature was needed on some papers."

"Then these must be those papers." Dawes produced the sealed envelope. Again he shifted uncomfortably. "Would you object to our remaining while you opened them?"

"Of course not." Thane tore open the seal and slid out the papers. He scanned them, his expression growing more and more puzzled as he read. "According to these documents, Father was in the process of selling a yacht he commissioned years ago. Mr. Delmore needed my signature to finalize the sale."

"And does that disturb you?"

"Disturb me? No. Frankly, I didn't even know Father owned a yacht; but then again, I didn't know the half of what my father possessed." His gaze flickered over Bryce. "I'm only now learning just how vast his assets were. But if you're asking me if the papers look out of order—no, I don't think so. Bryce?" He offered the pages to his brother.

Bryce pored over the document. "This appears to be a standard sales contract. The late duke had clearly decided to dispose of his yacht—due to illness, I would guess, judging from the recent date on these papers. His asking price seems more than reasonable—generous in fact—as do his terms. Delmore himself was the buyer, whether as a personal purchase or a temporary holding, these documents don't specify. The point is that at this time no other party was involved."

Handing the papers back to Thane, Bryce shrugged. "This is hardly a transaction involving enormous sums of money. If I had to speculate, I'd say that Delmore wanted to hold this meeting today as much for you as for himself. He probably assumed you'd want to tie up all the loose ends of your father's estate as soon as possible. So he waited a respectable period of time following the late duke's death, then contacted you about the completion of this deal."

"So you see nothing that would link today's murder to that document?" Dawes asked.

"No, I don't."

"Well, that's that," Dawes pronounced, shutting his notebook and shoving it into his coat pocket. "Mr. Delmore's visit here was evidently a routine and unrelated event, making his murder an unfortunate case of being in the wrong place at the wrong time." He gestured to his partner. "Let's be on our way, Webster. We've troubled the duke long enough." A quick glance at Bryce. "You'll be staying here, Mr. Lyndley?"

"Yes." Bryce was reexamining the papers, verifying that he'd missed nothing unusual.

If there was something questionable here, he sure as hell couldn't detect it.

Then why did his instincts scream otherwise?

"I'll have my driver take you both to the railroad station," Thane told the policemen.

"Thank you, sir," Webster replied. "We'd appreciate that."

Thane summoned Couling, who had the carriage brought around immediately.

Minutes later Dawes and Webster took their leave, shutting the study door in their wake.

"I can't thank you enough for coming," Thane told Bryce the instant they were alone. He crossed over to the sideboard, poured two goblets of brandy, and handed one to his brother.

"I'm pleased you feel that way." Bryce gave up his scrutiny before lowering himself into a chair and taking a healthy swallow of brandy. "I was a bit concerned you'd think I was intruding. But when I heard Delmore was on his way to Whitshire, my thoughts went immediately to you. And to Hermione, as well. Does she know about the murder?"

"Yes." Thane rubbed the back of his neck, sinking wearily onto the sofa. "I notified her as soon as I heard. As you'd expect, she was distraught. But I had to tell her. The roads are clearly unsafe for travel."

"Fortunately, the residents of Nevon Manor seldom leave the estate," Bryce reasoned aloud.

"Seldom, yes." Thane scowled. "The frightening and ironic thing is that yesterday was a major exception to that rule."

"How so?"

"Hermione and Gabrielle rode to Whitshire yesterday afternoon."

That brought Bryce up short. "Did you say Gabrielle was here?"

"Yes." Thane rolled his goblet between his palms, gazing steadily at his brother. "I realize how surprising that sounds, given how violently she reacted after her last visit." Assessing Bryce's startled expression, he added, "I know about the sleepwalking incidents—as well as the fact that you rescued Gabrielle from harm on two occasions. Hermione told me." With that, Thane explained Dr. Briers's suggestion and Gabrielle's decision to give it a try. "She was very courageous," he concluded. "When she arrived at Whitshire, her nerves were clearly frayed. Yet she pressed on anyway."

"How did the visit go?" Bryce demanded, moving to the edge of his seat.

"Very well, from what I could determine. The staff worked hard to make Gabrielle's day a happy one. Not that it was a difficult thing to do, nor that they objected to doing it. Clearly they all adored Gabrielle as a child. Their stories made me wish I'd been here to see that little imp constantly causing trouble, treading underfoot, hiding in countless unknown places." A chuckle. "In any case, the staff's efforts seemed to pay off. Gabrielle was relaxed, smiling—not to the extent that she is when she's at Nevon Manor, of course, but close." A flicker of worry crossed Thane's face. "Until the sun began to set. Then she seemed to tense up a bit. Hermione sensed it at once and whisked her off."

"I have to make sure she's all right," Bryce decided, coming to his feet. "Between yesterday's visit to Whitshire and, on its heels, this appalling murder, I'm sure Gabrielle is extremely unnerved." He set down his glass. "Hermione, too, for that matter." He shot Thane a quizzical look. "Would you object if I rode there now? I could come back as soon as I made sure . . ."

Thane was waving Bryce's offer away, standing up and crossing the room as he did. "No. Don't come back. Stay at Nevon Manor. From what I hear, you have an uncanny way of soothing the residents there. And Lord knows they'll need soothing, given what's happened. Besides, I have a stack of papers to go through. I'll spend the evening clearing my desk, then ride to Nevon Manor first thing in the morning. How would that be?"

"Excellent. At that time we can continue this discussion about your father's yacht."

"Something about that deal is bothering you, isn't it?" Thane was reaching into his desk drawer as he spoke.

"Yes. The problem is, I'm not sure what. Other than the fact that you didn't know of the boat's existence."

Thane stood, a dark object in his hand. "As we're both aware, there are a great many things about my father I didn't know." He extended his arm, offering Bryce the pistol he held. "Take this with you. None of us should travel unarmed until that highwayman is caught."

"Agreed." Bryce accepted the weapon. "That highwayman—or whoever it was who committed this crime."

Chaunce abandoned his post the instant he saw the long-awaited carriage round the drive. Hurrying down the hall, he flung open the door to the sitting room where Gaby and Hermione were taking their tea.

"Yes, Chaunce?" Hermione started, her pallor intensifying as she assessed Chaunce's uncustomary lack of composure. Given this morning's distressing news—which she'd shared only with Chaunce—his atypical behavior struck an ominous chord in her heart. "Has something else happened?" Hermione cast an anxious glance at Gaby, who'd been kept uninformed about the murder because she'd had such a distressing, sleepless night. Her drawn expression and lack of color supported that decision twofold.

"No, madam." Instantly, Chaunce read Hermione's mind and reassured her, emphasizing the positive nature of his intrusion by recovering his composure and clasping his hands behind his back. "Or rather, yes, something has happened, but certainly nothing upsetting. Quite the contrary, in fact. I wanted you to know that—"

"He's here!" Peter interrupted to announce. Rushing past the sitting room, his limp nearly indiscernible, he poked his head in, eyes shining as he elaborated on his announcement. "I just saw his carriage coming up the drive! He's back!"

With that, he disappeared, his footsteps echoing toward the entranceway door, along with his repeated calls of, "He's here! He's back!"

Doors slammed throughout the manor. Hurried footsteps echoed from every direction, converging in the hall that led to the entranceway door.

Hermione rose, staring at Chaunce with wide, hopeful eyes.

"Yes, my lady," the butler confirmed with a smile. "It is indeed Mr. Lyndley. I saw his approaching carriage myself."

"Thanks heavens," Hermione murmured, nearly sagging with relief, then recovering herself and moving purposefully toward the door. "He's earlier than expected, but given the circumstances, I can understand why he would alter his schedule and—" She halted, turning to cast another anxious glance in Gaby's direction.

She needn't have worried. It was obvious Gaby had paid no attention to her aunt's words, if in fact she had even heard them. Gone was the vague, anxious look in her eyes, the ashen cast to her skin. Abruptly, her cheeks were flushed with color, her eyes aglow with anticipation. She came to her feet, meeting Hermione's gaze, excitement clearly singing through her like a beautiful melody.

With a dazzling smile she hurried toward the doorway.

"Slowly, love," Hermione suggested, her lips twitching as she held up a detaining palm. "Give everyone else a chance to greet him. Save the best for last."

Gaby paused, her expression quizzical. "You think I should stay inside?"

"Definitely not. I think you should race outside—eventually. For now I think you should walk only as far as the vestibule near the entranceway. Then count to one hundred. At that point I suspect you'll see the perfect opportunity to go out and greet Bryce in exactly the way your heart tells you to."

"But—"

"Trust me, Gaby," Hermione said, caressing her niece's cheek. "Do as I say."

With that, she turned, giving Chaunce a triumphant nod, then hurrying forward as he held the door open for her to pass.

She had work to do—namely to provide Bryce with a proper welcome.

And to arrange the proper order in which that welcome would occur.

Bryce had scarcely climbed down from his carriage when the front door of the manor was flung wide and Peter emerged, leading Jane, Lily, Henry, and Charles on a wild rush toward him amid a chorus of "Mr. Lyndley! Mr. Lyndley!"

Close behind were Cook and Mrs. Gordon, both beaming as they hastened down the stairs and waved their hellos—Mrs. Gordon so excited she forgot herself, trod directly through the patch of dirt alongside the drive, and when she realized what she'd done, shrugged it off with a total lack of interest.

After that, the entranceway door seemed to explode from its hinges as the entire staff of Nevon Manor spilled out, shouting their greetings and waving. Wilson emerged from the garden, wiping mud from his face as he strained to see what was happening. Realization struck, and he abandoned his work and sprinted toward the drive at a dead run, nearly colliding with Goodsmith, who'd charged from the carriage house, determinedly trying to fit the buttons of his uniform into the correct casings as he dashed forward.

Bryce was speechless as he watched the scene unfolding before him. Too overcome for words, he merely stared from one welcoming face to another, absorbing their genuine pleasure at his return and for the first time admitting to himself just how much he'd missed the wonderful residents of Nevon Manor.

Gaby was right, he perceived in a flash of insight. It wasn't just *they* who needed *him*. *He* needed *them* as well.

"You brought Sunburst!" It was Lily who shattered his introspection, exclaiming aloud as Sunburst poked his head out of the carriage, curious about the cause of the commotion.

"I did indeed," Bryce affirmed. "He couldn't wait to see you."

As if to refute Bryce's statement, the kitten cringed at the sight of the growing crowd and, reconsidering his original intentions, desperately tried to retreat into the quiet safety of the carriage. But before he could hide, the girls snatched him up, hugging him and promising him a reunion with his brothers and sisters. Evidently the combination of affection and promises worked, because in no time Sunburst was purring contentedly in Lily's arms.

"Mr. Lyndley!" Flushed with exertion, Peter pushed his way forward. "I've taken really good care of your books. And I've even tried to read some of them."

"Excellent." Bryce laid a palm on the boy's shoulder. "You and I will have to find time for a legal discussion. A long one, I suspect, given that I've written out all the answers to your questions on the Elementary Education Act."

"Really?" Peter beamed. "Can we do it this evening?"

"I don't see why not." Bryce patted his coat pocket. "We'll set a time to meet right after dinner. I'll jot it down in my new writing pad so I won't forget."

The elation in the lad's eyes was humbling.

"Welcome home, Bryce." Hermione descended the steps with all the regal grace of a queen, hands extended to seize Bryce's. "You've been deeply missed."

"As have you," Bryce answered, bending to kiss her cheek. "Are you all right?" he asked worriedly.

"Now I am, yes."

"Thane said he spoke with you. Have you told the staff and . . . ?"

"No," she replied with a quick shake of her head. "Let's discuss the matter when we're alone." Abruptly she paused, darting a brief look over her shoulder. Then, with a determined lift of her chin, she backed away, clapping her hands for attention. "Everyone, please listen. Let's allow poor Mr. Lyndley to settle in. We'll have plenty of time to chat with him later." Hermione's probing gaze assessed Bryce as the staff immediately, albeit reluctantly, filed back into the manor. "We will, won't we?"

"Yes, Hermione," he replied adamantly. "We will."

"Splendid." She nodded, turning to Chaunce, who was now beside her, extending a personal greeting to Bryce. "Will you arrange for Bryce's bags to be taken upstairs?"

They exchanged glances.

"Certainly, madam," Chaunce assured her. "You

join the others inside. I'll make sure Mr. Lyndley's room is properly prepared. Then I shall see to his bags." He studied the area surrounding the drive, saw that it was now quiet, as the last of the children—and Sunburst—were making their way into the house.

Satisfied, he turned and offered Hermione his arm. "I'll escort you up the stairs."

"I can do that," Bryce proposed.

"No, no." Hermione had already gripped Chaunce's elbow and was retracing her steps. "You wait here while we ready things for your arrival."

"Very well. But just tell me, how is—"

"We'll talk in a few minutes. Be patient." With that, Hermione entered the manor with Chaunce, muttering something that sounded—at least from where Bryce stood, like ". . . both so impatient."

He frowned, wishing he'd had the chance to ask about Gaby and wondering why whenever he arrived at this house he felt as if he'd walked into the middle of some intricate scheme.

A flash of color caught his eye, and he looked up at the open doorway to see Gaby hovering on the threshold, watching him with a kind of wary uncertainty. "Hello, Bryce," she said, giving him a tentative smile.

"Gaby." He was taken aback by the surge of emotion that knotted his chest, and he moved forward, not even realizing he was doing so. "I'm so bloody glad to see you. I just couldn't shake the feeling that somehow you needed me and I wasn't here to—" He broke off, realizing how absurd he sounded.

Evidently Gaby didn't agree. All hesitation having vanished, she gathered up her lime-green skirts and flew down the stairs, not stopping until she stood directly before him. "I missed you," she confessed softly.

Bryce didn't answer. He simply reacted. Unthinking, he reached for her, drawing her against him and pressing his lips into the shining crown of her hair. "And I missed you," he told her fervently.

She tilted back her head, those cornflower-blue eyes that had haunted his thoughts now scrutinizing him thoroughly. "Did you?"

"Yes."

An impish grin. "Good."

Studying her beautiful features, Bryce could make out the dark shadows of fatigue beneath her eyes, the lines of tension etched about her mouth. What had caused them? he wondered. Was it the sleepwalking or the news of Delmore's death? He didn't dare ask, just in case Hermione's decision to remain silent about Delmore's murder extended to Gaby.

Gaby startled Bryce out of his thoughts by saying, "You kissed me good-bye. Won't you now kiss me hello?"

A spontaneous chuckle rumbled in his chest. "I thought I just did."

"On my head? That wasn't a kiss. Even *I* know that," she returned in a teasing voice. "Oh, I realize you hate to act impulsively. Still, you did so once. Couldn't you make just one more exception?"

Apparently he could, because what he did next came from anywhere but his mind. He framed her face between his palms, lowered his head, and covered her mouth with his.

This kiss was slow, deliberate, possessing none of the abruptness or uncertainty that had tinged its predecessor. Beginning as a tender caress, it soon intensified into something more, something compelling and heated and searching. Wordlessly, Bryce drew Gaby into his arms, deepening the kiss until he felt her lips soften, part, open beneath his gentle pressure.

His tongue claimed hers, and with a shivering sigh Gaby pressed closer, responding to his unspoken demand, giving him her tongue and taking his in return.

For one brief instant reality receded, hovering in some remote part of Bryce's brain, allowing him to indulge in this totally irrational, wondrous moment. He molded Gaby against him, tangling his hands in her hair and kissing her with a desperate yearning that seemed to swell rather than diminish, spreading through him like a raw, bottomless ache.

An ache that throbbed not only through his soul but through his loins as well.

That awareness brought sanity back with a crashing blow.

With staunch determination, Bryce tore his mouth away, breathing unsteadily as he stared into Gaby's dazed eyes. "My beautiful Wonderland," he muttered, his thumbs caressing her cheekbones. "What comes over me when I'm with you?"

"I don't know, but I hope it never stops," she whispered.

Bryce drank in her delicate features, flushed from the impact of their kiss. "Were my actions impulsive enough for you?" he heard himself ask, stunned to hear his own husky, teasing tone, bewilderedly contemplating this total stranger who seemed to be living inside him.

Gaby looked neither shocked nor amused. "They were perfect," she assured him softly. "Absolutely, utterly perfect." She stood on tiptoe, brushed her lips across his chin. "You've given me something new to dream about."

Her assertion brought him back to reality. "Have you been sleeping enough to dream?" Bryce's question was gentle but direct.

With a sigh, Gaby stepped away, her lashes fanning her cheeks. "There have been some . . . developments since you left for London."

"I know about your visit to Whitshire." At Gaby's puzzled look, he carefully added, "I stopped at Whitshire on my way to Nevon Manor. I had some business to review with Thane. He told me what Dr.

Briers had suggested—and what you attempted. I'm very proud of you. Was the visit successful? Did it assuage your fears and stop the sleepwalking, at least thus far?"

Gaby swallowed. "No. Last night was a horror, the images more vivid than ever before. It was excruciating. Even after Chaunce managed to awaken me, I couldn't seem to break free of that gnawing sense of terror. Neither he nor Aunt Hermione could help me . . . and they're both so tired . . . I'm so worried about their health, especially Aunt Hermione's—" Gaby's voice broke.

"I'm here now." Bryce tugged Gaby into the circle of his arms yet again, this time offering her his strength as a balm to her pain. Dammit, his instincts had been right. She *had* needed him. So had Hermione and Chaunce. Well, this time he wouldn't abandon them.

"We will combat this, Gaby," he vowed. "I promise you we will." His gaze took in the sky, noted that the day was fast slipping away. And he had much to accomplish before he posted himself outside Gaby's door tonight, which he fully intended to do. But first he had to speak with Hermione, learn everything about Gaby's experience at Whitshire and the ensuing sleepwalking episode, and touch on some of his questions about Delmore's business dealings with Richard Rowland, the late Duke of Wiltshire. As for today's murder, it was clear Hermione hadn't told her niece anything. And seeing the state Gaby was in, he could well understand why.

"Let's go inside," he suggested gently. "I must spend some time with Hermione before dinner. Afterward Peter and I have an appointment to go over some legal terms, and then I want to make sure Sunburst is behaving himself, not destroying what little of Lily's room Crumpet left undamaged. Once that's done, you and I will sit down in the music room and talk. All right?"

Gaby leaned back, studying his face. "Bryce, you don't have to—"

"I don't *have* to. I *want* to. Besides"—he traced the bridge of Gaby's nose with his forefinger—"I want to tell you all about the concert I attended—and about the one I mean for *you* to attend."

That had the desired effect, bringing a sparkle of excitement to her eyes. "Really? Have you thought of a way?"

"As a matter of fact, yes." Bryce cleared his throat. "How is Marion faring these days? Is she any steadier on her feet?"

"I wouldn't know," Gaby replied, a hint of a smile curving her lips. "Her feet haven't touched the floor in two days—since she and Goodsmith became officially betrothed."

"Excellent. That's just what I was hoping to hear."

"You knew about the betrothal?" Gaby blinked in surprise.

"Hermione mentioned it as forthcoming, yes."

Puzzlement supplanted surprise. "I'm glad you share their joy, just as the rest of us do. Still, I'm confused. What has Marion's steadiness to do with my attending the symphony?"

"I'll tell you later." Bryce caught Gaby's arm and led her toward the manor. "After dinner."

Gaby halted in her tracks. "You intend to keep me in suspense?"

A grin. "Initially I didn't. But now that I consider how delightful the anticipation will be—for both of us—I've changed my mind." Bryce's grin widened. "Something that impulsive people often do."

Their shared laughter echoed up the drive.

At the morning room window, Hermione released the drape she'd pulled aside so she could witness the reunion taking place before her delighted eyes. "Do you know, Chaunce," she mused aloud, turning around to gaze up at him. "I had originally thought a summer wedding would be lovely. But I'm beginning to think late spring would be even more spectacular. What do you think?"

Chaunce gave an unequivocal nod. "Definitely spring. In fact, given that rather extreme show of affection, I should think mid-spring rather than late."

Hermione laughed. "Don't be so priggish, my friend. It was only a kiss. A rather wholehearted one, to be sure, but a kiss nonetheless. I wouldn't worry about Bryce's intentions. He's nothing if not a gentleman. Once he recognizes his feelings for Gaby as what they are, he'll do the honorable thing. Yes, I quite agree. Mid-spring it is. The end of May, perhaps. I'll begin compiling the guest list this very night. Of course we'll keep the ceremony private and the reception small and intimate, given that this will all be occurring just a few months after Richard's death. Still, I'm determined not to let protocol stand in the way of Gaby and Bryce's future. What's more, I refuse to allow my brother to thwart Bryce's happiness ever, ever again." With that, Hermione gave a dismissive wave of her hand, her eyes growing misty with emotion. "Oh, Chaunce, I can hardly wait to see Gaby in her bridal gown."

"Nor can I." A glimmer of amusement flickered across the butler's face. "For the time being, however, might I suggest you temper your exhilaration a bit? With all due respect, you are allegedly weak and ailing—a condition that must persist until this union is a fait accompli. Right now you look more like a young girl on the verge of her own coming-out than like an elderly widow clinging to life—a remarkable feat, might I add, given the precious few hours' sleep you had last night. Nevertheless, I suspect Mr. Lyndley *is* on his way in to see you, and I don't think he expects to find you quite so jovial, or so lovely."

"Why, thank you, Chaunce." A becoming blush stained Hermione's cheeks. "What a charming thing to say. But of course you're right. I must look suitably depleted." Her exuberance faded. "Which, in light of this morning's tragedy, won't be difficult, even though Bryce arrived in time to soften the shock." Abruptly she raised her chin, determination emanating from every fiber of her being. "No matter how trying today's events have been, they don't alter the fact that Bryce is home and that he and Gaby belong together. I shall therefore give silent thanks to the heavens and pray we can soon celebrate the achievement of our goal."

Gathering up her skirts, she moved swiftly toward the door. "I'll be in my chambers, Chaunce. Give me five minutes to ready myself. Then you may show Bryce up."

Chapter 12

"So you're saying that Gaby was fine yesterday until it began to grow dark. Then her apprehension returned."

Pacing about his aunt's sitting room, Bryce summed up all Hermione had just recounted.

"Exactly." Hermione leaned back against the settee cushions, answering Bryce's questions in a worried voice that was totally unfeigned. "It was as if something came over her the instant she realized night was coming. We all sensed it: Thane, Averley, even Couling. I couldn't wait to get her home."

"And then she endured another horrible night—a *more* horrible night, according to Gaby. Dammit." Bryce sliced the air with his palm. "We've got to help her. I just don't know how. She mentioned to me that last night she experienced more vivid snatches of memory than ever before, which I have to assume were brought on by her trip to Whitshire. So do we abandon Dr. Briers's notion entirely and keep her away from the estate?"

"I don't know, Bryce." Hermione sighed. "That

visit seemed like such a good idea. It *was* a good idea—until the end. You should have seen her: laughing and romping about the grounds as she relived the happy moments of her childhood."

"Until she realized dusk was falling." Pensively, Bryce rubbed his jaw. "I'm not a physician, Hermione, but common sense tells me Dr. Briers was right. The visit to Whitshire did do Gaby some good. It just didn't address the problem. In fact, I'm beginning to think we're approaching this whole dilemma backwards."

"Meaning?"

"Gaby's sleepwalking episodes are happening for a reason. Keeping her away from Whitshire obviously didn't solve the problem, nor did countering her bad memories with good ones. Maybe what Gaby needs is not to silence the memories but to draw them out." With that, Bryce nodded, suddenly quite sure of the direction in which he was headed. "The first night I spotted Gaby sleepwalking and took her to her room, she was physically hurt and emotionally overwrought. But little by little she began telling me details of the night of the fire: how she'd left her bed to check on the robins and soothe them with the notes of 'Für Elise,' how she'd eventually sought shelter in the shed, how she'd awakened to see flames leaping around her, and how desperately she'd tried to get to her parents. Forcing herself to talk about all this was painful, yes, but at the same time it seemed to give her a measure of peace. Maybe these worsening episodes are a sign that she needs to bring to the surface the rest of her pain and contend with it. And maybe it's our job to help her do just that."

With each passing word of Bryce's theory, Hermione had sat up straighter, her eyes now wide with wonder and disbelief. "Gaby spoke to you of that night?" she breathed in amazement. "To my knowledge, she's never confided those details to anyone. Not even to me. Heaven knows I've tried, delved as gently as I could. But to no avail. She simply refused to discuss it. Yet she told you."

"It wasn't a matter of trusting me over her family," Bryce countered swiftly, misinterpreting Hermione's reaction as one of hurt. "Surely you know how much Gaby adores you, but she's worried sick about burdening you with more than you're able to withstand. And—"

"Bryce, stop." Hermione held up a deterring—and trembling—palm. "I'm so relieved, so grateful, that Gaby finally spoke to someone. And I'm overjoyed that someone was you." Wetting her lips, Hermione paused, clearly bringing herself under control. "So she'd gone to tend to some robins. How very like Gaby. And how wonderfully ironic that because she cared for others, her life was spared." A determined lift of her chin. "In any case, you're right. Given what you've just told me, it's clear that Gaby needs to give voice to whatever she's remembering, the anguish those memories incite. You're also right that I'm not the one to provide that much-needed ear. She's too preoccupied with my failing health."

"An obstacle that doesn't apply to me," Bryce pointed out with a meaningful look. "Thus, it's my responsibility to see this plan through."

Hermione's brows rose ever so slightly. "How do you propose to do that?"

"By taking over for you and Chaunce tonight. You're both exhausted; Lord knows you need the relief. I'll stand vigil outside Gaby's room. Should she experience another sleepwalking episode, I'll deal with it. Perhaps when the memories and the panic are fresh, I can coax them out. Maybe that will enable her to make peace with them."

"And how do you suggest we explain this to Gaby? She'll be expecting Chaunce at his customary station outside her door."

"No she won't. I've already told her I'd be taking

over for Chaunce, to give you both an opportunity to rest."

"Did you?" Another lift of Hermione's brows. "And she was amenable to the idea?"

"Yes." Bryce cleared his throat. "As I said, she's very worried about your well-being—yours and Chaunce's."

Silently Hermione gazed at her nephew. "You care a great deal for Gaby, don't you?"

A prolonged pause. Then: "Yes, I do. I also feel for her, comprehend at least some of the internal anguish she's struggling to combat. Making peace with the past can seem like an insurmountable challenge—especially in Gaby's case, where the past consisted of losing her parents to a violent death."

"Or in your case, where the past consisted of losing your identity and having your entire foundation snatched away," Hermione added softly.

Bryce's expression remained impassive. "We're not talking about me. We're talking about Gaby—and the best way to help her. Do you agree with my reasoning? Will you let me take over as tonight's sentry?"

A weary sigh. "I do and I will. My only prayer is that your plan works. Frankly I'm not sure just how much more Gaby can take."

"You didn't tell her about Delmore, did you?" Bryce asked quietly, shifting to the other topic that was nagging at him.

"No." Hermione massaged her temples. "I decided to keep the news from her, as I did from the rest of the family. I don't customarily shield Gaby as fiercely as I do the others. But this case is different, given the magnitude of the crime and the severity of Gaby's current state. I know my niece. News like this would devastate her. It wouldn't matter that she wasn't acquainted with Mr. Delmore. The idea of a man being murdered so close to home—worse, a fine man, with a wife and a family, now left alone—Gaby would have been crushed." Hermione inclined her head at Bryce. "I suppose you think I'm foolish, trying to protect my family to this extent. You're a barrister. You believe in facing life's harsh realities. Well, I don't—at least not in all cases. And when it comes to my family, I safeguard them with every fiber of my being. I always will."

Warmth softened Bryce's voice. "I, better than anyone, know that. And you're wrong, Hermione. I don't think you're foolish. I think you're every bit the grand lady I perceived when I was a boy. As for Gaby, you made the right decision. She's in no condition to deal with news of a murder."

Hermione's lips trembled. "Thank you for your faith."

"I seem to be acquiring a fair amount of that these days," Bryce murmured, half to himself. Snapping back to the issue of Delmore, he folded his arms across his chest. "Hermione, do you know anything about a yacht your brother commissioned years ago?"

A quizzical pucker formed between her brows. "A yacht? What yacht?"

"One he was planning to sell to Delmore." Bryce filled Hermione in on all the missing details he'd learned at Whitshire, from the purpose of Delmore's visit to the contents of the document delivered to Thane. "I wonder if there could be any connection between Delmore's destination this morning and the fact that he was murdered. Frankly, I find the idea of a highwayman committing this crime to be a bit far-fetched."

"Far-fetched—why? Thane is a very wealthy man, and the road leading to Whitshire is heavily treed and private. Why wouldn't a highwayman choose such a spot to lie in wait?"

"Perhaps. But if he had, wouldn't Thane have been his target? Or at least one of Thane's titled and affluent associates? Wouldn't it defeat a thief's purpose to attack a plain, modest carriage—not to mention doing so in broad daylight?"

"I see your point," Hermione concurred. "It is odd that he would choose Mr. Delmore as his victim." She frowned. "But to return to your question, I haven't a clue what yacht you're referring to. As far as I know, Richard owned no yacht, nor would he have wanted to. The man loathed the water. He always did, from boyhood on. He never set foot on a boat, even as a passenger."

"Yet I know for a fact that he *did* own one," Bryce mused. "I read the contract of sale; it's quite authentic. This mystery grows more puzzling by the minute. If your brother hated the water, why would he purchase a yacht? Unless, of course, he did so strictly for investment purposes. Even so, it seems strange that neither you nor Thane knew anything about this boat's existence."

Bryce gave a hard shake of his head. "Something doesn't feel right here. It hasn't from the onset. I don't yet know what it is—but I will. Thane will be riding to Nevon Manor first thing in the morning to discuss this subject. I'd like you to be present when we meet. Perhaps the three of us can come up with a plausible explanation for all this." Bryce cast an anxious glance at his aunt, who was already nodding her compliance. "That is, if you're up to it. Thus far, we've only danced around the subject of your health. I'm not terribly pleased by what I'm seeing. You're extremely pale. *And* extremely exhausted—which doesn't surprise me. You've had a harrowing day, a harrowing week." A heartbeat of a pause. "Part of that is my fault. I should have stayed at Nevon Manor—for many reasons. I'm sorry I didn't."

"You're wrong, Bryce." Profound wisdom registered in Hermione's eyes. "You had to leave—for the very reasons you're alluding to. The important thing is that you're here now. And I'm glad. Very glad."

Something tugged inside Bryce's chest. "No gladder than I."

With a delicate cough, Hermione glanced at the clock. "Oh, dear, look at the time. Have we covered the most pressing matters? I think we have." She provided her own answer. "You'll act as Gaby's sentry—and, I hope, as her confidant—tonight, and I shall meet with you and Thane tomorrow. And on that note"—slowly, Hermione rose to her feet—"I must dress for dinner." A twinkle. "You'd best prepare as well. Given your week-long absence, I suspect that mealtime will consist of a deluge of questions and an outpouring of news. So brace yourself for the onslaught." She smiled, gazing up at Bryce with a tender expression. "You'll soon see how much you were missed, by the children, the adults—everyone."

"I'm looking forward to it," Bryce assured her. "By the way, you have my word—although you haven't requested it—that I will not mention Delmore's murder to anyone at Nevon Manor other than you or Chaunce."

"I haven't requested your word because I knew I had it," Hermione stated simply.

The knot in Bryce's chest tightened, and he nodded, pivoting slowly and heading toward the door.

"Bryce?"

He turned.

Hermione's heart was in her eyes. "Welcome home."

The rest of the evening flew by, a series of rush-and-tumble events that left no room for thought or even sustained conversation. Dinner felt like a cozy robe Bryce had slipped into—one he'd misplaced and whose familiar warmth and comfortable fit he was only now rediscovering. Marion and Goodsmith proclaimed the news of their wedding, set to take place in a fortnight. Wilson bellowed that he had a whole new batch of primroses to describe. On the other side of the table, Bowrick waved his newer, thicker-lensed spectacles in the air, and Mrs. Gordon brandished Dora's walking stick, which she had polished to a gleaming shine. All the while, Cook beamed as she carried out trays of food and listened to Peter recite the facts he'd gleaned from Bryce's texts. The rest of the children withstood the legal chatter for as long as their patience could hold up. Then they interrupted with their own news: Crumpet's latest mischief, the kittens reunion with Sunburst, Lily and Jane's handmade doll.

The turmoil was heartwarming.

So was Bryce's ten-minute lesson with Peter, during which time he learned just how sharp the boy's mind really was and how quickly he was able to learn despite sophisticated concepts and a wealth of interruptions, from people and pets alike.

Bryce's music room chat with Gaby was even shorter, lasting less than three minutes before Lily, Jane, and the kittens exploded into the room, dashing in circles as they chased each other about.

Needless to say, nothing significant got discussed, including Bryce's plans for Gaby to attend the symphony.

The rest of the evening passed in equally chaotic warmth as the activity shifted upstairs, both in an effort to get Bryce settled in and as a gentle reminder to the children that bedtime had long since come and gone. Cook delivered tray after tray of refreshment to Bryce's chambers, chuckling as Henry and Charles tripped over each other in their haste to unpack his bags, while Sunburst watched sleepily from his newly claimed position on the windowsill.

It was nearly ten o'clock by the time the children had calmed down sufficiently enough to be put to bed, and half after midnight before the last of the adults ambled off to their rooms. A weary but radiant

Hermione said good night along with the children, allowing Bryce to escort her to her chambers only after she'd seen for herself that Chaunce was indeed relinquishing his post by the entranceway door in order to get some rest. The butler nearly sagged with relief at the prospect of a good night's sleep, thanking Bryce in his customarily dignified manner before dragging himself off to bed.

Long after silence settled over Nevon Manor, Bryce sat in his armchair, looking around his chambers and reflecting on the events of the day, the extremes that had defined it.

The morning had begun with the cold and shocking finality of death, the senseless murder of an innocent man. How tenuous it made life seem, how very dark and futile.

Then, just hours later, Bryce had experienced the embodiment of life at its richest: his arrival at Nevon Manor.

With a surge of wonder, he marveled at the overwhelming reception he'd received—an abundance of affection that not only humbled him but also provoked in him the most unexpected and profound mixture of emotions. He felt proud, touched, grateful—surfeited with a sense of caring and belonging.

He felt at home.

And at the very heart of that home was a beautiful, sensitive young woman who, simply by virtue of being herself, compelled him to do things he'd never done, crave things he'd never craved, and feel things he didn't even understand.

A young woman who needed him.

That realization spawned another—that being how very late it was getting. Somewhat disoriented, Bryce rose, shaking his head in the hope of recommencing rational thought, putting an end to the unsettled direction his musings had taken.

His attempts were unsuccessful. Nonetheless, he

knew where he had to be. Gathering up a legal text to peruse during his nighttime vigil, he drew a steadying breath and left his chambers.

The hallway was dark and quiet as Bryce made his way around the twisting corridor that led to Gaby's room. Fortunately her chambers were in the same wing as his and Hermione's, separate from the rest of the residents. As a result, Chaunce's presence outside Gaby's door had gone undetected, and no one else was aware of the ongoing trauma that had taken place here this past week.

Not that anyone could remain awake as late or rise as early as Gaby anyway, Bryce reminded himself with a wry grin. Given how little sleep she required, it was doubtful anyone was about when Chaunce either took up or left his station. Gaby's energy was inexhaustible, her need for rest almost nil.

As if to support his premise, the tinkling notes of Gaby's music box reached his ears, the beautiful strains of "Für Elise," broken only by the sound of the grandfather clock down the hall as it chimed one. Reaching the closed door, Bryce paused, listening to the rustling movements from within and contemplating the fact that Gaby was obviously still awake.

The very notion that they were the only two people about at this hour felt oddly right, curiously intimate. Abruptly, Bryce suppressed that thought, berating himself yet again for behaving more like a poet than a barrister. What in God's name was wrong with him tonight?

With a self-censuring frown, he pulled up the chair that stood nearby and was about to lower himself into it when the bedroom door flew open.

"Bryce." Gaby was modestly belting her wrapper as she spoke. "Come in." Eagerly she beckoned, standing aside to allow him to pass. "I've been waiting forever for you to arrive. I'm bursting with curiosity and excitement. Tell me what you arranged with regard to my attending the symphony."

Clad in white, illuminated by the subtle glow of gaslight, Gaby looked as delicate and captivating as an angel, the living epitome of heaven.

Bryce nearly groaned aloud. Instinctively he steeled himself, searching for and finding the ragged filaments of his self-discipline. He resisted the urge to comply with her request, forcing himself to consider the lateness of the hour, the inappropriateness of the situation—and of Gaby's attire. He knew how impatient she was to discuss the symphony, but everything about these circumstances was wrong, especially given his uncharacteristically muddled frame of mind. He was still reeling with first-time perceptions, struggling to understand this new and unanticipated surge of sentimentality he was feeling, and Gaby, as its most fundamental cause *and* its most vulnerable recipient, was the last person he should be alone with. At night. In her bedchamber. When she was wearing nothing but a thin gown and wrapper.

"Bryce, please." Oblivious to his inner turmoil, Gaby stepped into the hallway, grasping his forearm and tugging him toward the room. "I won't shut an eye until you tell me."

He had to refuse. To do otherwise was too bloody dangerous. Bryce's defenses were down, his reserve dissipated, his emotions raw.

The refusal hovered on his lips—and died as he gazed into those bottomless blue eyes. "All right," he heard himself say. "But only for a minute. Then you must promise to go to sleep. It's already after one."

"Very well. I promise."

With a quick glance along the deserted hall, Bryce entered her chambers and shut the door.

He commanded himself to stare at the dressing table, but his gaze was immune to the order. Instead, it focused on Gaby, shifting from the anticipatory glow on her cheeks to the sparkle in her eyes to the delicate curves of her body, accentuated by the fine material of her nightgown and wrapper.

Every fiber of his being reacted—physically, emotionally. Warning bells pealed their censure, as the stern voice of propriety issued an alert.

Coming in here had been a flagrant mistake.

One he couldn't seem to reverse.

"Gaby," he began, unable to stop staring at her, drinking her in from head to toe. "Let's wait until morning. I think—"

"When can I go?" Still engrossed in her thoughts, Gaby rushed forward, clutching the lapels of Bryce's coat, a thousand questions in her eyes. "Soon? With whom?"

"With me," he heard himself say.

"With you?" she repeated carefully. A pause. "What about Miss Talbot?"

Who? Bryce almost found himself asking. "She's not interested in returning to the symphony." Bryce threaded his fingers through Gaby's hair, knowing damn well he shouldn't be touching her and finding he was unable to stop. "And I'm not interested in taking her." He cupped Gaby's face between his hands. "Will you accompany me?"

Awareness had begun to dawn in Gaby's eyes, followed by a sparkle of exhilaration. "Alone?" she breathed without a shred of reticence.

God help him, he was drowning. "We'll take Marion along. She'll serve as your chaperon. She can keep Goodsmith company on the ride to London. If Hermione's up to it, she can join us, too. If not, or if the staff becomes too unnerved by the thought of her absence, she can remain at home. Either way, you'll have both an escort and a chaperon. How will that be?" He didn't give a damn how it would be. In fact, he was having a hard time remembering what they were talking about.

Gaby's cheeks were flushed with pleasure, and now she rose up on tiptoe and kissed Bryce's jaw. "Thank you. Your solution is ideal. I can hardly wait."

Bryce didn't answer. He simply pulled her to him,

tugged her head back, and covered her mouth with his. "Gaby," he breathed against her soft, willing lips, "kiss me."

She did, without pause or question, her arms gliding up to twine about his neck as if she understood his turmoil, sensed the rawness of his emotions.

The kiss began slowly and deliberately, their lips moving together in exquisite harmony, touching, tasting, then blending like two perfectly contoured pieces of a puzzle, only to break apart and begin anew. Again and again, they repeated the kiss, each time longer, hungrier, their mouths clinging more fully as they sought a deeper joining.

Bryce's hands shook as they clenched in Gaby's hair, his lips hardening, moving more insistently as they urged hers apart, issued a silent command—or perhaps it was a plea.

Gaby responded instantly, her lips parting in unwavering invitation. With a shivery sigh, she pressed closer, her fingers tightening about Bryce's neck, sharing rather than yielding to the intensifying embrace, fusing their mouths more completely.

Their tongues touched, Bryce's stealing inside to meld with hers, to claim the sweetness he'd sampled earlier that day. Gaby's breath caught, her entire body trembling as she savored the new, heart-stopping sensations this deeper joining aroused. Bryce indulged her—and himself—his tongue stroking hers in slow, heated movements meant to awaken the budding sensuality hovering just inside her.

He awakened himself instead.

With erotic innocence, Gaby reciprocated his caress, her tongue gliding into his mouth, tentatively stroking his, her breasts flattening against the hard wall of his chest as she strained to get closer.

It was as if a dam inside Bryce had burst, releasing a torrent of need, revealing an empty, famished stranger whose entire soul craved fulfillment. His arms tightened around Gaby like steel bands, locking her against him, and his lips seized hers, possessing her in a series of endless drugging kisses. His tongue plundered her mouth, gliding over every tingling surface before withdrawing and plunging again, desire exploding within him like cannon fire. Again and again his tongue captured hers—melding, mating, parting, beginning anew—his urgency so fierce he could taste it.

Gaby shivered, and Bryce savored her whimper of pleasure, lifting her from the floor and molding her entire body to his.

For the barest of seconds, she tensed, their first explicit contact making her blatantly aware of Bryce's hardening contours, despite the inhibiting confines of their clothes. A heartbeat later she relented, melting against him, her warm, soft body fitting his so perfectly that it was staggering.

This time Bryce couldn't stifle his groan, and it rumbled from his chest into Gaby's open mouth. His hands were shaking violently, one anchoring Gaby against him, the other caressing her as they kissed: her hair, her face, the silky column of her throat, the delicate curve of her shoulder. His lips followed suit, leaving hers to blaze a trail of hot, hungry kisses down to the neckline of her gown.

"Bryce." She whispered his name, and the sound was an exquisite blend of profound emotion and newborn desire. She threaded her fingers through his hair, pressing his mouth against her skin, and Bryce responded to her need, branding her with his kisses, blazing a path along the hollow between her breasts.

Her wrapper had fallen open, the thin muslin of her gown providing little barrier between Bryce and his goal. He could clearly make out the perfect swells of her breasts, flushed with need, their nipples tight with desire.

He lowered his head, surrounding one taut peak with his lips, tugging it into the warm cavern of his mouth.

Gaby cried out again, this time in wonder, and Bryce repeated the caress, drunk with longing, wild to taste more of her—all of her. He shifted to her other breast, frustrated by the interfering garment that hindered his quest. With that thin scrap of cloth between them, he was unable to savor her as he craved to do—deeply, totally—to fulfill the burgeoning need that surged through his veins, pounded through his loins. He needed her naked, clinging, reaching for him, and taking him inside her melting warmth. He needed her urgent, wild, as desperate for him as he was for her.

He needed her now.

Raising his head, he gauged the distance to the bed, then gazed into Gaby's eyes, recognizing the wonder and longing that mirrored his own.

"Bryce," she breathed, stretching up to kiss his throat, "make love to me."

It was her words—the meaning they conveyed, the essence of which he was only now discovering—that stopped him, shattering the aura of unreality that had governed the past few sequestered minutes, leaving the truth staring him in the face: he was on the verge of taking Gaby to bed.

With a harsh groan, Bryce took hold of his senses—whatever fragments of them still existed—and set Gaby on her feet, shaking his head as he denied her, denied them both, the fulfillment they sought. "Ah, Gaby . . ." His voice was raw, hoarse, rough with unquenched desire and unimaginable feelings. "I can't. Not now. Not here. Not like this."

Not ever, his conscience ordered reflexively.

His conscience was dead wrong. *That* Bryce knew—suddenly, unequivocally, and with every fiber of his being. This union was as inevitable as that of dawn melding with day, as natural and irrefutable as it was right. He'd just been too blind, too stubborn, too terrified, to see it.

Still, the timing, the location, the circumstances—

those were all wrong. In fact, the very idea that he'd almost allowed this to happen—*caused* it to happen, here, now—was totally insane.

"What in God's name am I doing?" he muttered, fighting desperately to regain rational thought and control. In one purposeful motion, he drew Gaby's wrapper together, then tugged her into the circle of his arms, as if the very warmth of her could shed some light on this madness. "I'm seducing you," he supplied. "In Hermione's house, no less. Under her roof—the fine woman who kept me alive, made sure that I became all that I am. A woman who trusts me. Whose family trusts me. And Hermione notwithstanding, I have no right to be doing this. Not now. Not when you deserve so much more. Dammit. What in the name of heaven was I thinking? More apropos, why wasn't I thinking at all? Gaby"—he framed her face between his palms—"I can't begin to explain—"

"*Why* have you no right?" Gaby blurted out, confusion and uncertainty clouding her features. "And why did you stop? Was it because of me? Am *I* the one you're protecting?" As always, her heart was in her eyes. "If so, don't. I want to be with you, desperately. What's happening is not an impulsive act, at least not on my part. I've dreamed about our making love since last week when you kissed me good-bye. I've prayed it would happen. Bryce, don't you understand?" She laid her palm against his jaw. "I love you."

Gaby's pronouncement sank in, its impact heightened by the delicate strains of "Für Elise" playing softly in the background.

"My beautiful Wonderland," Bryce murmured at last, his voice husky as he turned his lips into Gaby's palm. "That's the most magnificent declaration I've ever heard, much less been offered. Thank you."

"I don't want your thanks. I want your love. Or do you still not believe such love exists?" She stepped away, crossed over to shut the lid of her music box.

Stark silence prevailed.

Bryce sucked in his breath, grappling with feelings he couldn't fathom, couldn't assign words to, still reeling as reality crashed into place. "Gaby." He came up behind her and gently turned her around to face him. "We have a lot to discuss. And, yes, our feelings—yours and mine—are among those things. But tonight is not the time. Your bedchamber is not the place." He swallowed. "I've already betrayed Hermione's trust as it is."

"What about Miss Talbot?" Gaby asked softly, her eyes searching his. "Have you betrayed her trust as well?"

"Yes." Bryce never averted his gaze. "I have. Far more extensively than you mean, more extensively than I could begin to fathom."

"I don't understand."

"Nor do I. But now I do." Bryce's thumbs caressed Gaby's cheeks. "The fact is, I started betraying Lucinda's trust long before I took you in my arms tonight. I started doing so nearly a fortnight ago—the morning Crumpet brought you rushing up to my carriage. I've been dishonest with Lucinda since that moment. And I've been dishonest with myself as well."

"I see." Hope shimmered in Gaby's eyes. "Does that mean—"

"Not tonight," he interrupted, laying a forefinger across her lips. "There's too much to say and not enough time in which to say it. Tomorrow. After I've had a chance to collect my thoughts, come to terms with the deluge of emotions that are churning inside me—emotions I never even knew I possessed."

"All right," Gaby whispered, her breath warm against his skin. "When tomorrow?"

Her impatience made him smile. "I'm meeting with Thane and Hermione right after breakfast. How about the instant we're finished?"

"Can't you delay the meeting?"

"I wish I could." Staring into those magnificent blue eyes, inhaling the fragrance of her hair, Bryce was tempted to do more than postpone his meeting. He was tempted to carry Gaby to her bed and damn the consequences to hell. Determinedly, he subdued that impulse. "Gaby, I've got to walk out of here, take up my post outside your door. Now. While I still can."

Reluctantly, Gaby nodded. "Bryce?" She caught his wrist, staying his departure. "I appreciate everything you just said about trust. But, with regard to Aunt Hermione, I hope you realize that, caring for us both as she does, she'd be delighted if we happened to begin caring for each other."

"I don't think she'd regard what just happened as caring for each other," Bryce returned dryly. "She'd regard it as my taking advantage of you. And she would be right. In fact, this was the very type of behavior she begged me to protect you from should I be called upon to oversee your future. Little did she suspect that when the situation arose, I would be the offender rather than the protector."

"Oversee my future?" Gaby frowned, her expression puzzled. "I don't understand. Why would you be called upon to oversee my future?"

Bryce wanted to kick himself. Damn his muddled state of mind! Hadn't it compelled him to do enough damage for one night? Now he'd made a stupid, irreversible slip—one that couldn't have come at a more vulnerable time for Gaby.

"Bryce?" Gaby pressed. "Why would you have to oversee my future?"

The harm was done, Bryce realized, silently berating himself once again. Now he had to face the repercussions.

Catching Gaby's shoulders in his hands, Bryce braced himself for her reaction. "Because Hermione asked me to. In the unlikely event that she isn't . . .

able to do so, she wants me to ensure that you are brought out next Season, shielded from the wrong men, introduced to the right ones. She wants to feel secure that you— Oh, Gaby, don't." Bryce caught her arms as she tried to twist away from him.

"Are you saying that Aunt Hermione asked you to act as my guardian in the event of her death?" Gaby's voice trembled with emotion.

"Gaby . . ."

"Is that what you're saying?"

"Yes."

"I see." Gaby's whole body tensed, and she backed as far away as Bryce's restraining hands would allow. "And you agreed. Is that why you've spent so much time with me? Why you were so worried about my questions with regard to intimacy and passion? Why you came here tonight to stand vigil? Has all this been about duty and principles, about your responsibility and commitment to Aunt Hermione? Is that why Miss Talbot has been so understanding about your comings and goings—because she knows I represent no threat to her? Did you tell her I was—"

"I told her nothing." Bryce hauled Gaby back to him, refused to let her go. "You can't possibly believe what you're saying, nor can you possibly believe that what happened here tonight had anything to do with duty or responsibility. Gaby"—he tilted her face up to his—"don't do this—especially after what just happened between us. Don't doubt me. Not now."

Clearly, Gaby was fighting back tears. "Why didn't anyone mention this guardianship to me? Given that it was my life being decided, didn't I have any right to know what was being planned?"

"Yes, you did," Bryce concurred. "But in Hermione's defense, I must tell you that she dreaded mentioning to you the possibility of her death. She detested the thought of causing you worry or pain. That was the only reason for her silence—and mine. As for my concern for you, yes, it started out of duty.

At least that's what I tried to believe. But I was deluding myself. And after what happened tonight, I think you know that."

A prolonged silence, as Bryce's words found their mark and sank in.

"You do know that, don't you, Gaby?" he pressed, his thumbs once again caressing her cheeks.

Slowly Gaby nodded, her distress receding beneath a more significant, profound truth. "Yes," she replied softly. "I know that."

Relief washed through Bryce in huge, restorative waves. "Until morning, then?" he murmured.

"Until morning." A whisper of a smile touched her lips. "You have much to contemplate, barrister."

"Indeed I do." Bryce threaded his fingers through Gaby's hair, savoring its silken texture against his skin. "In an area that's totally unfamiliar to me, one that offers no texts for reference or statutes for guidance."

"You'll find your answers," she assured him, that age-old wisdom shining in her eyes. "They're hovering inside you, waiting to be savored, like the strains of a symphony. I told you, Bryce. You're capable of far more than you realize. I know it. It's time you did, too."

With a rough sound, Bryce drew Gaby against him, lowering his head to seal their mouths in a brief, heated kiss. "Sweet dreams, Wonderland," he said huskily. "I'll be right outside your door."

The sweet dreams were not forthcoming.

Initially it was wakefulness that precluded their occurrence.

Later it was the sleepwalking.

For over an hour after Bryce left her chamber, Gaby tossed and turned on the pillows, unable to shut her eyes, too overcome by the miraculous events that had just taken place in this very room—physical *and* emotional events that would forever change her life.

Bryce had all but said he loved her, his defenses crumbling in a rush, his thoughts and responses caught up in a turmoil whose cause she only partially understood. Something had happened inside him—a perceptible transition—the end result of which had been the unlocking of a wealth of emotion he'd never before acknowledged, much less allowed himself to feel. And his reception at Nevon Manor was only part of that transition's cause—its culmination, Gaby suspected. Something else had incited it—an event in London, perhaps that had caused Bryce's confusion, the internal battle he was now fighting. And unknowingly, Gaby had intensified that battle, beckoning him into a situation that had toppled his reserves, pushed him over the edge.

Thank God.

Rolling onto her back, Gaby stared at the ceiling, her heart pounding with excitement, her thoughts leaping from one memory to another.

Her lips still tingled from Bryce's kisses, her breasts throbbed from the erotic tugs of his mouth.

Dear Lord, the way she'd felt, the way she *still* felt—was this the miracle of passion? The weak, hot, shivering sensation that had poured through her body like liquid flame, the unfamiliar but relentless need Bryce's caresses had kindled inside her, the yearning for more that had scarcely begun yet clamored to be heard, intensified in seconds, and prevailed even now—was this the magical exhilaration reserved only for lovers?

If so, not even the most magnificent symphony could compare.

Smiling, Gaby curled up on her side, cradling the pillow in her arms. She and Bryce were each poised on an exquisite threshold: she was about to venture farther into the realm of intimacy, and Bryce was about to start believing in romantic love—if he hadn't already.

Thank goodness morning was but a few hours away.

It was on that happy thought that Gaby drifted off, her mind saturated with images of the joy yet to come.

The ticking of the clock on the mantel signaled the passing of night—two o'clock slowly becoming three.

Bryce . . . Bryce . . . Pictures of the man she loved floated through Gaby's dreams, then abruptly altered, shattered, and were swallowed up by a wild, deadly inferno. Fire exploded inside her head, all around her, orange flames leaping everywhere, devouring her thoughts, her body.

Mama . . . Papa . . . She struggled out of her warm cocoon, scrambled to her feet, groping about until her small hand found the music box, pressed it against her. Desperately she battled the heat, fought her way across the room. Distant voices rumbling, then raised, sharp with pain and fear, were muffled by crackling flames, swallowed up by death. With every ounce of her strength, she shoved against the door, using her nightgown to turn the hot handle, coughing as the smoke invaded her throat.

Suddenly she was outside, the sickening smell of wood mingling with something sweeter, a musky fragrance, assailing her nostrils as she pushed toward the grass. *Mama! Papa!* She had to reach them. Something slammed against her, halted her progress. A towering wall that refused to relent, would not let her pass. *No. No. I have to get by. I must reach them.* She beat her fist against the wall, managing only to awaken it, cause it to battle back.

"Gaby!" Bryce's voice came to her from a great distance, commanding her to respond. "Gaby!"

Why did he sound so urgent?

Oh, God, was he trapped as well?

"Bryce . . ." She struggled weakly, trying to escape the wall and locate Bryce at the same time. "I can't . . . the fire . . . the wall—"

"Gaby, wake up." Hard hands gripped her shoulders, shook her out of the nightmare.

The wall was Bryce.

Utterly disoriented, she responded, opening her eyes warily, awaiting the cloud of smoke that would inevitably assault them.

She saw only Bryce's handsome, worried face.

"Bryce?"

The grim lines about his mouth relaxed as she uttered his name, and he drew her to him, wrapped a protective arm around her as he eased her through the doorway and back into her room.

"The sleepwalking . . ." She was still dazed, but not so dazed that she didn't realize what had just occurred. "Oh, not again."

"It's all right, sweetheart. I'm here." Bryce guided her to the armchair by the window, then lowered himself onto the cushioned seat, tugged her into his lap. "You're awake now." He cradled her against him, stroking her back in slow, soothing motions.

Gaby began shivering, her teeth chattering uncontrollably as she burrowed into Bryce's warmth, her music box still clutched in her hands. "They won't go away. Those horrible memories, like scenes torn from a book."

"Tell me about them." Bryce's breath ruffled the top of her hair. "Talk to me, Gaby, while the memory is still fresh. Tell me what you're remembering."

"You already know."

"About the fire, yes. You're trying to get to your parents. Describe it to me."

She squeezed her eyes shut to seal out the pain but succeeded only in resurrecting the very images, smells, and sounds she was desperate to forget. "I awaken," she managed in a high, thin voice. "The room is hot. I hear voices—loud, frightened voices that are swallowed up by nothingness. Flames erupt around me. They're everywhere. I grab my music box, shove my way across the shed. The door handle is hot. I use my nightgown to wrench it open. I tumble outside. Everything is enveloped in an eerie orange light. It smells peculiar—smoky and sweet all at once. I look around, see the wall of fire devouring the servants' quarters. I run with all my might, but I can't get to Mama and Papa, no matter how hard I try. My music box falls to the ground, but I don't care. I just keep pushing at the wall, but it won't let me through. I see the ground rushing at me, all brown and barren, and then . . . I see nothing at all."

Bryce frowned, continuing to stroke Gaby's back. "The voices you hear in your dream, are they coming from outside?"

"No. Inside—but not in the shed where I am. The men are trapped, though. Both of them. Neither one wants to die."

"'Men'? 'Both of them'?" Bryce's hand stilled. "You're sure there are two voices, both of them belonging to men?"

Gaby's trembling intensified. "Yes."

With a hard swallow, Bryce continued, "They must be nearby for you to know that, as well as to perceive their fear."

"I think so . . . yes. In the coal room maybe. Or the woodshed." Gaby fought her growing panic. "I think the men were talking when I fell asleep. It's hard to recall. But when I awaken in my dream, the crackling of the flames is the sound that dominates all others. The voices are in the background, broken and indistinct. Then abruptly they're silent."

"Do you recognize them?"

"I'm not sure." Valiantly, she struggled to remember, the attempt heightening her sense of dread. "But I must have known them if they lived at Whitshire." She twisted around, gazed up at Bryce. "Could that mean something?"

"I don't know, sweetheart." Bryce fell silent, looking strained and pensive.

"Bryce, please." Gaby jerked to an upright position, her desire to master her own destiny overshadowing her fear. "Don't protect me the way you did with the guardianship. I won't have it. This is my life we're discussing. What is it you're pondering? I need to know."

He nodded, making no further attempts to conceal his suspicions. "I'm wondering if it's possible you endured an even greater trauma than we all realized. I'm wondering if you actually listened as two men you knew died."

Chapter 13

"HIS GRACE HAS ARRIVED, MY LADY," CHAUNCE announced from the drawing room doorway.

"Thank you, Chaunce," Hermione replied absently, her worried gaze fixed on Bryce. "Please show him in."

She and Chaunce exchanged concerned glances before the butler nodded, disappearing into the hallway.

"Bryce, what is it?" Hermione ventured, watching her nephew stare broodingly into his coffee—as he had been doing since Ruth served it ten minutes ago. "You've scarcely spoken a word since breakfast, and even then you were obviously keeping up a cheery front for the children. I realize how distressed you are by Mr. Delmore's death; at first I attributed your somber mood to that and to lack of sleep. But I'm beginning to suspect it's something more." She leaned forward anxiously. "Is it Gaby? Was there another sleepwalking episode last night? And if so, why didn't you mention it to me?"

Bryce lifted his head—a colossal effort given how

much it ached from fatigue and tension. How odd that he should feel so distraught in some ways and so utterly at peace in others. Tired? Yes, he was tired. He'd spent the hours preceding dawn perched in the armchair in Gaby's chambers—the only way he could be sure she would get a few hours of unbroken rest. Following their discussion, she'd been far too upset to go back to sleep—a reality that was totally unacceptable given that, after more than a week of these tormented nights, she was on the verge of physical and emotional collapse. So he'd stayed with her, vowing not to leave, murmuring quiet, soothing words until finally exhaustion won out and her eyelids closed.

He'd spent the duration of the night watching her, worrying about her, simultaneously delving inside himself as he pondered the host of issues plaguing his mind, assailing his heart.

The ultimate resolution had come along with the first rays of dawn.

"Bryce?" Hermione's voice broke into his thoughts—and Bryce could hear the panic lacing her tone. "You're frightening me. What is it?"

"Yes, there was another sleepwalking episode last night," he replied, shoving aside his cup. "A bad one. I'm sorry I didn't mention it immediately. I have a great deal on my mind this morning."

"Tell me what—"

"Good morning. Here I am, as promised." Thane strolled into the room, halting at once as he sensed the crackling tension around him, realized he'd interrupted something. "Forgive me," he apologized, looking from Bryce to Hermione. "Chaunce suggested I come straight in. If you'd like, I can wait—"

"No." Bryce rose, rubbing his jaw and gesturing for his brother to enter. "Come in. Close the door behind you. Hermione and I are discussing something that concerns you, too."

"Very well." Thane complied, shutting the door

and leaning back against it. "Has something more happened?"

"Not with regard to Delmore, no. With regard to Gaby." Bryce began pacing about the room. "She had a bad sleepwalking episode last night. When she tried to leave the room, I stopped her, awakened her. But instead of simply settling her back in, hoping she'd nod off, and praying the whole episode wouldn't repeat itself an hour later, I insisted we talk immediately, while the memories were still fresh. We did. And what Gaby said disturbed me greatly." Bryce paused, then relayed the entire conversation to Hermione and Thane. "In my opinion," he concluded, "there's every possibility that Gaby heard those two men die—their cries for help, their pain, Lord knows what else."

"Dear God," Hermione whispered.

"Thane, how many people died in that fire?" Bryce asked his brother.

"Dozens." Thane had gone pale listening to Bryce's theory. "The fire destroyed the entire service wing— all the structures from what was then the coach house to Whitshire's rear entrance—all but the stables." He swallowed. "Worst of all were the losses in the servants' quarters. Nearly the whole staff was asleep. They hadn't even time to react, much less escape."

"Where was the storage shed located with respect to the servants' quarters?"

Thane dismissed that notion with a shake of his head. "Not adjacent to it. The only room that abutted the storage shed was the coal room. On the other side of the shed were the servants' entrance and dining hall. Their quarters followed that."

"So the voices Gaby heard couldn't have been coming from the staff's quarters." Bryce raked a hand through his hair. "Could there have been people in the coal room?"

"I suppose so. The voices could also have been coming from the staff's dining hall. But if you're asking if it's possible that Gabrielle overheard lives being lost, the answer is yes. I was away at Oxford at the time, but I came home as soon as I got word of what happened. It was a tragedy—one in which dozens of people died a horrible death. And for a five-year-old to be subjected to that . . ." Thane paused. "It's no wonder she can't forget."

"This is still purely speculation," Bryce reminded him. "But frankly I'm worried sick about it. Because if what I'm suggesting did occur, Gaby has an enormous hurdle to overcome. Not to mention that it's going to be extremely difficult to test my theory. You weren't at Whitshire on the night of the fire, which leaves only the surviving servants—those who were employed by your father at the time—to tell us what they recall. And that's assuming all of them have either stayed on these thirteen years or left forwarding addresses where they can be reached."

"Do you really think we should bring this entire tragedy to light again?" Hermione managed, her hands trembling with emotion. "Will dredging up all this pain do Gaby any good?"

"Keeping it buried somewhere inside is destroying her," Bryce returned quietly. "And I won't allow that to happen. You and I both know Gaby is strong, Hermione. Once she fully understands what's gnawing away at her, she'll come to grips with it. I'll help her; we'll all help her. But she can't fight what she doesn't recall. So we've got to get at the truth."

"I'll talk to my staff immediately," Thane promised. "To my knowledge, all those who survived the fire have remained on these thirteen years, so locating them won't be necessary. I'll summon each and every one of them and ask if they knew of anyone who was in the coal room, the dining hall, even the woodshed when the fire struck. Maybe they'll have some answers for us."

"Thank you," Bryce said. He turned to Hermione. "Speaking of Gaby's ability to cope with difficulty, there's something else you should know: Gaby is aware of your plans with regard to my potential guardianship. I inadvertently let it slip. I hope you're not upset."

That revelation seemed to divert Hermione's worry—and to interest her rather than upset her. "How did she react?"

"Badly at first." Bryce cleared his throat, choosing his words carefully, so as not to divulge the circumstances surrounding this particular conversation. "But I explained your reasons and eventually she understood."

"What guardianship?" Thane interrupted.

Again Bryce cleared his throat. "Hermione asked me to act as Gabrielle's guardian, in the event I'm needed."

A dry chuckle escaped Thane's lips. "That's one situation that will never come to pass."

"I agree," Bryce replied. "Hermione is more than capable of filling that role for as long as Gaby needs her."

"Which won't be for long," Thane added.

Bryce's brows drew together in puzzlement. "What does that mean?"

Thane crossed over and poured himself some coffee. "That means," he answered with a grin, "that Gabrielle will never become your ward, but not because of Hermione's stamina, although I fully believe our aunt will live forever. Gabrielle won't become your ward because you're so bloody in love with her, you can't see straight."

Bryce's jaw dropped and he stared at Thane, only vaguely aware of Hermione's soft peal of laughter in the background. "What did you say?"

A lingering sip of coffee. "I think you heard me."

"How can you make a statement like that? How on earth would you know?"

"Apparently everyone knows, Bryce," Hermione put in gently. "Everyone but you." Her amusement faded, and she studied Bryce for a long, astute moment. "I stand corrected. I believe you've finally joined the ranks."

Bryce walked back to the settee and sank down heavily. "I've spent three or four days at Nevon Manor and three or four hours at Whitshire. How is it that, in so short a time, everyone around me perceived something of such great magnitude, something I myself clearly missed?"

"Seeing you and Gabrielle together, it wasn't hard." Thane sat as well, stretching his long legs out in front of him. "You scarcely take your eyes off her, you worry over her incessantly, and there's an astounding chemistry between the two of you; one can actually feel it. In addition, you're always fleeing either to her or from her." A twinkle. "Yesterday you nearly knocked me down in your haste to ride to Nevon Manor and check on her well-being, while last week you nearly bolted from Nevon Manor in your haste to return to London and forget her. I'm a man. I recognize the signs. Shall I continue?"

"No." Bryce shook his head. "You've made your point."

"Have you made yours?" Hermione asked eagerly. "Have you told Gaby—"

"Hermione, please." Bryce cut her off with a firm wave of his hand. "This conversation has gone far enough. I know you keep a scrapbook of my life, and evidently Thane has inherited your fine insight, but I'm not accustomed to openly discussing my private life. I refuse to be interrogated about my actions and intentions toward Gabrielle."

"Whatever you say, dear." Looking not the least bit perturbed, Hermione serenely resumed sipping her coffee.

Thane gave a discreet cough. "If I overstepped my bounds, I apologize."

"Don't. I asked." Bryce brought the conversation to an abrupt halt by introducing an equally pressing, though infinitely less sensitive subject. "Let's get to the reason for our meeting: Delmore. Thane, I told Hermione about our talk with the police yesterday. Like you, she knows nothing about your father owning, much less selling, a yacht. In fact, according to her, he loathed sailing. So why would he have commissioned a boat to be built?"

"For investment purposes, perhaps?" Thane suggested.

"I considered that, but the modest sum he was asking from Delmore certainly wouldn't generate any real profit."

"I'm sure Father originally intended to ask a far more substantial price. But, as you yourself pointed out, he probably modified his expectations once he became ill, decided to forgo his profit in order to sell the boat as quickly as possible."

"That was what I initially assumed, but since then I've had time to think. And I have to wonder why your father felt it necessary to make that sacrifice. What was his urgency to sell? After all, he could have turned the entire matter over to you, asked you to negotiate the highest price, whether or not he was still alive when the deal was consummated. You're a fine businessman. You would have secured a large profit." Bryce shot Thane a dark look. "And please don't tell me he did it to spare you the burden of disposing of the yacht. It's hardly a complicated transaction, and Richard Rowland was hardly a selfless man."

"I wasn't going to suggest that," Thane assured him. "Your reservations are valid, Bryce. In fact, everything you just said makes a world of sense. The problem is, I have no answers for you. I don't profess to have understood my father's thoughts or his motives."

"Here's another question: where is the title to this yacht? There has to be one. I assume, since you knew nothing of the yacht's existence, that the title wasn't among your father's papers."

"Definitely not. I've gone through every legal document Father possessed. No such title is there." Thane tapped his leg thoughtfully. "Could he have forwarded it to Delmore when they struck a verbal agreement and Delmore began preparing the contracts?"

"That's a distinct possibility." Bryce nodded. "Let's get back to Delmore's murder, and the highwayman who supposedly killed him."

"'Supposedly'?" Thane repeated. "I take it you don't believe a thief did this."

"Let's say I have my doubts—strong doubts. Think about it. Delmore's body was discovered some distance from his carriage, concealed in a cluster of trees. Highwaymen don't linger at the scene of a crime long enough to hide a body. They simply shoot their victim right where he sits, seize whatever they can, then gallop off as swiftly as possible."

"Perhaps the thief lured Mr. Delmore out of his carriage before shooting him," Hermione speculated.

"Using what as bait?" Bryce asked. "Delmore's life? Very well, then—why? Simply so he could conceal the body? What benefit would there be to that? To buy himself more time before someone realized a man had been murdered? The risk of discovery would far outweigh whatever gain that would afford, especially since it was broad daylight and the thief could have been spotted at any moment. No, the wisest course would have been to shoot Delmore, then flee like the wind."

"Your reasoning is sound," Thane concurred. "So let's assume for the moment that the police are wrong, that a highwayman didn't commit this crime. Where do we go from there?"

"To a motive other than burglary," Bryce supplied. "There was no sign of a struggle. In my opinion, that means one of two things. Either Delmore was shot in his carriage, then tossed into the trees—a possibility we can easily check into by asking the police if there were any bloodstains on the carriage seat."

"Or . . . ?"

"Or Delmore left his carriage willingly and alive, and the murderer shot him after they reached the roadside."

"Why would Delmore willingly leave his carriage, knowing he'd be shot?"

"He wouldn't. He would willingly leave his carriage only if he was unaware of the murderer's intentions."

Thane sucked in his breath. "You're suggesting Delmore knew his assailant."

"I think it's something we must consider."

"But Delmore was on a private road leading to Whitshire. Who would he know—" Thane broke off, all the color draining from his face. "Oh, no."

Hermione gasped. "Bryce, are you implying that one of Whitshire's residents killed Mr. Delmore?"

"I'm not implying anything, at least not at this point. I'm merely considering all the possibilities. We have no evidence to support my theory—or any other, for that matter. But has it occurred to me that someone from Whitshire might have killed Delmore? Yes. It has." Bryce rubbed his palms together. "Either that or someone knew he was headed to Whitshire and followed him there. That, too, is a distinct possibility. The point is, we have a puzzling robbery and an equally puzzling legal transaction, both of which involved the same man. I think that coincidence bears looking into."

"So do I." Thane set down his cup. "I take it you have a plan?"

"Not a plan, a step. Two, actually. First, I want to ask the police about the condition of Delmore's carriage. Next, I want to visit Banks. I want your permission to examine any or all documents pertaining to the construction or sale of that yacht, including the original title, if it's in Banks's possession. Perhaps

283

those documents will shed some light on this mystery."

"You don't need my permission, Bryce," Thane reminded him quietly. "Richard Rowland was your father, too."

"But nobody knows that." Bryce's jaw set. "And I don't intend to change that fact, as I've already told you."

"All right." Thane accepted Bryce's decision without further protest. "I'll pen you a letter right now. You can take it to London, give it to Banks."

"Does that mean you're leaving again?" Hermione jolted upright, lines of distress tightening her mouth.

"Only for a day or two," Bryce replied. "Hermione, I must. Given the circumstances, I have no choice." He hesitated. "And there are other reasons for my trip—reasons I'm not ready to discuss. You're going to have to trust me."

The lines on her face softened. "You know my answer to that."

"Good. I intend to leave as soon as possible— before noon today. I'll talk with the police, visit Banks, then take care of the other matters I need to address. I'll ride back to Nevon Manor the instant I can—tomorrow, I hope. By that time Thane will have spoken to his staff about the fire, and perhaps we'll be better equipped to help Gaby." A scowl. "I won't be here to keep vigil outside her door tonight."

"Chaunce and I will manage," Hermione assured him. "We had a good, unbroken night's sleep, thanks to you; certainly we can withstand resuming our post for one more night, especially knowing how soon you'll be back."

"Thank you. Also, I want you to promise me that no one will leave Nevon Manor. As Thane pointed out yesterday, the roads aren't safe. So please don't use them."

"We won't." Hermione attempted a smile. "Goodsmith will be delighted to abandon his driving duties and give his full attention to Marion and their upcoming wedding." A sudden worried look crossed her face, and she turned to Thane. "Speaking of safety, what if Bryce's theory has merit? What if there's a murderer living at Whitshire? You could be in danger."

"Doubtful," Thane responded. "Whoever this killer is, I'm evidently not a threat to him." A reassuring smile. "Don't worry. I'll be extra cautious."

"That's a good idea, Thane," Bryce concurred. "I agree you're not in any immediate danger, but still, keep your eyes open."

"I intend to." Thane cocked his head quizzically at his brother. "Is there a reason you aren't leaving here until noon? It's just ten o'clock now. You could get an earlier start—unless you have another appointment, that is."

"I do." Bryce met Thane's curious gaze. "A very important appointment. With Gaby. I have a great deal to discuss with her." His glance shifted to Hermione. "And, with your permission, I'd like one of those things to be Delmore's murder. As Gaby pointed out to me last night, she's not a child who needs protection. She has a right to know about events that affect her life—which this will, given that she'll have to cancel any return visits she might have intended to make to Whitshire. She also has a right to know why I'm leaving Nevon Manor when I promised I'd stay. The others will forgive me a day of pressing business, so long as I vow to return. But Gaby . . ." A small smile touched his lips. "I don't think she'd accept my explanation. In fact, I don't think she'd even believe it."

An understanding glint lit Hermione's eyes. "You're right," she conceded. "She should be told about the murder—by you. For all the reasons you just named. Also, selfishly, I'll be relieved to have someone other than Chaunce with whom to share this burden as well as to aid me in my crusade—that is, keeping the news from the others. Chaunce and I can intercept just so many newspapers. And Chaunce can restrict just so many conversational tidbits to the rear entrance when deliverymen arrive." Hermione sighed, leaning her head back against the cushion. "Gaby is so softhearted and delicate, at times I forget how very strong she is. But I shouldn't. She's always been my sunshine and, along with Chaunce, my strength. She's overcome a tragedy that would have destroyed most others. True, she'll be heartbroken that an innocent man was killed, but she'll take the news in stride, if only to help protect the rest of the family."

"Not to mention that protecting the family will give her something positive to focus on," Bryce added. "Something other than her sleepwalking."

At that, Hermione's lips curved. "Something positive to focus on? That job, my dear Bryce, I shall leave to you. And, as always, you shan't disappoint me."

It was half after eleven, the sun glinting between the branches of the oaks as it ascended to their peaks, when Gaby and Bryce reached the flat rock beside which they'd said good-bye a week earlier.

They'd walked here in silence, not a strained silence, but an expectant one, as if they both knew that the words they needed to exchange were too precious to be uttered in passing.

Gaby gathered up her skirts and sat down, beckoning for Bryce to follow.

"Did you get any rest?" she asked softly.

"I didn't try to," he replied, lowering himself beside her. "If you recall, I had a great deal of thinking to do. Besides, I wanted to make sure you slept undisturbed."

"Thank you." She inclined her head, gazed up at him. "I don't want to discuss the sleepwalking. Not now. Tell me what great revelations you came to while I was asleep—and before."

Bryce smiled. "Several. First, that I've either changed completely these past few weeks or that I never really knew myself at all."

"Both," Gaby supplied. She tucked a stray lock of hair behind her ear. "You opened up an extraordinary heart that you only just discovered. And in return, you've acquired a whole new outlook—and a whole new family."

"They are astounding, aren't they?" Bryce concurred, staring off into space. "I couldn't stop thinking about them when I was away: wondering how Peter was faring with my texts, how Marion had reacted to Goodsmith's proposal, how Chaunce was faring during his nighttime vigils, how Hermione's health was holding up." A baffled shake of his head. "The entire week I was in London, my thoughts were in turmoil. Everything that had only days before been real suddenly seemed meaningless, and everything that had been nonexistent suddenly seemed essential. I felt as Alice must have when she was toppling down that tunnel into Wonderland."

"But you've arrived." Gaby laid her hand over his.

"Yes." He gazed at her delicate fingers, his chest growing tight with emotion. "I've arrived, thanks to my new family, and you."

"Does this mean you finally believe love exists?" she teased softly. "Not just compassion, mind you, but love—both familial and romantic?"

Bryce lifted her fingers to his mouth. "My beliefs have changed quite a bit these past weeks. I'm drowning in feelings and emotions. So, yes, I believe love exists. And not only in general. In me." He pressed her palm to his lips, kissed it gently. "Ah, Gaby, I have so much to say to you, so much I need you to understand—so much *I'm* still in the process of understanding."

With acute insight, Gaby studied his face. "I'll begin for you. Something happened yesterday— something serious. Whatever it was, it drove you back to Nevon Manor. It was heightened by seeing all of us. It was also responsible for the intensity of your mood last night and for making you lose control the way you did. What was it?"

His head jerked around, and he gave her a stunned look. "Do you read my mind, Wonderland?"

"Sometimes. Mostly I read your heart. Now tell me what it was that affected you so profoundly."

"I intend to. But first I want to clarify something. You were right when you said something happened, something serious, and that it drove me back to Nevon Manor feeling raw and vulnerable—a vulnerability that was driven home by the inspiring welcome I received. But you were wrong when you said it made me lose control last night. Only one thing did that: you. I wanted you so badly I was shaking with it. I still do." Bryce swallowed. "All right?"

"Oh, more than all right," Gaby murmured, caressing his jaw. "Perfect. You see, I felt—*feel*—the same way."

An ardent silence.

"Gaby," Bryce said at last, his voice husky, "if I take you in my arms now, I'll forget everything on earth except you . . . us . . . how badly I want you. And there's too much that needs to be said before I do that. So let me say it."

"And then can I fling myself into your arms?"

"No. Then I'll drag you into them."

"Very well. Continue."

Bryce drew a lingering breath. Then slowly, candidly, he told Gaby what had happened: Delmore's murder, the police officers' suspicions, his own doubts and concerns, the puzzling sale of the yacht.

As he spoke, all the color drained from Gaby's face. "Murdered—my God." She wet her lips with the tip of her tongue, clearly trying to bring herself under control.

From a distance, the sound of a slow-moving carriage reached their ears.

Gaby's chin shot up, and she stared off in the direction of the drive. "You're returning to London," she announced quietly. "That's your carriage Goodsmith is fetching. You're riding to Town to see Mr. Delmore's partner."

"Sweetheart, I have to." Bryce gripped Gaby's hands between his, watching her face to gauge her reaction. "I'll only be gone overnight. You have my word. I don't want to leave you now, with all that's happening between us and with the new recollections you have of the night of the fire. You need me. I want to be here for you. And, yes, I want to be here for us, for the family, and—most astonishing of all—for myself. But an innocent man has been killed, and if I can help determine why . . ."

"Bryce." Gaby stopped him with a gentle shake of her head. "Stop. You don't need to explain. I'm the one who keeps reminding you what a wonderful, compassionate man you are. I appreciate why you have to go. I'd do the same thing, if I were you. Dear God, that poor man." She shuddered. "And his poor, grieving family."

Gaby's words awakened in her precisely the reaction Hermione had predicted. Bryce saw her back stiffen, saw a fierce, protective spark kindle in her eyes.

Slowly she pivoted to face him. "Thank you for confiding in me," she acknowledged softly, aching determination lacing her tone. "Now I can make things easier on Aunt Hermione, help keep this dreadful news from the others."

"You are too beautiful for words," Bryce said fervently. "I have no doubt you'll protect the family like a lioness shielding her cubs. As for your own situation, I don't want you to worry about potential sleepwalking episodes. Hermione has already told me that she and Chaunce feel strong enough to take up their posts outside your door tonight. By tomorrow night I'll be back to relieve them. And, Gaby"—

Bryce slid his hand beneath her silky tresses, caressed the nape of her neck—"I meant what I said: we're going to get to the root of your sleepwalking, and then we're going to overcome it. I've already taken steps to do so."

"Steps? What steps?"

"I've elicited Thane's help." Bryce went on to fill her in on his and Thane's intentions.

"I thank you both," Gaby responded in a choked voice. "I feel incredibly fortunate—and incredibly optimistic. With all our efforts combined, I have no doubt we'll resolve my past, relegate it to where it belongs. You and Thane—" Abruptly, she broke off, sunshine illuminating her features, chasing away the emotional gravity of the past few moments. "Bryce, wouldn't it be wonderful if helping me brought you and Thane closer together?"

Bryce smiled. "Only you would think of my relationship with my brother when we're discussing your turmoil."

Her dazzling glow intensified. "You just called Thane your brother. And earlier you referred to everyone at Nevon Manor as your family. Have you any idea how happy that makes me?"

"How happy?" Bryce murmured.

"Ecstatic. Overjoyed. Elated."

Instead of laughing, Bryce became solemn. "I'm glad, because making you feel ecstatic, overjoyed, and elated is what I intend to do—not only now but for always."

Bryce could actually see her breath catch.

"Gaby." He drew her closer, tilted her chin up to his. "I have another reason for going to London." He held her gaze. "I need to see Lucinda."

If he expected dismay or even a token protest, he didn't get it. Gaby simply nodded, instantly grasping the underlying meaning of his announcement. "You're going to end it."

"Yes. But I'd feel like a cad if I didn't do it in person."

"I understand." *Now* came the flicker of remorse. "Will she be devastated?"

Only Gaby would feel sympathy for a woman she didn't even know—one who, until now, had been heralded by the newspapers as *the* woman in Bryce's life, his obvious and preeminent choice for a wife.

More fools they.

"No, sweetheart." Bryce's knuckles caressed Gaby's cheek. "Lucinda won't be devastated. Devastation is not something she'd experience—it's far too strong an emotion. She'll feel a trace of disappointment, perhaps a surge of surprise. Then she'll consider my decision, acknowledge its merit, and move on with her life. Besides," he added, with a rueful grin, "I suspect, considering my recent behavior, that she'll be secretly relieved at our parting. Judging from her comments regarding my affinity for Nevon Manor, my fondness for its unorthodox residents, I do believe she thinks I've gone mad."

A cloud of sadness crossed Gaby's face. "That, of course, I can't condone. Still, I feel for the loneliness she's bound to endure."

"I can promise you that Lucinda won't be lonely. She has a dozen suitors waiting in the wings, all of them eager to compete for her affections." Even as Bryce spoke, it startled him to realize how utterly detached he felt about a woman to whom he'd almost pledged his future. It just proved what a void he'd been existing in, how oblivious he'd been to his own needs.

Until Gaby.

"Lucinda is a charming and uncomplicated woman who knows just what she wants out of life," he concluded. "She's gracious, practical, and even-tempered; she'll make the perfect wife and hostess for an equally uncomplicated man."

"But not for you."

A definitive shake of his head. "No. Most definitely not for me."

Gaby's smile was tinged with wonder. "In other words, she's unable to feel the music."

"Neither the notes nor the melody," Bryce concurred. "Not now. Not ever."

"I'm sorry for her."

"I'm not. One doesn't miss something one doesn't know exists." Bryce brushed Gaby's lips with his. "On the other hand, one is eternally grateful when one's heart is opened to music that has always lived inside him but has until now gone unheard."

"Bryce—"

"Enough about Lucinda," he murmured, capturing Gaby's protest with his mouth. "Our parting will be quite civil, I promise you. After which I'll be leaving the old Bryce Lyndley behind—not my work or my causes but the hollow shell of a man who existed a fortnight ago." Another kiss, this one deeper, more fervent. "And when I return, I'm going to have a very important question to ask you."

Tears welled up in Gaby's eyes, trickled down her cheeks. "Really?" she whispered. "What a coincidence. I'm going to have an equally important answer to give you."

"Gaby . . ." Bryce tugged her against him, his thumbs capturing her tears, wiping them away. "God, I don't want to leave you even for a day. What I'm feeling . . ." He gazed deep into her eyes—exquisite, damp pools of cornflower blue. "It's unimaginable, overpowering. It's humbling, especially for a man who's never believed such feelings were possible, never believed such constants existed."

"Say the words," Gaby breathed, twining her arms around Bryce's neck. "Please, Bryce. I need to hear them."

"I love you." He tangled his hands in her hair, covered her mouth with his. "With every fragment of my newly discovered heart, I love you. With all the music you've awakened in my soul, I love you."

"And I love you," she whispered. "So much."

Their kiss was heated, consuming, a bottomless wealth of emotion mixed with a burgeoning, spiraling passion. Gaby pressed as close as she could, shivering with pleasure when Bryce pulled her onto his lap, molded her body to his as he devoured her mouth in a series of hot, drugging kisses. She slid her hands inside his coat, savored the warmth of his skin through his shirt, and thrilled to the sensation of his heartbeat as it accelerated, slamming against hers.

"Gaby . . ." Bryce shifted, tumbled them both to the grass, then stretched out full length beside her, fitting her body to his. "I want you so much," he muttered, wrapping her fiercely in his arms. "So damn much." He kissed her mouth, the pulse beating frantically at her neck, the scented hollow of her throat, threading his fingers through her hair and savoring every inch of her exposed skin.

"Ummm." Gaby's eyes slid closed, her body vitally alive, her senses swimming with discovery. She was keenly aware of the cool grass beneath her, the warmth of the sun above, but mostly Bryce, Bryce—his hands cradling her head, his mouth claiming her purposefully, possessing every inch it touched.

With a painful effort, he rose up, propped himself on his elbows. "One minute more," he managed, his breathing harsh, uneven, "and I'm going to forgo every bloody principle I possess and make love to you right here, right now."

"That sounds exhilarating," Gaby murmured, opening her eyes to see his handsome face taut with the struggle for restraint. "Let's abandon your principles." She wrapped her arms about his neck, tugged him toward her.

"No. Let's not." Bryce caught her arms, gently disentangled them, kissing her palms as he lowered them to her sides. "When I make love to you, it's going to be for hours, without the inhibiting worries of discovery and previous entanglements and pressing departures for London. It's going to be everything you deserve, everything I want for you." A muscle worked in his jaw. "Everything I never knew existed but am blessed enough to have discovered."

Gaby kissed him ever so tenderly. "For a practical barrister who's governed strictly by logic, you've turned out to be an impossible romantic."

"True." Bryce's eyes twinkled, and he hoisted himself to his feet, tugging Gaby up beside him. "Appalling, isn't it?"

"Intolerable." She brushed blades of grass from her gown. "A most inopportune time for you to step out of character." A dazzling smile. "Then again, not completely out of character. Your principles still govern all else."

"I think not." Bryce caught Gaby's shoulders, drew her back into his arms. "In fact, I think when I return we'll need to review some of those places you mentioned where couples go to be alone."

Gaby giggled. "I'll take copious notes while you're gone."

"Do that." He tipped up her chin. "I'll miss you."

"I hate saying good-bye to you," she answered fiercely, all traces of humor gone.

The sound of the carriage horses, stamping about impatiently, drifted to their ears.

"Go," Gaby said firmly, countering her previous admission as she saw the indecision warring on Bryce's face. "Do what you must. I'll be fine—I promise."

"And I'll be back tomorrow—I promise."

She laid her palm against his jaw. "I know you will. This time for good."

Bryce captured her palm, pressed it to his heart as he leaned forward to kiss her. "I love you, Wonderland."

Then he turned and was gone.

* * *

Gaby stood utterly still, gazing after him for a long trancelike moment. Then she strolled over to a solitary oak, leaning against its solid strength and peering through the grove of trees that overlooked the drive. She brushed a windblown tress from her face, watching as Bryce said his good-byes, climbed into his carriage, and urged the horses into motion.

It wasn't until his carriage had disappeared from view and the sounds of the horses were no longer audible that she reacted.

Jolting upright, Gaby touched her fingers to her lips, the enormity of what had just happened striking home in a rush.

"Aunt Hermione," she breathed, taking a reflexive step in the direction of the manor. "Aunt Hermione!" This time it was a shout, as Gaby gathered up her skirts and made a mad dash for the door.

She burst into the house like a cyclone, nearly knocking Chaunce down in the process. "Aunt Hermione!"

Her aunt hurried out from the drawing room, moving as quickly as her limbs would allow. Her eyes widened in astonishment as she took in Gaby's rumpled state and noted Chaunce's skillful attempt to regain his balance. "Darling? What is it?"

With an apologetic squeeze of Chaunce's arm, Gaby flung her arms around her aunt. "He loves me," she breathed, joy rippling through every word. "Oh, Aunt Hermione, he loves me. He told me so."

Hermione's hands trembled as they stroked her niece's hair, and—over Gaby's shoulder—she and Chaunce exchanged a joyous and triumphant glance.

"Oh, Gaby, how wonderful," she murmured. "I'm so very, very happy for you." She held Gaby away, her lips twitching as she searched for the telltale signs of Bryce's declaration. "I assume you heard this splendid news during your stroll?" she inquired, plucking several blades of grass from Gaby's gown.

Gaby was far too excited to be embarrassed. "Yes. And, Aunt Hermione, that's not all. Bryce also said that when he returns from London he'll have an important question to ask me."

This time tears welled up in Hermione's eyes. "Oh, Chaunce, did you hear that?"

"I did indeed, madam." Chaunce cleared his throat. "And it appears that important question isn't coming a moment too soon."

Hearing the protective note in Chaunce's tone, Gaby glanced down at herself, blushing as she realized how obvious it was that she'd been in Bryce's arms. "Thank you, Chaunce," she said softly, her expression tender. "Thank you for always worrying about me. But I assure you that Bryce is the most honorable person in the world." A twinkle. "More honorable than I am."

A flush crept up Chaunce's neck. "I'm relieved to hear that, Miss Gaby."

"Ah, now it makes sense," Hermione realized aloud, paying little attention to Chaunce's puritanical concerns. "When Bryce said he had other business to attend to, I'll venture a guess that he meant severing his ties to that ice maiden."

"Aunt Hermione!" Gaby began to laugh. "That's a dreadful thing to say about Miss Talbot."

"It's not dreadful, it's true. She was wrong for him from the start—as were all of her many predecessors. Only you could awaken Bryce's soul, permeate that self-protective wall he's built around himself since childhood, just as I anticipated, as I've always known in here." She patted her chest where her heart was located, then clapped her hands with glee. "Oh, this is the most glorious news!"

"Bryce does intend to end his liaison with Miss Talbot," Gaby confirmed. "He feels strongly about closing that chapter on his old life in an honorable way before beginning his new . . ." Gaby broke off, inclining her head in puzzlement. "What do you mean, just as you anticipated? You sound as if you planned this whole thing."

"I?" Hermione's brows arched in innocent surprise. "Don't be silly, darling. How on earth could I possibly have planned for two people to fall in love? Only fate can do that."

"True, but then why did you say—"

"Pardon me, my lady, but it's time for your medicine," Chaunce interrupted. "Might I suggest you go upstairs and I'll bring it to you?"

"Of course. Thank you, Chaunce." Hermione gave him a sunny smile. "As always, you're indispensable."

"I'll walk you up," Gaby offered.

"Excellent, my dear." Hermione took Gaby's arm, moved toward the stairs. "This way you and I can have a splendid woman-to-woman chat while Chaunce fetches my medicine."

"That sounds perfect."

Chaunce gazed after them, waiting patiently as Gaby and Hermione ascended the stairs, rounded the second-floor landing, and disappeared from view.

Then he allowed himself one brief self-congratulatory moment, chuckling aloud and rubbing his palms together in exultation. Abruptly he remembered himself, squelching his ear-to-ear grin and clasping his hands behind his back before hastening off to fetch the lemon water from the pantry.

Just inside the sitting room, Marion flattened herself against the wall so as not to be seen, pressing her forefinger to her lips to remind the others to stay quiet. Then, she ruffled Jane and Lily's heads and gave Peter, Henry, and Charles a proud nod before turning to Mrs. Gordon and the rest of the female staff.

"Thank heavens we listened to the children last week when they insisted this was happening," she whispered. "They were right." She glanced at the housekeeper, who was frowning at a smudge atop her own shoe. "Mrs. Gordon?" Marion leaned toward her, righting herself as she stumbled on the edge of the rug. "Will the gown be ready?"

Mrs. Gordon pulled herself up like a British general marching into battle, her twiglike head held high. "Of course it will. Ready *and* spotless. The purest of whites."

"I sewed the last of the tiny pearls on before dawn," Ruth confided in an excited hiss. "Now only the ribbons are left."

"The remaining yards of satin were delivered on schedule," Mrs. Gordon announced. "I myself shall attend to the ribbons as well as to all the other last-minute details. The gown will be exquisite—a bride's dream."

"As will the veil," Ruth confirmed. "Wilson has selected only the finest orange blossoms, and the lace you ordered, Mrs. Gordon, is as delicate as Miss Gaby herself. It's beautiful."

"Naturally," the housekeeper replied with a haughty sniff.

"I've prepared the menu," Cook chimed in. "The midday meal following the ceremony will be a feast fit for a king"—a sparkle of joy—"and his queen."

"That's what they deserve." Marion's round face glowed with pleasure. "Now all we need to do is wait. And," she emphasized, glancing about the room, "keep all this a secret. Remember our agreement: Lady Nevon and Chaunce deserve to be guests at this long-awaited event. We mustn't let them know what we're doing, or they'll start right in helping. We want them to be as surprised as the guests of honor, don't we?"

A murmur of assent rippled through the room.

"Tell that to Goodsmith," Mrs. Gordon informed her sternly. "He does more chattering than all of us combined."

"Don't worry about George," Marion assured her.

"He's busy polishing the carriage that will be taking Miss Gaby and Mr. Lyndley to the local inn after the reception. Besides," she added, loyally defending the man she loved, "George knows how important this wedding is—to Miss Gaby *and* to me. It means equally as much to him. He promised not to say a word to any of them: Miss Gaby, Mr. Lyndley, Lady Nevon, or Chaunce."

"Then that's settled," Cook declared. "Goodsmith would never break a vow to you."

Even Mrs. Gordon grudgingly agreed with that statement.

"I wish I could do more," Dora murmured, her creased face lined with regret as she leaned heavily on her walking stick.

"Dora, your job has yet to come," Marion inserted quickly. "You've been Lady Nevon's personal maid for how long?"

"Over forty years, ever since she married Lord Nevon," Dora returned, pride lacing her tone.

"And for twelve of those years you've sat beside her in the music room, listening while Miss Gaby played."

"Since the child began taking lessons at six." A nostalgic sigh. "She played like an angel, then and now."

"I agree. The point is that you, better than anyone, know which minuets and symphonies are Miss Gaby's favorites. I'll need you to tell me each and every one so I can give a list to the musicians."

"Of course." Dora's narrow shoulders lifted, and a spark of vitality lit her eyes. "I know them all well."

"Good." Marion's smile was tinged with relief.

"Will we be allowed to throw rose petals, Mrs. Gordon?" Lily asked tentatively. "I know they're messy—but just this once?"

Mrs. Gordon scowled, the word "no" hovering on her lips. Then she noticed the pleading look in the child's eyes—and her frown magically eased. "Will you promise to keep your shoes clean?" she demanded gruffly.

Both Jane and Lily nodded eagerly.

"Very well, then." The housekeeper turned to Henry, Charles, and Peter. "But it's up to you boys to make sure they do. Also, you'll have to show the guests to their seats."

"It will be our pleasure, ma'am," Peter assured her.

"The primroses will be in full bloom," Ruth announced. "Wilson promised me. He also promised he'd fill the chapel with colorful, fragrant wildflowers. So the room will look lovely for the ceremony, and the garden will be perfect for the party."

"The whole wedding will be perfect," Marion concluded. "Just like the bride and bridegroom."

"It's up to us to see that it is," Mrs. Gordon said with a rare show of sentimental fervor.

"I agree," Marion concurred, looking from one determined face to the next. "Miss Gaby and Mr. Lyndley have given us so much. It's time we gave them something in return—something they'll remember for the rest of their lives." An anticipatory sparkle. "And I think we've found just the thing."

Chapter 14

Dusk was contemplating its descent when Bryce walked purposefully into the sitting room of Banks's London town house. It felt like weeks rather than hours since he'd left Nevon Manor. He was weary, baffled, and restless, and all he wanted was to tie up the loose ends of his life and go home—to Gaby.

He'd made good use of his afternoon in London, though. First, Doctor's Commons—the sole uplifting visit he'd planned *and* one that had yielded satisfying results—followed by a chat with the Metropolitan Police. Banks's house was Bryce's third stop of the day, with but one remaining: Lucinda.

Both were necessary, neither agreeable.

"Thank you for seeing me, Frederick." Bryce lowered himself into one of the walnut chairs, declining the refreshment offered him by Banks's butler. "I realize you're still in shock. Had this not been important, I wouldn't have intruded."

The solicitor sighed, dismissing his manservant and refilling his brandy snifter. He tossed off the contents in a few shaky swallows. "I haven't gone back to the office yet," he said quietly. "I know I must—William's wife needs assistance removing his personal things—but I thought it best I take another day to compose myself. I wouldn't be doing her any good in the state I'm in. Besides, I told the police they could find me here if they had any questions." Banks massaged his temples wearily. "What can I do for you, Bryce?"

"I'd like to discuss Whitshire's yacht."

"The yacht." Banks seemed to collect his thoughts. "According to what I heard from Officers Dawes and Webster, that avenue yielded no results. The duke's son knew nothing of the fact that his father was in the process of selling his boat to William."

"That's true. In fact, Thane had no idea that his father owned a yacht, much less that he was selling it."

"That's odd."

"I thought so, too. Tell me Frederick, to whom did William intend to transfer title of the yacht?"

"He didn't intend to transfer it to anyone," Banks replied with an element of surprise. "He intended to keep the yacht for himself." A flicker of realization. "Ah, I see. You thought William might have been acting as an intermediary. He wasn't. Clearly you didn't know what an avid sailor he was. He already owned two smaller craft—not nearly as lavish as Whitshire's, of course, but fine boats nonetheless. He felt honored when the duke opted to consider him a potential buyer for his yacht, especially since the two men had never sailed together. Of course, William certainly would have preferred it if happier circumstances had prompted Whitshire's decision to sell." Banks's shoulders slumped. "Still, deteriorating health or not, the duke couldn't have made a better choice. William would have taken excellent care of his craft."

"I'm sure he would have." Bryce leaned forward.

"Frederick, do you recall when Whitshire purchased the ship? Also, do you know if there was a contract authorizing its construction? And with regard to the title, have you any idea where it is? Neither it nor any other papers pertaining to the building or sale of the yacht seem to be in Thane's possession."

Banks frowned. "That does seem unusual, given that the yacht belonged to his late father. The missing title I can explain. I seem to remember William mentioning that Whitshire had forwarded it to him several months ago when they began negotiating the terms of the sale. But as for any related documents, I can't even hazard a guess. This entire transaction was William's matter to handle. I had no part in it. With regard to your first question, all I know is that William said something about the craft being in perfect condition, despite being over a decade old. Exactly when it was built—again, I have not the slightest idea."

"Could you check? When you go back to the office, could you go through William's papers and locate the title and any other letters or papers pertaining to this matter, maybe even something bearing the name of the company that built the yacht?"

"I suppose so." Banks blinked, his eyes red-rimmed from grief and lack of sleep. "Why are you pursuing this? What exactly is it you're looking for?"

"I don't know," Bryce replied honestly. "All I know is that I don't agree with the conclusion of the police that a highwayman was responsible for William's killing, nor am I certain robbery was the motive. I voiced all my reservations in your office yesterday. There are just too many details that don't fit: Why would a highwayman choose William as a target when Thane was far richer? Why would he strike in broad daylight? And why wasn't William's body left in his carriage—if, in fact, he was shot there? I've already stopped at the offices of the police, spoken with Officer Dawes. He informed me that Delmore's carriage was undisturbed—no bloodstains, no torn leather, no sign of a bullet. To me that suggests William might have been murdered on the roadside rather than in his coach. And if that's the case . . ." Bryce inhaled sharply. "Let's just say I want to make sure that Delmore didn't know his assailant and that there's no connection between where he was killed and the papers he was delivering."

"Yes, you did mention that yesterday, but I was too dazed to pay attention," Banks said, paling. "Now that I'm focusing better, I realize you're implying that someone at Whitshire might have committed this crime."

"I'm *speculating* that someone at Whitshire might have committed this crime," Bryce corrected. "Either that or someone knew Delmore's destination and followed him there. But to get at the truth I need your help. Can I count on receiving it?"

"Of course." Banks nodded, mopping at his brow. "Whoever killed William, I want him caught and punished. I'll do whatever I can to make sure that occurs quickly and efficiently, regardless of what it takes or whom it incriminates. I'll go into the office first thing tomorrow. The title to Whitshire's yacht is doubtless among William's current papers, either on or in his desk. I should locate it without any trouble." Banks paused, considering the remainder of Bryce's request. "As for any other documents—documents that date back to the time when the craft was commissioned—those will be a bit trickier to unearth, assuming William had them in his possession at all. Since it's been more than a decade since the yacht was built, any related papers would be in our storage room, buried in the old, inactive files. I'll need some time to sort through those—a few days, at least. How would it be if I send for you the moment I finished doing so? By then I will have amassed all the pertinent material."

Bryce rose. "That would be excellent. If I might impose upon you a bit further, I'd appreciate your sending me two messages: one to my house here in London and the other to Nevon Manor. I'm not sure in which of the two places your note will find me."

"Consider it done." Banks shoved aside his brandy snifter and leaned forward to shake Bryce's hand. "Thank you. I realize your motive is twofold in this matter: you're propelled not only by your long-standing association with us but by your business relationship with Thane Rowland as well. Still, I greatly appreciate your commitment to discovering the truth."

"With all due respect, Frederick, my ties to both you and Thane are secondary in this matter. An innocent man was murdered. I want his killer caught. Now. Not only to bring him to justice but to keep him from harming anyone else."

At that moment, twenty-five miles away, Thane Rowland was preoccupied with his own search for answers.

He stood rigid at the head of Whitshire's library as some forty servants filed in, looking distinctly concerned by the summons they had received—concerned not for themselves but for the young woman they suspected was to be the topic of this meeting, as she had been of the meeting His Grace had called several days ago: Gabrielle Denning. At the previous gathering, the duke had explained Gaby's plight, announced her upcoming visit to Whitshire, and elicited their help.

They'd gladly offered it.

Now they waited with varying degrees of curiosity and suspense, wondering if their efforts had paid off, if the delightful child they remembered from years ago had benefited from her day's outing at the estate, and if the duke had something more to ask of them.

All of them would eagerly comply.

All but one.

"Thank you for coming," Thane began, flattening his palms on the desk. "As I'm sure you've guessed by the particular group of you I've assembled today, this gathering pertains to Gabrielle. First, I want to thank you all for your kind efforts in making her day here an enjoyable and memorable one. That was, after all, our primary goal." A sigh. "Unfortunately, it appears Gabrielle's painful memories are buried deeper than we realized."

Clearing his throat, Thane glanced around the room, warmed by the anxious expressions he saw, from Mrs. Darcey's furrowed brow to Mrs. Fife's drawn mouth, from Thomas to Averley and even to Couling, whose impassive features were now troubled, taut with concern.

"I visited my aunt at Nevon Manor this morning," Thane continued. "It seems that Gabrielle's sleepwalking episodes have worsened and her fragmented memories of the fire have become clearer and more distinct. Evidently, when she awakened in the storage shed that night and saw the flames blazing about her, she overheard two men shouting, crying out for help, before she stumbled across the room and made her way to safety. Judging from the proximity of those voices, I suspect the men were trapped either in the coal room or the woodshed. Do any of you recall one of your colleagues heading in that direction prior to the fire?"

Silence.

"Please think hard. Your answer could help Gabrielle understand what she was inadvertently subjected to that fateful night—in addition to her grief at losing her parents and her helplessness at being unable to prevent their death. I was away at Oxford at the time, so I'm of no use in recounting specifics. All of you, however, were here. So try to remember. Did any one of the servants who perished in the fire strike out toward the coal room or mention his intention to do so?"

"Dowell." It was Thomas the groom who spoke up, abruptly naming the man who had been Whitshire's head gardener at the time of the tragedy.

Thane whipped about to face Thomas. "Dowell? Are you sure?"

"Positive, sir." The groom nodded vigorously. "I'd forgotten about it until just now when you asked your question. I guess I was so shaken up by that night that I did my best to block out any memory of it. But Dowell was definitely in the coal room. I passed him on his way there. I was heading toward the stables, just a half hour or so before the fire broke out. Dowell seemed very distracted, lost in thought. I asked him if he was all right, and he said he was fine but needed to get going because he had business to take care of before he went to bed. I remember looking back over my shoulder when I reached the stable door. I saw him going into the coal room, probably to borrow one of the shovels that were stored in there. So if Miss Gaby heard someone calling out, it could very well have been Dowell."

"He was alone?"

"Yes, sir. All alone."

A frown. "Did you see anyone else—before that, perhaps?"

Thomas puckered up his face, thinking.

"Pardon me, Your Grace, but Thomas was no more than a lad when the fire struck," Couling interjected. "Surely he can't be expected to remember every detail of an event that occurred thirteen years ago."

"People often remember details surrounding a tragedy," Averley countered thoughtfully. "Broken images become ingrained in the mind, along with the horrors of the event itself. So it's not surprising that Thomas's memory of what happened just before the fire is so vivid. I myself shall never forget that night." A sorrowful pause. "None of us will."

"Thank God you spotted the flames when you did," Thane reminded Averley, with a wealth of gratitude. "Otherwise I shudder to think how many more people would have died."

"I'm thankful I was in the right place at the right time," Averley replied. "But as to your question . . ." He pursed his lips. "I too recall the minutes preceding the fire. I was making my way back from the tenants' quarters. A handful of people were still about when I neared the service wing. I remember seeing Thomas, as he just told us, crossing over toward the stables. I didn't see Dowell, but I did spot two or three footmen heading toward the carriage house and a maid leaving the dining quarters on her way to bed. Do you think that information might be helpful?"

"The way the service wing was constructed then, the carriage house was just past the coal room and the woodshed," Thane mused with a nod. "So it's possible that one of the footmen you noticed came upon Dowell and stepped inside to speak with him, then became trapped by the flames." He ran a frustrated hand through his hair. "Do you recall which footmen in particular you saw?"

Averley frowned. "Not offhand, Your Grace. I'm sorry."

"Don't be. I'm asking you to think back thirteen years. Furthermore, this entire avenue I'm pursuing is still pure conjecture. But it is a start." Thane's gaze darted from one servant to the next. "I want all of you to keep racking your brains to see if you remember anything more. In the meantime, I'll pass the information you've just given me on to Lady Nevon. She's extremely worried about Gabrielle."

"We all are," Mrs. Darcey inserted, wringing her hands.

"You're right—we are," Thane agreed. "I don't know what's prompting Gabrielle to remember all these terrifying details at this particular time, but we've got to try to uncover the cause of her sleepwalk-

ing. Should any of you recall anything of conse-
quence, please let me know immediately." Thane
dismissed the staff with a fatigued wave of his hand.
"Thank you, Thomas, Averley. Thank you all. Your
cooperation is greatly appreciated."

The staff filed out as pensively as they'd arrived. On
the surface, nothing had changed.

But the pernicious seeds had been planted.

Moonlight filtered through the window of Bryce's
bedchamber, illuminating the slowly moving hands of
the mantel clock.

Three o'clock.

There would be no sleep tonight, he realized with a
resigned sigh. Despite his weariness, his thoughts
simply would not permit him to rest.

He folded his hands behind his head, staring up at
the ceiling and reviewing the events of the day.

His business with Banks had gone as well as could
be expected. The poor man was still in shock, and the
request Bryce had made of him was both tedious and
time-consuming. It would also be painful, given that it
necessitated sorting through Delmore's papers so
soon after his death. Nevertheless, Banks had agreed,
just as Bryce had anticipated, if for no other reason
than to ensure he'd done everything he could to
unearth his partner's murderer. Now all Bryce had to
do was wait. After which, with a modicum of luck,
Banks would provide the documents Bryce needed to
either substantiate his theory or silence his qualms.

His visit with Lucinda had been a good deal more
difficult.

Not that she'd made a scene. Quite the opposite, in
fact. She'd listened patiently, accepted his decision
with her customary grace and dignity, even wished
him well when she bade him good-bye.

All of which had made him feel like a cad.

It hadn't eased his guilt to hear himself insist on
taking all of the blame for the way things had turned

out. After all, that was nothing more than a truism, given it was he and not she who had changed. Nor had it helped that she didn't shout out accusations or shed a tear when he explained the feelings he'd developed for Gaby, feelings he felt compelled to mention, given his plans for the immediate future.

What *had* helped was Lucinda's response when he told her who Gaby was.

"I don't understand," she'd said her expression genuinely baffled. "The woman you've come to care for is that waif Lady Nevon took in? Bryce, are you sure you know what you're doing? What in the name of heaven do you two have in common? You're a renowned barrister, on your way to being the youngest barrister ever to become Queen's counsel. She's a sheltered provincial girl whose only frames of reference are an eccentric old woman and a houseful of peculiar servants. I know the depths of your compassion, but please try to remember that taking someone on as a cause is quite different from taking her on as a . . . a . . . romantic companion or, even worse, something more permanent. Dear Lord, Bryce, consider your future, your reputation."

Never had Bryce been more aware of the stark differences between himself and Lucinda than at that very moment.

Two weeks ago her speech would have enraged him.

Now, thinking of Gaby, the beauty she'd brought to his life, Lucinda's speech succeeded only in inspiring pity.

"I *am* considering my future," he'd replied with absolute candor, "quite clearly and carefully. The very fact that you can ask me those questions is a perfect illustration of why, even if Gaby were not involved, you and I could never build a life together. We simply see things too differently. Perhaps we always have." A tactful pause. "Let's leave it at that," he'd concluded, scooping up his coat. "Feel free to tell people this parting was your decision. Not that it matters. You're well aware that you have many admir-ers, all of whom will leap at the opportunity to take my place in your life. An hour after you make the announcement, you'll be bombarded with invitations from men far better suited to you than I." He'd managed a cordial smile. "I wish you the best, Lucin-da. Truly I do."

She'd nodded, still looking utterly baffled. "I wish you the same."

You needn't, he'd thought silently. *I already have it.*

On that uplifting thought, he'd taken his leave and gone home.

Well, not truly home, he corrected himself. A temporary stopover, cold and impersonal compared to Nevon Manor.

Gazing up at a patch of moonlight that danced across his ceiling, Bryce smiled, thinking of what Gaby's reaction would be when he flourished the two gifts he meant to take with him—gifts he'd be picking up at midday tomorrow. He had already arranged for the more significant one. Oh, he'd had to exert a fair amount of influence to obtain it on a day's notice. But one of the advantages of being a well-established barrister was knowing enough influential people so that when, at times like this, he needed to expedite a bureaucratic process, he could manage to do so. Unwilling to accept defeat, Bryce had put forth his case and had gotten a positive—actually, a good-natured—response. Thus, the paper he sought would be signed and ready just after noon.

Which left the morning hours to purchase Gaby's second gift: tickets to the symphony.

He could hardly wait to brandish them before her delighted eyes, share her jubilation.

Sharing. That was an act he'd never have deemed himself capable of taking part in, much less yearning for. The truth was that, after thirty-one years, he'd all but convinced himself that the only one he could truly count on in life was himself, that anyone else was transient and could vanish at any moment. His skepticism was understandable even to him—given his childhood, the knowledge of his father's abandonment. Still, he'd truly thought himself a loner by nature, a practical, logical man whose career was his life.

It had taken Gaby to prove him wrong. Gaby, who had shown him both the impulsive, lighthearted side of himself and the passionate, emotional side of himself—a man with more dimensions than he'd ever imagined.

A man capable of a deep abiding love.

Gaby. God, how he missed her.

Bryce rolled onto his side, punching his pillow and closing his eyes. Eager for the night to pass, he tried focusing on mundane issues, such as the paperwork he needed to finish up before he headed back to Nevon Manor.

That didn't work. Instead, he found himself wondering what Thane had learned at Whitshire and, more importantly, if Gaby was resting peacefully.

An uneasy feeling told him she wasn't.

Thane's note arrived at Nevon Manor just before lunch the next afternoon.

Chaunce delivered it directly to the sitting room, where Hermione and Gaby were sipping tea and chatting about the future—an attempt by Hermione to keep Gaby from dwelling on what had turned out to be yet another unsettled night.

"Does Thane say if the servants remembered anything?" Gaby asked, pushing aside her saucer and watching her aunt scan the letter.

"Yes, he does." Hermione cleared her throat and read aloud the detailed account of what had taken place at Whitshire the previous day.

"Dowell. He was the head gardener at the time." Gaby frowned. "Could he have been one of the men I overheard?" A dull throb began vibrating inside her head, and, and, resignedly, she massaged her temples. "This is so frustrating. Last night I had two more sleepwalking episodes. Each time I awakened, I was able to envision the shed and all my activities as clearly as if they were unfolding before me. Yet when it came to the rest, all I could remember was what I remembered with Bryce: the terror in the men's voices and that sickening smell of fire."

"The memories will come back to you," Hermione assured her, folding the letter and slipping it into the side-table drawer. "Besides, Thane has only just begun this crusade. He intends to reconvene his staff again soon. You know how badly they want to help. Eventually something conclusive will emerge. In the meantime"—Hermione tossed her a mischievous smile—"Tonight Bryce will be home."

Gaby's entire face lit up, just as Hermione had hoped. "I know. I can scarcely wait." She leaned forward. "Do you think he'll ask to speak with me right away?"

A chuckle. "I don't think you'll give him a choice."

The joy on Gaby's face faded a bit. "Do you think I'm being too obvious?"

"No, darling. You're being you. And that's precisely who Bryce fell in love with." Hermione gave a delicate cough. "There is something we haven't discussed, something I'd like to bring up, if I may."

An impish grin. "You needn't worry, Aunt Hermione. As I told Chaunce, Bryce has more self-control than I. He's been a complete gentleman—too much so, if you ask me."

Hermione dissolved into laughter. "That isn't the issue I intend to broach, but I'm relieved to hear Bryce is so restrained in his ardor. For now," she added. "I suspect that will soon be a thing of the past."

"Is making love wonderful?" Gaby asked with her customary directness.

"For you and Bryce, it will be—yes." After thirteen

years Hermione was unsurprised by Gaby's straightforward manner, which, given her limited exposure to the outside world, had remained uncluttered by artifice or shame. "When the time comes, it will be everything you're dreaming of and more."

"I doubt it could be more. My dreams are extraordinary."

Another chuckle. "Let's leave that to Bryce, shall we?"

"All right." Gaby sighed. "I just wish the hours between now and evening would fly by." A questioning pucker formed between her brows. "If intimacy isn't the issue you wanted to discuss, what is?"

"The guardianship. Bryce told me he mentioned my plans to you. Are you very angry with me?"

"Not for selecting Bryce, no. I was upset that neither you nor he chose to include me in the conversation you had concerning my future, but Bryce made me realize you were only trying to protect me." Gaby leaned forward, seized her aunt's hands. "I have two additional replies to your question. First, you needn't worry over my future, or anyone else's for that matter. You're going to be with us forever. I intend to see to it. And second, please stop trying to shield me. I'm a grown woman now, Aunt Hermione, not a little girl. I'm strong enough to share your problems and your plans, just as I've shared your love for our family— and our mutual determination to shelter them."

Tears filled Hermione's eyes. "We've done a good job at that, haven't we?"

"The best." Gaby's smile was watery. "Then again, that's not a surprise. You *are* the best."

"I quite agree." Chaunce stood in the doorway, nodding his approval at Gaby's statement. "Pardon me, ladies, but Lily has advised me that Master Crumpet has once again escaped from his warren. She and Jane are combing the gardens, but I'd prefer they not venture into the wooded areas alone. Shall I ask Bowrick to relieve me at the door and go with them?"

"No, thank you, Chaunce." Gaby rose to her feet. "I appreciate your offer, but I'll assist the girls."

"I wonder if that's a wise idea." Chaunce frowned. "You didn't sleep a wink last night and—"

"Chaunce," Gaby interrupted, "as I just said to Aunt Hermione, you must stop worrying about me." She gazed lovingly from Chaunce to her aunt and back again. "I love you both with all my heart, but I'm not a child anymore. It's *I* who should be helping *you*, not the other way around. I realize I'm going through a difficult time, and you're concerned about me. I can't tell you how grateful I am for your caring and support. But let the truth be known, I feel horrible about the fact that my sleepwalking compels you to spend your nights standing guard outside my bedchamber door, and all to protect me from myself. So please, for my sake, relinquish that role during the day, when it's totally unnecessary. All right?"

Hermione nodded, smiling through her tears. "All right."

Gaby leaned down to kiss her aunt's cheek, then crossed over and stood before Chaunce. "You'd best recover your strength," she said softly. "I suspect that after Bryce asks me his important question, I'm going to have an equally important question to ask you." With a tremulous smile, she rose on tiptoe, pressed a kiss to Chaunce's jaw. "I hope you won't refuse me. You are, after all, like a father to me—the only father I've known for thirteen years."

With that, she hurried off to search for Crumpet.

Hermione dashed the tears from her cheeks. "She really has grown up, Chaunce. Just now, watching her, listening to her speak, it struck me in a rush. I'm sure you think me foolish for crying, but I find this whole situation wonderful and painful all at once."

When Chaunce didn't answer, Hermione looked up, inclined her head in his direction.

There were tears glistening in his eyes.

* * *

It was nearly three o'clock.

Bryce was halfway to Nevon Manor, his carriage moving at a rapid clip, the gifts he had chosen for Gaby tucked carefully in his pocket.

Abruptly, that feeling struck.

It was the same feeling he'd had last time, the nagging sensation that he was needed.

Only this time it was stronger. Stronger and more specific.

It wasn't just anyone who needed him. The person who needed him was Gaby.

Jaw set, he shifted forward in his seat, slapping the reins and commanding the horses to quicken their pace.

The carriage raced toward Nevon Manor.

"Crumpet! Where are you, you wretch?"

Gaby traipsed along the wooded path, cupping her hands and shouting for her pet in the hope that she'd startle him into making a rustling sound, thus revealing himself.

The search was taking longer than usual—nearly three hours, to be exact. Jane and Lily had been sent back to the manor ages ago, their small bodies weary, their eyes half closed with exhaustion.

At this point, even Gaby was getting irritated.

She'd covered the entire area surrounding the gardens, scoured the woods on either side of the manor as well as behind it. Now she was retracing her steps to see if Crumpet had tired himself out and headed home for his warren.

She had a few unpleasant words for her pet when she found him.

Cutting through a thick grove of trees, Gaby was just about to break into a run when she heard the telltale rustle she'd been waiting for.

"Crumpet?" She veered in that direction, winding her way through the trees and calling out as she walked. "Where are you?"

The sound came from just behind her.

Gaby whirled about, on the verge of grabbing her pet and scolding him.

Her words died on her tongue as a dark, masked figure loomed over her, clutching a rock in his hands. Before she could react, he raised his arms and brought the rock down on her head.

Colors swam before Gaby's eyes, and an oddly familiar musky smell pierced her nostrils as pain exploded inside her head.

Then she was sucked into a swirling tunnel of blackness.

And finally . . . nothing.

Chapter 15

FIRE.

It was blazing inside her head, all around her body, only this time her skull ached too much to lift it, her eyes burned too much to open.

Oh, God, would this nightmare ever go away?

Gaby shifted, shards of pain bursting in her temples, weighing down her mind. And her leg.

Her leg?

Dazed, she tried to move her left leg, only to find that it was trapped, anchored by something too powerful to dislodge.

What was happening to her?

The sound of crackling flames reached her ears, intensifying heat radiating through her body. And that smell. That horrible sweet, musky smell. The smell of death.

She had to get out.

Again she tried to move, and again her leg refused to cooperate. Beneath her, the ground was softer than she remembered, more like grass than dirt.

With every drop of will she possessed, she forced

her eyes open, shifted her weight to her elbows, and tried to see beyond the splitting pain in her skull.

She could see nothing but leaping flames—the heinous orange glow she recognized only too well.

Only this time the fire was real.

Like the first time.

"No," she choked out, peering about to determine where she was.

Again that tug on her leg.

Gaby looked over her shoulder, shifting so she could see the lower section of her body.

She was lying alongside Crumpet's warren, and her leg was jammed into the opening, pinned there by rocks.

Pinned there by someone.

In a rush, Gaby remembered—the assailant, the rock, the smell.

Fire.

Whoever had hit her, had also trapped her here.

And then he'd left her to die.

With a cry of fear and pain, she clawed at the stones, frantically struggling to free her leg. Her forehead was bleeding; she could feel the trickle of blood oozing down the side of her head, and the pain was excruciating. So was the dizziness. But she couldn't give in to them, couldn't lie down and succumb to the slumber her body craved. To sleep would mean to die.

Racking coughs seized her as the fire spread, blazing a trail across the grass, igniting everything it touched. Thank heaven this area immediately surrounding Crumpet's warren wasn't heavily wooded. The lack of trees would slow down the fire's progress and buy her some time.

Or make her death that much more agonizing.

No. She couldn't think that way.

Gaby gave in to the coughing, crying out at the resulting pain in her head, yet knowing that the pain would help to keep her awake. Frustrated by her impotence, she pounded at the rocks that wedged her foot tightly inside the narrow opening in the dirt.

They wouldn't budge.

"Help!" She pushed herself as far upright as she could, shouting hoarsely, hoping someone would hear her or spot the fire. For the first time she wished Crumpet's warren weren't located in such a remote area; if only it were near the gardens, where Wilson might see her, or closer to the coach house, so Goodsmith might notice. How long would it be before the flames were visible from the manor? Quite a while. They were low to the ground, burning only grass and dirt, as there were no tall trees to catch fire.

God help her, she didn't want to die.

"Help!" Alternately coughing and yelling, Gaby held her head to still its agony, squeezing her eyes shut to block out the smoke.

Minutes slipped by—only a few, but each one seemed like an eternity.

The dizziness intensified, and unconsciousness became more and more a reality, her body's demand for sleep more acute.

Mama . . . Papa . . .

Gaby felt tears sting her already burning eyes, and she dug her fingers into the ground, grasping clumps of grass between her fingers. "Help," she called out, her voice thin, a mere wisp of sound. "Help." It was a whisper.

Pounding.

The ground vibrated as if it were about to swallow her up. Or was it just the drumming in her head?

More pounding, followed by a shout of "Gaby!"

The pounding was footsteps.

The voice was Bryce's.

"Bryce." She wasn't sure if she said his name or just imagined she did. All she knew was that he was beside her. She didn't even need to open her eyes to know it. He was there.

"Gaby." He swore violently, the wrenching motions and rustling sounds telling Gaby he was tearing off his coat. An instant later it was around her and Bryce was gathering her up to lift her.

"My . . . leg—" she choked out, then dissolved into coughing.

Another oath, and Bryce dropped to his knees, wresting the rocks away in a few powerful yanks.

Gaby felt the blessed relief of freedom.

"I've got you, sweetheart." He lifted her gently, cradling her against his chest and striding away from the heat, the smoke, the smell.

An unknown number of strides later, she heard him shout, "Wilson! There's a fire at the warren!"

"A fire?" More pounding footsteps. "Dear Lord, Miss Gaby!" Wilson's frightened exclamation came from right beside them.

"I'll take care of Gaby," Bryce instructed. "You get that shovel of yours and throw as much dirt as you can on the flames. It's not out of control yet. But it will be. I'll send help from the manor."

"I'll bring all my shovels. Send Goodsmith. We'll put out that blaze. You just make sure Miss Gaby's all right."

"I intend to." Bryce was moving again, and the motion was almost overwhelming.

"Bryce," she whispered, her head swimming, "I . . . don't think I can . . ."

The tightening of his arms about her was the last thing she remembered before she fainted.

A sea of voices surged about her, worried voices, taut with strain and fear. Something cumbersome lay on her head, and her body burned and ached as if she had a fever.

Did she?

With a supreme effort, she forced open her eyes.

"Welcome back, Wonderland." Bryce's words were light, but his expression was grim, his gaze anguished as it searched her face. "We missed you." He captured her hand in his, bringing her fingers gently to his lips. "God, I've been so worried."

Gaby gave him a puzzled look. "Your face is charred," she started to say, but a fit of coughing stopped her. Her chest felt tight and raspy, eclipsed only by the unbearable pain in her head, a pain that increased with each successive cough.

"Shhh. Don't try to talk." Bryce kissed her palm, pressed his forefinger to her lips. "You inhaled a fair amount of smoke. It will take a while for your lungs to clear. And coughing will only worsen your headache."

Memory flooded back.

Instinctively, Gaby tried to sit up, then thought better of it as throbbing waves swept over her.

"You're in your bed," Bryce supplied. "Nearly the entire family is here—all but Cook, Wilson, and Goodsmith. They're in the kitchen. Cook is tending to the minor burns Wilson and Goodsmith got when they put out the fire. They did an astonishing job. There's very little damage to the property other than the area directly surrounding the warren. Everyone is safe. Including Crumpet. And you."

Gaby's eyes filled with tears. "Aunt Herm—"

"I'm right here, darling." From the chair on the opposite side of Gaby's bed, Aunt Hermione leaned over, stroking her niece's hair with a shaking hand. "I wouldn't be anywhere else."

"I'm here, too, Gaby," Lily's small voice chimed in. "Crumpet's staying in my room until you're well. He was behind the stables, munching on some tossed-out vegetables when we found him. He's real sorry to have caused so much trouble. And he can't wait to see you."

Gaby managed a tiny smile.

"Hot tea for the patient." It was Chaunce's voice, brisk as ever. The butler made his way through the room, placing a tray on Gaby's nightstand. "Ah, Miss Gaby. I'm delighted you're awake. The tea is hot and—" His voice broke and it took a full moment for him to recover himself. "I'll pour you a cup," he managed at last, his hand trembling as he did.

"I'm going to help you sit up a bit," Bryce told her quietly. "I want you to drink the tea. Chaunce laced it with a bit of brandy, just as Dr. Briers instructed. It will relieve the pain and help you rest." Bryce leaned forward and, in full view of the staff, brushed his lips to Gaby's. "I know you ache everywhere right now, but that will pass. We were very lucky. The rock that evidently struck your head hit only hard enough to cause a minor concussion. And quite a hefty gash. Your leg is swollen and bruised, but not broken. In short, you'll heal. Rapidly. We all intend to see to that."

A chorus of fervent yeses reached Gaby's ears.

"We'll all be here when you awaken. So drink the tea and go to sleep. We'll talk later."

"All right," she whispered, letting him help her to a half-sitting position. "Bryce?" she murmured between sips of tea.

"Hmm?"

"Thank . . . you."

"Don't." He shook his head emphatically. "It wasn't only you I was thinking of when I stalked through those flames. It was me. I couldn't survive if anything happened to you. It wasn't a choice, Gaby. I had to get to you. So I did."

Tenderly Gaby caressed his jaw. "That . . . important question . . . you had to ask me . . ."

For the first time a smile touched his lips. "The instant we're alone. I promise."

Gaby finished the tea, then allowed her eyelids to droop. "G'night," she slurred.

Bryce swallowed past the lump in his throat. "Good night, Wonderland."

Evening melted into night.

Gaby faded in and out of consciousness several times, each time drifting awake amid a sea of concerned faces, murmured voices, and gentle reassurances.

It was during the deepest hours of night that she opened her eyes to a dark room and silence.

"Bryce?" she whispered into the blackness.

A rustle of movement and he was by her side.

"I'm here, sweetheart." Slowly he sank down on the edge of the bed, brushing strands of hair from her face.

He was wearing the same charred clothing he'd been wearing earlier, except that the sleeves of his shirt were rolled up now and he'd washed away the telltale black streaks from his face.

He was not only the handsomest of men but the most welcome sight on earth.

"Are we alone?" she asked, looking about.

He smiled, following her gaze. "For the moment. However, I wouldn't hold out much hope of that lasting. Chaunce and Hermione are probably already on their way back to check up on you. They've scarcely left your side all night." He paused. "Your voice sounds much stronger. Is your breathing easing?"

"Yes. My chest doesn't feel nearly as raspy as it did. Now I just feel weak."

"Thank God for that. According to Dr. Briers, you must have regained consciousness soon after the fire was started. That's why your burns are minor, and your difficulty breathing minimal. Evidently you had been lying amid the flames for only a few minutes when I arrived."

"It seemed like an eternity." Gaby shuddered. "As for thanking God, I do. But I also thank you. Had you not found me when you did . . ."

"Don't even say it."

"How did you know I needed you?"

"Just a feeling. This time I was smart enough to heed it." Bryce leaned down, brushing Gaby's lips with his. "Are you in any pain?" His fingertips grazed the weight on her head ever so slightly—a weight Gaby realized was a bandage.

"The pain has subsided a lot." She reached up, caressed Bryce's jaw. "Please. We can talk about everything else later. But, as you said, I doubt we'll be alone for more than a few minutes. So . . ."

"So let's get to my question," he guessed with tender amusement. "Or rather, my questions. I have two. They accompany the two gifts I brought you from London." He reached over to where his coat lay on the chair—the same coat he'd wrapped her in when he carried her to safety. Groping in his pocket, he extracted the tickets he'd procured. "Question one. Will you accompany me to the symphony next week? If you're not up to it by then, we can exchange the tickets for a later performance."

"Oh, Bryce, thank you." Gaby touched the tickets gingerly . . . if a shade disappointedly. "I'll be all healed by next week, I promise. I'd love to accompany you to the symphony. You know how badly I've wanted to go."

"But . . . ?"

"But it's just that I thought . . . that is, I hoped—"

"Now for the second gift," Bryce continued mysteriously, once again reaching into his pocket. "Acquiring this one took quite a bit of maneuvering, so I hope you'll be more excited about it than you are about the tickets. In fact, I hope you'll be exhilarated about it— as exhilarated as I am." He extracted a folded piece of paper, flourished it before Gaby.

Gaby frowned, unable to read the paper in the darkness. "What is it?"

"A special license." Abandoning his mock composure, Bryce placed the license beside them and, with aching tenderness, framed Gaby's face between his palms. "I love you, Gabrielle Denning. You've filled a void inside me I never knew I possessed, much less recognized as empty. Will you do me the supreme and extraordinary honor of becoming my wife?"

Two tears slid down Gaby's cheeks. "I've imagined this moment at least a thousand times since yesterday, prayed I hadn't misunderstood the question you mentioned," she whispered. "And now that my prayers have been answered, now that this moment is actually here, I want somehow to capture it, to make it last forever."

"There will be an eternity of moments equally as treasured. This is but the first. I promise." Bryce's thumbs caught her tears, caressed the delicate contours of her cheekbones. "Now tell me, in your thousand imaginings, did you happen to provide me with an answer?"

Joy illuminated Gaby's face. "Yes, I provided you with an answer—the same answer each and every time: Yes. With all my heart, yes, I want more than anything to become your wife." She drew his mouth down to hers. "Bryce, I love you so much."

With a husky sound, Bryce kissed her, a deep, reverent kiss that flowed through her like warm honey, soothing and inflaming all at once.

"Stay with me," Gaby breathed. "Don't leave."

"Never again, Gaby." Bryce's meaning far transcended Gaby's more immediate one. "Never, ever again." He molded the softness of her lips to his, touching her, tasting her, savoring her flavor. "I won't leave you or Nevon Manor—ever." He threaded his fingers through her hair, buried his lips in hers for an endless, timeless moment. "This time I'm home to stay."

"Nothing could make me happier than hearing you say those words."

Along with Hermione's fervent declaration, a shaft of light from the hall splintered the darkness, ending the magical spell of privacy that had prevailed during Gaby and Bryce's moments alone.

Breaking apart, they turned toward the doorway, noting that both Hermione and Chaunce hovered on its threshold, having heard at least some portion of Bryce's vow.

Judging from the rigidity of Chaunce's stance, not the initial part.

"I've dreamed of this moment for as long as I can remember," Hermione proclaimed, her voice trembling as she stepped into the room.

"Indeed," Chaunce agreed, following her in and eyeing Bryce with decidedly less approval. "I'm equally delighted that you've elected to remain with us. However, don't you think you might declare your intentions to do so while sitting in the chair? Miss Gaby is hardly up to so . . . strenuous a visit."

Taking in Chaunce's disapproving look, his less than subtle censure, Gaby laughed—laughter that ended on a moan as she clutched her head.

"Chaunce, please, it hurts when I do that. And to answer your question, no, Bryce could not have declared his intentions while sitting in a chair. Because one of those intentions—the one you obviously arrived too late to overhear—involved not Nevon Manor but me. Or, to be more exact, us." Gaby's enthralled gaze shifted to Hermione. "Bryce has asked me to marry him."

"Oh, Gaby." Hermione pressed her hand to her heart, joy shimmering through her like rays of sunlight. "I retract my original statement. *This* is the moment I've dreamed of forever, the moment destined to make me happier than any other. Chaunce"—she turned to him—"did you hear that?"

"I did indeed." In contrast to his clipped reserve of a moment earlier, Chaunce was now actually smiling. "And I couldn't be more pleased." He guided Hermione toward Gaby's bedside, clasping Bryce's hand as Hermione leaned over to kiss her niece.

"When shall we plan this splendid occasion?" Hermione murmured. "A month from now? Two? That will give us ample time to make all the arrangements: the gown fittings, the musicians, the menu—"

"Three days," Bryce interrupted quietly.

Hermione blanched. "Three days?"

"Yes. Three days."

A heartbeat of silence ensued.

Flattened against the wall just outside the open doorway, Lily clapped a hand over her mouth to silence her cry of delight. Carefully, she tiptoed away; then, when she'd reached a safe distance, tore off to report this new and exciting development.

Unaware of what was transpiring elsewhere in the manor, Bryce rose, folding his arms across his chest as he explained his position to Hermione and Chaunce. "I procured a special license while I was in London," he began, gesturing toward the sheet of paper at Gaby's bedside. "At the time, I did so because I wanted Gaby to have the freedom to choose whichever wedding day she wanted. But after what happened here this afternoon, what almost happened"—Bryce swallowed—"waiting is no longer an option. Hermione, someone tried to kill Gaby. There's no guarantee that whoever it was won't try again. I intend to ensure he doesn't succeed."

"But we'll contact the police. Surely they'll investigate."

"Oh, they'll investigate. The first thing they'll do is to question the residents of Nevon Manor."

"Oh, Bryce—no," Hermione breathed. "Our family believes the fire was an accident. They wouldn't be able to comprehend, much less accept the fact, that someone actually tried to kill Gaby. And questioning? They'd succumb under the strain."

"Exactly. And since we know that no one here had anything to do with Gaby's attack, the whole process would be unnecessarily destructive, and thoroughly unacceptable. It's our job to protect our family, to spare them that emotional devastation."

"The police might perceive a connection between Mr. Delmore's murder and Miss Gaby's assault," Chaunce said thoughtfully.

"I agree. That's a strong possibility, given the proximity of the two incidents. In which case, the police will assume one of two things. Either they'll assume they're dealing with coincidental assaults by the same desperate and somewhat ineffective thief who's unable to discern a rich victim from a poor one, or they will reconsider my original suspicion with regard to Delmore's destination and link the two crimes to someone at Whitshire. Which, at this point, is the last thing we need, because if they question Thane and his staff, the murderer might very well become alarmed and try again. And if Gaby is right here within striking distance . . ." Bryce broke off, a muscle working in his jaw.

Insight registered in Hermione's eyes. "You're going to take Gaby away," she inferred.

Bryce's nod was definitive. "Until we figure out the identity of that madman—yes, I am. We won't go far, only to my home in London, but that's far enough to put a safe distance between the murderer and Gaby. It's the only way, Hermione, until we can determine who this scoundrel is, find concrete proof of his guilt, and see him imprisoned in Newgate." Bryce turned to Gaby, reaching down and clasping her hand. "I'm sorry, Wonderland. Were you dreaming of a large, elaborate wedding?"

"I was dreaming of marrying you," Gaby stated simply, unsurprised by Bryce's line of thought or his authoritative tone. She well understood the reason for his reaction, and she loved him all the more for his determination to protect her and their family. True, her dreams of being married had always included a traditional wedding with a flowing gown and a joyous party amid the lush gardens of Nevon Manor. But all that paled beneath the dire issues confronting them now.

So she would become Bryce's wife—in whatever manner he deemed best.

"Gaby?" Bryce prompted, watching her expression.

Gaby's fingers tightened in his. "I agree with everything you just said. And if circumstances preclude a few of my dream's secondary aspects, so be it, as long as I become your wife." She chewed her lip. "But with regard to London . . . we will return to Nevon Manor as soon as this nightmare is behind us, won't we?"

"The instant the murderer is caught." Bryce kissed her fingertips. "I want to be here as much as you do."

A reassured nod. "I know."

"Mr. Lyndley's logic is sound, my lady," Chaunce concurred, laying a soothing palm on Hermione's shoulder. "Miss Gaby's life is in danger. Keeping her safe comes before all else."

"Of course it does," Hermione agreed, her dismay eclipsed by loving concern.

"Sweetheart," Bryce continued, touching Gaby's cheek, "now that we've broached the subject, I'd like to pursue it—for just a few minutes. I realize you're exhausted and still suffering some degree of pain and shock. But can you tell us what you remember about this afternoon?"

Gaby nodded again, staunchly gathered her thoughts. "I never actually saw the man who tried to kill me." For the first time she said the words aloud, and she began to tremble with reaction. "He was wearing a mask. I was some fifty yards from Crumpet's warren when I heard rustling in the brush. I turned, thinking it was Crumpet. It wasn't. I caught a glimpse of a masked figure in black, clutching a rock. He raised his arms, brought the rock down on my head. That's all I remember until I awakened amid the fire. That and a musky smell—the sickening smell of death."

"Burning grass and wood," Hermione murmured.

Bryce nodded. "Do you remember anything else about him?"

"No," Gaby said after a moment. "I only saw him for a fleeting instant."

Hermione swallowed hard. "I think the more important question is why. Why did he do this to Gaby?"

"You can guess the answer to that—evidence or not," Bryce returned quietly. "We all can."

"Yes." Gaby shivered. "He was alarmed by my recent, more distinct memories of the fire. Whoever he is, he was afraid I'd remember something he didn't want anyone to know about. Something that would implicate him." A tormented pause. "Bryce, that leads me to only one conclusion: what I overheard the night of the fire—the men's voices—wasn't just two people trapped in an accidental death; it was murder."

"And I'm willing to bet that whoever committed the murder also started the fire," Bryce agreed. "Probably to cover up his crime. I'm sure he never intended for the fire to blaze so completely out of control, to claim so many lives. But it did. After which, it became even more imperative for him to avoid discovery, which he managed to do effortlessly, given that everyone believed the fire to be a chance occurrence. In fact, he wasn't even at risk—until you remembered the voices in the coal room. That showed things in an entirely new light, which unnerved him enough to try to silence you."

"So one of the voices I overheard was his, and the other, his victim's." Gaby met Bryce's gaze. "Clearly you believe that whoever this killer is, he lives at Whitshire."

"It certainly makes sense. After all, you were attacked the very day after Thane reassembled his staff and told them about your reawakened memories. That's *too* striking a coincidence. Also, as we mentioned a few minutes ago, Delmore's murder now looks doubly suspicious, given its location and timing. All these incidents are connected somehow—I just don't yet know how. But Delmore's partner, Frederick Banks, is in the process of assembling all the documents relating to the late duke's yacht. He's agreed to send for me the moment he's through. I suspect those papers will fill in some of the missing pieces. So . . . do I think the murderer is living at Whitshire? Definitely. And I'll wager that whoever he is killed Dowell that night."

"But who? And why?" Again Gaby rubbed her head. "Dowell—every time I hear his name, my head begins to ache. That must be a sign we're getting close. I just wish I could remember more." She winced as her fingers brushed her bandaged wound.

"You will—but not tonight." Bryce reached over to the nightstand and poured a cup of tea, then added a few drops of laudanum to it. "We've done enough conjecturing for now. You've been through an ordeal. You need your rest in order to recover. We'll all be here, as will the mystery, when you awaken." He supported her shoulders and held the cup to her lips. "This is a fresh pot of tea. Chaunce brought it up while you were asleep. It's still warm. I want you to drink the entire cup, then lie down and close your eyes."

He waited while she complied, then eased her back down, tucking the bedcovers about her and watching the laudanum take effect.

"All right." Gaby's eyelids were already drooping. "I suppose I am a little tired." A yawn. "Bryce?" she said abruptly, her lashes fluttering.

"Hmm?"

"You did say three days?"

Bryce leaned down, brushed a chaste kiss on her mouth. "Yes, Wonderland. Three days and we'll be married."

"Chaunce . . ." Clearly, she was fighting the affects of the drug.

"Miss Gaby, you really should rest," Chaunce chided her gently.

"I will." She gave him a faint smile, her blue eyes—though glazed and battling to remain open—soft with tenderness. "But first I need to ask you my important question. Will you walk me down the aisle, give me to Bryce . . . not away but to a new life that will also encompass all the beauty of my old one?"

A muscle worked at Chaunce's throat. "I'd be honored, Miss Gaby."

"Thank you. And Aunt Hermione . . ."

"I'll be your aunt and your bridal attendant all in one," Hermione vowed.

"No. My best friend and my mother," Gaby's words were slurred, but not too slurred to have an impact.

Joyous tears slid down Hermione's cheeks.

"And the whole family . . . will be . . . there . . ." Gaby sighed, a wisp of sound that was as awed as it was faint. "Mrs. Bryce Lyndley." A faraway smile. "Much better than Wonderland."

With that, she slept.

Lily knocked on Marion's door, then dashed inside the instant she heard the mumbled "Come in."

"Lily, why are you awake at this hour?" Marion asked, worry lacing her tone as she sat up in bed. "Is it Miss Gaby? Is she worse?"

"Oh, no." Lily scrambled onto the bedcovers, kneeling beside Marion with a wide grin. "She's much better. She was awake for a long time, Marion. And I heard her and Mr. Lyndley talking to Lady Nevon and Chaunce." An impatient tug at the sleeve of Marion's nightgown. "Guess what they said?"

"What?"

"They're getting married. In three days."

"Three days?" Now Marion was wide awake. "Are you sure?"

"Uh-huh. I heard them say so. Mr. Lyndley, especially. He didn't want to wait."

"Let's go." Marion sprang out of bed, yanked on her wrapper in a few clumsy tugs, and snatched Lily's hand. "We've got to awaken Mrs. Gordon, make sure the gown is finished and find out what else is left to do. Everything's got to be perfect." She tripped over the belt of her wrapper, shoving it aside impatiently, only to trip on it again.

Pausing, she jammed the belt into her pocket and leaned down to give Lily a hard hug. "Lily, you're the best eavesdropper in the whole world!"

Like thieves in the night, they darted through the hallway, racing purposefully toward Mrs. Gordon's chamber.

Chapter 16

GABY'S WEDDING DAY DAWNED WITH ALL THE RADIANT splendor that filled her heart: dazzling sunshine, twittering birds, and one exuberantly screeching woodpecker.

"Vicar Kent will be here in an hour," Hermione reported to Gaby, flitting about the sitting room as the grandfather clock inched its way toward 9:00 A.M. "He was charmed by your desire to be married right here at Nevon Manor and, therefore, delighted to perform the ceremony in our chapel."

"He's a wonderful man," Gaby proclaimed. "Today the whole world is wonderful!" She whirled across the room to hug her aunt.

Chaunce strolled in, arched a brow at the two frolicking ladies. "I came to see what the commotion was about, thinking perhaps you required my help. Instead, you require my advice." He glanced first at Hermione. "My lady, you'll tire yourself out before the ceremony if you continue in this manner. And, Miss Gaby"—he turned to the bride—"need I remind you that just three days ago you were nearly killed? Dr. Briers cautioned you to stay in bed for a day; you were out the next morning. He instructed you to limit your activities, to move about a bit at a time; you were frolicking in the woods by yesterday. And he insisted you spend the morning of your wedding abed—a reasonable enough suggestion, since the ceremony is to take place at ten o'clock, but you've been up since dawn, fluttering about like your crazed woodpecker. If I hadn't bolted the door, you'd be running outside with the children." Chaunce rolled his eyes. "What am I to do with you?" A pointed glare at Hermione. "With both of you?"

"Why not join us?" Hermione suggested with a twinkle. "I feel stronger than I have in weeks, like a young girl myself. And Gaby . . ." She inclined her head at her niece, who was now waltzing about the room, alternately humming and greeting the sunshine that spilled through the windows. "Does she look peaked to you? I think not. Besides, I'm quite sure she'll agree to retire early this evening, won't you, my dear?"

Gaby tossed her aunt a conspiratorial grin. "You have my word, Aunt Hermione."

"There," Hermione proclaimed with a flourish. "That should ease your unfounded worry. In addition, today is a joyous celebration, the culmination of years of praying, months of planning—"

Chaunce's warning cough was interrupted by a question from Gaby: "What months of planning?"

Hermione recovered herself gracefully. "Very well, then—days. Humor me, darling. I'm trying to pretend I actually had the month or two I yearned for to plan a romantic, dream-come-true wedding for you. I wanted your day to be perfect."

"It is perfect," Gaby assured her. "My family is here, and I'm marrying Bryce. Not only that, but Bryce has asked Thane to stand up for him as his groomsman. Now, what could be more perfect than all that?"

"A well-taken point," Chaunce conceded. "However, unless you plan to be married in your worn-out day dress, with a bit of this morning's custard on your cheek, I'd suggest you improve upon perfection by going upstairs to change."

"Goodness! You're right." Gaby stared down at herself in dismay.

"There's still plenty of time," Chaunce assured her. "Marion said to tell you she's drawn you a bath and laid out the dress you requested." He frowned. "I had hoped Lily and Jane would be here to help Marion weave a few flowers through your hair, but they and Ruth are nowhere to be found. Dora offered to take their place; I think between her and Marion, they'll do a splendid job of arranging your tresses, flowers or not. Oh, and Mrs. Gordon has ordered everyone away from the dining room and yellow salon; apparently, she's scrubbing them both free of some scuff marks that were allegedly left on the floors and on the windows overlooking the garden. She's none too pleased about the situation, either; she nearly bit my head off. Of course there was no one else about for her to chastise and warn away. Nonetheless, given her rather piqued frame of mind, I'm more than happy to stay out of her way."

Hermione's brow furrowed in puzzlement. "Now that you've called it to my attention, the entire manor has been unusually quiet since breakfast. Even the boys are nowhere to be found, although Peter is probably in Bryce's chamber reading his legal texts while Bryce prepares for the wedding. Thane is also up there—in his case, to assist the bridegroom. But there's been not a thud or a shout or even a peal of laughter in hours. Where is everyone?"

"Perhaps they're all getting dressed, just as I should be," Gaby proposed, brushing a stray lock of hair off her face with more than a touch of self-censure. "And with the vicar arriving in less than an hour, I'd better do so—and swiftly." She seized Hermione's hands.

"Will you come up with me? I know you need time to dress, but—"

"I'll sit with you while you prepare for your bath," Hermione offered at once. "We'll have a lovely pre-nuptial chat. Then I'll go to my chambers and dress. After which Dora and Marion can arrange our hair in my sitting room. How would that be?"

"Ideal." Gaby hesitated, a flicker of worry dimming her exuberance. "Aunt Hermione, are you sure Thane's staff wasn't upset about not being invited to the wedding? Mrs. Darcey, Mrs. Fife—so many of them are very dear to me, and I hate the fact that we were forced to exclude them. I understand we had no choice, that the decision was made for my protection, but I just can't envision any one of those wonderful people trying to harm me."

"But one of them might have," Hermione said firmly. "The way Thane handled the situation was the only way to ensure your safety, Gaby. He was extremely diplomatic, explaining that you were still weak and shaken by your ordeal and that, as a result, we were limiting the guest list to those at Nevon Manor so as not to overtax your strength. He added that you were still in shock and somewhat dazed, and he ended with a pointed mention of the fact that your concussion had left your memories of the *accident*— he stressed that word—muddled and indistinct. Thane's explanation was intended to accomplish two objectives: to eliminate the potential for hurt feelings, and to lull your assailant into a false sense of security in the belief that you, like everyone else, believe the fire to have been accidental." Hermione wrapped an arm about Gaby's shoulders. "So put your worry over the Whitshire staff from your mind. Today is your wedding day, darling. It's going to be the most wondrous day of your life. I want nothing to taint it. Now, let's go up and get ready, all right?"

The glow reappeared on Gaby's face. "All right."

* * *

Twenty minutes later Gaby stepped out of her bath and sailed into her room.

"I guess you're ready to get dressed?" Marion asked with a twinkle.

"Yes." Gaby studied the pale yellow frock on her bed with a frown. "Marion, do you think I made the right choice? I wanted to select a color as close to white as possible. My beige gowns are drab; this is the only one that has full skirts and a bit of trim about the sleeves. Do you think it will do?"

"I don't know." Marion helped Gaby into her underclothes, studying the yellow gown with apparent concentration. "Actually, now that you mention it, the gown is all wrong for the occasion. It looks more like a party frock than a wedding gown. It's bright and cheerful, but not very devout-looking. After all, you are getting married, even if it is in a plain old chapel."

Gaby felt as if she'd been punched. "Then what shall I do?" she asked. "I have nothing more suitable."

"I'll send for your aunt," Marion suggested. "Maybe she'll have an idea."

She disappeared, only to reappear minutes later with Hermione, who was clad in a dressing robe.

"Gaby? What is it, darling?" Hermione went straight to her niece. "Marion says you're upset with your dress. Why?"

"I'm being silly," Gaby replied, straightening her shoulders. "Bryce won't care what I'm wearing. It's just that . . ."

"The dress is all wrong for today," Marion supplied. "It's too . . . well, yellow; too ordinary. I don't blame Miss Gaby for her feelings."

Hermione whirled about, giving Marion an utterly astounded look. "It's not like you to be cruel, Marion. You know we didn't have enough time to create—"

"No, you didn't, but *we* did."

A puzzled expression. "You did . . . what?"

"Have enough time." With that, Marion smiled,

walking over and opening the bedchamber door. "I hope you like it, Miss Gaby," she said fervently. Then: "Come in."

Like a general leading her troops to battle, Mrs. Gordon marched in, followed by Ruth, Lily, and Jane, each of whom clutched a different part of the most exquisite shimmering white creation Gaby had ever seen—trimmed with lace, strewn with pearls, its billowing skirts a rich, vibrant satin.

It was every bride's dream come true.

On command they halted, waiting, anticipation swelling as they watched Gaby's face.

"Oh, my," she breathed, unable to absorb the enormity of what was happening.

"Do you like it?" Marion demanded.

Gaby couldn't speak.

"It's a wedding dress, Miss Gaby," Lily supplied helpfully. "We made it. For you. Don't worry about it being the wrong size. We borrowed one of your dresses so we could measure. We did it really fast, so we could return your dress before you noticed it was gone. We were afraid we wouldn't be able to finish it in time, but Mrs. Gordon sewed the last stitch at half after four this morning—just before you woke up." Lily's small brow furrowed as she studied Gaby's overwhelmed expression, the tears gliding down her cheeks. "Don't you like it?" she asked anxiously.

Slowly Gaby turned toward Hermione, who shook her head, her own eyes damp. "I knew nothing about this," she managed.

"We didn't want you to," Mrs. Gordon reported crisply. "Not you or Chaunce. The two of you had enough on your mind. Besides, this is a gift from us to Miss Gaby." She glared at Gaby, but an iota of uncertainty flickered through her caustic veneer. "You do like it, of course."

"It's the most breathtaking gown I've ever seen in my life," Gaby whispered, somehow finding her voice. "It's . . ." She walked forward, gingerly touching the satin bodice. "I never imagined . . . How did you . . . When did you . . ." She sucked in her breath. "Thank you all." She hugged each of them, alternately laughing and crying as the full impact of what they'd done sank in. "You must have spent days stitching, sewing, trimming . . . My God, you must have gone without sleep." Reverently Gaby stroked the lace, ran her fingertips over each translucent pearl. "I don't know what I did to deserve this, but I'm more grateful than you'll ever know. It's the most beautiful, loving, meaningful gift I've ever received in my life, with the exception of your love."

"*That* goes with it—and so does this," Ruth announced, stepping forward to hand Gaby a frothy lace veil, its coronet of orange blossoms crowning the sweeping, diaphanous cascade of white that draped gracefully to the floor.

"Oh . . ." Gaby cradled the veil in her arms, gazed at it in wonder. "It's as if a vivid fragment of my dreams just came to life."

"That's what a wedding day is all about," Marion replied, her round face beaming with joy.

"Everyone helped," Jane chirped. "Even the men. Reaney and Bowrick met the delivery men at the gates so you wouldn't see the materials arrive." She paused, reconsidering her words. "Well, Reaney did have to guide Bowrick across the grounds—but just a little. And Bowrick carried all the heavy parcels, because of Reaney's gout. So it all evened out." A giggle. "And every one of us learned how to keep a secret. We did a good job, didn't we, Marion?"

"Not a good job—a *great* job," Marion corrected with a grin. "Without you children, none of this would have been possible. It was all of you—and your fine eavesdropping—that let us know this wedding was about to take place." She looped her arms about Jane's and Lily's shoulders. "We each did our part. We worked together. But that's what being a family is all about."

Gaby looked from her gown and veil to the beloved people who'd crafted them. "I have more blessings than any bride could pray for. I . . . thank you."

"Enough chatter," Marion interrupted, clapping her hands. "The gown will do you no good draped across your arms. It's time to turn you into the fairy princess you truly are. Let's go, ladies." She gave Gaby a quick wink. "Besides, I think there might still be a surprise or two in store for you."

Thirty minutes later Gaby entered the chapel on Chaunce's arm, nearly gasping aloud when she saw the room's grand transformation. Wildflowers decorated the aisle, the arches, and the iron fixtures, enhancing the high vaulted ceilings and stained-glass panes, transforming the modest-sized chapel into a miniature version of a grand and splendid cathedral.

Near the altar stood Vicar Kent, a broad smile creasing his elderly face as he watched Gaby begin her slow march down the aisle.

An awed murmur escaped the lips of the staff as they caught their first glimpse of the bride, a myriad of emotions crossing their faces—emotions that flashed by Gaby in rapid succession as she passed, but etched themselves on her heart nonetheless: pride, elation, joyous tears. At her feet, rose petals strewn by Jane and Lily heralded her approach beckoning Gaby and Chaunce through the throng of beloved well-wishers. In the front row sat Aunt Hermione, her hands clasped tightly together, her blue eyes soft with the love and serenity derived from knowing how right this union was, her back very straight and sure as she met Gaby's exhilarated smile.

Gaby's gaze shifted, found Thane, who gave her an encouraging wink, then moved on to the magnificently handsome man beside him, the man who was about to become her husband.

Bryce's black frock coat hugged his broad shoulders, his light waistcoat and gray-striped trousers an elegant tribute to the importance of the day. His forest-green eyes darkened as he beheld his bride, drinking her in with pride, admiration, and an emotion too profound to describe, too vast to contain.

Their gazes locked, and Bryce smiled—a slow, enveloping smile that wrapped itself around Gaby's heart, drew her closer, carrying her toward him and their future.

Chaunce gave her to Bryce with an aura of certainty, stepping aside with a flourish to allow Gaby to begin her new life.

She took Bryce's proffered arm, and together they stepped forward to speak their vows.

Perhaps these very words had been spoken by countless people through countless ages; yet in Gaby's mind they were being uttered for the first time—beautiful, meaningful words that would forever bind her to the man she loved, and him to her.

The ring Bryce slid on her finger was exquisite, a rich gold circle as solid and pure as the love behind it, as meaningful as the brief, profound brush of her lips with his.

"I love you, Wonderland," he said fervently, beginning to raise his head. Abruptly he paused and, heedless of everything but his bride, threw propriety to the wind. "For you, Mrs. Lyndley," he murmured for Gaby's ears alone. "The impulsive husband you coaxed forth."

With that, he tipped up her face and buried his lips in hers for a heated, far-too-long-to-be-proper kiss. An appreciative chuckle reverberated through the chapel, and Gaby had to clutch her husband's arms for support when at last he eased reluctantly away. "Acceptable?" he inquired, his eyes twinkling.

"Commendable," she assured him breathlessly.

Capturing Gaby's arm, Bryce led his new wife through the chapel.

The cheers that accompanied them were far too raucous to be deemed appropriate, but no one cared.

Not even the vicar, who gazed from the rose petals that covered his feet to the children dancing in the aisles—even Peter, who'd completely forgotten his limp—to the rest of the embracing servants who composed Hermione's family, all of whom were clearly impaired in ways that mattered not a whit, and blessed in ways that made them whole. Vican Kent reverently bowed his head, giving thanks to the Lord for allowing him to share this day.

As if in reply, the organ commenced playing, emitting the first magnificent tones of the musical celebration chosen by the staff to be the glorious and fitting culmination to Gaby's wedding ceremony:

"Ode to Joy," the finale of Beethoven's 9th symphony, echoed through the walls.

The staff filed past the bride and groom, bidding them a series of heartfelt but fleeting congratulations before making a hasty retreat in the direction of the yellow salon.

"Why is everyone in such a hurry?" Gaby asked, still dabbing at her eyes in a futile attempt to stem the emotional tears that had been flowing steadily since she'd glimpsed the chapel. "I have so much I need to say, so much gratitude to express."

"I suspect you'll have your chance," Hermione observed thoughtfully, looking after their retreating guests. She turned to Bryce and Gaby, took their hands in hers. "I'll echo the very words you just used: I have so much I need to say, so much gratitude to express." Her voice broke, and she swallowed, determined to retain her composure. "Every prayer in my heart has been answered," she stated simply. Swiftly she glanced about, ensuring that only Chaunce and Thane remained.

Hermione continued, "My beloved niece and my deeply cherished nephew, I've known for years you belonged together. Thank God He shared my sentiments." She pressed a trembling kiss, first on Gaby's cheek, then on Bryce's. "Love and nurture each other. Share not only your strengths but your weaknesses as well, for that will make you all the stronger. And most of all, be happy—now and for the duration of time."

"You'll be a part of that happiness, Aunt Hermione," Gaby whispered. "Always. I absolutely insist."

A spark lit Hermione's eyes. "But of course. Why, after today I agree wholeheartedly with Thane's assessment: I shall indeed live forever. Who else would look after the three of you?" A sidelong glance at Thane. "Who would find the right mate for my other handsome—and as yet unclaimed—nephew? Who would properly advise all your children in matters of love?" Hermione shot Thane an angelic look, smiling as he groaned aloud. "You're safe for the time being," she assured him, linking her arm through Chaunce's. "At the present, I'm preoccupied with the current bride and groom—who, by the way, are expected in the yellow salon for their wedding feast. My guess is that the staff is eagerly awaiting their arrival. Come."

Bryce wrapped an arm about Gaby's waist, chuckling as he saw Thane roll his eyes to the heavens. "Hermione's intervention could be a blessing in disguise," he suggested. Sobering, he gazed down at his new wife, an expression of profound emotion crossing his face. "It's made me the happiest man alive."

Gaby's throat tightened, and she pressed closer to Bryce's side.

"I see your point," Thane conceded quietly. He then tactfully walked ahead with Hermione and Chaunce, leaving Gaby and Bryce for a moment of privacy.

"I love you," Gaby breathed.

Bryce tucked aside her veil, cupped the nape of her neck and drew her against him, covering her mouth in a deep, heated kiss of binding love and absolute possession. "And I love you—so much it defies words."

"We'd better join the others in the yellow salon," Gaby murmured, making no move to free herself from her husband's embrace.

"Yes, we'd better. Or we won't go at all." Bryce kissed his bride again, then—with the greatest of efforts—released her. "But soon, Wonderland. Soon I'll have you to myself."

"I can hardly wait." Abruptly, Bryce's comment to Thane registered in Gaby's wondrously dazed mind. "So you *do* think Aunt Hermione had something to do with our meeting, with the extensive amount of time we spent together."

A broad grin. "Did you doubt it?"

"She denies it."

"Of course she does."

Joyously, Gaby smiled up at her husband. "No. I don't doubt it. She arranged this every step of the way—with Chaunce's help, naturally."

"A brilliant woman." Bryce's lightheartedness vanished, and he brought Gaby's fingertips to his lips, kissed them with solemn awe. "Once again Hermione Nevon has saved my life."

With that, he guided Gaby through the chapel doors and toward the yellow salon—and their future.

The room surpassed anything Gaby had even remotely anticipated.

"Oh, my," she gasped, clutching Bryce's sleeve as they stood in the doorway, gaping at the magnificent banquet laid out before them.

"This is inconceivable," Bryce muttered thickly, as moved as Gaby by what their family had done—a family who now huddled together in one corner of the room, beaming, watching Gaby and Bryce's reaction and reveling in the success of their plan.

The salon had been totally transformed, its mahogany tables draped with elegant cloths, covered with tray after tray of the most elaborate and mouth-watering dishes imaginable. Potted lobster and salmon, turkey in jelly, caramel baskets filled with bon-bons and other sweets, fruits of all kinds, pastry sandwiches and orange-flower cakes—and in the center of the head table, a magnificent wedding cake, decorated with cupids and gold charms. It was like being in the palace of the Queen herself.

In the corner, three musicians played, lilting strains of Beethoven's Minuet in G filling the room with warmth and festivity.

The glass doors along the far wall had been thrown wide, beckoning everyone to the courtyard and the gardens beyond.

And what gardens! Wilson had outdone himself, each flower pruned to perfection, a stunning rainbow of brilliant color and intoxicating scent. At the heart of the arrangement were the peonies, now in full bloom, their bright petals open to the sunlight as if celebrating the occasion.

For the dozenth time that day, Gaby was speechless.

This time, so was Bryce.

"This is the loveliest wedding breakfast I've ever seen," Hermione pronounced, coming to the newlyweds' rescue. "From Gaby and Bryce, and from me, I thank you. Every one of you has outdone yourself." She smiled at Gaby and Bryce. "Clearly you've made two very special people extremely happy."

"Three," Chaunce amended, giving Hermione a meaningful look.

"Four," she corrected, directing her smile at him. She glanced back at the group. "We love you all. Now, shall we begin the celebration?"

A chorus of yeses ensued.

It took long moments for Gaby to compose herself enough to join Bryce in walking about the room, personally thanking all of the members of her family for their incomparable contributions to this day.

"My shovel and I did good, huh?" Wilson proclaimed with a lopsided grin. "Almost as good as

Cook, who didn't come out of the kitchen for three nights so she could do her fussin' without you findin' out." He looked at Cook, gave her a clipped salute. "We could all get used to meals like this," he suggested good-naturedly.

"Don't," Cook advised, her entire face suffused with pleasure as she took in not only Gaby and Bryce's joyous expressions but Hermione and Chaunce's as well. "Fooling these four isn't easy. I'm not eager to try again." A twinkle. "Until Marion and Goodsmith's wedding—the one rumor has it might not be theirs alone, might, in fact, boast two brides and two grooms." She squeezed Ruth's shoulders as the girl blushed scarlet. "Is that true?"

Wilson stood up tall. "Yup, it sure is! I finally got up enough nerve to ask her yesterday. And what do you know—she said yes!"

Everyone clapped.

"Then another feast it will be," Cook vowed. "Only this time I won't have to prepare it like a thief in the night."

Laughter filled the room.

The party went on for hours, and it was half after three that afternoon when Hermione finally separated herself from the group and signaled to get everyone's attention.

"I think it's time the bride and groom were on their way," she began.

"That's been taken care of as well," Marion inserted quickly. "George has the carriage polished, gleaming, and ready to take the newly married couple to the village inn."

"You even thought of that?" Gaby exclaimed, shaking her head in wonder. "You're astounding." A tender glance at Goodsmith. "Thank you. I'll go up and change and be ready in a few minutes."

"My pleasure," Goodsmith assured her.

Bryce and Thane exchanged a quick look.

"The gesture is deeply appreciated, Goodsmith," Bryce began. "The trouble is, Gaby and I will be going from here to London for a few days. And—"

"I have an idea," Thane interrupted. "Why don't you and Gabrielle spend your wedding night as these fine people have planned? When Goodsmith drives you to the village, I'll follow behind in your carriage, which I'll then leave at the inn. That way, you and Gabrielle can ride on to Town whenever you wish, and I'll travel back here with Goodsmith."

"Excellent," Bryce agreed with utter relief, having loathed the disappointment he'd seen flicker across Goodsmith's face. "I wasn't much in the mood for a long trip after this superb celebration anyway."

Goodsmith's broken-toothed smile was back in place. "I'll fetch the carriage."

"Thank you," Bryce muttered to his brother.

Thane grinned. "Think nothing of it. I suspect there's more than a bit of truth to your statement about not wanting to travel too long today." A quick glance at Gaby's retreating figure. "Nor do I blame you." He extended his hand to Bryce. "My best to you both. I wish you a long and happy life together."

Bryce clasped his brother's fingers, the warmth that had sprung up between them an added bonus to his newfound joy. "Thank you." A flicker of amusement. "Incidentally, I look forward—in the not-too-distant future—to watching Hermione work her miracles on you."

An hour later—including fifteen minutes of preparation and forty five minutes of good-byes—Gaby and Bryce were on their way.

"I doubt any bride ever had a more perfect wedding day," Gaby told Bryce with a contented sigh, settling herself on the carriage's polished leather seat as Goodsmith guided the horses onto the main road.

Bryce nodded, swinging across to sit beside his bride. "I don't know how they managed everything.

You were right—our family is extraordinary." He tilted Gaby's chin up, his knuckles caressing her cheek. "And so are you. When you first walked into that chapel, you nearly brought me to my knees. That's how beautiful you looked."

"It was the gown."

"No. It was the bride." Bryce's thumbs grazed Gaby's cheekbones, stroked the delicate contours of her face. "You're mine now," he said fervently.

"Ummm." Gaby made a small, appreciative sound, reaching up to stroke her husband's jaw. "Yours. I like the sound of that."

Lowering his head, Bryce kissed her, the sensual exploration sending tiny skyrockets of desire through them both.

"Thane was right. I'm suddenly *very* glad we aren't traveling all the way to London," Bryce murmured huskily. "In fact, even the inn seems too far away."

With a shiver, Gaby wrapped her arms about his neck. "I promised Aunt Hermione I'd retire early," she breathed against his lips.

"Because of your head?"

"No. Because of my husband."

A harsh groan vibrated through Bryce's chest and he literally tore himself from Gaby's arms, wrenching down the window to shout: "Goodsmith, pick up speed."

Goodsmith's good-natured laughter reached their ears, and an instant later the carriage lurched forward as the horses broke into a rapid trot. "I'll have you there in twenty minutes," Goodsmith called back. "Try admiring the scenery."

"I am," Bryce muttered, his restless gaze roving over his wife. "That's why I'm in a hurry."

For once Goodsmith didn't chatter endlessly.

Upon their arrival, he merely assisted Gaby and Bryce with their bags, wished them a fine life together, and took his leave—after reminding the innkeeper that this was *the* newly married couple whose arrival he'd been told to expect and whose treatment should be every bit as regal as had been previously arranged.

The innkeeper nodded sagely, then registered Gaby and Bryce as quick as a wink and escorted them to the loveliest room in the inn. "You have a choice view from your window . . . Never mind," he interrupted himself. "I don't suppose you'll be doing much star-gazing." With a discreet cough, he added that they shouldn't hesitate to ask for anything their hearts desired, including any food they wanted sent up—day or night. He droned on a bit more—words Gaby and Bryce scarcely heard—and then, seeing the way the bride and groom kept staring at each other, he took his leave.

Heated tension crackled in the air the instant the inn door shut, leaving Gaby and Bryce finally and blissfully alone.

Gaby watched Bryce bolt the door, her heart pounding so hard she feared it might explode from her chest.

"There's wine on the nightstand," Bryce noted, never taking his eyes off Gaby. "Obviously another romantic touch arranged by our family." He crossed over, caught Gaby's shoulders in his hands, massaged them with his thumbs. "Would you like some? I could pour—"

"No." Gaby shook her head, her cheeks flushed with anticipation. "Not now. Later. Now all I want is us."

"Gaby." Bryce caressed the nape of her neck. "I have two questions for you."

A hint of a smile. "That seems to be becoming a habit."

Bryce didn't return her smile. "First, are you in any pain or discomfort, or do you feel weak?"

"No," she answered without hesitation. "I'm far

too exhilarated to hurt. And weak?" Her palms glided up his waistcoat. "Only my knees are weak. And that has nothing to do with my injuries."

A sharp intake of breath. "Second, are you in any way nervous or unsure about what's going to happen between us? Because if so, I want to ease those uncertainties now. Once I take you in my arms, I want there to be nothing but—"

"Wonderland?" she teased breathlessly. "Because that's all there will be." Reaching up, she unfastened the top buttons of Bryce's shirt. "No, I'm not nervous. I'm also not unsure." She stood on tiptoe, kissed the warm expanse of skin she'd just bared at his throat. "I have a keen imagination and exceptional instincts." She dispensed with another button, tugged at his tie. "And when I falter, I'm confident that my brilliant barrister husband will provide the proper counsel." An inquisitive lift of her brows. "Have I answered both your questions?"

With a shudder of need, Bryce caught Gaby's hands, placed them around his neck. "Kiss me," he commanded, tugging her against him. "Let me drown in your sweetness."

Gaby complied eagerly, lifting her mouth to Bryce's, whispering his name as his lips closed over hers, molded and tasted her with dizzying thoroughness, unwavering purpose.

She opened her lips to his tongue, warmth seeping through her in sharp waves as the kiss grew more urgent in its intensity. Bryce cupped her head in his hands, cradling it so as to shield it from pain as his mouth devoured hers, their breath mingling in harsh, broken pants.

"I want to make this last," Bryce rasped, shaking in an effort to slow down. "But I'm not sure how much control I have. Sweetheart, I want you so much . . ."

Even his words made Gaby's body tighten, her breasts tingling with awareness, a liquid warmth converging inside her, pooling low in her abdomen.

"Control is not for wedding nights," she murmured. "Control is for court hearings." She pushed the frock coat from his shoulders. "I've ached for you since that night in my bedchamber. Please, Bryce, make the ache go away."

With a low growl, Bryce relented, dropping his coat to the floor, then dispensing with the buttons on Gaby's gown, tugging it down and away from her. He lifted her in his arms, carried her to the bed, divesting her of petticoats and stockings as he walked. By the time he laid her on the bedcovers, only a thin chemise and silk drawers separated him from his goal.

Pausing, Bryce gazed down at his wife, reaching forward to pull free whatever pins still remained in her hair. Slowly, his fingers glided through the satiny tresses, spread them over the pillow in a shimmering chestnut waterfall.

"You're so beautiful," he said reverently, his palms sliding down the sides of her neck, over the curve of her shoulders to the top of her chemise. "I wish I could prolong this moment, stand here for hours just absorbing your beauty, exploring every inch of you with my eyes and my hands." Holding her gaze, he began unbuttoning the chemise, his fingers hard, urgent, his expression taut with desire. "But I can't." An incredulous pause. "I just can't."

"Don't." Gaby was quivering under Bryce's touch, her untutored body clamoring for the pleasures she knew lay ahead. She shifted restlessly, willing each button free of its casing, squirming free of the undergarment the instant she could.

Bryce tossed aside the chemise, his hands molding Gaby's breasts, cupping their weight, his thumbs skimming the tightly budded nipples—once, twice—his caresses hot, fervent.

Gaby whimpered aloud, sensations burning through her like wildfire. She arched up from the bed, seeking closer contact with her husband's hands, desperate to feel more of his touch. Bryce exhaled sharply, releasing her only long enough to yank open the buttons of her drawers, slide the silken garment down her legs, then cast it to the floor.

For a brief moment Gaby lay still, watching her husband's reaction to her nudity. "Bryce?" she asked tentatively.

"Too exquisite for words," he replied in an aching whisper. He worshiped her with his eyes, then his fingers, caressing her legs, her hips, her thighs. Ever so gently he eased her thighs apart, brushing the dark cloud between them with butterfly strokes that sent skyrockets of pleasure coursing through her—and made lying still a virtual impossibility.

Scrambling to her knees, Gaby yanked at the remaining buttons of her husband's shirt and waistcoat, willing her fingers to stop shaking long enough to complete their task.

Bryce did it for her.

He wrenched off his clothing in a few tugs, not pausing until he stood before her, gloriously naked. Gaby inched forward on the bed, staring and touching all at once. She rested her palms on Bryce's chest, marveling at the warm, hair-roughened surface, the rippling muscle beneath. She could feel the wild beating of his heart, feel each rasping breath as it vibrated through him. Her thumbs skimmed his nipples, watched in fascination as they reacted much as hers had, tightening and hardening with each caress. Continuing her explorations, she swept her hands across the broad expanse of his shoulders, down the powerful muscles of his arms.

Abruptly, she shifted, and Bryce's abdomen contracted as her fingers grazed it, hovering as she stared wonderingly at the glorious evidence of his arousal, the rigid length of him that proclaimed him a man. Without hesitation or modesty, Gaby touched him there, her forefinger gliding along the taut surface of his manhood, discovering it to be rock hard yet satin smooth. She wrapped her small hand around him, savoring his size, his texture, the exhilarating pulse-beat of life that throbbed within him.

"Oh, Bryce," she breathed, lifting her enchanted gaze to his. "You're magnificent."

That seemed to break what little control Bryce had left.

With a guttural sound of need, he seized her wrist, dragged her hand from its goal. "Stop," he commanded. "Now." He hauled her into his arms, toppled them both to the bed, rolling Gaby beneath him and devouring her mouth with his—again and again—shuddering as she wrapped her arms around him, met his urgency with her own.

Neither of them could breathe. Neither of them cared.

In one fervent motion, Bryce nudged her thighs apart, tearing his mouth from hers so he could watch her face as his fingers opened her, glided over her satiny wetness, then slipped inside.

Gaby's breath caught in her throat, every nerve ending shimmering to life, converging into a frantic yearning right where Bryce's fingertips had just teased. "Oh . . ." Her eyes widened, her entire body melting and tightening all at once as it responded wildly to her husband's caress. With a will all their own, her hips lifted, urging him to take her deeper into this enthralling vortex of sensation. Bryce gritted his teeth, stroking softly, intimately, his fingers gliding more fully inside her, his thumb simultaneously caressing the tiny bud that screamed for more.

"Bryce . . ." Gaby wondered if she'd die, the pleasure was so acute.

"Yes," he responded through clenched teeth, sweat beading on his forehead. "God, you're so small. So tight. So bloody perfect." A hard shake of his head. "I won't hurt you."

"Hurt me?" Gaby was frenzied with sensation. Hurt her? In some part of her passion-drugged mind, she remembered there was to be pain the first time.

But at that moment, the very idea seemed incomprehensible. How could there be pain when every inch of her was vibrating with pleasure?

"Damn," she heard Bryce mutter, battling himself as he deepened his presence in her body. "So incredibly soft. You feel like hot silk." His thumb caressed that magical spot once more, making Gaby cry out, shift restlessly on the bed.

"Again," she pleaded, moving against his hand as she sought that unbearably thrilling and elusive contact. "What you just did . . . please . . . do it again."

Groaning, Bryce complied, caressing her exactly where she needed him—not once, not twice, but in slow, breathtakingly exciting continuous circles. "Like this?" he breathed into her parted lips.

"Oh . . . God . . ." Gaby couldn't speak. She clung to her husband, unaware of anything but his touch, the havoc it was wreaking on her. Molten flame spread through her loins, and her eyes slid shut, every fiber of her being concentrated on some unknown pinnacle of sensation that hovered just out of reach.

She felt Bryce shift his position, his fingers never halting their sensual onslaught, and all at once the full, wondrous weight of him was upon her. His thighs pressed hers wide apart, wedging themselves between, exposing her more completely to the intimate stroke of his fingertips. Reflexively she molded herself to him, lifting her legs to hug his flanks, her hips wild in their undulations.

"Gaby . . ." His mouth was on hers again, his tongue taking hers in unbearably erotic strokes— deep, slow—matching the gliding presence of his fingers.

Then the gliding penetration vanished, leaving Gaby suddenly and acutely empty, devoid of Bryce's presence inside her. His thumb continued to make its dizzying circles, but it wasn't enough to fill the emptiness. She needed more.

"No!" She shook her head wildly, then moaned in

pleasure when she felt him entering her again. "Don't . . . go."

"I won't." His hips were moving now too, his thighs rigid between hers. "God help me, I can't."

It was different this time. He was stretching her, taking her more totally, and the ecstasy building beneath his thumb burgeoned, intensified by the thick, full feel of him inside her. He was hot, throbbing, forging a path inside her where none had existed but which yearned for his possession.

He was joining his body with hers.

Gaby's eyes flew open as realization mingled with sensation. "Bryce . . ." She was utterly and abruptly aware of this moment—this moment and her husband, his shoulders taut with the exertion of restraint, his features stark with need, slick with sweat, his rigid shaft pressing deeper and deeper inside her.

"Does it hurt?" he rasped, his hips rocking back and forth, faster, more urgently with each motion, his progress eased by her slick, pliant flesh as it yielded eagerly to his penetration.

"No. Oh, no." Instinctively, she arched when he pushed, feeling the resulting pressure and not giving a damn. "You're inside me," she breathed, her heart touched as deeply as her body. "It truly is a miracle." Another undulation of her hips. "Bryce, don't hold back. I want to feel everything."

Throwing back his head, Bryce emitted a desperate sound of primal male need. "God, Gaby, so do I." He was pushing harder now, unable to continue modifying his pace so as to enter her by the measured degrees he'd been allowing. "Sweetheart!"

Suddenly he went very still, his muscles flexed, his thumb pausing in its assault.

Startled by the suspension of pleasure, Gaby felt her focus alter sharply, reconverging on her own body and the screaming protest that jolted through it at this unbearable lull. She hovered at the very brink of sensation, unwilling to retreat, unable to reach the peak she so desperately craved. Frantically she arched, whimpered, begged Bryce to take her over the edge.

He did.

The deliberately withheld, now deliberately bestowed caress was neither slow or tentative. It was total, erotic, Bryce's fingers gliding directly over the tight little bud that throbbed for his touch and remaining there—rubbing, stroking—until it became too much.

Gaby shattered.

Screaming Bryce's name, she dug her nails into his back, arching upward, her legs gripping him tightly as her body clenched, then unraveled. She dissolved into climax, convulsing again and again in exquisite spasms of release, gripping the entire length of Bryce's engorged manhood in fingers of fire.

With a triumphant shout, Bryce thrust forward, burying himself in her climax, tearing the thin veil of her innocence and plunging immediately over the edge. His hips pumped wildly as he gave in to the clawing demand of his loins, exploding inside her in a scalding, unending release, pouring himself into the very mouth of her womb.

Gaby cried out again, everything inside her opening in a rush, reveling in the sensation of Bryce's seed as it spurted hotly into her. The intimacy and magnitude of his climax only served to intensify hers, and her contractions began anew—harder, more powerful this time, spiraling higher and higher until the very room seemed to spin away.

Perhaps she lost consciousness; perhaps she only drifted.

Awareness returned in increments—the softness of the bed beneath her, the blissful weight of her husband's body blanketing hers, even the slowing of their heartbeats, the shallowness of their breathing as it gradually returned to normal.

Savoring this glorious aftermath, Gaby gave a shivery sigh, tracing the damp planes of Bryce's back, the muscles now utterly relaxed beneath her fingertips. She felt weak, boneless and replete, her entire body suffused with a joy too profound to describe.

Bryce shuddered at her touch, murmuring her name as the lingering droplets of his seed trickled into her.

Another long moment passed.

"Gaby." Ever so slowly Bryce raised his head, struggling to recapture his strength, his ability to think. "Sweetheart"—his fingertips brushed her face—"are you all right?" He made an attempt to move, then gave it up, instead rolling to one side and taking Gaby with him. "Gaby?"

"Ummm." Gaby hadn't the strength to open her eyes. She merely smiled, snuggling against her husband's chest and pressing her body close to his.

She winced at the resulting discomfort.

"Dammit." Bryce began to ease away, but Gaby would have none of it.

She caught at his arms, her eyes flying open as she shook her head. "Stay inside me. Please."

"I'm hurting you. I already hurt you. God, I lost every shred of sanity and reason I possess."

"In that case I hope you never regain either." Raising her chin, Gaby gave Bryce a melting smile. "What just happened between us was like touching heaven."

The harsh lines on Bryce's face softened. "That isn't surprising. Because heaven is what I'm holding in my arms." He kissed her with aching tenderness, a soft, reverent caress that whispered through Gaby like a summer breeze.

"Was it the Wonderland you expected?" she breathed against his mouth.

"Not even close." Another, deeper kiss. "Wonderland pales in comparison."

"I'm glad."

As if remembering something crucial, Bryce drew

back, frowning as he touched the fading bruise on Gaby's forehead. "Damn. I could have made this worse. What the hell was I thinking?"

"You weren't. Nor was I." Gaby caressed her husband's clenched jaw. "Stop berating yourself. I forgot all about my wound."

His anxious gaze searched hers. "Are you all right?"

"I'm euphoric." Gaby twined her arms about his neck. "In every way. It's as if my body is singing. And there's no pain—not in my head, not *anywhere,*" she added meaningfully. "You made our first joining perfect, everything a bride could wish for."

"I hurt you."

"I scarcely felt a twinge. You made sure of that. What I did feel was . . ." She broke off, searching for a way to describe the sensations she'd just experienced, and finding none. "There are no words," she whispered, awe reflected in her eyes. "None but these: I love you, Bryce."

Emotion darkened his gaze to a deep forest green, and he gathered her closer, enfolded her against his heart. "Not nearly as much as I love you."

They lay like that for a timeless time, their bodies joined, their hearts beating as one. At last—and amid Gaby's protests—Bryce disengaged himself from her clinging warmth, but only to cross over and pour some water into a basin, dampen a towel and bring it back to the bed. That done, he eased Gaby's legs apart, cleansing away the evidence of her lost virginity, then gently stroked the towel between her thighs, soothing away the minor aches caused by their lovemaking.

"Better?" he murmured.

"Ummm . . . yes." Gaby sighed, her entire body glowing from his tender ministrations.

Seeing the slumberous look in her eyes, Bryce tossed aside the cloth, peeled back the bedcovers, and settled Gaby and himself beneath them, her body curved into his. "Would you like to sleep?" he asked.

She glanced at the window, saw the last filaments of daylight still drizzling through, and shook her head. "It's not even dark yet. Why would I sleep?"

Bryce chuckled. "Some people rest during the day as well," he informed her, tracing the delicate curve of her spine. "In fact, most people need more than your scant four hours of slumber each night."

"Then I pity them. Sleep is such a waste of time." Gaby stretched like a contented kitten. "There are so many inspiring things to do that are precluded by long hours abed." Her eyes glinted mischievously. "Then again, I might reform now that I'm wed." She pressed closer—and was rewarded by Bryce's sharp intake of breath, his already aroused manhood surging against her. "In fact I'm certain of it. The bedroom is looking infinitely more alluring as of today."

"Is it?" Bryce pulled her over him, drew her mouth down to his.

"Oh, yes," she breathed, shivering as Bryce's hands began to work their magic. "More alluring by the minute."

They made love for endless hours—exquisite, passion-drenched hours—until dusk was transformed, first to evening, then to night. Gaby's senses shimmered with the wonders Bryce introduced her to—wonders that seemed as astonishing to him as they did to her.

She didn't need to ask why. This was as much Bryce's night of discovery as it was hers.

Sometime before dawn, Bryce cradled her against him, threaded his fingers through her tangled mane of hair, and softly said, "Now you really *must* sleep. You're still recovering from a concussion."

With a resigned sigh, Gaby nestled against Bryce's chest. "I know. Well, at least now I have some beautiful memories to dream about—and many more to make."

Bryce smiled against her hair. "Your music box is at Nevon Manor. Shall I hum 'Für Elise' for you?"

"There's no need," Gaby replied solemnly. "As I told you once before, with you here, I need no music box. I've simply traded one melody for another."

Her husband's smile vanished, and his voice grew husky. "You, my love, are all exquisite melodies combined. You fill my life and my heart with music. You're my symphony, and I love you." He paused, and Gaby could actually sense his mood alter, feel his thoughts shift back to the ugly realities that today's joys had held at bay.

His next words confirmed it.

"Gaby, these past few nights you've taken laudanum for the pain. Tonight is your first night without it."

"I don't need it."

"I realize that, and I'm thankful. But I want *you* to realize it was the laudanum that induced your uncommonly prolonged hours of sleep—the kind of drugged sleep that bars any chance of sleepwalking. Tonight that benefit will be absent." Bryce tipped up her chin. "I'm not trying to frighten you. Quite the opposite. I'm trying to remind you that from this moment on, I'll be beside you. Every night. *All* night. If you so much as stir, I'll feel it. You're not going anywhere. What's more, nothing will ever hurt you again. I intend to see to that."

"I know." Gaby swallowed, a knot of apprehension gripping her stomach. "And I'm not afraid of the sleepwalking—or of anything else—when I'm with you. But, Bryce, we both know this is no longer a matter of simply protecting me from a painful memory. What I overheard as a child was a murderer, someone who—it's becoming increasingly likely— killed Dowell. It's also likely that the same man murdered Mr. Delmore and tried to kill me. So hiding me away is not the answer. We need to find this savage, find him and see him punished for his crimes, before he can hurt anyone else. And it's obvious I'm the key to his identity, if only I could remember everything I overheard. So, yes, I'm afraid—not of being hurt but of the unknown. I'm also frustrated, because it's clear that I'm getting close. Why else would he have risked his neck by coming after me, in the open, at Nevon Manor?"

"Sweetheart, don't." Bryce tightened his embrace as if by doing so he could ward off all the evil Gaby was describing.

She shuddered, squeezed her eyes shut. "What happened the other day—it was like reliving my most terrifying nightmare. Not the assault, but seeing those flames, feeling trapped—and breathing that unforgettable musky smell. That deceptively sweet smell of death—I recognized it at once, knew I was amid a fire even as I lost consciousness. I inhaled, and I knew."

In the midst of sifting strands of her hair through his fingers, Bryce paused. "You recognized it *before* you lost consciousness? That makes no sense. Whoever attacked you didn't start the fire until after he'd moved you and trapped your leg in the opening to Crumpet's warren. So you couldn't have smelled the flames as you fell. Your memory must be fuzzy on that point." Bryce frowned, reconsidering. "On the other hand, now that I think about it, you described the events in that same order just after the incident occurred. You said that all you remembered was the masked figure who struck you and the sickening, musky smell of death—*until* you awakened amid the fire. I didn't ponder the order of events then, but now . . . I wonder."

Twisting about, Gaby gazed up at her husband. "Do you think it means something?"

"I'm not sure," Bryce replied thoughtfully. "But none of your memories have been inaccurate thus far. So my instincts say we shouldn't ignore what your mind is telling you. And if you're right, and if the timing of that smell does reveal something about the fire, we'll figure out what it is. I promise you, we will."

With that, he kissed the worried pucker between

Gaby's brows, settled her against him. "But not now. Now I want you to rest, at least for a few hours." She felt him smile against her hair. "After which you may awaken me in whatever manner you choose."

His teasing words had their desired effect, and Gaby relaxed in her husband's arms. "In whatever manner I choose? Ah, the possibilities you've taught me tonight." Her eyes widened as a new and wondrous prospect struck—one that eclipsed every iota of ugliness from view. "Bryce . . ." Her palm strayed to her abdomen. "Do you realize that at this very moment I could be carrying our child? Or, if not, that I could conceive any time from this day on?"

Bryce's smile vanished, and his voice, when he spoke, was rough with emotion. "Yes, darling, I realize that. And it enthralls me almost as much as it humbles me."

Tears filled Gaby's eyes, and she reached up, drew his mouth down to hers. "I want to give you a child," she whispered. "I want that so much."

"Gaby . . ." Bryce's arms trembled as they brought her against him.

"What's more," she confessed breathlessly. "I don't want our wedding night to end."

"Nor do I." He rolled her onto her back, raising her arms above her head, interlacing their fingers as he covered her body with his. "And I did promise to make it last, didn't I?"

Gaby's nod was solemn. "Yes, you did."

With that, the notion of sleep was forgotten.

Chapter 17

"THAT WAS BREATHTAKING!"

A full twenty minutes after leaving the concert hall, Gaby was still enchanted, her blue eyes bright with wonder as Bryce steered their carriage toward his town house. "Oh, Bryce, even my most vivid dreams couldn't conjure up the exquisite blending of sounds, the richness, the emotion . . ." She turned her glowing face toward his. "From the bottom of my heart, thank you."

Bryce pressed her head to his shoulder. "Watching your face was all the thanks I need. It was like watching a child at her first Christmas." He kissed Gaby's shining crown of hair. "Just as the music surpassed your wildest expectations, so did your reaction surpass mine."

"I've never felt more alive, more exhilarated . . ." She broke off, tossing him a mischievous grin. "At least not during occasions where I'm clothed."

A husky chuckle. "Which you haven't been for almost three days, except during our drive to London. I've kept you abed nearly every breathing instant."

"I've attempted sleepwalking only twice in all that time," she pointed out.

"You've slept only twice in all that time."

"Ummm, that's true." Gaby smiled dreamily, even the sleepwalking and all its ramifications unable to dim the pleasure of the past three days.

While awaiting Banks's summons, they'd taken full advantage of their time alone, spending long, lazy hours in Bryce's bed, talking, laughing, and of course exploring all the dazzling nuances of passion in each other's arms. Tonight had been their first venture out, and Gaby had been so enthralled by the music and its splendor that it had nearly driven away the anxiety she experienced over making her initial appearance into Bryce's glittering world. But the episode hadn't been nearly as frightening as she'd expected. The people had been cordial, even welcoming. By the end of the evening she'd grown quite accustomed to the introductions, the polite how-do-you-do's. Why, she'd even survived the awkward meeting with Lucinda Talbot and her newest escort during the concert's brief intermission.

"She's lovely," Gaby had whispered to Bryce the instant they were alone. "And extremely gracious, given the circumstances."

Bryce had shrugged. "That's Lucinda, always gracious." He'd taken Gaby's hand in his. "Thank you for making the situation bearable. You were warm and charming—your usual exuberant self."

"I can afford to be," she replied with her customary candor. "I have you." A twinkle. "However, if you'd actually taken her to any of those private spots I questioned you about, my behavior would have been far less courteous."

"Speaking of those private spots"—Bryce's fingers had tightened about hers—"the instant we leave here, we're returning to my bed. It's been hours."

Gaby's heart had thumped wildly. "Definitely."

She stepped closer, murmuring in a voice only Bryce could hear. "I'm glad we're moving to your room at Nevon Manor. It's not only larger than mine, but farther away from the other wings and from Aunt Hermione's room." The look she gave him was sheer seduction. "I'm not very good at staying quiet."

"I'll swallow your cries of pleasure with my mouth," Bryce vowed huskily.

"And yours?"

He sucked in his breath. "You'll do the same."

"That's not always possible," Gaby reminded him, her forefinger tracing a line down the front of his waistcoat. "Sometimes our mouths are otherwise—"

"That did it." Bryce had drawn her closer, kissed her then and there, in front of anyone who happened to be watching.

All in all, the evening had been perfect.

Gaby's smile vanished as they approached Bryce's house and saw the messenger sitting patiently on the doorstep.

"Bryce?" She sat up straighter, peering around to study the man. "Do you think Mr. Banks sent him?"

Bryce, too, had seen the messenger, and his entire demeanor changed. "I assume so," he answered, bringing the horses to a stop. "Let's find out."

Sure enough, the message was indeed from Banks, informing Bryce that he'd spent the entire week poring over old files and had, at last, uncovered all the papers in William's possession that pertained to the late Duke of Whitshire's yacht.

Bryce sent a return message, thanking Banks and saying he'd be at his office the next morning at nine o'clock sharp.

The clock in Banks's office was chiming nine when his clerk ushered Bryce and Gaby in.

"Bryce." Banks greeted his colleague with a bit more energy than he had the last time, although his eyes were bleak, puffy from lack of sleep. "I just heard about your marriage." He smiled in Gaby's direction. "Congratulations. I see now why Hertford held so much appeal."

"Frederick, this is my wife, Gabrielle. Gaby—Frederick Banks."

"A pleasure." Banks said, half bowing.

"I'm happy to meet you, sir," Gaby replied. "And I'm terribly sorry about Mr. Delmore. Bryce told me how many years you two had been partners. I'm sure this is very difficult for you."

"It is. Thank you for your sympathy." Banks turned to Bryce. "I won't keep you long, since you've been married a scant few days. But I knew how eager you were to have those papers." He offered Bryce an envelope. "In there you'll find the original title to the yacht, along with the letter that accompanied it when Whitshire forwarded the title to William several months ago. Both those papers are authentic. The title was signed by the builder, conveying the yacht to Whitshire, and the letter of correspondence was penned by Averley, Whitshire's steward, since the duke was on his deathbed. As I suspected, both those pages were in William's desk."

"And the other, older documents you mentioned?"

"That was the tedious part. I had a great deal of searching to do, years of old files to pore over. And I wanted to be thorough, to make sure I found every pertinent letter or document that might aid your investigation. Unfortunately, there wasn't much. The only other papers I came upon were letters between Whitshire's steward and the builder who constructed the yacht." A questioning look. "That was what you wanted, anyway, wasn't it?"

"Definitely." Bryce tore open the envelope, scanning the pages within, his jaw tightening fractionally. "Robert Smythe. Is that the builder's name?"

"Yes. He was an established fellow, well past middle years. He retired about eighteen months ago, turned the business over to his sons."

Bryce tensed. "But he's still alive, and in England, I hope."

"The answer to both questions is yes." Banks pointed at the envelope. "I thought you might want to talk to Smythe. As luck would have it, he lives in a little cottage right in Hertford. The address is written on a slip of paper behind the correspondence. I verified it and, at the same time, requested Smythe's permission to give it to you. He had no trouble saying yes."

"We'll go there immediately. Frederick, I appreciate this more than I can say." Bryce clasped the older man's hand.

"You can show your thanks by determining who killed William," Banks replied. "The police still have no clues and no suspect. So if there's any merit to your theory that William's business at Whitshire and his death are somehow connected, find out what that connection is. And then find out who killed him."

"I intend to." Bryce caught Gaby's arm, headed toward the door.

"Again, the best of luck to you both," Banks repeated. "I hope this investigation doesn't detract from the joy of your new marriage. I wish you great happiness."

"Thank you." Bryce guided Gaby through the doorway, his entire body whip-taut. "I'll let you know the instant I learn anything."

In the waiting area he stopped, intently examining the letters still peeking out of the envelope.

"Bryce?" Gaby murmured. "What is it?"

"The date on these letters. *And* the one on the deed." He shoved all the documents back inside, facing Gaby with a purposeful expression. "Whitshire's yacht was built in March 1862."

Gaby's eyes widened. "Just over thirteen years

ago," she realized aloud. "Two months before the fire."

Robert Smythe was a gray-haired man with a full beard and a gruff, somewhat wary manner. "What can I do for you?" he asked, having admitted Gaby and Bryce to the tiny sitting room of his Hertford cottage. "Banks said you wanted to see me, but he didn't say about what."

"About a yacht your company built," Bryce supplied. Perching on the edge of the well-worn sofa, he opened the envelope and extracted the title and letters. "Evidently it was quite a beauty. I was wondering what details you could provide me with, about the construction of the yacht itself, the specific details of the transaction—anything."

"And why do you want to know all this?"

Bryce cleared his throat. "I'm not at liberty to discuss my reasons, at least not at this time."

Smythe scowled, leaning his elbow on the arm of his chair. "I'm familiar with your name, Lyndley. I know you're a barrister. Well, let me tell you straightaway that my sons and I are completely honest. Always have been. So if you're looking for anything shady, you've come to the wrong place."

"Nothing like that," Gaby assured him in a soothing voice. "This is a personal matter, Mr. Smythe—*our* personal matter. Your integrity is not in question, nor is your family's. On the contrary, according to Mr. Banks, your reputation is excellent."

"Yeah, well, he's right." Somewhat mollified, Smythe leaned back in the armchair. "This deal you're asking about—did I oversee it? Or did it take place after I retired?"

"Your signature is on the title," Bryce told him. "And it definitely preceded your retirement; this yacht was built thirteen years ago."

"Thirteen years ago?" Shaggy gray brows shot up.

"Lyndley, my company has built hundreds of boats. How the hell would I remember anything about a deal that took place thirteen years ago?"

Bryce had been prepared for this potential problem, and he proceeded with the strategy he hoped would eliminate it. "Mr. Smythe, the boats your company builds—they're mostly small recreational craft, aren't they?"

"Small, but well-built, yes."

"I don't doubt that. How many elaborate yachts did you construct over the years?"

"More than a few." The builder's head came up defensively. "As I said, our reputation is excellent."

"And, as *I* said, I don't doubt it. This particular yacht I'm looking into was commissioned by a wealthy, titled nobleman. The duke could have gone anywhere for his yacht. But he chose your company. I think that speaks for itself."

"The duke?" Recognition—immediate and absolute—flashed in Smythe's eyes. "Why didn't you say so in the first place? I've had a couple of aristocrats as patrons. But only one duke." He stroked his whiskers thoughtfully. "Yeah, I'd say thirteen years sounds about right." Leaning forward, he added, "Let me see those letters."

"They're from His Grace's steward to you and vice versa," Bryce explained, placing the papers in Smythe's palm. "Averley handled all his employer's business correspondence."

"Sure—Whitshire, that was the duke's name." Scanning the pages, Smythe gave an emphatic nod. "His steward wrote to me, but the duke himself came to supervise the work. He was real lavish with his praise—and his payment. It was nice doing business with him. Always hoped I'd have the chance to build him another boat one day. Not that he'd need it. That beauty I crafted for him was all any man could want. He could hardly wait to sail her away."

371

Bryce frowned. Smythe's depiction of Richard Rowland's enthusiasm for sailing was inconsistent with Hermione's view.

"You're certain His Grace meant to keep the yacht for his personal use?" he probed. "Isn't it possible he intended to buy it as an investment, then sell it at a substantial profit?"

"Sell it?" Smythe started. "Hell, no. Every detail of that yacht was designed for the duke's taste. We even changed the dimensions of the captain's cabin to make it more comfortable for him. He didn't need those high ceilings. Instead, he wanted bigger quarters and a wider berth so he wouldn't feel crowded." A chuckle as Smythe patted his protruding middle. "Not that I can afford to talk. I've put some extra meat on my bones since I retired; been eating too much of my wife's fine cooking."

Gaby had gone very still. "Mr. Smythe, would you describe the duke for us, please?"

He scratched his head. "Describe him? Like I said, he was a real gentleman. Always dressed in fine wool suits and polished shoes. He wasn't too tall, and, again like I said, he was a bit round about the middle. But then, he wasn't a lad anymore, either. About my age, I'd guess, with ruddy cheeks and thinning hair. I don't have that problem myself." Smythe ran a hand through his thick gray mane. "Anyway, he was also real generous. Paid me twice what I asked for, so long as I promised not to design the same boat for anyone else and not to talk about our deal with anybody. I guess he was afraid I'd let some of the construction details slip if I did. Well, it didn't matter to me. I was happy to honor his request, since there wasn't much call for a boat that fancy. He gave me my money and a bottle of that cologne I always admired. After that, I never saw him again."

Reeling with what he was learning, Bryce jumped on the last statement. "Cologne?"

"Yes, sir. The duke told me it was imported from

Paris, made special for him. Even the bottle was elegant. Whitshire gave me my own bottle of the stuff as a gift for a job well done. I used it only on Sundays when I went to church, so it lasted a long time. When it was finally gone, I kept the bottle as a memento."

Bryce was torn between his own growing tension, spawned by the realization that their goal was in sight, and the spiraling apprehension emanating from Gaby—a palpable entity he could actually feel, and one that worried him greatly.

Gingerly he took the next step. "May we see this bottle?" he asked Smythe.

A shrug. "I guess so. If you want to, although I can't imagine why. I'll get it." Smythe rose, left the room.

"Gaby, are you all right?" Bryce asked the instant they were alone. His wife had gone very pale, and her breath was coming in short, shallow pants.

"Richard Rowland was tall and broad-shouldered, much like you and Thane," Gaby replied in a high, thin voice.

"So I've been told."

Gaby stared at her husband, her blue eyes glazed with shock. "Bryce, the man Mr. Smythe just described . . . His description fits Mr. Averley."

"I know, sweetheart." Bryce captured her hand in his, speaking in a deep, soothing tone. "Let's not panic or jump to conclusions. Let's just hear Smythe out and take it from there."

"I can't." Gaby jumped up, her eyes wide, terrified. "I can't continue this."

Swiftly Bryce rose, drawing Gaby against him and holding her tight. "Yes you can. I know you can." He could feel her trembling—a reality that was as damning to Averley as Smythe's description. "We're nearing the end."

She didn't answer, just pressed closer.

Smythe cleared his throat as he reentered the room. "You two newly married?"

"Hold on, Wonderland—I'm with you," Bryce

whispered fiercely before turning to face Smythe, one arm wrapped protectively about Gaby's waist. "Yes," he replied. "As a matter of fact, we are."

"I could tell." A gruff chuckle. "Anyway, here's the bottle." He held out the empty gilded flask.

"May I?" Bryce asked.

"Sure." Smythe uncapped the top. "Just be careful."

"I will." Bryce brought the bottle to his nose, inhaling deeply.

The lingering scent was still very much present—strong, distinctive, and thoroughly unmistakable: Averley's eau de cologne.

Another incriminating piece fell into place.

But Bryce needed confirmation. And there was only one person who could give it to him.

Meeting Gaby's alarmed gaze, he nodded slightly, telling her without words what she already knew: that this next step was crucial—and that it was hers. Tightening his hold about her waist, he murmured, "Remember—I'm here."

He waited for her answering nod. Then he eased the bottle under her nose, proud of her unfailing inner strength, praying he wasn't overtaxing her already depleted emotional reserves.

She swallowed hard, clearly steeling herself for whatever impact lay ahead. Then her lashes drifted downward and, slowly, she inhaled.

A choked cry escaped her lips. "The fire . . ." she whimpered. "That smell . . . Oh, God." Backing away, she whipped about, pressing her fist to her mouth as ghosts exploded into her consciousness.

"What's wrong?" Smythe demanded. "What's going on?"

Bryce knew Gaby couldn't take any more right now. She was at her breaking point.

"Mr. Smythe," he said quietly, placing the empty bottle on the table beside the sofa. "I need some time alone with my wife. May I impose upon you to give us that time? I realize you don't even know us and that none of what's happening here makes any sense to you. But I assure you, the business that brought us here is of the utmost importance. Lives are at stake."

Smythe's eyes had gone as wide as saucers. "Lives?"

"Yes. And if that's not enough incentive, I'll be willing to pay you, say, fifty pounds."

Smythe waved away the offer. "Keep your money. One look at your wife tells me this is serious. I'll go read the morning newspaper. Call out when you're done talking."

"Thank you. We will."

Bryce waited until he and Gaby were alone. Then he came up behind her, caught her quaking shoulders in his hands. "That's the musky smell you were describing?"

Gaby's nod was shaky, her voice when she spoke, faint and faraway. "Yes. It was so deeply ingrained in my memory of the fire . . . that I attributed it to the blaze itself."

"Instead of attributing it to the man responsible." Bryce's mouth set in grim lines. "Well, this certainly explains why your sleepwalking resumed along with your return to Whitshire—*and* worsened after Averley's visit to Nevon Manor, for that matter. The scent he wears is not one that's easily overlooked; it's strong and sweet. I recognized it as his the instant I held that bottle under my nose. Unfortunately I never connected it with the musky smell you kept describing from the night of the fire."

Bryce drew Gaby back against him, buried his lips in her hair. "I wish to God we had more time. You need to deal with this bit by bit, not in a crushing onslaught. But we don't have much time, sweetheart. We need to assemble all the pieces now, while we're still in Mr. Smythe's company. We need his word as evidence. Then we need to act—quickly, before Averley figures out what we're up to and eludes us. Gaby, I know what this is doing to you. If there were any other way . . ."

"There isn't." Gaby turned. Tears were coursing down her cheeks, but the glazed look in her eyes had vanished. "Nor would it matter. Fragments of my memory are flickering back on their own, like tiny sunbursts of recall. The gaps between them are still hazy, but the overall picture is clear, as are my instincts. Averley is the one we're looking for. He's a liar, a thief, and a murderer." Gaby's hands balled into fists. "I don't care how painful this is for me to discuss or to thoroughly recall. Averley must pay for what he did." Marching over to the sofa, she lowered herself to the cushion, her back rigid with purpose.

"I'm proud of you," Bryce said simply, sitting beside her and taking her hands in his, frowning at how icy cold her fingers were. Staunchly, he reminded himself that, strong or not, Gaby was battling severe emotional shock.

He had no intention of allowing it to win.

"Considering the information Smythe just provided, I must agree that Averley is indeed a liar and a thief." Deliberately, Bryce began with the obvious, deferring the most painful of Gaby's accusations until she felt ready to address it. "Averley commissioned a yacht, pretending to be the duke, doubtless using the duke's funds. Given the circumstances, he never expected his theft to be discovered. After all, why *would* it be? He was Whitshire's steward. He had total freedom with the books, and thorough knowledge of all the duke's business contacts. Why, he even handled all correspondence with those contacts, including Smythe and Delmore—a task that is perfectly natural for a steward to perform. And such an exemplary steward at that—one whose books were, as he boasted to me, in perfect order."

"'The books are in perfect order,'" Gaby whispered, that odd, faraway light glimmering in her eyes. "Averley did say that to you. In fact, he was uttering those very words the day I walked into your meeting at Nevon Manor." She massaged her temples, one recollection spawning another. "He also shouted them at Dowell on the night he killed him."

Bryce swallowed hard, studying Gaby's tormented expression. "You know that for a fact?" he asked, keeping his voice low and calm. "You actually overheard Averley use those words?"

"Yes." She shifted forward and was instantly assailed by the potent smell of cologne emanating from the empty bottle that sat on the table beside her.

Details crashed into place.

"I heard yelling—*before* the fire started, not after. I knew it was Averley and Dowell. The wall separating the shed from the coal room was thin. I could make out everything they were saying; I didn't understand what all the words meant, but I knew both men were angry. I covered my ears and tried to fall asleep. But I couldn't. Even my music box couldn't play loud enough to drown out their shouting. Dowell was yelling that he wanted money. He kept accusing Averley of stealing, said he'd followed him and knew about the boat. Averley yelled back that he was crazy. That's when he said 'the books are in perfect order.' I remember that phrase because I wondered how books were ordered—were the important ones those with more pages or more pictures?"

Gaby was staring ahead, once again the five-year-old child who was seeing the walls of the storage shed, hearing the voices from next door. "Dowell laughed, but it wasn't a nice laugh. He called Averley some names, said if he didn't share, he'd go to the duke and tell him what was going on. Mama used to tell me to share, too, so I understood why Dowell was angry. Then I heard a commotion and a dull thud, as if something had fallen. It must have been Dowell, because after that, Mr. Averley started stamping around, ordering Dowell to get up. Dowell didn't answer, and Mr. Averley stopped asking. There was a funny, hissing sound, and then a door slammed. It got warm and quiet after that, so I curled up in the blankets with my music box and lay there until I fell asleep. The next thing I knew I woke up and the wing was on fire." She blinked, dragging herself back to the present, no longer a cowering little girl but a cognizant, fully grown woman who was as horrified of the truth as she was certain of it. "Dowell blackmailed Averley. And Averley killed him for it."

"Not only him, but everyone else who died that night," Bryce added, focusing on the final part of Gaby's recollection. "My guess is that Averley stole much more than just that yacht. In fact, based on the argument you just recounted, I suspect Dowell stumbled upon major discrepancies in the household accounts. Who knows? Maybe Averley inflated the quantity of garden supplies he purchased. I'm not certain. All I know is that Dowell figured it out and wanted a share of the profits.

"I'd also venture a guess that the hissing sound you heard was a match igniting some rags, and that your shed got much warmer after that because the coal room was burning. Averley obviously tried to cover up what he'd done by setting fire to the place so everyone would think Dowell perished in a tragic and accidental blaze. But things got out of hand. The fire didn't stop with the coal room, or even the woodshed. It burned the whole damned wing to the ground, killed everyone in it. Averley must have been panic-stricken; that's why he reported the fire so quickly—he was hoping to limit its destruction."

Gaby's entire body was trembling, but she shook her head when Bryce reached for her, determined to see this ordeal through. "That explains Averley's murders of thirteen years ago. It also explains why he

378

tried to kill me when he learned about the male voices I remembered: he was afraid I might implicate him. But where does Mr. Delmore's murder fit into this?"

"My guess?" Bryce replied, aching to absorb Gaby's pain. "When Richard Rowland fell ill, Averley was probably frantic to sell the yacht before it passed to Thane, who might question the existence of a boat he'd never seen or heard of, purchased by a man who loathed sailing. Averley knew from Whitshire that Delmore was an enthusiastic yachtsman. He figured he'd sell the boat to him at an excellent price and wash his hands of the whole matter before Whitshire died. Only it didn't work that way. Whitshire died before the title was transferred. Averley was in the midst of a transaction with Delmore, pretending, through his correspondence, to be acting on Whitshire's behalf. He would have been vulnerable as hell, *if* anyone had linked him to his fraud."

"Which Mr. Delmore could do."

"If he met with Thane and discovered that Richard Rowland never bought the yacht he was allegedly selling, yes. So when Averley learned that Delmore was on his way to Whitshire to conclude the transaction, he knew he had to stop him. And he did." A contemplative pause. "Now that I think about it, that's why Averley asked me so many questions about my credentials that first night I visited Whitshire, and why he was so uncomfortable about my examining the records. He was probably scared to death that I'd notice a discrepancy or that my business association with both the Rowlands and Delmore might put me in the position of inadvertently discovering something that would implicate him."

"Have we covered everything?" Gaby asked weakly, turning away from the lingering scent of cologne that hovered nearby.

"Yes." Bryce shoved the bottle to the far edge of the table, then drew Gaby against him, enfolded her in his arms. "As I told you once before, you're extra-ordinarily strong," he said fervently, his lips in her hair. "I'm prouder of you than you can imagine." His expression hardened. "One more day, Gaby, and all this will be over—forever."

She tilted back her head, gazed up at him. "What are we going to do?"

We. The fact that she could still say that, after all she'd endured—such courage was astounding.

"We're going to expose Averley for the murderer he is," Bryce responded. "All we need is a bit of help from Thane and a confirmation from Mr. Smythe, both of which I'll arrange for immediately. When we're through with Averley, the only cabin he'll know is a very small cell in Newgate."

The critical note was dispatched to Whitshire post-haste. The chat with Smythe was terse and candid—and yielded instant results.

By late afternoon, Bryce's carriage rolled into the drive at Nevon Manor, where Thane was waiting, the requested items in his possession.

The meeting was short, the outcome decisive.

And the plan was devised.

The new day was just under way when Averley approached the duke's study the next morning, knocking politely at the door. "You sent for me, Your Grace?" he inquired, stepping inside.

Early morning sunlight drizzled through much of the room, but the far corner was still cast in shadows, awaiting the first blush of day.

"Hmm?" Thane sat hunched over his desk, leafing through some papers and looking thoroughly piqued, while Bryce paced about, scowling at a document in his hand.

Averley cleared his throat. "You did want to see me?"

Thane glanced up, as if noticing his steward for the

first time. "Ah, Averley. Yes. I did." He rubbed the back of his neck. "Mr. Lyndley and I were conducting some legal business, and we came upon a document that pertains to a purchase my father made. Supposedly this purchase was made some time ago, but there seems to be a discrepancy about the timing. Given your long-standing position as Father's steward, we are hoping you can shed some light on the matter."

"I'll be happy to, sir."

Pausing near the French doors leading out to the courtyard, Bryce leaned against the doorframe, still frowning at the document in his hand. "Averley, do you recall when the late duke commissioned his yacht to be built?"

A bit of the ruddiness faded from Averley's cheeks. "Yacht?"

"Yes. Take a look at this." Bryce waved the paper in the air.

With an uneasy cough, Averley walked over, skimming the title Banks had supplied Bryce with. "Ah, the sailing vessel His Grace commissioned. You'll have to forgive my memory, Lyndley. It's been some time since that transaction occurred. But, yes, I remember it. His Grace contracted Mr. Smythe's company to build him a rather luxurious yacht. That's the title transferring ownership of the craft from Smythe to His Grace. I don't understand where the discrepancy lies. The date is clearly penned on bottom: March 14, 1862."

"Precisely," Thane concurred, leaning back in his chair. "But the problem is that all my records—correspondence, old business drafts—indicate that Father was in Scotland on a prolonged venture when this transaction occurred."

A frown. "That's impossible, sir."

"Exactly. Which could only mean that the title is dated incorrectly." Thane shoved his papers aside, raking a frustrated hand through his hair. "Since your records are far more painstaking than mine, would you kindly check your books and determine when, in fact, Father purchased the yacht so we can amend my papers?"

The slight tension permeating Averley's stout frame was the only indication that he was unnerved. "Of course, sir. I'll fetch my records for the entire year and bring them to you at once."

Bryce and Thane waited until the steward's footsteps had faded away.

Then Bryce whipped about, yanking open the glass door and beckoning for the man outside to enter. "Well?" he demanded as Smythe stepped into the room.

The builder shook his head in stunned disbelief. "I never would have believed it—always thought myself a good judge of character."

"Is that the man you sold the yacht to?" Bryce pressed.

"It sure is. He's older, grayer, and a bit portlier, but that's definitely the man who called himself the Duke of Whitshire."

"You're sure?"

"Positive. I'd recognize him anywhere. Like I said, I only had one customer who was a duke . . ." Smythe broke off, his lips thinning into a grim line. "Or rather, one customer who pretended to be a duke. The bloody bastard." A deep sniff. "There's that cologne of his, too. You can't miss it. Yeah, it's him all right."

"Good." Thane folded his hands neatly before him. "Then we have only to wait for my honorable steward to return."

Bryce glanced toward the far corner of the room, still untouched by daylight. "Sweetheart, are you all right?" he asked quietly.

Gaby stepped forward for one brief instant. "I'm fine." Her small jaw was set with purpose. "And I'm more than ready to do my part."

"Soon," Bryce promised. "Averley should be back here any minute to report the missing books."

As if on cue, the steward's footsteps resumed, a bit slower than last time.

Gaby withdrew into her corner.

"I don't understand it," Averley began, reentering the study. "The books for that year are nowhere to be found . . ." His voice trailed off as he stared at Smythe, his mouth dropping open.

"Hello, *Your Grace.*" Smythe nodded curtly. "I see you remember me."

With a great deal of difficulty, Averley composed himself. "No, I'm sorry, I don't believe I do."

"I'll refresh your memory," Bryce offered smoothly. "This is Mr. Robert Smythe, the man who sold you—or rather, you posing as Whitshire—the yacht we were just discussing. Oh, and the books you couldn't seem to find amid your records? His Grace is holding them in his hands." He gestured toward Thane, who waved the ledgers in the air. "No surprise that they confirm the date on the title as accurate. So it seems, given the Duke of Whitshire's whereabouts at the time, that he never did purchase that yacht."

Smythe corrected him bitterly. "Yeah, he did. He just didn't realize he'd purchased it."

Averley shifted from one polished shoe to the other. "I don't know what you're talking about, Lyndley. I never met this man before in my life. As for the discrepancy, I can't explain it. Only the duke can. And unfortunately he's dead."

"Yes, he is. And he's not alone, is he?" Bryce inquired. "William Delmore also died recently. Of course, Delmore wasn't permitted the peace of a natural death. He was murdered. Tragic, wouldn't you say?"

Sweat beaded on Averley's brow. "Yes, very."

"Banks tells me that Delmore was in the process of buying Whitshire's yacht when the late duke died. Speaking of which, how is it that you couldn't remember anything at all about a yacht whose sale you were conducting for His Grace mere months ago? Or have you forgotten that as well?" Bryce held up the pages of correspondence, all written in Averley's hand. "Would these refresh your memory?"

Averley's gaze narrowed. "Even if I was handling that sale for the late duke, it proves nothing other than that I was doing my job. As for this person's accusations"—he gestured toward Smythe—"they're groundless. And need I remind you that it's his word against mine. With my impeccable record—"

"A record I've thoroughly discredited with the fraudulent entries I've discovered in this one-year time period alone," Thane informed him icily. "Give it up, Averley. We've established you as a liar and a thief ten times over. And we have more than enough proof to support our claims."

"Then there's the matter of Delmore's murder," Bryce reminded him. "We have yet to extract a confession for that."

"A confession?" Averley's eyes nearly bugged out of his head. "To murder? Are you deranged? Rewarding myself with an occasional monetary bonus is hardly in the same realm as killing someone. As for the yacht and whatever other niceties I helped myself to, I more than earned them. And Richard Rowland could well afford them—and a great deal more. The coldhearted bastard never paid me what I was worth anyway. But murder? I don't know what you're talking about."

"Delmore represented a potential threat to all those lovely niceties you just mentioned. He might have deduced the same ugly truth we just discovered—*if* he'd been allowed to reach Whitshire and compare his documents to Thane's. If so, he'd doubtless have realized that Richard Rowland never bought that yacht. All the doubts and questions would have led to you—and your undoing. You didn't dare take that risk. So you met Delmore's carriage as it made its way to Whitshire, summoned him to the roadside under some false but believable pretense, and shot him dead."

A sardonic smile. "That's quite a story, Lyndley. Highly entertaining. Unfortunately for you, there's no way of proving its truth. I don't intend to admit to anything. Only Delmore could lend merit to your ludicrous accusations. And he's dead, so he can't very well incriminate me."

"Well, I'm not, and I can." Gaby marched out of the corner, her face flushed, eyes ablaze. "Perhaps you have a more vivid memory of your attempt on *my* life. If not, I'll enlighten you. You tried to kill me a week ago. Fortunately, you failed. So I'm alive and well—and extraordinarily eager to incriminate you in precisely the way Mr. Delmore cannot. In fact, nothing will give me greater pleasure than to turn you over to the authorities."

Averley's whole demeanor changed, his breath coming faster, his fists clenching and unclenching at his sides. "You're bluffing. You have no way of knowing who your attacker was. He was masked, dressed in black."

"And how would *you* know *that?*" Gaby countered, anger and the need for vindication eclipsing all traces of fear. "I never publicly described my assailant. Only Bryce, Aunt Hermione, and Chaunce knew how he was dressed, which means, Mr. Averley, that you've just implicated yourself." She didn't wait for a reply but pressed on. "But even if you hadn't, it wouldn't matter. Your mask did nothing to conceal your identity. I recognized you by the scent of your cologne—that special fragrance you import from Paris for you and you alone, except for that one bottle you gave to Mr. Smythe in gratitude for a job well done. And I recognize it from another night—a night on which you murdered dozens of innocent people, including my parents. Do you recall that night, Mr. Averley? Because, luckily, I now do. I remember it all, from your argument with Dowell to his accusations of theft, from your striking him down to the match you lit when you set fire to the coal room. I now remember every moment of the tragic night that has haunted me all these years, the details of which never quite surfaced until the night I returned to Whitshire. Then it all came surging forth, first in my dreams, then in my awareness. You triggered that awareness, Mr. Averley, just as you started that fire. You're a murderer many times over. And as the one living witness to that night, as well as the one you tried to kill for remembering exactly what happened in that coal room, I will attest to your guilt before every magistrate in the country."

"Damn you." Something inside Averley seemed to snap. "I won't let you do this to me, you audacious chit." He stalked toward Gaby, fury contorting his features.

Before he'd taken his third stride, Bryce was on him, slamming his fist into Averley's jaw and sending the older man reeling. "Lay a hand on my wife and you'll wish you'd died in that fire." He dragged Averley to his feet, gripping his coat in tight, furious fists. "If you have something to say, say it to me."

Sweat was pouring down Averley's face. He was cornered and he knew it, condemned by his own deeds, backed into an admission he'd fought thirteen years not to make. "I didn't mean to kill Dowell," he gasped, terrified by the look of sheer animal rage on Bryce's face. "The bastard was blackmailing me. We each threw a few punches. When Dowell went down, he hit his head on a coal bucket." A harsh indrawn breath. "I begged him to get up. I shook him, slapped him. When I realized he was dead, I didn't know what to do. With all those cuts and bruises on him, no one would have believed he tripped. They'd know there was a fight. And they'd know with whom, because my lip was bleeding, my face swollen. Sooner or later they'd figure out what we were fighting about. I couldn't risk it." Another shuddering breath. "I never meant for anyone else to die. I couldn't believe how fast that fire spread. . . ."

Pausing, Averley shot a bitter sidelong glance at Gaby. "I heard that damned music box playing. I knew she was in there. But she was just a child. I prayed she hadn't heard anything and, if she had, that she hadn't understood. When Lady Nevon took her away, I was relieved as hell. I didn't want to hurt anyone else; I was horrified at the fire, all the lives it had claimed. I just wanted to bury the whole thing, forget it ever happened."

"Forget it ever happened?" Gaby burst out, her eyes wide with appalled disbelief. "You killed an entire wing of people just to conceal your thefts, and you wanted to erase that crime from your mind as if it had never occurred? How in God's name could you expect to do that? In truth, you should be haunted by your heinous acts every moment of your life."

"What about Delmore?" Bryce demanded, his grasp on Averley's coat tightening. "That wasn't accidental. That was premeditated murder."

"It was self-defense," Averley shot back. "So was getting rid of Gabrielle. If everyone had only stayed away, minded their own business—"

"Then what, Averley? Then you could have disregarded the fact that you'd committed murder? And you could have continued stealing from my family for another decade?" Thane shoved back his chair, leaping to his feet with a revolted expression on his face. "Bryce, I've had enough. Couling is in the hallway with Officers Dawes and Webster. They're awaiting our signal to take Averley away. I'll summon them." He stalked over to the door, yanked it open, and waved for the authorities to enter.

"Good." A muscle was working furiously in Bryce's jaw, and he flung Averley at the officers with near-violent intensity. "The bastard confessed to everything. Now get him out of my sight."

Dawes stepped inside, seizing Averley's arms and locking them behind his back. "With pleasure." He glanced at Gaby, whose expression was composed, though she looked inordinately pale and shaky. "We have your statement, Mrs. Lyndley. But if we need your verbal accounting—"

"Then we'll both be there to supply it," Bryce interrupted swiftly.

"No, we'll *all* be there to supply it," Thane amended, handing the incriminating ledgers to Webster. "Between the three of us and Mr. Smythe here, I think we can put Averley away for the rest of his life."

"Put him away?" Dawes scowled at his prisoner. "Hell, he'd better hope you're feeling generous. With what you told me, you could ensure he hangs."

"No." Gaby marched forward, her arms folded across her chest to still the uncontrollable shudders racking her body. "There's been enough killing already. Please—no more. Just throw him in prison." Her voice broke. "And make sure he never hurts anyone again."

"We will, ma'am," Dawes assured her. "You have my word." He and Webster led Averley from the room.

"Gaby?" Bryce was beside her in a heartbeat. He drew her into his arms, holding and warming her all at once. "You were astounding. Are you all right?"

She nodded, feeling her husband's love pervade her, obliterate the darkness of the past hour. "Bryce?" she whispered, her voice muffled by his waistcoat.

"Yes, sweetheart?"

"It's over. Do you remember what you promised we'd do the minute it was over?"

A profound smile curved his lips. "Indeed I do." He tilted up her chin, kissed the tears from her cheeks. "Come, Wonderland. Let's go home."

Chapter 18

"SCREECH IS ANNOYED," GABY ANNOUNCED.

Grinning, Bryce cradled his wife's warm body against his, very much aware of the distinctly sated, unconcerned tone of her voice. "So I hear—and have been hearing since five A.M." He shifted a bit, drawing the bedcovers up over them in an attempt to shut out the new day—and the unrelenting shriek of Gaby's woodpecker.

Laughing softly, Gaby kissed the damp column of Bryce's throat. "He's still not accustomed to the fact that I have new sleeping quarters."

"Or how much time you spend in them." Bryce rolled Gaby beneath him, wanting nothing more than to sink deeper into his wife and make love to her the entire day.

"Ummm." Gaby sighed contentedly, twined her arms about Bryce's neck. "He'll get over it. He'll have to. Just as I've gotten over my sleepwalking."

"Those episodes are gone forever, just as I predicted," Bryce proclaimed, feeling utterly smug and thoroughly aroused. "Although you do sleep even fewer hours now than you did before."

"Fewer, perhaps, but sounder," Gaby reminded him. "My slumber has been heavenly—deep, dreamless, perfect. It's brief, only because staying awake is infinitely more exhilarating, just as I imagined it would be." Gaby shivered as the hardening of her husband's body inside hers made his intentions clear. "Do we have time?" she breathed, already lifting her hips to his.

"We'll make time." Bryce withdrew, then pressed deeper, penetrating her in exquisite increments of pleasure.

"But it's nearly nine o'clo— Oh, Bryce." Gaby whimpered as he withdrew again, then reentered her in one deep, inexorable thrust.

"We'll dress quickly." His voice was thick, husky with passion. "You did ask me to be impulsive, did you not?"

"Yes." She wrapped her legs around him. "Absolutely, yes."

"Good." He groaned, his control shattering as she melted and tightened around him all at once. "God, Gaby." He gave in to the wildness, cupping her bottom, dragging her up to meet the frenzied motions of his hips, plunging into her again and again. "I couldn't stop . . . if I tried."

"Don't try." Gaby was about to break apart, everything inside her coiled, poised, waiting. "Bryce . . ."

"Now . . . right now," he rasped, melding their loins for one fierce, unendurable instant.

They shattered together, dissolving into a thousand brilliant fragments of sensation, clinging to each other as the passion peaked, then ebbed, banking into the wondrous aftermath that was as magical as the minutes preceding it.

"I love you," Gaby breathed, her limbs sinking weakly to the bed.

"Each moment, each day, I fall in love with you all over again," Bryce murmured, kissing her soft, parted lips. "But that's the miracle of Wonderland."

Gaby lifted her lashes, and the look she gave him was filled with aching tenderness. *"One* of the miracles of Wonderland," she corrected. "You, my darling husband, provide quite a few of your own."

A stampede of footsteps intruded on their privacy.

"Gaby?" Lily knocked soundly on the door. "Are you and Mr. Lynd—I mean Bryce—still asleep? Chaunce said we should leave you alone. But I knew you wouldn't want that. 'Cause the vicar will be here in a half hour for—you know, the rehearsal."

One glance at the clock, which now read nine-thirty, confirmed Lily's announcement.

"We're awake, Lily." Gaby was already scrambling out of bed. "We're just . . ." Frantically, she searched for an excuse.

"We're just late," Bryce supplied, swinging his legs over the side of the bed. "But we'll be there in plenty of time. I promise."

"Oh, good." Lily sounded thoroughly relieved. "Did you hear that?" she declared to whoever else was with her. "They're just late. Let's go wait for them in the chapel."

The stampede of footsteps resumed, then faded away.

"We're just late?" Gaby repeated, as she hastened toward the bathroom. "Is that the most original excuse you could conjure up?"

Bryce's eyes twinkled. "Not original, but incredibly fitting. I borrowed it from Alice's white rabbit."

The chapel was in chaos when Gaby and Bryce arrived.

Marion and Ruth were whispering in the rear, repeating the wedding vows aloud in the hope of learning them. Along the right side of the room

Goodsmith and Wilson paced up and down, muttering nervously about rings and the proper time to lift the bride's veil for a kiss.

The rest of the staff was rushing from one end of the chapel to the other, alternately calming down the grooms and reassuring the brides.

In the center of the room, Chaunce was conducting a card game with the children to keep them occupied, and at the altar, Hermione was conversing with Vicar Kent, probably seeking the help of some higher being to ease the hysteria that pervaded the chapel.

"We haven't missed anything, have we?" Gaby asked brightly.

"No, no, of course not." Vicar Kent smiled down at them from his sanctified position. "Although I do wish your aunt wouldn't worry so much. It isn't good for her health."

Hermione frowned. "My health is fine, Vicar. I'm simply upset that four people I happen to love, each of whom adores his or her betrothed, are getting married tomorrow and are distraught rather than excited about the nuptials."

"Still," Bryce observed, "Vicar Kent is right. You really shouldn't become so overwrought. Think of how weak you've been."

"Actually, Aunt Hermione has been much better these past weeks," Gaby informed her husband. "Why, I haven't seen Chaunce fetch her medicine once, have you?"

"Now that you mention it, no."

Chaunce and Hermione exchanged glances.

"Dr. Briers doesn't feel I need as many doses as I once did," Hermione explained. "Evidently I'm regaining my strength."

"How wonderful!" Gaby said, her entire face aglow.

"Indeed it is," Bryce concurred. "To what does Dr. Briers attribute your recovery? Whatever it is, we'll have to ensure you receive more of it."

A loud wail from Ruth interrupted their conversation.

"Ruth, what is it?" Hermione asked, hurrying over.

"Oh, ma'am, I don't know what to do," Ruth replied, wringing her hands. "I love Wilson so much, but I just know I'm going to say the wrong thing or do the wrong thing and embarrass him."

"You?" Wilson bellowed from the other side of the room. "It's me who's goin' to ruin things. I'm not used to speakin' my mind to anyone but a shovel. And you're too precious to stutter even one word to."

"I've whipped this ring out of my pocket a dozen times," Goodsmith announced. "And I drop it each time. What kind of bridegroom drops his bride's ring?"

"And I trip every time I practice walking down the aisle," Marion chimed in. "I'm convinced I'm going to knock the vicar over and land at George's feet."

"Please, all of you, stop." Hermione waved away their complaints, pulling her petite form up in that remarkably regal way she had. "You're all just nervous. That's perfectly natural. But I don't want—"

"What in the name of heaven is going on in here?" Thane demanded, stepping inside the chapel. "I came to attend a wedding rehearsal. Instead, I'm walking into a brawl. What's the matter?"

Four overwrought voices began explaining at once.

"Wait." Bryce waved his arms to silence everyone. "You all watched and listened as Gaby and I took our vows. As you saw, there was nothing to it."

"You're a barrister," Wilson muttered. "You're good at talkin'. I'm a gardener. I'm not."

"Wilson, the words come from your heart, just as the feelings do," Gaby said softly. "I assure you that anyone can say them." Seeing his skeptical expression, she shot a pleading look in Chaunce's direction.

The butler rose from his card game. "I'm not a barrister, Wilson. Will it reassure you if I show you how it's done?"

Wilson looked as if he wanted to kiss Chaunce, who was unofficially but undeniably the male head of the family. "You'd do that for me?"

"Certainly." Clearing his throat, Chaunce walked solemnly down the aisle, positioning himself in front of Vicar Kent.

"Now what?" Goodsmith called out.

"Now I await the bride."

Marion let out a whimper. "How do I know how fast to walk? Or how slow? How do I take the proper steps?"

Hermione rolled her eyes. "I shall demonstrate." She glanced at Thane. "Since Chaunce is acting the part of the bridegroom and can't fill his role as escort, would you mind ushering me down the aisle?"

A chuckle. "My pleasure."

"Now watch—Marion, Ruth." Taking Thane's arm, Hermione walked sedately down the aisle, placing one foot in front of the other as she made her way toward Chaunce. "Just look straight ahead and take measured steps. That way you won't trip or fall. All right?"

"All right." Marion's brow furrowed as she watched Thane turn Hermione over to Chaunce. "And now?"

"Now comes my part," Vicar Kent advised her. "I read as follows . . ." He recited the ceremony, substituting Chaunce's and Hermione's names for those of the brides and grooms.

"Reginald?" Lily piped up in surprise. "I didn't know Chaunce's name was Reginald."

"I didn't know Chaunce *had* a name," Henry whispered loudly.

"Of course he has a name," Peter explained. "Everyone has a name. Reginald is his given name, Chaunce his surname."

"Shhh," Jane hissed. "This is the good part. I remember from Gaby and Bryce's wedding."

They all fell silent, listening as Hermione and

Chaunce exchanged vows, demonstrating to the others how it was done. The vicar dug in his pocket, producing a spare ring he evidently kept for emergencies like this one.

Chaunce slipped the ring on Hermione's finger.

There was a brief moment of quiet.

Then Hermione turned to face the room. "So you see? There's really nothing—"

"I now pronounce you man and wife," Vicar Kent trumpeted proudly. He waited for one long, patient moment, then gave Chaunce a gentle nudge. "You may kiss your bride," he said with a meaningful glance at Hermione.

"Pardon me?" Chaunce inquired.

"I said, you may kiss your bride." A broad grin. "I'm sure she'll enjoy it."

"Vicar . . ." Hermione inclined her head in his direction. "What on earth are you—"

"I'm marrying you two," he replied, "as I've wanted to do for years. Correction: I've just married you. Now you must kiss and greet your well-wishers."

Both Hermione and Chaunce stared, stupefied, from the vicar to each other, to the roomful of people all gazing expectantly at them.

"Go ahead, Chaunce," Thane urged. "We've awaited this day with bated breath—nearly as eagerly as the two of you have."

"And a good deal more impatiently," Gaby chided good-naturedly. "Honestly, at least Bryce and I had the good sense to realize we'd fallen in love. How long did you intend to ignore the obvious?"

"On the other hand, your dawdling did give us the opportunity to concoct this splendid plan," Bryce pointed out. "We accomplished two great feats in one: uniting two people who were made for each other *and* affording ourselves the pleasure of outdoing the masters." His lips twitched. "Surrender, you two. You've been bested. Our match is as well-devised as yours, and as cleverly and secretly arranged. *But* we accomplished it without feigning a need for medication—rather, lemon water—or inventing guardianships. We found something more effective than either: our family." He made a grand sweep with his arm, indicating all the scheming conspirators now beaming at the gaping bride and groom. "A remarkable group of actors, wouldn't you say?" Bryce's teeth gleamed.

Hermione's dazed glance darted from Wilson and Goodsmith to Marion and Ruth. "You mean you didn't . . . you weren't . . . you aren't . . ." She never finished her sentence.

Everyone understood nonetheless, and a rumble of laughter reverberated through the room.

Marion answered for the four of them. "Quite the contrary. Yesterday, during our *real* practice ceremony, Ruth and Wilson spoke their vows with not a single stammer, George flourished my wedding ring in one smooth motion, and I walked down the aisle without so much as a wobble. So, no, ma'am, we didn't want your help. What we wanted was your happiness."

Hermione's lips trembled as the reality of what was happening slowly began to sink in. Her misty gaze drifted over the group, settling on Bryce and Gaby. "You knew about the medicine, about the guardianship—about everything?"

A broad grin split Bryce's face. "Aren't you the one who insists that I have a brilliant legal mind? What kind of barrister would I be if I couldn't recognize manipulation and deduce its objective?" He wrapped an arm about Gaby's waist. "An incomparably flawless objective, I might add. As for my wife here, she's not only insightful, she never sleeps. Put the two together and you have a keen mind that's perpetually in motion."

Gaby laughed, enjoying the expression of utter incredulity on Aunt Hermione's face and, more astoundingly, on Chaunce's. "Once Bryce and I combined our suspicions, we unraveled your scheme like a ball of wool. Of course, we needed to be sure, because we were eager to return the favor. So we did the only practical thing. We went to see Dr. Briers. We explained our intentions to him, and he was more than willing to help, since he also happens to think you two make an ideal couple. He divulged the truth about your supposed illness. That was all we needed. The rest was easy, thanks to our family." Gaby cast a tender look about her. "We all know how much you two love each other, how right it is that you become husband and wife. But we also know you never consider your own needs. You're too busy worrying about ours. Well, it's time you understood that your joy is ours." Tears glistened on Gaby's lashes, and she gestured for Chaunce to seal his marriage as the vicar had advised. "Enough chatter. Kiss your bride, Chaunce. We're all waiting. It's up to you to make our family complete."

Chaunce swallowed, his eyes damp. Then, rife with emotion, he gave a brief nod and turned to face Hermione.

The two of them smiled at each other, a sense of rightness hovering between them, and Chaunce lowered his head, brushed Hermione's lips with his.

A jubilant cheer erupted in the chapel and the entire family surged forward, surrounding the bride and groom in a sea of good wishes and love.

"I'm beginning to relish these weddings I conduct at Nevon Manor," Vicar Kent declared to Gaby and Bryce, after offering his congratulations to the bride and groom. "One could become accustomed to these delightful, unorthodox displays of emotion."

"Then isn't it fortunate you'll be back here tomorrow when Marion and Goodsmith, Ruth and Wilson, truly do wed," Gaby laughed.

"And don't forget Thane," Bryce added blandly, keeping a perfectly straight face. "I'm sure his day of reckoning won't be far off if Hermione has her way. Why, I'm sure she's already begun concocting enticing plans for his future—with the help of her ingenious new husband, of course."

"Didn't we plan an extended wedding trip for those two?" Thane demanded. "If not, I think we should."

"No, thank you, Thane." Hermione appeared at his side, patting his arm reassuringly. "Thanks to all of you, I have everything I want right here at Nevon Manor. Chaunce and I will be remaining at home, won't we?" She turned glowing eyes up to her new husband, who'd come to stand beside her.

"Absolutely." Chaunce's lips twitched. "Now that our lemon water has been unmasked, we'll have to be even more resourceful in our next venture." Abruptly, his amusement vanished, and he gazed solemnly at Thane, Bryce, and Gaby. "Thank you. I'm not a man of words, but I want you to know . . ."

Gaby stood on tiptoe, kissed his cheek. "We love you, too," she whispered. With that, she moved to her aunt, hugged her fiercely. "Be as happy as we are. I can wish you nothing more miraculous than that."

Stepping back, she clapped her hands to get the crowd's attention. "Everyone, Cook has prepared a mouthwatering feast—"

"In secret again," Cook called out good-naturedly. "I'm glad tomorrow's wedding breakfast can finally be prepared out in the open."

More laughter.

"Let's escort the bride and groom to the manor and begin the festivities," Gaby concluded.

"There's no music for them to exit with," Marion murmured in dismay. "We didn't have time to arrange for—"

"Ah, but there is." Eagerly, Gaby dug into Bryce's coat pocket, extracting her music box and opening it to release the silvery strains of "Für Elise." "What better way to begin a marriage than with a music box that now holds nothing but joy?"

"Joy and Beethoven—I can't think of a more perfect combination," Bryce replied, drawing Gaby to his side, "other than the breathtaking woman who brought them into my life and the lucky man she married." Tenderly, he kissed her.

On that note, the chapel doors were flung wide, and everyone poured outside, running, stumbling, even limping toward the manor—a family bound by something more profound than the eye could see. Limitations ceased to exist, supplanted by the deeper knowledge that life's truest blessings were indeed theirs.

The music box played on.

And Wonderland reigned at Nevon Manor.

> When I used to read fairy tales, I fancied that kind of thing never happened, and now here I am in the middle of one.
> —Lewis Carroll, *Alice's Adventures in Wonderland*

Author's Note

IT IS MY GREATEST HOPE THAT, IN READING *THE MUSIC* BOX, you've just shared all the emotions I experienced in writing it—that you laughed, cheered, and perhaps at times wept along with Gaby, Bryce, and the special residents of Nevon Manor. I, like all of them, truly believe that nothing is more powerful or binding than the ties of the heart, which can overcome all obstacles.

I leave Nevon Manor in the best of hands, and instinct tells me we won't be saying good-bye forever. Not only because, as always, I hope you'll feel compelled to reread Gaby and Bryce's story but also because I have a nagging suspicion that neither they nor Hermione and Chaunce will be able to resist meddling in Thane's love life. There are a few stories that I need to tell first, but one day Thane Rowland will meet his match!

Speaking of other stories about characters spawned in previous books, it's time to fill you in on my next undertaking. Remember little Noelle from my story "Yuletide Treasure" in the holiday anthology *A Gift of*

Love? The precocious little four-year-old you've all been clamoring to hear more about? Well, guess who's grown and just as much trouble as when she was little? I feel sorry for Ashford Thornton, her dashing (and daring) hero, who happens to be the son of Daphne and Pierce Thornton from *The Last Duke*. Talk about the proverbial apple not falling far from the tree.

Noelle and Ashford are thrown together by their mutual search for a sinister figure from Noelle's past—one who threatens to destroy the very life he himself created.

I hope the preview Pocket Books has provided you of *The Theft* whets your appetite for the incomparable (and combustible) combination of Noelle and Ashford and for the suspense and intrigue that envelop them. I always enjoy hearing from you, either by post or by E-mail. You can write to me at

P.O. Box 5104
Parsippany, NJ 07054-6104
(Include a legal-size SASE if you'd like a copy of my latest newsletter.)

Or E-mail me at:

WriteToMe@andreakane.com

And visit my exciting web site at:

http://www.andreakane.com

Love,

Andrea

**POCKET STAR BOOKS
PROUDLY PRESENTS**

THE THEFT
Andrea Kane

**Coming Soon
from Pocket Star Books**

**Turn the page for a preview of
The Theft. . . .**

Farrington Manor, Dorsetshire, England
June 1869

He should have anticipated her request.

But he hadn't.

Maybe that was because of the enormous love that existed within his family. Or maybe his reasons had been more selfish, a fervent wish that the past could remain as it was, dead and gone.

Still, Eric admonished himself, he'd been a damned fool.

After all, this was Noelle. And when, in the dozen years of her young life, had Noelle allowed the slightest detail to escape her? When hadn't she demanded to know the answer to every tiny, bloody question under the sun?

And this involved far more than a simple question.

This involved her birth, her lineage, the physical roots of her very existence.

"Papa?"

Abandoning his thoughts, Eric Bromleigh, the seventh Earl of Farrington, leaned back in his library chair, regarding his elder daughter with a dark scowl. "What, Noelle?"

"I asked you . . ."

"I heard what you asked me." He made a steeple with his fingers, rested his chin atop them. "I'm just not sure how to answer you."

"You're not *sure* how to answer me? Or you don't *want* to answer me?" With her typical candor-bordering-on-audacity, Noelle met her father's gaze, her sapphire-blue eyes astute, assessing.

"Both."

"I see. So you really don't know his name."

"Not his name or anything about him."

"And you're not the slightest bit . . . ?"

"No. Not even the slightest bit."

Noelle sighed, twisting a strand of sable hair about her forefinger—a childlike gesture Eric found greatly comforting, especially in light of the circumstances. Actually, he amended silently to himself, as Noelle grew older he was finding himself more and more grateful for the infrequent reminders she afforded him that she was not really a short, unusually straight-figured woman, but rather a normal, if extremely precocious, twelve-year-old girl.

One whose mind and tongue were quicker than a whip.

Heavyhearted, Eric cleared his throat, seeking his own essential answers. "Why are you asking me this—now, after all these years? Why are you suddenly curious about your real fath . . . about the man who sired you?"

Something of Eric's anguish must have conveyed itself to Noelle. Abruptly, her probing look vanished, supplanted by a flash of regret and a wealth of unconditional love. "Oh, Papa . . ." She jumped to her feet, rushing over to fling her arms about Eric's neck. "You don't truly imagine I consider that horrible man—whoever he is—my father, do you? You don't think my question has anything to do with my feelings for you and Mama?"

"No. But still, I have to wonder . . ." Eric broke off, wishing he knew what the hell to say.

"Good. Because you and Mama are my parents. My *only* parents." Noelle hugged Eric fiercely. "I love you both so much," she whispered. "If my interest in knowing who *he* is hurts either of you, I'll forget the entire notion."

Tenderly, Eric stroked Noelle's hair, reflecting on how very typical this entire display was. Noelle was fervent about everything. Her love. Her curiosity. Her allegiance.

Her hunger for knowledge—knowlege that, in this case, she was more than entitled to be granted.

Yes, she was his daughter, his and Brigitte's, but

it hadn't been that way from the start. She'd been born his niece, the unwanted illegitimate babe of his sister Liza. Liza and some nameless Italian aristocrat who'd thrown her aside the instant he learned she was with child. Not that Liza had proven to be any more principled than her lover. As always, she'd hastened straight to Eric, seeking him out as her inexhaustible source of love and protection. And, as always, he'd offered her both, convincing himself that she truly repented her reckless behavior, that she was ready to forgo her selfish whims and assume responsibility for the life of her unborn child.

What a fool he'd been. Liza had given birth to Noelle on Christmas Day, then abandoned her at the onset of the new year—forsaking Farrington Manor to sow her wild oats, only to die shortly thereafter, leaving Eric with a bitter heart, a deluge of self-censure, and an untenable dilemma.

Noelle.

God help him for his reaction. He'd been a wounded animal, incapable of feeling or forgiveness—especially when it came to himself. Uncertain of his sanity, unable to endure even the slightest reminder of Liza, Eric had wrested Noelle from his life, determined to live out his days in self-imposed isolation.

It hadn't happened that way.

And not because of any heroic transformation on his part. No, Eric harbored no illusions on that score. His unexpected awakening, all its ensuing joys—every one of those blessings he owed to one extraordinary, incomparable woman.

Brigitte.

As his courageous bride, Brigitte had marched into Farrington Manor just shy of Noelle's fourth birthday, a wife in name, a governess in fact.

Or so Eric had intended.

Within weeks Brigitte had undone four years of hell, healed all of Eric's and Noelle's emotional wounds, and transformed the future from bleak to miraculous.

Thanks to Brigitte, there was joy, there was unity, and there was family—a family that grew to include not only their beloved Noelle but their equally beloved Chloe, who made her appearance the summer before Noelle turned five.

Both girls had flourished—happy, nurtured, secure in the knowledge that they were loved.

Fortunately, Noelle had never had to know the selfish woman who'd given her life.

Or the despicable man who'd aided in the same.

There was no reason for that to change. No reason but one.

Noelle. Noelle and her inexhaustible curiosity.

"Tempest," Eric murmured, easing Noelle away from him and gripping her small hands in his large ones. "Even if I knew who the scoundrel was who—that is, the scoundrel who was responsible for . . . for . . ."

"Impregnating," Noelle supplied helpfully. "The scoundrel who was responsible for impregnating Liza." She smiled a bit at the ashen expression on Eric's face. "I do know how babies are made, Papa."

"Why did I doubt that?" he muttered, shaking his head. "In any case, even if I knew his identity, I'm not certain I'd share that information with you. What would you do with it? Write him a letter? Ask why he'd chosen to walk away from his unborn child, why he wanted no part of the life he'd created?"

"Of course not." Noelle gave him a you-can't-be-serious look. "I know why he wanted no part of my life: he was, or is, an unfeeling coward. It was his loss, Papa, not mine. I have no misgivings or self-doubts on that score, believe me. Still, I am dreadfully curious. I'd like to know what he looks like, thinks like, what traits I might have inherited from him. Surely you can understand that?"

Eric swallowed audibly. "Yes, I can understand that." A contemplative pause. "Noelle, he lived in Italy. I explained that to you when Brigitte and I told you all we knew of him, all Liza relayed to me after their relationship ended. Assuming he's still alive, finding him would be like searching for a needle in a haystack."

Soberly, Noelle nodded. "I realize that. And I've given it much thought. We could hire someone—an investigator. Surely he could travel to Italy, find someone who actually saw this man and Liza together. No matter how discreet they were, they were bound to be noticed. Liza was a very beautiful woman."

And you look just like her, Eric added silently. "Yes, she was," he said aloud. For a long moment he studied Noelle's earnest expression. "This means *that* much to you?"

"I can't bear wondering and not having answers. You know how I am, Papa."

"Yes, I certainly do." With that, Eric came to a decision. "All right Noelle, I understand your curiosity. And I'm willing to indulge it—in my own way."

She leaped on his words. "What does that mean?"

"It means I'm proposing a compromise."

"What kind of compromise?"

"I'll do as you ask, hire an investigator to see what he can unearth about this blackguard." Seeing the excited glint in Noelle's eyes, Eric clarified hastily: "Bear in mind that this procedure could take months, maybe longer—years—if he's moved from city to city or, worse, from country to country."

Noelle appeared not the least bit deterred. "And once you've uncovered what I want to know—whenever that might be—you'll share your findings with me?"

"Not immediately," Eric replied, meeting

Noelle's honesty with his own. "I adore you, Tempest, but you're as impulsive as that reckless cat of yours. Don't bother denying it." He held up his palm to silence her protest. "We both know it to be true. If this scoundrel should turn up in India or Tibet or even Tasmania, you'd be on the first ship traversing the globe. I can't and won't take that kind of risk. So I'll find out what I can, *with* the stipulation that the information I unearth stays with me."

"Forever?" *Now* Noelle looked crestfallen.

"No, not forever. Only until you're older—old enough to think not merely with the intelligence of a woman but with the maturity of one. When I can be certain you'll properly employ whatever details I convey to you. At that point, if you're still interested in pursuing this matter, I'll turn all my findings over to you."

"Older? When is older? When I'm fifteen?"

Eric arched a sardonic brow. "That's hardly a woman, Noelle. How does twenty-one sound?"

"Ancient. How does sixteen sound?"

"Youthful." A hint of a smile curved Eric's lips. No matter how dismal the subject, Noelle had a way of infusing it with filaments of joy—and a healthy dose of debate. "I'll meet you halfway. Twenty-one is a woman; fifteen is a child. Shall we say eighteen?"

Noelle scrutinized him, her lips twitching slightly. "Is that your final offer?"

"It is."

"Very well. I accept. Eighteen." Lightly, she jumped to her feet, her chin set in that all-too-familiar way that made Eric's gut knot, obliterated whatever hope he'd entertained that time might diffuse his daughter's determination to locate her sire. Eric knew that particular look, and it meant only one thing: waiting for Noelle to change her mind would be like waiting for the sun to grow cold.

"Thank you, Papa," she called out, skipping over to the doorway and turning to give him a victorious grin. "I feel ever so much better."

"I might fail to find him," Eric warned.

"You might. But you won't. You've never disappointed me yet." Noelle's glowing faith was absolute, her enthusiasm irrepressible. "My eighteenth birthday is just five and a half years away. On that Christmas Day I'll learn all the missing pieces of my heritage."

"And then?"

"Then my curiosity will be satisfied, and I can bid the past good-bye." With a conclusive nod, Noelle dismissed the subject. Blowing Eric a kiss, she gathered up her skirts and scooted out of the library.

Eric gazed solemnly after her, the wisdom of adulthood cautioning him that the situation wouldn't resolve itself quite that easily.

In fact, he had a sinking feeling that precisely five

and a half years from now all hell would break loose.

Look for
The Theft
Wherever Paperback Books Are Sold
Coming Soon
from Pocket Books